Liam and Beverley Moore live in North Wiltshire and are owned by four cats. Liam is a nurse and Beverley teaches English. When they met Liam and Beverley discovered a mutual interest in writing and shortly after they married they decided to work together to achieve their dream of becoming published authors.

'Under a Ghostly Moon' is the first novel created by this new writing team. The inspiration for 'Moon' came while Liam was living in Bristol, which boasts many haunted pubs and possibly the most haunted hospital in England.

UNDER A GHOSTLY MOON

Liam &Beverley Moore
___

UNDER A GHOSTLY MOON

Vanguard Press

VANGUARD PAPERBACK

© Copyright 2011
Liam and Beverley Moore

The right of Liam and Beverley Moore to be identified as authors of this work has been asserted by them in accordance with the Copyright, Designs and Patents Act 1988.

All Rights Reserved

No reproduction, copy or transmission of this publication may be made without written permission.
No paragraph of this publication may be reproduced, copied or transmitted save with the written permission of the publisher, or in accordance with the provisions of the Copyright Act 1956 (as amended).

Any person who commits any unauthorised act in relation to this publication may be liable to criminal prosecution and civil claims for damages.

A CIP catalogue record for this title is available from the British Library.

ISBN 978 1 84386 654 1

*Vanguard Press is an imprint of
Pegasus Elliot MacKenzie Publishers Ltd.*
www.pegasuspublishers.com

First Published in 2011

**Vanguard Press
Sheraton House Castle Park
Cambridge England**

Printed & Bound in Great Britain

'To all our friends and acquaintances in Bristol who have inspired this book, both the noisy living and the unquiet dead.'

Prologue

It was a dank, lightless place, which smelt of damp rust and mildew. Festoons of ancient spider webs hung like ragged black lace from high corners and iron beams. The oldest had taken on an odd permanence where rusty water had transformed their silken strands into ruddy stalactites. In one dimly lit corner, where a single shaft of sunlight was grudgingly admitted by a rusty ventilation grill, stood an indistinct figure illuminated by the rippling reflections cast from a ruddy pool. It wore a dark, round brimmed hat, a dirty, white, open-collared shirt with rolled up sleeves and moleskin trousers tucked into the tops of a pair of worn hob-nailed boots. A pick-axe was gripped in a pair of pale, work-scarred hands, which rose and fell as it dug silently into the floor, leaving not a mark and making not a ripple in the rusty puddle that filled the bottom of this iron chamber. On his left hand, where a wedding ring might fit, a silver claddach ring glinted, as if with the light of a different sun. The ring's twin lay, six metres below under earth and concrete, blackened and twisted, around a skeletal phalange in the hand of an ancient corpse. It recalled the memory of a promise made to a Kerry girl so many years ago, now never to be kept. But Connor O'Flynn would keep on trying, till Doomsday if necessary, to complete Brunel's wonderful bridge, ever toiling unaware that the structure that he laboured long to complete, in the construction of which he had lost his life, now towered above him in all its glory and had done so for over a hundred and fifty years.

The mind of a ghost can be very single-focused and dedicated to a pin-point purpose. Connor remembered some fuss at the bottom of the foundation pit, a bit of confusion before he was back on the job. He often wondered vaguely why his workmates had started ignoring him and why they had eventually disappeared, but his main concern was to get this thrice bedamned pit work done so he could be paid and off home to marry Mary and buy her a farm. Very little pierced his focus but one thing did now. It was a nasty little sound, a snake-slithering, spider-clicking sound, which spun him round to be pierced by a pair of glowing blue eyes that hung above a mouth of sharp fangs.

"I have come to end your toil, navvy," a voice like the greyness of death hissed dryly through those teeth. "You should thank me."

Then Connor felt his purpose drain away as bluish tendrils of life-force snaked away from his spectral form into the empty blackness of the being that faced him. "Mary!" he cried wretchedly as his consciousness dwindled. Finally, all that remained was a tiny blue speck, floating above the rusty puddle with nothing but the faintest memory to hold it there.

"Ah!" hissed the dark spectre with obvious satisfaction. "Farewell, little shade," it said as it dissolved into the lesser shadows and disappeared.

Chapter 1

In Bristol Royal Infirmary's Casualty Department's Resuscitation Room the uneasy calm of a, so far, unusually uneventful night was shattered as the Resus staff gathered into an ordered huddle around one of the trolleys where, at the centre of a web of wires and tubes, a teenage girl hung on the edge of death.

"Did we get the toxicology results back yet?" Gary Wong, the medical senior house officer, asked the team in general.

Jerry Moon, a staff nurse, ran to the bedside waving a flimsy printout slip. "Right here," he said, steeling his sense of smell against the mixed odours of vomit and urine emanating from the girl's soiled clothing. Normally, he would have quipped something like: "hot off the press," but he wasn't in a joking mood. He had read the printout when he had taken it from the printer and knew the kid had taken a highly effective combination of killer drugs. A deep sinking feeling in his gut told him they were going to lose this one. All in all it was far too high a price to pay for being jilted by some spotty sphincter of a seventeen-year-old, who she'd have forgotten all about in a year or so. "It doesn't look good."

Seething with impotent irritation, Wong ripped the printout from Jerry's unresisting fingers. "Let me be the judge of that, Moon!" His eyes quickly scanned the printout. "Oh bugger," he sighed, his Tyneside accent, made more pronounced by emotion, seemed out of place with his Asian appearance; Wong was a fourth generation Chinese immigrant whose family had moved to Newcastle in the 1900s. "How the shit did the stupid kid manage to get her hands on both morphine *and* antidepressants?"

"Her mother has advanced breast cancer," replied Jenny Wilson, the 'Major End' Sister. "Shelly here, must have raided her mum's medicine cabinet."

"Respirations are far too low and her blood oxygen saturation level's in her boots. We need to get some Narcan into her now!" urged Wong. Moon grabbed a vial of the anti-morphine injection from a nearby trolley and showed it to Jenny, who checked the medication and its use-by date and then took the proffered syringe, drew up the drug and handed it to Wong, who quickly injected it.

The child's respiratory rate picked up gradually, but there were other problems. The vital signs monitor began to alarm again as Shelly's heart rate became erratic.

"Fuck!" exclaimed Wong, as the monitor trace degraded to the aimless wavering pattern of ventricular fibrillation. "She's arrested! We'll have to shock her! Hook up the defibrillator please, Jenny." However, despite their best efforts, they could not revive the girl. The lethal cocktail she had taken had done its deadly work before her mother discovered her lying comatose in her room. The few minutes it had taken for the ambulance to arrive had taken her over the fine margin they had needed to save her.

Putting an oxygen mask over her face to prevent the other patients from realising that there was a corpse passing by them in full view, Moon helped push the trolley bearing Shelly's body out of the resuscitation area. He noticed Wong and Jenny heading for the relatives' room to inform the girl's parents. *Poor sods*, he thought, trying to ignore the dim figure that he sensed drifting at his left-hand side – *"Not now, Love, wait until we're alone."*

Later, after he and Tracy, a health care assistant, had finished laying Shelly out, he muttered a brief excuse and slipped back into the side cubicle where Shelly's pitifully small looking corpse now lay. She was cleaned and wrapped in a disposable shroud. A shadowy figure seemed to melt out of the darkness gathered in one corner of the unlit room as the girl's shade moved to hover, indistinct but still recognisable, at the end of the trolley. *"So that's me?"* she said softly, *"or should I say, 'Was me'?"*

"Yes," replied Moon knowing that only he could hear that peculiar thought-emotional wavelength the dead used.

"...I didn't mean it to go this far, you know."

"I know," replied Moon in a low whisper, "kids your age seldom do." Ghostly silver tears shone on her face. Moon watched her coming to terms with her own death, aware that Tracy was waiting and might appear any time looking for him.

"Look, we don't have much time here…"

Suddenly, a huge apparition emerged from the left hand wall and leered at Shelly. Its crimson eyes glared and flashed as it snapped at her with a maw full of needle-like teeth. The young ghost withdrew sharply through the wall with a terrified shriek. Moon waved his hand, dispersing the ghoulish creature with a grin on his face.

"Don't let Gordy upset you. He's just an old tramp who died here a few years ago and still hangs around now because he likes to put the wind up newcomers and passing psychics."

"You're no fun, Mooon!" moaned Gordy as he coagulated into the form of a shabby old man and drifted away through the closed door of the cubicle leaving behind a parting whiff of cider-breath and unwashed body.

Shelly cautiously reappeared through the opposite wall and blinked her eyes tearfully at Moon, *"What do I do now?"*

"Well, that's pretty much up to you, but if you want my advice I'd suggest you head for the Source and complete your destiny. That's what most people who pass on here seem to do. It's pretty easy to identify from your side according to the one or two people who've stopped long enough to chat. A 'big bright light like a beacon lighting up the spiritual plane' so they say."

"But… My mum, she'll be frantic!"

"Not wanting to sound unduly callous, but you should have thought of that before you took all those pills. If you try to sort it out now you'll only make things worse."

"I could try to explain…"

"She wouldn't hear you, very few of the living can. Ghosts who hang around on Earth, trying to fix the things they've left undone, tend to end up stuck here. After a few years they forget why they stayed and degenerate into a run of the mill haunting. Do you really want to hang around as a ghost for centuries until you finally just fade away?" Shelley shook her head, her long silken curls dissolving at the tips into vaporous wisps. The unearthly beauty of this effect caught Moon by surprise and it was a second before he caught his breath to continue, "I thought not. There are rules to how things should happen, even in death, you know. The *Powers that Be*, whoever or whatever they are, seem to have it all worked out."

A sharp, malicious smile spread over Shelly's shadowy features. "Nothing wrong with giving Sean and that slag Sally Hopkins a good scare though, is there. I'll teach them to go together behind my back!"

"I wouldn't..." Moon began, but Shelly had already evaporated in a cloud of ectoplasm. "Just don't hang around too long!" he called after her as loudly as he dared then shook his head. Some people would never listen. He walked out of the cubicle waving his pen, the retrieval of which had been the excuse he had given for going back into the room.

"Took your time," observed Tracy curiously.

"It was caught in the shroud." He tucked the pen back in his pocket. "It was a bugger to find!"

"Ugh!" Tracy pulled a disgusted face. "I'd have left it, it's only a ballpoint."

"Yeah, but you know how hard it is to get hold of a pen in here. They're like gold dust."

"You're a skinflint, Jerry Moon. I buy my own."

"Just add it to my long list of endearing eccentricities," replied Moon with a wan grin.

Tracy smirked back. "That list's too long already, Moon, as you well know."

"I didn't know you cared." Moon was glad that Tracy's love for trading insults had distracted her from the length of time he had spent supposedly searching Shelly's corpse. He could cope with being labelled a skinflint in preference to people thinking he had an unhealthy obsession with death.

Moon finished handing over his patients to the day shift at about seven-thirty a.m. The rest of the night had been pretty typical Accident and Emergency fare: the usual parade of drunks, heart attacks, drug overdoses and nursing home referrals (for some reason there were always a few of these each night). He'd been threatened with a knife once and had to change his hospital blues twice. Once because he'd been vomited on and the second time because a patient had bled all over him (while attempting to threaten him with a knife). There had been two deaths: Shelly, and a male cardiac arrest victim, who was DOA and had presumably left his spirit hovering somewhere along the M32 motorway in the wake of the speeding ambulance. He was glad he only did the occasional Bank Nurse shift in Casualty, as a regular job it would be too demanding.

It was a thirty-minute walk from the Infirmary to the second floor flat Moon rented in a large Victorian house in Redland. He usually enjoyed the walk, which helped him calm down after his shifts but today he was still too worried about Shelly for the journey to be of much benefit. It was bad enough for the other healthcare staff having to cope with the death of such a young patient, but Moon had to worry about whether he could have handled things better after she died. Could he have said anything that would have stopped her rushing off and potentially wrecking her afterlife?

Moon had no real explanation for his special 'gift'. He supposed he had always sensed atmospheres and intense emotions but, he had dismissed most of that as a mixture of good body language interpretation as well as being endowed with an over-fertile imagination until he realised that he was beginning to see and hear the dead. His latent talent had truly awakened shortly after he had made his career change into nursing. It was probably his first experience of death at first hand that had been the catalyst, but, regardless of what had caused it, he now had to share most of his waking hours with the restless spirits of the dead.

Moon had completed his nursing diploma five years before and had worked in a couple of ward-based posts before finding his niche working on the night pool at Bristol Royal Infirmary. Nursing during the dark hours in that ancient building, parts of which had sheltered the sick for nearly three hundred years, had exposed him to the wide variety of spirits and spooks that inhabited its wards and corridors. As a nurse he felt responsible for his patients but he felt it really should end when they passed over, unfortunately, they had other ideas. Often he came home more exhausted because of the problems of the departed than those of the living and he had become a reluctant expert in the afterlife just to cope with it all.

His journey home took him up Marlborough Hill, which ran along one side of the newer of the Infirmary's two sites, and through Cotham, the affluent area that dominated the hilltop behind the more recently built part of the hospital. At the top of the hill he crossed over a small grassy area. Here he paused to look back over the city where it lay, misty and new, splashed with gold by the rising sun. He then turned right along Cotham Brow, which breasted the hilltop, his path taking him past an old, Victorian gospel hall, the front of which was still in shadows, untouched by the new day, as he passed. Glancing at the dark doorway, he was surprised by a faint, glimmering motion in the darkness. He drew closer and was amazed to see three dancing blue globes spiralling in the gloom. "What are you?" he whispered, stretching his right hand towards them. "Ghost moths?"

As one of the ghost globes passed through his hand he felt a shudder of cold and what seemed to be a distant memory of the tearstained face of a young girl, perhaps three or four years old, passed through his mind, accompanied by a sense of inconsolable loss. Another brushed against his head and the image of a hand holding a bloodied knife passed through his memory for an instant, bringing with it an intense wave of guilt and shock. Moon was perplexed, these were obviously some kind of spirit form but unlike anything he had previously encountered. Fascinated, he watched their dance for a minute or so, experimenting by passing his hands through their substance, but all that each seemed to hold was a single overpowering memory and the ghost of the emotions that went with it. The third globe's memory was no more enlightening, Just a vivid image of a pair of Victorian woman's shoes married to the desperate desire to own them. Eventually he gave in to his growing fatigue and stumbled his way back to his flat unaware that, almost invisible in the sunlight, the three tiny globes detached themselves one by one from the doorway and followed, dancing in his shadow.

Chapter 2

It was ten past eight by the time Moon entered his building, a handsome, four-storey, Bath sandstone edifice that had once housed a wealthy merchant's family and servants. Now it was owned on a buy-to-let mortgage by a shady individual who Moon suspected had underworld connections. Ideally, Moon would rather not have to deal with this dodgy character but he had found that could not afford to buy his own place on a nurse's salary, when he returned to Bristol after his training, because of the inflated state of the housing market. At least the rent was manageable; in some parts of the city people who the mortgage companies considered too poor to afford a mortgage were forced to rent for twice the amount that a mortgage would have cost them. Moon had never been able to fathom the logic behind this.

As he climbed up to the second floor landing he peered a little nervously through the banisters but to his relief no one was there so he quickly traversed that section of staircase and unlocked the door to his flat. A faint fragrance of violets tingled in his nostrils and a tiny, plaintive voice echoed up the stairwell, *"Jerry, come and play!"* This was what he had feared.

"Hi, Anna," replied Moon with a weary smile, peering over the banisters to where a pair of huge brown eyes hovered in an indistinct face shaped mist. "I'm sorry, I can't play at the moment; I've been working all night."

"Oh, pooh!" said Anna, and Moon caught the hint of ringlets shaking in agitation on either side of her face. *"No-one ever plays with me now!"*

"I'll come down and talk with you later," he promised.

As he turned to enter his flat Anna's querying vibe floated up to him. *"Why did the big girl hurt herself?"* Drat, he had never found out how this worked but spirits seemed to be able to sense when someone else had died.

"It was a mistake, mostly, Anna. When you're that age emotions seem far too important, they can make you very silly sometimes."

"Well then! I'm glad I'll never be that age," replied the tiny ghost emphatically. And that was why Moon had tried to avoid her. Lovely as she was, Anna's own personal tragedy always made Moon feel sad when they were together. Shelly's suicide made this even more poignant, chaffing like a raw wound and making him relive all the emotions he had hoped to smooth over before he slept.

Anna would never be older than four because, some time in the early nineteen hundreds, her father had thrown her downstairs in a drunken rage. During the early days of his psychic awakening, while he was trying to validate his gift and desperate to prove that he wasn't going crazy, Moon had confirmed this in the local archives. He was only glad that he seldom had to brave the fourth-floor landing where the guilty drunk had hanged himself in a fit of grief and remorse. His restless spirit now made life a misery for the upstairs tenants, who thought he was a combination of bad wiring and very noisy mice.

With a final goodbye to Anna, who poked her tongue out at him as he blew her a kiss, Moon stumbled into his flat. He was dead tired, and wanted to get some decent sleep in before the evening so he would be well refreshed and able to pursue his true passion in life, journalism. Moon hoped he'd eventually be able to make a living from his efforts as a freelance journalist. He had already had a couple of features printed in Bristol's entertainment magazine, *Venue*, and had even had one small article accepted by the Guardian newspaper. He tended to view his nursing career as primarily financing his eventual rise to media stardom. Impressed by a recent article he had written for them about the lifestyles of the travelling traders who toured the local music festivals, *Venue* had contacted him earlier in the week to ask if he would write them a two-pager on the local Goth sub-culture. Eager for the work, Moon had agreed, so now he had a deadline to meet.

It was a sunny Friday in late March and bright sunlight filtered through Moon's bedroom curtains making him sleep fitfully. The noise of the road works outside drilled through his earplugs, adding to his discomfort, and he eventually woke at quarter past two from a dream in which Shelly and Gordy twirled faster and faster in a staccato demon's dance, while he tried frantically and unsuccessfully to break them apart. It was unseasonably warm and sleeping in the sun blazing through the curtains had left him sweaty and dehydrated. Thirst and an overfull bladder propelled him out of bed and he shuffled zombie-like to the bathroom for double relief. A shave, a shower and a few minutes in his kitchenette later and he was happily ensconced in a dangerously prolapsed armchair, watching afternoon TV and eating sugar-coated kids' cereal dry from the box while washing it down from a pint mug of tea with Dennis the Menace grinning from one side of it. On the telly Quincy had just watched a dozen police cadets faint while he autopsied a corpse and Moon grinned for probably the thousandth time at the joke, which accompanied the show's credits. Being able to watch *Quincy* on afternoon TV was one of the things that made night shifts not too bad.

After *Quincy* finished, Moon went out to do a bit of shopping and to get some money out of a nearby cash point. He returned home to potter about, do a few household chores and then play with his latest computer game before he went out later to a Goth venue to start his research. Anna was absent both when he went out and returned, having gone wherever ghosts go during the full daylight hours. On the whole spirits seemed to prefer the night to full daytime and the colder months to summer. He had theorized that perhaps solar radiation interfered with their ability to manifest. When he had first begun to perceive the spirit world, he had tried to find some decent guidelines on how to cope with this new intrusion into his life but had been disgusted by the sheer unreliability of the books written on the subject. If it hadn't been written by an old biddy with sugarplum fantasies about the afterlife it would be by some oily American con-man out to make a quick profit by starting his own cult. Moon was a scientist at heart, he liked cold, hard facts, but it seemed that a person's experience of these phenomena was always coloured by their own beliefs. He had even spent a few weeks with the Spiritualists, but he had quickly been put off by the religious emphasis of their teachings and eventually realised that he would have to make his way through this particular maze alone. He realised he would probably end up colouring his findings with his own views just like everyone else, but at least they would be *his* views and not someone else's.

So far it had been very confusing. For instance there seemed to be no predictable set of reasons why someone would become a ghost. The 'unfinished business' concept was a loose explanation but, while some cases, like Anna and her father, were understandable, other spirits just seemed to hang around to see what happened. For instance, Moon had been surprised on one ward meeting to find that the girl wearing a sister's uniform who sat in a corner during handover and said very little was actually the shade of a ward sister who had died seven years earlier but who liked to look in to make sure everything was running properly. Perhaps dedication to work could become a kind of 'unfinished business', he mused before being rudely drawn back into the present as he watched his barbarian hero be hacked to pieces by ferocious skeletons. "Damn!" he swore, reloading his last save game. "My life is forever being complicated by dead people."

Later, Moon debated with himself what to wear to the Goth band-fest he was going to that night. The venue was the *Hangman's Rest*, an old coach inn near the modern day centre of Bristol. It was a notorious hang-out for the Bristol Goths and he didn't want to stand out too much. He knew the general Goth colour scheme was black and silver, with a touch of blood red or purple, all with a twist of dark fantasy and a hint of vampirism. He regarded himself in the half-length mirror set in his wardrobe door. He was below medium height, stocky in build and had thick, wavy sandy-coloured hair, a genetic heirloom from his Scottish grandmother, cut short so as not to offend the older patients. There was very little dark or Byronic about him. He knew the Goths went in for piercings and tattoos and he did fare a little better on that count, as his left ear was pierced, and also his tongue, which had been done as the result of a drunken dare when he was a student. Tattoos again came under the 'don't upset the patients' category, besides he had been thoroughly put off tattoos when he was on a student placement in a liver transplant ward. Many of the Hepatitis C patients were heavily tattooed and he had wondered how many had caught the disease that way.

Eventually, he opted for a plain black T-shirt, black jeans and a black leather biking jacket, which he had not worn for several years. He still felt he didn't look very Gothy but at least he had made an effort. Slipping a small Dictaphone into his pocket, he exited his flat, greeting Anna cheerfully as he headed down the stairs. The small ghost was engrossed in a game of some kind. Moon looked over her shoulder and was unsettled to find her playing with four glowing blue globes like the ones he had seen earlier. "What are they, Anna?" he asked. "Do you know?"

"Pretty," vibed Anna, *"I like them."*

"I've seen them before," said Moon, trying to be patient. "But I don't know what they are. I'd like to know, Anna."

Anna shrugged. *"I don't know? They're friendly, see they like it when I tickle them."* Anna caught one of the globes and tickled it, making it glow brighter suddenly and increase to nearly twice its size for an instant. Anna giggled. *"And they remember things, old things, some of them not very nice."* She shook her head so her ringlets jiggled.

"I know," replied Moon. "Can you touch them, Anna, or do your fingers go through them?"

"Oh, yes I can touch them. They feel like icy feathers."

So they were like ghosts, thought Moon, or at least made of the same stuff, whatever that was. "Thanks, Anna; you've been a very helpful girl."

Anna stared quizzically at Moon's retreating back. For some reason her new pets had decided to follow Moon to the *Hangman's Rest*. A very adult expression of concern invaded her chubby face as she stood and smoothed the nebulous frills of her lacy dress with her tiny hands. *"Oh, Jerry Moon,"* she said to herself. *"I don't know what you're getting yourself into but I think you're going to need some serious help."* Then she shrugged moodily and went off to tease Mrs Foley, the middle aged widowed bank clerk, who rented the flat directly beneath Moon's.

Chapter 3

The *Hangman's Rest* was situated on one of the main roads into the centre of Bristol, within walking distance of Moon's flat. The light was just reaching the cusp of dusk and true darkness when he strolled into the pub's car park, which used to be an enclosed courtyard and still looked like it should be a refuge for coaches and horses, rather than the cars and motley collection of motorbikes which were parked along two sides of the pub. Moon usually avoided visiting the place because the local gallows had once stood nearby and with his 'gift' he was never sure which of the clientele were alive and which were deceased villains revisiting their old drinking grounds. That it was now a favourite dive for Goths and bikers made his task all the more difficult.

Over the pub doorway hung a sign in garish colours, depicting a gallows framed by moonlight from which a rope extended into the foreground, where it was tied in a noose around the neck of a grinning corpse, which winked out at the beholder, holding up a tankard of Ostrich beer. Beneath was the caption: 'Worth coming back for!' which Moon thought was in exceptionally bad taste, especially because the corpse was the spitting image of one of the resident spooks, who was currently leaning on the drainpipe beside by the pub door and eyeing up the local Goth chicks as they entered.

The entrance queue looked like a 'Transylvanian rejects' convention. Moon wondered what they wore during the week; he doubted if many of those with day jobs got away with wearing that sort of costume at work. Most of the people present were teenagers or in their early twenties, but Moon was surprised to see quite a few older people there. Then, perhaps he shouldn't have been. According to his research, Goth had been born out of the ashes of the punk and new romantic genres in the early eighties, so it was perfectly possible that two generations were queuing up to enjoy the show.

When he got to the door an anaemic-looking girl with long, dyed black hair scrutinised him doubtfully from behind a beer stained table, which served as a makeshift ticket counter. Moon wondered vaguely how these Goth chicks always managed to look so pale. Was it all make-up or did they really sleep all day and shun the light? "Sorry," she said, "but I can't let just anyone in, we've had some trouble."

This completely bemused Moon, who was used to just wandering in to see pub bands in Bristol with little hassle except for the occasional entrance fee. He wondered whether his lack of piercings and tattoos and his general normalness had somehow marked him out for this treatment. "Well, I'm not out to cause trouble, I'm just here to see the bands, like everyone else."

"Yes," replied the girl. Her eyes seemed huge and dark behind all that purple eye shadow half hidden behind a spider web pattern veil, which was held in place with a hairclip fashioned like a crushed purple rose. Moon's eyes dwelled with momentary fascination on a small black widow spider tattoo which seemed to be in mid-scurry up the left side of her cleavage. She was actually quite plump, he realised; it was amazing what pale make-up and good corsetry could contribute towards achieving the half-starved undead look. "But, like, do you know anyone here?"

Moon struggled to remember the name of the tall, leather-clad Goth who, after several free pints for the sake of research, had suggested he try the Friday band night for a slice of Goth culture. 'Spuggy', was it, or 'Sproggy'? Oh, yes, "Stroggy! He told me this gig was worth a look in."

There was a gasp from a skinny girl behind the ticket seller. "Stroggy! But he's the one who arranged the gig. He's the lead singer for *Stoker's Kiss*. You'd better let him in, Avril!"

Avril shrugged. "Five quid then. Give us your hand." Moon handed over the fiver and smiled at Avril's friend while the back of his hand was stamped with what, on examination, turned out to be a black pentagram.

Avril's friend grinned back, exposing a set of gleaming white fangs. The effect would have been better if she was more physically imposing. Unfortunately, with her long hair and dark eyes, she reminded him of an over-friendly spaniel who had fallen in love with his left leg while he was visiting an ex girlfriend's parents for tea. As Moon entered the pub she came up to him and asked, "So, how come you know Stroggy?"

"I'm doing an article on local Goth culture," he replied, "Stroggy helped me a bit with my research." He pointed over to the bar. "Can I get you a drink?"

"I'll have a Green Fairy, White," she replied with another spiky grin. "My name's Sonia, by the way."

"Jerry Moon," he replied, having to shout over the death metal band who were playing first set. "Most people just call me 'Moon'."

"I like Jerry. It's a friendly name." She grinned again, exposing double canines on either side of her mouth. "Do you like my fangs? I got them off the Internet."

"Very impressive," lied Moon, beckoning to the bargirl to order their drinks. He frowned at the guttural roar coming from the stage. "Is this really what you guys are into?"

"What? *Coffin Shaker*?" Sonia grimaced. "Some of the guys like them but I prefer the more romantic bands like *Stoker's Kiss* or *Phantail*. Goth's a real subculture. There's quite a lot of variety, really."

Moon nodded, as he watched a teeny Goth girl walk up to the bar. She was dressed like a cross between a Manga schoolgirl and Wednesday Addams. Over one shoulder was a tote-bag shaped like a black coffin. In a gesture of individuality the kid had stuck a 'baby on board' car sticker on the back of the bag. He smiled, these people certainly had his sense of humour. "So, how did you get into all this?"

"My older sister was in at the start. She's eight years older than me and I thought she looked really cool and the music she listened too was so much better than all the boy-band crap everyone else was into."

Moon nodded again, "Anything's better than boy-band crap," he agreed. *Except Hip-Hop*, he added in his head. If people claimed to make music they could at least have the decency to try to sing.

He scanned the audience. It was strange, for most of the pub bands he went to see the audience was like any pub-full of people: little groups of friends with the odd loner thrown in. This was more like a class reunion; everyone seemed to know each other. Then suddenly time seemed to slow down to an eternity. For an interminable instant his eyes locked with those of a tall leather-clad figure with burning blue eyes and waist length blond hair. A light blue aura seemed to surround him and his pale, blue tinged features looked like they had been hewn expertly out of marble. He was flanked by two stunningly beautiful girls, who seemed to have got everything right that Sonia and Avril had got wrong. They had effortlessly achieved the elegance and style that the other Goth girls in the room aspired to. They were stunningly clad in clinging red-tinged black velvet each wearing matching chokers with a silver ornament at the throat in the shape of a flying bat. Then the moment passed and he found that he was just staring at a trio of particularly attractive but fairly 'normal' looking Goths.

Coffin Shaker finished their set with one final cacophonous growl from their lead singer, a short Goth with Alice Cooper-like make-up on his face and wearing what looked like a PVC basque with bones piercing it at odd intervals. Then the band members leapt down from the stage to embrace and chat with friends and lovers, who seemed to constitute a sizeable fraction of the audience. "Does everybody here know everyone else?" asked the surprised Moon.

"Well, it's quite a close-knit scene," explained Sonia, sipping her Green Fairy absinthe. "Most of the bands are local and we all hang out in the same places so, of course, we tend to have at least a nodding acquaintance with everyone else."

Moon changed track. "What was that your friend on the door said about having some trouble?"

"Well, we tend to have the occasional bit of bother from people who don't like us being different and think Goth bashing's a good night's fun." She drew closer and Moon caught her making a furtive glance in the direction of the beautiful trio, who were chatting with Coffin Shaker's drummer. "But things have got very odd recently; a few regulars have dropped out of sight without telling anyone where they've gone."

"So you're saying people have just disappeared? How many?"

"Three, so far," replied Sonia, "and, you know it's funny, but now I think of it they all seem to have stopped coming along after one of these band nights... But, I mean, shit, people move on, you know. Maybe they just got jobs elsewhere or went to college or they may have 'seen the light' and got 'born again'. It happens occasionally and they tend to be warned off Goth by the church they've joined after that."

"'Born again'?" Moon understood what the term meant but he had never heard it used as if it were some kind of natural hazard before now.

"Yeah, Bristol's crawling with Fundamentalist Christians of one flavour or another and they tend to single out Goths. You know, we're obviously 'lost' souls. Of course most of us are revelling in the fact but they occasionally catch someone in a lonely or vulnerable moment. Normally, at least a close friend or their partner knows what's happened and tells everyone. Not with these guys though."

"Three people have gone missing and no-one's told the cops?"

"Yeah, well, it's not like we know something bad's happened to them and all three of them came from somewhere else. You know, moved here to work, lived in bedsits, no family here; for all we know they could all have given up on Bristol and gone home."

"Still, it's very odd. Someone should tell the police."

"We're not too hot on the police. They don't like people with alternative lifestyles and we're nearly as alternative as you can get. If one of us called in at the station and told them some crazy tale about Goths going missing, well, let's say I don't think they'd be very sympathetic and leave it at that."

Moon remembered that odd glance at the trio on the dance floor. "Do you think anyone here knows more than they're telling?" he asked watching her face closely.

Again, she made that tiny glance. "No... Well, rumours that's all."

"Care to let me in on them."

"Not really, crazy stuff, that's all. Stuff I wouldn't bother telling a 'mundane'."

"'Mundane', eh?" *If only you knew*, he thought. But instead he quipped, "I doubt the guys in A&E would agree with you!"

"A&E?" Sonia looked puzzled behind her bat's wing eye shadow.

"Oh, yeah, I didn't tell you. I only write articles part-time. Mainly I work as a nurse."

"Cool, do you get to see lots of... like, dismemberments and stuff?" For once Sonia's teeth did look menacing, wrapped up in a bloodthirsty smile. It seemed Goths did occasionally live up to their morbid stereotype.

The night powered on to the beat of the bands. Sonia introduced Moon to some of her crowd and the alcohol helped to break the ice. Glad that he had hidden his Dictaphone in his pocket before leaving his flat, Moon managed to gather plenty of information for his article. He doubted that he'd remember half of it by morning otherwise because he was having far too much fun.

At ten o'clock *Stokers Kiss* started an hour long set with a lively comic song called 'Carpe Jugulum', inspired by the Terry Pratchett book of the same name. It was fun to listen to but something about the music struck Moon as a bit odd. He gave Sonia a puzzled look. "This is Country and Western, isn't it?"

Sonia laughed prettily despite her fangs. "Yeah, but don't try to tell them. They get really upset if you suggest that it's anything other than Goth."

Otherwise, the band was extremely high-quality and Moon decided to give them a special mention in his article. By the time they were performing their last set number, 'Dark Caress', a sinisterly erotic song about vampiric love, Moon was dancing very close and very sexy with Sonia. *I'm in with a chance here*, he thought, as she beckoned him into a shadowy corner for a passionate, if rather toothy, snog. Moon remembered a joke he had heard or read somewhere about the dangers of French kissing vampires. Sonia's fangs may only be plastic but he was slightly worried he was in danger of losing his tongue.

The band finished with a double encore of their more rocky numbers, but by then, Moon was too engrossed with Sonia to do more than vaguely register that they were quite good. Then, during the sudden, shocking quiet of 'drinking up time', Sonia looked up at him shyly and asked, "Would you like to come back to my place?" Moon made a quick mental check of the expiry date of the condoms stored hopefully in his wallet for just such an opportunity, then joyfully agreed.

Chapter 4

The outside air was mercifully cool and smoke free after the heat and fug in the pub. Moon stood as patiently as possible with his arms around Sonia while she and Avril said goodbye to almost everyone who had come to the gig. Avril, it turned out, was going out with the bassist of *Unquiet Grave*, one of the bands that had played during the first half of the programme, before Moon had arrived. He continued to be impressed by the family-like atmosphere between these people. It was almost as if becoming a Goth was like joining a different race which had its own identifying features and customs.

The parade of goodbyes finally drew to an end and they left the courtyard to board the cab that Avril had phoned for earlier. As they piled into the taxi, Moon glanced back at the pub and with a start glimpsed a pale figure beckoning to him from the darkness of a nearby alley, which ran behind the main building. He recognised it as a spirit; its deathly pale face was framed by the shadowy ghost of long black hair and a dark red stain glistened wetly at the right hand side of its neck. The dark hollows of its eyes seemed to bore into Moon, accusing him of indifference, as he climbed guiltily into the cab.

Avril and Sonia shared a flat in Bristol's Hotwells area, not far from the Ebenezer Chapel and just up the road from where Isambard Kingdom Brunel's famous steam ship, the *Great Western* was moored on permanent display across the harbour. It was a part of Bristol Moon didn't visit often as the only attractions were the docks, a large Army & Navy store and a couple of fairly mediocre pubs. The taxi pulled into an Edwardian terrace and the Afro-Caribbean driver, his head made huge by the dreadlocks packed into his red, yellow and green woollen hat, asked for eleven pounds fare. Feeling magnanimous, Moon paid for all of them. The girl's flat was in a semi-detached Edwardian house about a hundred yards uphill from the main road. Most of Bristol is either up or downhill from somewhere because it was built around the Avon Gorge. However, the roads around the Hotwells area run down the sides of the Gorge itself and are very steep, so Moon was feeling quite winded by the time they reached the front door. "I hope you're up for this, Lover!" whispered Sonia, perplexed by his shortness of breath.

"Oh, yes! I'll be fine. I'm just not used to consorting with cliff-dwellers."

Sonia gave a short laugh. "I suppose it is pretty steep. You just get used to it."

The walls of the flat were painted a standard landlord's magnolia but Sonia and Avril had done their best to hide it, using a general colour scheme of purple and black with a heavy emphasis on the macabre. In the living-room a cobweb made out of black headed drawing pins joined together with black thread took up the entire top left corner of the hall-side wall, while on the opposite side of the room a modest collection of resin and pottery skulls grinned from above the fire-mantle. In the midst of these, Moon was surprised to see a small silver trophy in the shape of a woman wearing a martial arts outfit. He decided to ask Sonia about this some time if he ever had the chance. A large framed poster depicting the Middle-Eastern demon/goddess Lilith, dark wings outspread, embracing a winged serpent holding a black rose in its jaws, dominated the back wall above the sofa. The shabbiness of this ancient piece of furniture was mostly hidden by a black and purple Celtic knotwork throw. Longhaired fluffy black cushions lurked by the arms of the sofa and the two similarly accoutred chairs, like small venomous beasts waiting to pounce. "You girls really take this Goth stuff seriously, don't you?" commented Moon, taking off his jacket and throwing it over the arm of one of the dubious chairs then sitting firmly on top of one of the sofa predators.

Avril smiled. "If you're going to follow a fantasy why not take it all the way? Coffee?"

"Yes please; white, no sugar." He smiled at Sonia, who had sat down beside him, and she smiled back a little nervously snuggling into the crook of his arm. "You okay?" he asked, kissing her cheek.

"Yeah, I suppose. It's just that I hate this part. You seem

like a nice guy, Jerry. You're not going to turn out to be another every-day bastard are you?"

Moon hesitated; he'd assumed Sonia was, like many of her contemporaries, the kind of girl who treated sex as a bit of fun. Now he realised there might be a future to tonight and, with some consideration and mild reservation, realised he was cool with that. She was a nice lass in her own peculiar way and it was hard to meet potential partners in his line of work. "I'm not the love-'em-and-leave-'em sort, if that's what you mean," he replied reassuringly. "We can take it slowly if you like."

She kissed him deeply, tickling the stud in his tongue with the tip of her own. "Oh, I don't see why we can't take it slowly and have our fun at the same time, eh, Jerry?" That hungry gleam had returned to her eyes and the false fangs suddenly made her look very sexy. He gave a short, throaty laugh and returned her kiss with interest. Sonia rose seductively from the sofa, drawing Moon up with her. "Avril, don't bother making coffee for Jerry and me!" she called over her shoulder as she led him towards the stairs.

Sonia's bedroom continued the Goth theme with a vengeance. The bed was bordered with a frill of black lace and a blood red duvet cover and matching pillows, similarly trimmed with black lace, complemented a black bottom sheet. Over the bed hung a black net canopy, trimmed with red lace, which gave the room a slightly Middle-Eastern feel. The walls were the same uniform magnolia but hung with framed posters, which had a common gothic romantic theme. The ordinary, second hand landlord's furniture had been transformed using a combination of red and black satin throws and drapes, plus gothic style ornaments. Gargoyles, dragons and skeletons covered most of the available surfaces in the form of candlesticks, boxes and goblets. A glass-topped drinks table with a huge, black dragon for a pedestal had pride of place in one corner of the room. Its top arranged with various ornaments and candlesticks to resemble an altar.

"Interesting room," Moon commented noncommittally, as he regarded his own pale reflection in a Gothic arch style mirror. He looked huge-eyed and unreal in the reddish light cast by the room's lantern-like ornamental lamp. In contrast the gargoyle at the top of the arch looked disturbingly real, its eyes glittering evilly above a spike-toothed grin.

"Yes, I've put a lot of work into it," replied Sonia, removing silver bat-shaped clips from her hair.

Moon perused her heavy-laden bookshelf. The Ann Rice novels he recognised but some of the other authors were less familiar. Sonia seemed to be heavily into gothic horror with a smattering of lighter fantasy. He heard her moving behind him. "Jerry..." she whispered and he turned to find her sitting on the bed wearing nothing but her basque, her loose hair falling to mid-waist level.

Silently, he moved to sit beside her, touching her face gently with his fingers and kissing her deeply on her mouth before slowly moving his lips to her neck and breasts. It was here he began to notice a bit of a problem. Her breasts, although small, were quite beautiful, but she had silver rings through both nipples, which clashed against his teeth and made them less fun to nibble than the unadorned variety. Whether it was a hangover from being breast fed or that he'd been weaned too late from his dummy, Moon didn't know, but there was a strong oral side to his libido and he found unexpected lumps of metal a bit of a turn-off. With a small sigh, he switched from tongue to fingers and started to kiss the unmodified flesh of her breasts themselves. Then Sonia's deft fingers undid the front of his trousers and slid underneath to gently caress the growing firmness they found there. A few frantic manoeuvres later and they were both naked on top of the bed with Moon tracing his tongue down between her breasts, over the white mound of her stomach and her spider shaped navel ornament and down further. He noted with mild humour that she was really a redhead. Then... bugger! Another ruddy piercing! A silver skull with red amethysts for eyes grinned out from among a tangle of tight little auburn curls.

"Do you like my little skull?" asked Sonia, grinning down at him. "I got it for my twenty-fifth."

"Quite... charming," replied Moon, cursing inwardly. The little bleeder was blocking his favourite bit.

With a mental shrug, Moon tried a few tentative tongue strokes. Great! The skull ring didn't get in the way too much and soon there was a tumult of appreciative sighs from Sonia as he teased and caressed her with his lips and tongue, building her up to a crescendo of joy. Then suddenly, "Ouch!" That didn't sound good. He stopped then tried to move his tongue; "Ow! Ooh! Jerry, what the fuck are you doing down there? It hurts!"

The awful truth dawned on Moon. "I'the god by thongue sthtud sthtuck id you're ickle sthkull."

"You what! Well, unstick it then. Ouch! No, don't move."

"I think wid a bith off jiggling..." said Moon, trying to extricate himself with his fingers.

"Owww! No! And don't try to talk either, it's agony." Sonia reached carefully for her mobile phone on the bedside. "I think we'll have to call an ambulance."

"No!" Moon panicked. "I workth there!"

"Ouch! Shit, I said don't talk. I'm calling an ambulance and that's that."

At one twenty a.m. Moon and Sonia were wheeled into a cubicle in Accident and Emergency on a single trolley. Moon, who had been hidden under a green cellular blanket in an attempt to preserve Sonia's dignity, suddenly found himself laid bare, blinking under the cubicle's strip lighting and gazing up at the face of Gary Wong, grinning sadistically and wielding a pair of surgical wire cutters. "Hello, Jerry," he sniggered. "My, have you been a naughty boy!" This brought a chorus of laughs from the three unnecessary nurses who had also crowded into the cubicle.

"Geth sthtuffed, Wong!" lisped Moon, eliciting a pained scream and a clip round the ear from Sonia.

"Just get it over with!" said Sonia through gritted teeth. "I want to get as far away from this moron as possible."

Fifteen minutes later Moon was dressing himself in a separate cubicle and wondering what the ambulance crew had done with his other shoe when Wong sidled through the curtain waving a transparent sample container in front of him then sticking it under Moon's nose. "You must have been going some, Jerry, my son." He unscrewed the lid, grasped Moon's hand, and tipped the container's contents into his palm. Moon gazed miserably at his tongue stud and Sonia's skull ring, the latter now cut open and bent out of shape, but he could still see the point where it had somehow twisted and locked onto the other. "Adds a whole new dimension to safe sex, doesn't it?" Wong was obviously determined to milk this for all it was worth.

"I'm not in the mood, Gary," Moon replied dangerously.

"No?" replied Wong. "But you obviously were. Where on earth did you find 'Vampirella', the local cemetery?"

"Not that it's any of your business, but I was researching an article for *Venue*."

"What into, necrophilia?" Wong laughed.

"Goth culture if you must know. And Sonia happens to be a very nice girl, despite her taste in fashion."

"Well, sorry to pour cold water on it, like. But I think you've spoiled your chances there, Kidda."

Moon sighed. "You're probably right." He really had to try to patch things up with Sonia somehow. They'd been doing all right up until everything had gone pear shaped and it wasn't very easy to meet potential partners as a nurse. He met some lovely female nurses while working, but it's hard to find the right moment to approach someone socially when your most intimate encounters usually involve a distressed patient and soiled bed-linen. At twenty-seven Moon was beginning to worry about his future.

He found Sonia crying in the next cubicle with Avril trying to comfort her. Her eyes narrowed as he peered around the curtain. "Sorry, Love..." he began lamely.

"'Sorry' doesn't cover it. Not by a long straw!" Sonia replied petulantly. "I'm so bloody sore I probably won't be able to sit down for a month. What the hell were you thinking? You know you have to be careful with piercings."

"Well, no I didn't, to be honest. I didn't realise there'd be a problem."

Sonia wasn't listening. "And that's another thing; twenty-five quid that little skull stud cost me at *Dusk-till-Dawn Fashions*. Not much use for anything now is it!"

"I'll pay for it," Moon fished in his pocket. "I've got nearly forty quid here, buy something nicer."

"Nicer? Oh I see, it was tacky, was it? My choice in

jewellery isn't good enough for you." Sonia started to cry again.

"Look, that's not what I meant..." said Moon still holding out his wad of cash. "Oh, look. I know you're pretty upset at the moment but I think we were both enjoying the evening up to that point." He fished one of the business cards he used for his journalist work out of his pocket. "If you feel differently once you've had a chance to think about it just call me. Okay?"

Sonia took the card, tore it in two, balled it and threw it into a corner of the cubicle. "You'll be twice as much history once I've had time to think about it, Mister Jerry bloody Moon!"

"Sorry you feel that way," he replied sadly, turning to leave the cubicle.

Avril retrieved his card then followed him out. "Look," she explained, "Sonia's had a really painful and embarrassing experience and it'll take her a while to calm down. It's too early to try to make peace just yet, you know. I think you're a good guy, Jerry, but she's had to put up with a few real shits in her life. If you're willing to stay the distance I think things might work out between you two. I'll even put in a good word for you. So hang in there and she might come around."

Moon smiled wryly. "I do like her, you know; enough to give her a little time to think things over anyway. I'll be around the *Rest* for the next week or so gathering more material for my article so the two of you might catch me there but, if you don't, call me if there's any sign of a thaw." He nodded towards the cubicle where a miserable looking Sonia could be seen trying to peer through the chink in the curtains. "You talk her round and I'll owe you big time, I mean it."

Avril smiled. "Be careful, I might hold you to that some time."

Moon winked at her. "You do that. Bye Avril, for now."

Moon headed out of the Minor Injuries section and through the double doors into the night, tiptoeing gingerly over where a drunk had thrown up on the entrance steps. He felt strangely elated by Avril's words, despite the embarrassing events of the last couple of hours. As he set off on his lonely way home he failed to notice the six tiny blue balls of light that detached themselves from the neon glare of the hospital and spiralled along above the pavement behind him.

Chapter 5

Moon awoke the next morning in response to a painful throbbing in his tongue. As the events of the previous evening filtered back into his brain he groaned with guilt and embarrassment. Grabbing a bubble pack of paracetamol from his bedside cabinet, he popped a couple of pills into his mouth, swilling them down with a mouthful of cold, grey tea from the unfinished cuppa that he had made when he had got home the previous night. Getting out of bed, he padded naked into his kitchenette where he made some fresh tea and buttered toast, which he took back to bed with him, switching on the TV as he passed it. Making himself comfortable, he sat up in bed watching a kids' computer graphic adventure series as he gingerly chewed his toast and planned his day.

One big advantage of working in the night pool was that he had a lot of control over his shift pattern so he worked in the middle of the week, allowing himself a longish weekend for his own projects. Today being Saturday, he thought the best use of his time would be to work on his article for an hour or so. Later, he would head out to the city centre for a little therapeutic shopping followed by an early visit to the *Hangman's Rest* to see if he could interview some of the bar staff before it got too busy.

Breakfast finished, he refilled his teacup and perched himself cross-legged in his executive chair with his keyboard in his lap. As he booted up his computer he rewound the tape in his Dictaphone and placed the machine next to the monitor. Taking a deep preparatory breath, he opened his 'Notes and Ideas' text-file, switched on the tape machine and began to type notes on the previous night's work, an exercise that he found helped him to organise his thoughts for the real task of writing.

Hearing Sonia's voice on the tape reminded him of the pale softness of her body against his the night before and that intriguing quirkiness, verging on downright weirdness, which he had found so attractive about her. He realised that he was actually hoping against hope that Avril would succeed in getting her friend to give him another chance. *I must be mad*, he thought, *she'll never change her mind after last night.*

As their taped conversation repeated itself, his curiosity was stirred again by Sonia's strange ambivalence concerning the missing Goths. It struck him as odd that she had seemed almost afraid to talk about them. Then he remembered that pale, beckoning ghost hiding in the alleyway. Okay, there were quite a few spirits who regularly haunted the alleys around the *Hangman's Rest* and the pub itself, not to mention some of the other less human entities that prowled Bristol's night-shrouded streets. However, the way it had felt to his extra senses told him this one had been a new addition and it had obviously been extremely anxious to communicate with him. Unfortunately, he was being paid to write about Goth culture, not missing persons. He couldn't let his curiosity jeopardise his work.

He played a little more of the tape and recalled Sonia's nervous glances towards that strange, beautiful trio of Goths he had noticed on the pub dance floor while they had been discussing the missing people. He wondered if Sonia thought they were somehow involved in the disappearances; perhaps he could quiz them about the missing Goths and interview them about their lifestyle at the same time. They were clearly the sort of characters he should be talking to anyway and he had a couple of weeks to his deadline so he could probably afford to indulge his curiosity just a little.

His notes completed plus a brief outline for the article sketched out, Moon saved his work to his hard drive and backed it up on disk. Now he felt he could head out to town, satisfied that he had made a decent start.

Anna wasn't on the stairs when he stepped out onto his landing but a tingling in his 'ghost sense' drew his eyes upwards to the balcony above his own, where he could see the pale face of Harry, Anna's father, peering over the banisters of the floor above. *"Where is she?"* he vibed. *"I only want to tell her I'm sorry... So sorry. It wasn't my fault. Her mother drove me to the drink, you know, always nagging me about how I'd never make anything of meself. Damn the woman!"*

Moon had heard this before and had enough experience to know it was self-centred rubbish. Harry's supposed contriteness was just veiled blame-shifting fired by raging guilt, as awful and destructive in some ways as his drunken rages had been when he was alive. Anna still hid herself from her father, recognising that this half-hearted repentance was no more than a self-centred sham. "Don't kid yourself, Harry. It was your fault. You got drunk and threw your four-year-old daughter over the banisters. You need to accept responsibility for your own actions before you can be forgiven for them, you know. Even Anna understands that and she's only a child." With a whimper of terror the drunk's spirit disappeared, apparently hoping to avoid further confrontation.

With a snort of disgust, Moon stomped off down the stairs, catching Anna's tearful face peering out at him from the shadows of Mrs. Foley's doorway on his way downstairs. Great! He hadn't made it out of his front door yet and his ghostly neighbours' domestic problems already had him in a bad mood!

The city centre was crawling with shoppers. Moon made a half-hearted effort to window shop around the Virgin Superstore but he couldn't shake his depression. Eventually, he decided he needed to do something positive and, in desperation, he caught a number 54 bus up to the top of Whiteladies Road, where the University rubbed shoulders with the high value residential areas of Clifton and Cotham. Once there he popped into a bakery and bought himself a couple of filled rolls and then took the most direct route he knew to St Andrew's Cemetery.

The now disused cemetery was close to Queen's Road, a fairly busy thoroughfare which ran between Whiteladies Road and the affluent area of Clifton Village. The most recent graves there dated from the early nineteen hundreds and the bombed out ruins of the adjoining St Andrew's Church had long since been demolished and converted into a park-like area bordered by ancient trees. The cemetery itself had a secluded feel to it, being sheltered by several large yews and other smaller trees. One side of it was closed in by a Georgian red-brick wall, the opposite by a formidable hedge and a paved avenue ran through its centre, separated from the cemetery proper by spiked iron railings and covered over by small trees trained to ironwork arches, which had earned it the name Bird Cage Walk. Moon had discovered it by chance one day when he had decided to go exploring and now it was one of the places he knew he could go if he wanted a bit of peace.

Until recently the graveyard had been quite overgrown but a local volunteer group had taken up its cause. They had cleaned up the graves, which Moon applauded, but they had also cut back the trees or in some instances even removed them, which had saddened him as it had diminished the cemetery's secluded atmosphere. However they *had* planted wildflowers, which had mollified him a little. As he entered through the first archway the twenty-first century seemed to slip away and his spirit relaxed in the peace of the place. He leaned on the fence and started to eat one of his rolls, watching a fat squirrel playing among the graves. It eyed him brazenly then scurried through the bars and, resting one foot on his shoe, gazed up at him demandingly. Chuckling at this boldness, Moon broke off a morsel of bread and gave it to the squirrel, which grabbed it between both front claws and devoured it daintily. "No wonder you're so chubby!" laughed Moon. Obviously, being so cheeky paid off in tidbits. The squirrel, startled by his outburst, ran a short distance back into the graveyard then turned and scolded him loudly. Moon laughed again, he loved visiting this place; it seemed to patch over a hole in his spirit that urban living created.

As he threw another morsel to the squirrel he recognised a strange ripple passing through the grass and wildflowers and felt an odd buzz of energy, which filled his extra senses with the feel of roots and flowers, of soil and growing things. He often suspected *this* was the reason why the place affected him so much more. He hesitated to think of them as 'fairies', perhaps 'nature spirits' was closer to the mark but, regardless of classification, their presence always had a healing touch to it. He had never attempted to communicate with them because they always seemed busy; not in any kind of driven sense, if anything there was a constant sense of enjoyment and play to what they did, but they obviously had a job to do and he respected that. For their part they seemed quite happy to share their energy with him, just like they did with any other piece of nature they encountered while maintaining the fabric of life, or whatever it was they were doing. Since his first visit he had grown to realise that the graveyard was quietly swarming with them and he treasured the unique mystery of their presence.

He leaned on the fence gazing into the dappled twilight over the graves and munching on his roll. This was what he needed; this place of death but so full of life recharged his soul and healed it from the bruises left by city living. "Thank you," he whispered to the place in general as he finished his meal, throwing out a few last crumbs for the squirrels. He rolled up his paper bag into a ball and tossed it into a convenient wastebasket as he headed back out of the past and into the noise and fumes of the present. *I really must try to come here more often.* He chided himself, hoping that his busy schedule would allow him to do so.

He meandered back through town, browsing in shops along the way and finally arrived at the *Hangman's Rest* in time to catch the kitchen open. He ordered a meal with his first pint and sat near the window, watching passers-by as he waited for his order. The *Rest* was fairly empty except for a few professional bar-proppers, who had probably been there since lunchtime, and a young couple who looked like they had wandered in at random in search of a meal. The bar throbbed with Death Metal music, which must have been the choice of the skinny Goth lad behind the bar, while muted satellite MTV heavy rock videos played on a large TV screen on a wall of the main bar and several smaller screens around the pub. Moon wondered why anyone in his or her right mind would like Death Metal; he supposed that there might be some comfort in knowing that once you finished listening to it life was unlikely to get worse.

When his chili con carne arrived, he found it was surprisingly good for pub fare and he dug in happily, as he watched the early evening crowd arrive. He recognised a few faces from the night before, most of them appearing a little less spectacular and a lot more human. The men wore little or no make-up and the girls were wearing dowdier less constricting clothing; this was obviously 'off-duty' Goth, not party Goth.

Moon made a mental note to mention this compromise with the 'mundane' world in his article.

His meal finished, he wandered up to the bar for a refill. The barman was serving one of the bar-proppers and as Moon waited his turn several young Goths came through the door and approached the bar. To Moon's surprise the barman finished serving the first customer then ignored him studiously and started chatting to and serving the newcomers. He was wondering whether he should complain when a cheery female voice said from his end of the bar, "Can I help you?"

"A baseball bat would come in very handy right now," Moon replied angrily, nodding towards the gaggle at the end of the bar, "but failing that I'd like a pint of Ostrich if that's not too much trouble."

The voice's owner, a diminutive thirty-something woman with short cropped almost white platinum blonde hair, frowned slightly then said, "Oh, is Moz being an arsehole again? Hey, Moz, I pay you to serve customers not to cozy up with that band of rejects! First come, first served, remember that?"

Moz looked away from his conversation with a skinny girl with pink and blue dreadlocks and replied, "Okay, sorry, Kate."

"Just remember, I've told you twice already, you're here to work not hang out with your mates. One more time and you're out on your ear." She turned back to Moon. "Sorry, we employ our staff mainly from the clientele and sometimes they forget which side of the bar they're on. Ostrich was it?"

"Yeah, look, are you the boss here?" Moon surveyed Kate's outfit: high-heeled black calf boots, black jeans and a studded black leather vest. The latter partly revealed Celtic tattoos on both shoulders which flowed into twin dragons on her shoulder blades, an impressive cleavage and a physique which hinted at many hours spent in the gym. She didn't look very much like a Goth, this lady and she was, frankly, much more impressive than most of the Goths he had met so far.

"I'm the manager, yes," replied Kate, handing him his drink.

"Have you time to chat a while? You see, I'm writing this article on Goth culture for *Venue* and I came here this evening hoping to interview one of the bar staff, seeing as this is the main Goth venue in the city."

Kate pondered for a second. "I suppose I could give you a few minutes. It's hardly busy in here, is it? Moz, I'm taking five!" She pulled herself a pint of lager then indicated a side table, where they installed themselves with their drinks. "What's your name?" she asked, pulling a tobacco tin out of her pocket emblazoned with a silver pentagram on a black background. Moon noticed the same device occurred elsewhere about her person in the form of rings and a pendant.

"Jerry Moon," he replied. "Most people just call me Moon."

"'Moon' I like," Kate replied, rolling a thin liquorice-papered cigarette. "The moon's always been associated with the Goddess, you know. Good omen." She smiled mysteriously.

This puzzled Moon slightly but he pressed on with his interview. "So how long have you been a Goth?" he began.

A wolfish smile spread across Kate's face. "I'm not a Goth; if anything I'm a biker, but I suppose it's an easy mistake to make; we have a similar fondness for black leather and tattoos. It's just that bikers have balls." The grin she flashed him would have looked at home on something large and furry.

Moon cleared his throat. "Sorry, I just assumed, with the pub's clientele…"

"The *Rest* was a biker pub long before the Goths moved in, Moon. We didn't choose them; they chose us because we didn't turn our noses up at them. The *Hangman's Rest* has always had a soft spot for s0ociety's rebels and misfits."

Yeah, and some of them hang on way past kicking out time, thought Moon, watching the shade of a regency highwayman float past behind Kate's head. "So, you didn't decide to target Goths, they just started coming along."

"Yeah, kids looking for somewhere to drink where they could Goth up in peace."

"'Goth up'?" Moon wasn't sure what she meant.

"You know, wear the gear. Pose a bit without some moron ragging them off or using them as a punch bag. Goth is an escapist sub-culture. They use a spoonful of fantasy to take the bitter edge off reality. That's easier to do somewhere where the harsher part of reality is out of the picture."

"So that's why they dress up? To escape from reality?" This was what he needed for his article, an objective, but informed, opinion.

"That and to create a sense of identity. A lot of them have had a hard ride from mainstream society somewhere down the line: bullying at school, boring day jobs, oppressive parents... It's a way to break away from the world you despise safe in the company of people who feel the same way. The gear is both a sort of uniform and a way of giving the rest of the world the finger. All subcultures work that way, from the skinheads to the fundamentalists."

"But why Gothic?" Moon asked the most obvious question. "Why dress up as vampires or corpses? Why toy with fantasies about being damned? What's the point?"

Kate laughed then drew hard on her cigarette. Blowing smoke out of her nostrils, she replied, "Ask me an easy one, why don't you? The answer to that must lie as far back as the first ghost story told around the first cooking fire and then down through the ages from countless folk-tales to Stoker and Shelly and the early Gothic writers. It's all about power and fear, I would say. Death is powerful and frightening, so if you toy with death then you take on some of its power. The dark is the primal fear and if you embrace the darkness you become fearsome. And vampires – well, they're just cool, aren't they? Modern folklore has transformed them from the bloated living corpses that terrified mediaeval peasants into chic, guiltless, beautiful predators who slide through the ocean of humanity like tiger sharks. Of course some people are going to want to look like them."

"But they're just fantasy," observed Moon.

A dark thought passed behind Kate's eyes. "Perhaps," she replied.

Something in Kate's reaction reminded him of the missing Goths. "I hear that a few of your clients have disappeared recently. Have you any idea where they may have gone?"

"Not really, some of our guests are pretty transient you know, especially the eighteen to twenties crowd. They get better jobs; go off to college, that sort of thing. It's just the fucked up ones who hang around forever, eh Tez?" This last was addressed to a nearby character whose straggly beard and long, slightly greying hair made it hard to determine his age, which could have been anywhere from thirty-five to fifty. He was wearing a black leather waistcoat covered in badges over a worn looking denim shirt, above dirty patched and faded jeans and down-at-heel cowboy boots. He seemed to have been listening in on their conversation and was obviously not at all bothered by being caught out.

"Takes one to know one, Kate," he grinned roguishly, showing off several missing teeth.

"I work here, you old bugger, what's your excuse?"

"I'm enslaved by your stunning beauty and maidenly charms," Terry replied, winking at Moon.

"I never knew," Kate fluttered her mascara-thick eyelashes. "Not that I think you're man enough, but thanks for the thought. Moon, this is Mad Terry, he's been causing trouble here longer than I've been manager, so he may be able to help you with your article. I'm afraid I'm long overdue back at the bar."

"'Mad' Terry?" queried Moon, examining his new acquaintance dubiously as he took the chair recently vacated by Kate.

"Yes, well..." replied Terry, "I was a lot younger when I earned that moniker. I tend to drink less and piss more nowadays, if you get my meaning. The real name's Terry Doyle. Glad to make your acquaintance."

Moon shook the proffered hand, trying not to wince as Terry's work-calloused digits ground his knuckles together. "You seemed to be interested in what Kate and I were discussing, Terry. The missing Goth kids: have you any idea what may have happened to them?"

Terry gave Moon a sidelong glance along his thin, aquiline nose. "Nothing that wouldn't have you thinking that I deserve my nickname, but then, you seem to be an open-minded feller, so perhaps you won't think me so mad after all."

Moon nodded in encouragement and Terry, with a deep frown of concentration, started his tale. "I was drinking in here one evening and they had a few of the Goth types in, chatting around the bar mostly, including a couple of gorgeous young things hanging around a lad that looked... well, like a modern day Viking god to put it poetically. Tall, blue-eyed, blond hair down to his arse, you know what I mean?"

"I think I've seen them," answered Moon with a grimace. "Your description matches that of a group of Goths I noticed at the band-fest on Friday."

"Yeah, well they hang around here a fair bit. Seem to be well in with the rest of the crowd. Anyway, I had to take a piss so I went through to the gents. There's a little narrow window that looks out into the car park, which was partly open, so as I was shaking off I glanced out the window and who should I see but Viking Goth boy and his two lovelies looking like they were heading off home. So I think: 'I wonder what sort of wheels he has'."

"As you do..." encouraged Moon.

"But he hasn't got any wheels."

"He hasn't?"

"No. And this is the part that'll make you think I deserve to be called *Mad* Terry." Terry drew conspiratorially close to Moon across the table.

"Really?" Moon was enjoying Terry's sense of theatre.

"Yeah. You see Viking boy and his girls look around as if they're afraid someone will see them then he puts an arm around each of their waists and they fly off into the night."

Moon choked on his beer. "They flew?" he sputtered.

Terry nodded while wiping bits of foam from his face. "Yeah, well *he* flew; seemed like he was the one providing the lift, straight up into the sky like a frigging super-hero. And I hadn't even had any blow that night, let alone anything stronger, so I wasn't hallucinating."

"And do you hallucinate?"

"Well, yeah sometimes. I like a bit of blow and I drop the occasional tab of acid or 'E' but not a lot nowadays and this wasn't one of my *normal* hallucinations. It was far too sensible."

Moon pondered this information for a second. Terry was obviously not the most reliable eyewitness ever to have walked the earth but Moon had himself noticed something odd about the

'Viking' and his girlfriends and he was used to trusting his gift where the supernatural was involved. He heard the bell over the door ring and looked over Terry's head towards the main entrance. Sonia and Avril had just walked in. "Look, thanks Terry, I owe you a pint, but I really need to talk with one of those girls who've just come in. Do you mind if we continue our conversation some other time?"

"No problem, Moon, old mate," said Terry draining his glass. "Mine's a Guinness." With a sense of trepidation Moon picked up their empty glasses and headed for the bar.

Sonia stood at the bar looking like a pretty anaemic in her white make-up. She was wearing a black trench coat, a furry black sweater decorated with silver beads, a black leather mini skirt, black tights and a pair of black laced boots with chrome decoration and two-inch thick soles. Over her shoulder she carried a black latex rucksack, which looked like an alien parasite. Avril was slightly more conservatively dressed in a black sweatshirt bearing a picture of a rose in a pool of blood with its petals twisted into the face of a skull and the legend *Stoker's Kiss* in gothic script beneath it. Over this she wore a black beaded jacket with a fluffy fake-fur collar and her legs were encased in very ordinary jeans over black, chrome-tipped cowgirl boots. Sonia regarded Moon with a grim expression. "Avril reckons I ought to give you another chance," she sighed. "I suppose you can't really be blamed for an honest mistake but you're going to have to prove you're worth the trouble you've caused."

Moon grinned. "Well, we could always take up where we left off," he replied, making Avril spin round and glare at him in exasperation.

"Why do men always think of *that* before anything else?" hissed Sonia. "It'll be a long, long time if ever before we get back to that, Mister. I'll have you know I spent most of last night with a bag of frozen peas clasped between my thighs to keep the swelling down, for what good it did me. I'm sad to say I now put *your* 'little soldier' to shame in that department, if last night's viewing was anything to go by." She gestured archly to the relevant part of Moon's anatomy but the pointed remark failed to hit home. One advantage of being a male nurse was that you saw enough of other men's anatomies to know where you were in the penis stakes. Moon knew he was about average as these things go and wasn't going to let a little bitchiness upset him. Visibly troubled by his lack of reaction, Sonia continued, "What I meant is that you need to show that you're serious about making a go of it even if we do have to wait a while to consummate things. What do you say?"

It took a second or two for Moon to gather his thoughts. For an instant the mixed feelings stirred up by the anger behind Sonia's earlier remark threatened to make him want to serve up a similarly bitchy reply, but a certain vulnerability in her eyes caught him off guard and reawakened the more gentle feelings that had been kindled the night before so he simply said, "I'd like to try," and took her right hand in both of his.

She smiled and kissed his cheek and said, "Then I'll have a vanilla Green Fairy and so will Avril."

Chapter 6

Moon and the girls found themselves an empty side table. Then he quickly delivered the pint of Guinness to Terry, who was already in deep banter with another ageing biker of similar aspect. The pair nodded to him without pausing in their conversation except for a foam-muffled "Thanks" from Terry. Moon returned to find both girls contemplating him with curiosity. "I didn't know you were pals with Mad Tez." Sonia made this sound like the least cool thing on earth.

"I'm not. Kate suggested he might be able to help me with my article."

"Why?" asked Avril. "He's not a Goth."

"No, but he's been a local at the *Rest* for years and Kate thought he might be able to explain how it became a Goth venue. He also has some *interesting* tales to tell…"

"Like the one about Uri and his two girlfriends being vampires?" Avril laughed. "That guy is such a druggy!"

"Are you talking about that very blond Goth who was here last night with the two girls?" Moon was surprised. "Terry seemed to think they had something to do with the missing people but he didn't say anything about them being vampires. Do you two know this Uri then?"

"Yeah, he occasionally plays violin for *Unquiet Grave*. I think he writes some of their lyrics too. He lives with Charli and Roanne, the two girls he's usually with, somewhere up near the Downs. They're a sort of open *ménage a trois,* not my cup of tea but very nice people all the same. They're a bit too heavily into the Goth game. You know, the type who sleep in coffins and only come out at night, but there are plenty of wannabee vamps on the scene, look at Sonia with her teeth."

"Oh, but that's just a bit of fun," Sonia was quick to explain. "At least they're not permanent like some people go in for. You can buy them on the Internet you know. I don't know about Uri though, Avril, there's something not quite right about him and his women. They give me this odd, creepy feeling sometimes."

"Is that why you kept looking over at them when you were telling me about the missing people last night?" asked Moon.

"I suppose so. Was it that obvious? Look, I thought you were writing an article about Goths, not missing persons."

"I am, but I hate loose ends and several people disappearing over a fairly short length of time are the type of loose end that my natural curiosity wants to unravel."

"Aren't you frightened what you'll find?" Sonia's eyes widened dramatically.

"Well, yeah, but if something bad's happening it needs to be stopped."

"So you'll be going after Uri with a stake and a crucifix?" asked Avril. "Seems a bit dramatic."

"I didn't say that. It's just that two people in this pub seem to think he's involved."

"I don't think Sonia's spooky feelings and Mad Terry's hallucinations amount to proof of anything." Avril raised her eyebrows sceptically as she sipped her Green Fairy.

"Yeah, but you can add some spooky feelings of my own to Sonia's and I tend to trust *my* spooky feelings."

"You get spooky feelings too?" asked Sonia. "That's great!"

"Not just feelings sometimes." Moon smiled at her. "Sometimes I see things too. Spirits, auras, that kind of thing."

"Oh, come on!" Avril's reaction was full of scorn. "You're as bad as Mad Terry, the two of you, seeing things and feeling things. I think I'll leave you both to your delusions." Grabbing her drink she flounced off to where a handful of Goths were chatting in a corner.

Moon was surprised by Avril's reaction. "Is she really that bothered by psychic phenomena?"

Sonia came round to the seat next to him and snuggled under his arm. "A bit," she replied. "Avril is bothered by stuff she can't control so the idea of all sorts of invisible stuff happening around her freaks her out but I think mostly she wanted to give us some time on our own. Plus, of course, Roger's here."

"Roger?" asked Moon.

Sonia nodded to where Avril was cuddling up to a tall, longhaired Goth with a goatee and mild acne. Moon recognised him from on the stage the night before. "Her boyfriend," explained Sonia.

"I would have thought being a Goth would mean you were automatically open to the possibilities of the supernatural," observed a bemused Moon.

"That's one stereotype that you can challenge in your article, isn't it?" Sonia kissed him on the cheek. "Just because someone likes the look and the people and may have a soft spot for the dark mythos, it doesn't mean they actually believe all that stuff."

"How about you?" asked Moon. "Do you believe in the supernatural?"

"Well, I've had my spooky feelings all my life and one or two experiences I can't explain, except in terms of the supernatural, so, yes I suppose I do believe. Although, I don't think I could really say exactly what I believe in."

"I don't know that I really have any choice in the matter," said Moon, steeling himself for ridicule or rejection. "You see, shortly after I started my first job as a nurse I had a patient die under my care for the first time. I was working in the High Dependency Unit and this old chap came in with a complicated heart problem. He was fairly conscious on admission but quickly deteriorated and because of his health problems he'd asked that we wouldn't try to bring him back if his heart stopped. When it was obvious that he wasn't going to make it we moved him into a side cubicle and he passed on shortly afterwards, but that's just it, he didn't…"

"Didn't what?" Sonia's eyes were wide with interest.

"Didn't 'pass on'; he just died and hung around. After his relatives had gone home, I went back into the cubicle with another nurse to lay him out and there he was, standing by his own corpse looking really confused. He recognised me from when I admitted him and flew over to me demanding to know what was happening and what was I going to do about it. He didn't realise he had died, you see, because he was comatose when it happened. This was the first time anything like that had happened to me and all I could do was whisper under my breath, 'It's okay you're just dead. Go towards the light.' The poor girl I was laying him out with must have thought I was bonkers but it seemed to work."

Sonia laughed. "I didn't know you could die and not realise you're dead."

"It happens quite a lot. I'd say about forty to fifty per cent of hauntings involve disorientated dead folk blundering around in confusion because for some reason they've died and not noticed it. What's worse is that most of them don't want to listen when you explain it to them. Believe me, I've tried."

"So you talk to dead people a lot, do you?" asked Sonia without any apparent sarcasm.

"Most of the time I try to avoid it, unless it's someone who's died under my care, then I think I still have a duty as a nurse to help them, but dead people often have a warped view of reality, they tend to be stuck in their own time. It's hard to reason with them, especially if they've been around for a few years. And often you have to find the right key to move them on to the next world."

"Key?"

"Yeah. Like you might find a soldier haunting his old post because he was never dismissed so you would have to try to find a sympathetic army officer to dismiss him, or a little girl might not rest until her favourite toy is returned to her, that sort of thing. Mostly they're scared of 'moving on' and make excuses for staying around. Personally speaking, I honestly don't have the time to pander to a load of cowardly spooks."

"You think they should get an *after*life," quipped Sonia with a grin. She had left her fangs at home this evening much to Moon's relief.

Moon laughed and hugged her to him. "Yes, I suppose you could say that."

Moon and Sonia continued to chat and cuddle, relaxing more into each other's company as the night progressed. They had already established what they felt for one another so now they were able to forget their earlier problems and just be themselves. Strangely enough, the fact that sex wasn't an option at present seemed to allow them to draw closer emotionally. To put it bluntly, they were falling in love and enjoying it immensely.

As drinking up time drew to a close Sonia grabbed Moon's hand. "It can only really be coffee tonight but would you like to come back to our place. We'll be alone; Avril is staying over at Roger's for the weekend."

"I'd like that," replied Moon, eager to spend more time together. "I don't have work tomorrow or anything that needs getting up early for." So they collected their belongings and exited the *Hangman's Rest* hand in hand.

As they left the car park they passed the dark entrance to the alleyway where Moon had glimpsed a spirit the night before. He glanced at it in passing and instantly regretted doing so. "Sonia, tell me, the missing Goths, does one of them have a skeleton tattooed on his left arm made to look like it's breaking through cracked porcelain?"

"You mean Dominic, yes, why?"

"Because he's standing in that opening beckoning to me, that's why." Moon pointed at the shadowy figure visible only to himself and a terrified alley cat that was cringing in the lee of one wall.

Sonia peered into the darkness. "No, he's not! Oh! You mean he's…"

"Dead, yes," replied Moon, following the retreating shade into the alley.

"Hi," vibed Dominic, looking back over one vaporous shoulder at Moon, *"is that right? You think I'm dead?"*

"I'd lay odds on it," replied Moon. "Sorry."

"Thought so," said Dominic with a resigned grimace, pointing to a pathetic bundle lying where his feet should be. *"This was a dead giveaway."*

Moon looked down at the pale-faced remains, which had once housed the spirit who hovered before him. "I guess so," he answered. "Any idea who killed you?"

"No, I just remember being hit from behind."

Sonia came up behind Moon, took one look at Dominic's corpse and screamed. "It's him, Dominic! Oh my god, you've killed him!"

"No, I did not!" Moon was shocked. "Look at him, he's been here a while."

"So how did you know he was here?" Suspicion darkened her features.

"He told me, remember?"

"You mean all that stuff about seeing spirits was for real? I thought it was just normal bullshit. You know, just to make yourself seem interesting."

"I wish!" Moon shook his head incredulously.

"I'm still not sure I believe you."

"Look, darling, I'm hardly going to take my new girlfriend to meet the corpse of my latest victim am I? It's bad that you're willing to think I'm a psycho but *stupid* as well? Give me some credit!"

Sonia thought for a moment. "Okay, I suppose."

"We're going to have to report this anyway. Have you got a mobile on you?"

The police arrived with uncharacteristic speed. Moon, who had once waited several hours after a burglary for a policeman to arrive just to lecture him on the foolishness of moving into the neighbourhood he then lived in, was very impressed. Within minutes the alleyway was sectioned off with police tape and he and Sonia were in the back of a police car heading the few hundred yards to Bridewell Police Station.

"It would have been quicker if we'd walked," complained Moon as they stopped at their second set of traffic lights.

"Ah," replied the officer at the wheel. "But if we walked you might get away."

"Shut up, Sid!" said the other policeman. "Sorry about that. Constable Newell tends to act as if everyone we take to the station is automatically guilty of something."

"Well, most of 'em are!" commented Sid emphatically.

"You ever read *Judge Dredd*, Officer Newell?" asked Moon, just knowing the significance of his comment would probably go over Sid's head.

"Never 'eard of 'im," replied Sid. "Is 'e one of them big London judges then? We don't often see that sort at the Bristol Crown Court."

"Oh, I think you'd approve of him if you'd met him," replied Moon archly. Sid's mate, who *did* recognise the significance, stifled a laugh, while Sonia nudged Moon in the ribs and glared at him to behave himself.

They arrived at the police station and were ushered into separate interview rooms by Sid and his mate. Moon sat gazing at the buff panelled walls and hoped Sonia had the sense to leave out the part about Dominic's spirit. The police were unlikely to take kindly to ghost stories.

Moon was studying the flaking paintwork and wondering how long they would keep him waiting when Sid's mate opened the door to the interview room and entered, followed by a plain clothes officer dressed in a shabby dark grey suit and carrying a vending machine cup full of steaming liquid. This second individual who introduced himself as Detective Inspector Whatley had the barrel-like build of a large athletic man who was slowly succumbing to middle-age flab. The way his rumpled white shirt strained around his middle spoke of too many nights down the pub and, the nurse in Moon noted grimly, impending heart disease, if the yellow stains on his right index and ring fingers were anything to go by.

Whatley pulled at his necktie, straining the already miniscule knot into something not much larger than a pea in his attempt to increase the ventilation via his open top button. *Suits are the curse of the modern working man,* thought Moon to himself. *I'm glad I don't have to wear one of the sods.*

"Mr Moon?" said Whatley in a West Country burr, as Sid's mate put a cassette in the large tape recorder at one side of the intervening table. Moon nodded.

"Interview with Jeremy Angus Moon of Flat 5, 43 Angel Terrace, Redland, Bristol. Interviewing officer, Detective Inspector Arthur Whatley; also present Constable William Wright. Interview commences twenty-three eighteen, Saturday, twenty second May, two thousand and four."

Whatley coughed. "Thank you, Constable. Now, Mr Moon, please tell me in your own words how you came to discover the body of Mr Dominic Llewellyn in the vicinity of the *Hangman's Rest* public house."

Moon decided to tell as much of the truth as he could get away with. "Well, let's see, Sonia and I…"

"That would be Miss Sonia Crest, the girl who was with you when you discovered the body. What is your relationship with Miss Crest? Friend? Girlfriend? Fiancée?"

Moon felt a small rush of emotion to hear Sonia described in these terms. "Girlfriend, I suppose, we've not been together long. Anyway, we'd spent the evening in the *Hangman's Rest* having a drink and chatting, then we decided to head back to Sonia's place. As we were leaving the pub we went past the entrance to the alleyway and I thought I heard someone cry out. I went into the alley to see if anyone needed help and saw the body lying on the ground but when I looked at him more closely I realised he was dead. The noise I heard must have been a cat. I saw one when I first went into the alleyway."

"You were sure Mr Llewellyn was dead?" asked Whatley, sipping from his Styrofoam cup. "God! I'll never know how the charlatans who vend this stuff get away with calling it coffee!" he grimaced with disgust.

Moon grinned involuntarily at Whatley's outburst. "I'm a nurse, Inspector, and I work in A&E quite regularly so I know a corpse when I see one. Besides, it looked like something had been eating him. I saw what looked like bite marks on his neck. That's why I didn't attempt to resuscitate him; no one could survive with that kind of wound. Not a lot of blood though. It looked like he'd been dead for some time and I'd guess the bites were post mortem or they'd have bled more."

"Did you know the deceased, Sir?"

"No, but Sonia did vaguely. He was part of the local Goth scene. I've not had much to do with it."

"But Miss Crest has, judging by her attire." Whatley sounded disapproving.

"Yes, well it's just a bit of escapism, isn't it," commented Moon. "I've been researching the whole thing; I do a bit of freelance journalism on the side, you see, that's how I met Sonia. I'm doing an article on the Goth subculture for *Venue.*

"And during this 'research' of yours have you come across anything that might relate to Mr Llewellyn's death."

Moon thought immediately of the other missing Goths, Sonia may not like him mentioning them but he thought it was about time the police knew about it. "Dominic was apparently one of a number of members of the Goth community who have recently disappeared from circulation. According to Sonia it's quite common for people to just move on or drop out of sight for other reasons, but I did get the impression that this has happened more frequently in the last two or three months."

Whatley's eyebrows rose. "Would you have names for these individuals, Sir?"

"No, but Sonia might," replied Moon. "Although, I'm not sure if it'll help you much, half these guys tend to go by silly nicknames."

After a few more routine questions the interview finally drew to an end; Whatley read back a transcript of Moon's statement, which he signed gratefully, hoping that this meant he could get to bed soon. "That will be all for now, Mr Moon," said Whatley, placing the statement in a cardboard folder. "Just don't make plans to travel away from Bristol in the next few weeks as we may need to ask further questions."

Moon had to wait another fifteen minutes for Sonia to finish her interview. She came out into the waiting area, hugging her jacket around her for comfort. The mixture of stress and fatigue on her face made her look like a lost child. "You okay?" he asked, kissing her forehead and caressing her hair.

"Just get me home, Jerry," she sighed. "It's been a long night. Do you mind if we get a cab?"

"Sure, there's a taxi rank just round the corner. Do you want me to leave afterwards? I'll understand."

She clung to him like a rock in a stormy sea. "No, Jerry, I don't want to be alone tonight. Too much happening all at once, already! Poor Dominic..." she held him tighter, tears forming stark, miserable rivulets of mascara on her pale cheeks. Moon nodded grimly and led her softly out into the night.

They travelled back to Sonia's flat in stunned silence and once the cab fair was paid, they made their way swiftly to Sonia's bed where they held each other in gentle nakedness until morning.

Chapter 7

Moon woke to find nothing but a scented hollow in the pillow beside him. Sunlight streamed through the gaps in Sonia's red taffeta and black lace curtains, punctuating the reddish glow in the bedroom with bars of brightness and starkly illuminating odd portions of her collection of gothic knick-knacks. He could hear the clink and clatter of china and utensils from the kitchen along the hallway. Memories of the previous night flooded back. The fear was that he might possibly be accused of murder, tempered by the joy of having spent the night with Sonia.

Sonia poked her head around the door. "Oh, you're awake at last," she said, entering the room, her pale skin showing in tantalising glimpses through the open front of a black silk kimono. "I brought you some coffee." She placed a steaming mug on the bedside table.

Moon studied the mug, which had a Manga logo on one side; on the other was a title frame from 'Blood – The Last Vampire'. "Actually, I don't drink… coffee," he said, wondering if she'd get the movie reference. "At least not in the morning, usually."

"Dracula 2001, yeah?" Sonia got the reference. "Cool movie. So can I get you some tea instead or do you really want the freshly drained blood of young virgins. Which I have to admit may be quite a tall order in this neighbourhood."

Moon grinned. "Oh, tea will do. I wouldn't want you to put yourself to any trouble."

"In a jiffy," promised Sonia, picking up the mug and sweeping out of the room. Moon caught a glimpse of the gothic rose and thorns tattoo on her right buttock as she opened the door. He had occasionally mused over the impact that the current fad for body art would have in the nursing homes of the future; he could imagine one teenage care assistant whispering to her colleague as they helped a ninety-year-old client bathe. "Is that a *bat* tattooed on Kylie's bum?" and her friend replying *sotto voce*,

"No. It's a butterfly. I stretched it flat once when I was drying her off," followed by giggles and sounds of disgust. Still, on Sonia's bum the rose looked good for the present at least.

Sonia returned with a mug shaped like a goblet, its stem fashioned into a dragon's claw, which held the bowl in a four-taloned grip. "Don't you have any normal mugs?" asked Moon.

"Oh, sure, we have a china set we keep for 'mundane' visitors. But I thought you'd like our wilder selection. It's more fun."

"Well, yes I suppose," Moon sipped his tea. "I just haven't drunk from anything quite so... exotic before."

"Wait until you see Avril's skull mug then. It's the biz." Sonia climbed back into bed and snuggled up to him.

Moon felt a familiar urge accompanied by undercover stirrings. "Did they say how long until you could... You know?" he asked, toying with the ring in her right nipple.

"At least a week." Sonia grimaced. "No, you know until the swelling's gone down."

"Damn! I'm partial to a bit of... 'you know'," sighed Moon, having to content himself with a kiss and a snuggle.

"So, why did your interview with the police take so long?" asked Moon. They were still lying sleepily in Sonia's bed, making the best of Sunday morning.

"Well, I thought I ought to tell them about the guys who've stopped coming to the Rest recently and they wanted details." Sonia shook her head. "More details than I was able to give them for the main part."

"You didn't say anything about me talking to Dominic's ghost, did you?"

Sonia fixed him with a steady eye. "Oh yeah, I told them how you were psychic and Dominic called you down the alleyway to help him out." At the look of shock on Moon's face her deadpan expression broke into a grin. "What do you think I am, stupid? The cops don't react well to anything off beam; it's bad enough that I'm a Goth without blabbing on about the supernatural. I just said you must have noticed something down the alley which sparked your curiosity."

Moon pulled a grumpy face. "You shouldn't joke about it like that. I was petrified they'd think I'd done it. *You* thought I'd killed him to start off with, didn't you?"

Sonia kissed him. "I didn't know what to think, Jerry, but I'm still here aren't I? I just don't think you're capable of murder, so you must be psychic, mustn't you?"

"Glad we've sorted that out. But it does mean someone connected with the *Hangman's Rest* is a murderer, perhaps even a serial killer." He looked directly into Sonia's frightened gaze. "Did you notice that something had *bitten* into Dominic's throat? I thought it must have been rats or that cat I saw but it's an odd place for an animal to start nibbling. You don't think…"

"You're beginning to think Uri had something to do with this after all?" Sonia's eyes widened. "He's the obvious culprit, you know, he's had most of us getting a bit of a thrill out of thinking he might just be the real thing ever since he turned up on the scene three or four years ago."

Moon frowned. "So he's not local?"

"Well, by all accounts he's lived in Bristol a long time but no, he's foreign, I think he's from Eastern Europe, possibly Russia or even Transylvania. Which is another thing, that's where vampires are traditionally supposed to come from, isn't it?"

"Well, yes," replied Moon, "and more recently the Cheeky Girls." His flippancy masked his unhappiness with the turn the conversation was taking. "You know, love, I may be able to see spirits and talk to the dead and all that but at heart I like to think I'm a rational man. I've seen enough weird stuff to give me an open mind but only ever in the spirit world. The idea of some sort of demon-human hybrid that lives on human blood goes a bit off limits even for me. There are good spirits and bad spirits, yes, just like there are good and bad people, but I've never met what I'd really call a 'demon'… I think I ought to interview Uri and see what I can sense from him. He'd be on my list anyway if he's as heavily into the Gothic fantasy lifestyle as you say he is."

"Well, he'll probably be at the Rest tonight, they tend to come in most nights over the weekend. Until then," she kissed him, "there are one or two things which are nearly as good as 'you know'…"

After about twenty minutes of something which was very nearly as good as 'you know' and a further ten minutes of basking in the afterglow Sonia turned to Moon and asked, "Do you like shopping, Jerry?"

Moon frowned. This wasn't a subject which had normally come up in his limited experience of pillow talk. "Depends on what sort," he replied, finishing off his mug of cold tea.

"I mean browsing, you know going round the shops to see what they've got and possibly buying the odd bit of jewellery or piece of clothing."

Moon was a card carrying window-shopper of long standing but he thought that he'd play the male stereotype for now, hoping to pleasantly surprise Sonia when they got out on the streets. "Well, I'll give it a go. Not too many clothes shops though, I never know what to say if a girl asks me how they look in something. My last girlfriend dumped me because I told the truth one time too many. Day-glow cerise...ugh! God should have been sacked for even imagining that colour."

"Well, you won't have that problem with me, will you? My colours are black, red, purple and occasionally white; you'd have to lobotomise me before I was seen dead in pink. Anyway, I was thinking more along the lines of browsing the book and record shops. There's a good selection down Park Street and in Broadmead. Most of the larger ones are open on a Sunday."

"Okay, why not?" Moon smiled, "it might help take our minds off last night."

"Oh, don't remind me!" Sonia grimaced. "Poor Dominic, he was a nice kid, you know, had a really dry sense of humour…"

Moon remembered Dominic making a joke of his own corpse. "Still has if last night was anything to go by," he smiled.

"Oh!" A look of shocked anger flitted over Sonia's face for a second before the truth hit her. "Yes, I suppose if you believe people don't really die it must give you a very different perspective on death."

"There's no 'believe' about it, darling, I'm subjected to it on a daily basis." Moon tried to convey the frustration of his relationship with the dead to her. "Some people say that dying is like a person going into another room. Me, I wish they bloody well would go into another room occasionally instead of harassing me with their problems."

Sonia was lost in thought for what seemed like an age. "You know, Jerry, people aren't given gifts like yours for nothing. Perhaps, instead of griping about them, you really ought to think about helping them. Maybe that's your real job in life."

Moon rolled his eyes at her. "No, my real job in life is nursing, hopefully with a bit of journalism on the side. Ghosts don't have to eat, I do!"

"Just think about it, huh." Sonia's eyes were serious as they gazed into Moon's, a hand's-breadth away. "Perhaps if you help solve Dominic's murder it'll begin to make more sense of things. Even knowing you for only the last few days I've learnt that you don't like loose ends. It'll niggle away at you until either you tie it up or someone else does."

Moon traced a fingernail around the dragon's claws on his mug. "You really think so?" he asked vulnerably.

Sonia sucked her teeth then kissed him on the cheek. "I know so, Jerry. Don't ask me how but I sense this. It's one of *my* spooky feelings." She said this last, leaning in so their foreheads and noses touched, her cinnamon eyes were open wide as she grinned up at him.

Moon laughed and kissed her smiling lips. Sonia returned the kiss, giggling and Moon threw back the duvet. "Okay, let's go shopping and leave the spooks to themselves for now."

Sonia and Avril's flat occupied part of the ground and first floors in an Edwardian town house on the Hotwell Road end of Ambra Vale. This was close to the old Bristol Harbour area in a part of town that is generally known as Hotwells, because of the old healing spring situated just off Jacob's Wells Road. Moon and Sonia walked arm in arm into the town centre along the harbour side, enjoying looking at the variety of ships. They paused to watch some cormorants fishing off the TV aerial of a houseboat for a while before they ambled on. Entering the Watershed area via the huge granite and concrete amphitheatre in front of the Lloyd's bank offices, they had to jump out of the way several times to avoid the skateboarders, who monopolised the area for their play.

The Watershed area itself took up the left side of the harbour as they walked towards town. It was comprised of numerous bars and cafés and the Watershed Arts Centre, from which it took its name. Its covered pavement, which fronted onto the harbour, was busy with street traders and groups of people at café tables drinking their Sunday beers, taking in the harbour and generally having a good time. The pavement led up via a flight of steps to St Augustine's Parade, where ranks of submerged fountains played into large shallow pools; children loved to play in these during summer but they were now empty apart from drifts of dead leaves washed up in the corners. Here Moon and Sonia bought ice-cream crêpes at a vending stall near the steps and sat down to eat them on a convenient bench.

After a short discussion they decided that they would go into Broadmead, the commercial centre of Bristol, and the Galleries Shopping Centre then make their way back up Park Street towards Jacob's Wells Road, so their afternoon became a happily aimless shopping spree around the centre of Bristol. In a small jeweller's at the bottom of Park Street Moon bought Sonia a silver enamelled pendant, which had the new moon in white enamel with her hidden face making up the rest of the disc in black. "Just so you'll always remember me," said Moon, gazing meaningfully into her eyes as he fastened the clasp behind her neck.

Walking up Park Street they entered the Bristol Museum, where they took in a visiting Egyptian exhibition and the ground floor gallery, which was showing a collection of comic-book art from the nineteen-forties to the present day. Sonia finally had to drag Moon, who was a bit of a comic-book anorak, away from a display of original *2000 AD* artwork so they could eat Sunday lunch in the museum restaurant before it closed.

Later, they wandered slowly back through town to the *Hangman's Rest*, window-shopping along the way. "I'll have to take you to the market some time," said Sonia. "There are one or two really good Goth stalls in there. It'd give you some idea of where we get stuff and the sort of clothes and accessories that are available. For your article, you know…"

"Oh, yeah," replied Moon. "That would be great but it would have to be next weekend, my deadline's in two weeks."

"It's a date then," Sonia smiled, toying with her new pendant. "Look, I can't stay too long in the Rest tonight; I've got work in the morning."

"That's okay, I'll try to get some dirt from Uri as soon as possible then I'll walk you home."

"Are you sure? It's just that going through the centre at night can be a bit dodgy, you know," She bit her lip nervously. "I don't usually come over here unless I've got someone to go home with."

"Look, it's fine love. I have to stay awake a bit late tonight anyway to get ready for working nights during the week." Moon shrugged. He knew it was scarier for a woman alone at night than a bloke and Bristol city centre could be scary enough for anyone during the weekend.

The *Rest* was quiet when they entered with just a few hardened regulars propping up the bar, some of whom were still human, but Moon wasn't entirely sure which. Sonia walked obliviously through a short, motherly looking lady who sported a badly permed bleach job and was wearing a lavender twin-set (this surprised Moon who would have bet good money that this was a 'live one') and greeted the barman, a short, skinny, cheeky faced young Goth, with a friendly, "Hi, Ragger!"

Ragger grinned brightly at them over the beer pumps. "Oh! Hi, Sonia, who's your mate?" He was very short and very slightly built with a pointed-chinned, high-cheekboned face like a Brian Froud pixie. He was wearing – almost inhabiting – an oversized Stoker's Kiss T-shirt and his long black hair was tied back from his face in a ponytail.

"This is Jerry, Ragger, he's doing an article about us Bristol Goths for *Venue*."

"Cool," said Ragger, extending a hand over the bar. "Hi Jerry."

Moon shook his hand. "Most people call me 'Moon'," he explained. "I'm not too keen on Jerry. It was my Grandpa's name and it's always felt a bit second hand."

"Okay, then. Hi, Moon," said Ragger, extending his hand again.

"Well, I like 'Jerry'," said Sonia emphatically. "I think it sounds friendly."

"Oh, I don't mind it from you love," Moon was quick to reassure her. "From you it sounds special for some reason."

"Do I detect a certain romantic rapport between you two," observed Ragger teasingly. "It's about time someone hooked our Sonia. I can see you're good for her too, she's got a bit of an unfamiliar sparkle about her for a change. What can I get you?"

A cheery Goth? thought Moon, *whatever next?* "Oh, a pint of Guinness Cold for me and whatever Sonia's having."

"Bacardi and coke," said Sonia. "Any idea if Uri's going to make a show tonight. Moon would like to interview him."

"Whooo...Uri!" replied Ragger pulling a spooky face and raising his hands like claws. "So you want to meet the creature of the night himself, eh?" Ragger did a very good Vincent Price impression for 'creature of the night', which made Moon snort in his beer.

"I take it you're not too keen on him?"

"Oh, Uri's all right I suppose, if you take him in small doses. But I think you can take your fantasies too far and he's way beyond the edge of madness if you want my opinion. You'd never catch me sleeping in a coffin, even if I could find one small enough. Anyway, he's in most Sundays so you should get a chance to talk to him, if you can get past his entourage that is. He has a quite a fan club, Uri. I suppose him being tall, buff and gorgeous must have something to do with it."

Moon and Sonia were sitting in a raised area with seats and tables on the right-hand side of the bar, sipping their drinks and chatting quietly together when Moon's spine suddenly tingled alarmingly. He noticed that the few resident ghosts who had been floating around the bar this early in the evening had quickly made themselves scarce. His head snapped up, like a dog that had suddenly caught an unusual scent, and he expanded his senses, searching for the source of the psychic disturbance. Then he realised Uri and his two girlfriends had entered through the barroom door. *How the hell did I ever mistake **that** for human?* he wondered, as the vampire stalked into the room with preternatural grace, waves of supernatural energy radiating out from him like a beacon. Uri belatedly caught Moon staring and a cloud of mundanity condensed into place around him like a sudden change in focus, making him look and feel normal. But it was too late; Moon knew exactly what he had seen and he would not be fooled again.

"What's wrong, Jerry?" asked Sonia, looking round. "Oh, it's just Uri, you looked like you'd seen a ghost."

"It's not the ghosts I'm worried about," replied Moon, nodding towards Uri. "Do you think you could introduce us?"

"Sure thing," replied Sonia, taking Moon's hand and leading him directly into the jaws of the largest predator he'd ever seen outside of a zoo.

Chapter 8

"Uri, I'd like you to meet Moon," said Sonia slipping her arm possessively around Moon's waist. "He's a freelance journalist writing an article on Goths for *Venue* and I suggested he speak to you because you, and your, uh... partners live Goth to the hilt, so to speak..."

"Indeed we do, indeed we do, Mr Moon." All through Sonia's introduction Uri had been eyeing Moon knowingly with a mocking gaze but when he spoke his tone was sincere. "Please, both of you sit down and you can interview us to your heart's content."

"Just 'Moon', please," said Moon, "and may I call you Uri?"

"Of course, of course, and my two playmates here are Charli and Roanne." The girls nodded and smiled at Moon. Again, they wore matching outfits. This time both wore black lace bodices with puffed velvet sleeves above tight black-leather trousers with laced up seams, which were tucked into knee high black suede stiletto-heeled boots. Each had an identical antique silver ring with a single large ruby set in it on her ring finger and wore a black lace choker around her neck with a silver rose at the throat. Though equally beautiful, they weren't identical. Moon realised on seeing them up close that Charli's dark hair was true blue-black and her eyes were the darkest of dark browns. Moon thought she had more than a hint of Spanish ancestry. Roanne's eyes, on the other hand, were a deep, dark blue, like the mid ocean, and her skin had that peculiar milky paleness that can only be found in the dark-haired, Celtic Welsh. Both of them, despite these differences, had a strange air about them that Moon couldn't quite put his finger on. Their beauty seemed to echo from a different time; perhaps this was because of the Gothic chic they wore, but Moon doubted it.

Moon smiled at the ladies then furtively turned on the Dictaphone hidden in his jacket pocket and asked his first question. "Uri, that's a Russian name, isn't it? But I don't detect much of an accent…"

"Byelorussian, actually," replied Uri. "But I've lived in England a long time and have lost most of my accent."

"Oh, how long?"

"Half my life," replied Uri with a grin. Were those real fangs? They certainly looked real. "Or should I play the Game and say: 'Half my death'?"

Moon laughed politely but was beginning to feel uncomfortable. He realised Uri hadn't really answered his question but couldn't think of a polite way to point this out. "So, why do you play 'the Game' so completely? You don't really strike me as someone who needs to run away from reality."

"Because, as they say in this country, Moon, it is fun!" He said this last with true Russian relish. "But also because I am a performer and it pleases my audience to think perhaps I might be the real thing, no?"

"I've been told that you play violin occasionally for *Unquiet Grave,* but surely that doesn't constitute a performing career."

"*Unquiet Grave* is not the only band I am involved with." Uri shrugged, "Charli, Roanne and I perform together as *Blood Velvet.* I play violin and guitar, Roanne, keyboard and vocals and Charli is our drummer, if that is a sufficient term for one so accomplished in percussion as she is. I am pleased to say we have quite a fan base among the Goth community, both here in Bristol and elsewhere."

"That's right, Jerry," interjected Sonia, "Uri and the girls have played at the *Rest* a few times but not so much in the last year or so."

"We went touring for a while," explained Roanne. There was definitely a hint of a Welsh accent to her voice Moon noticed. "And we've been resting on the proceeds while we put together the material for a new album."

"So how come I haven't heard of you if you're so successful?" asked Moon

"We aren't mainstream and it is unlikely that we ever will be in this present wishy-washy musical climate," replied Uri with a grimace. "Our music is too strong meat for the current pop-obsessed generation. Too much 'bite' you might say." He grinned darkly, showing an impressive set of double upper and lower fangs. *Talk about hiding in plain sight!* thought Moon with grudging admiration.

Despite himself Moon was beginning to like Uri; his playful flamboyance was quite infectious, although Moon found himself wondering whether one reason Blood Velvet would never make mainstream might be that none of the performers would register on videotape. Having spent several minutes in close contact with their auras he was now convinced that all three were vampires, although Uri was by far the most powerful. "So you *aren't* a vampire, Uri?" he asked, hoping to catch him unawares.

"Ah, ah!" replied the vampire, shaking one long forefinger in Moon's face. "If you are going to publish this, Moon, then I need to keep the audience guessing. Let them make up their own minds."

"Aren't you playing a very dangerous game, if you don't mind my saying so? Maintaining a reputation as a blood-sucking monster; especially at a time when there have been several recent disappearances within the Goth community associated with this pub?" As far as he was aware the news of Dominic's death had not yet been made public so Moon felt it best not to mention it.

"Hmm. You have a point there. However, most Goths who're well versed in the vampire mythos would inform you that vampires don't need to kill to take enough blood to survive. *Bozhe Moi!* A human body contains several litres of blood, where a litre would probably be enough to fill the greediest vampire's stomach."

Moon was surprised. "Really? But I thought the legend, as I recall it at least, is that vampires drain the blood from their victims, thus killing them and infecting them with vampirism at the same time."

"Medieval church propaganda exploited by Hollywood for cheap thrills, I say." Uri gently banged his fist on the table in emphasis. "The vampire legend is older than both and does not always involve the death of the victims, or even in some stories the taking of blood. If there are vampires in truth I suspect that they do not kill those they feast from or they would long ago have wiped out their food supply. Don't you think, Sonia?"

"I suppose so," replied Sonia. "I've not really thought about it." She pondered the question for a moment then continued, "You know, I think you're right: the films and books don't seem to agree at all. Some have the vampire draining a person in a single feed while others make it take a lot longer or say that they don't kill at all."

"Fascinating," said Moon, who had heard enough. "But we're getting off the main purpose of this interview. Uri, the thing I've found most interesting about the Goth scene is the music. Some of the bands I heard the night before last were excellent and, as you mentioned, very innovative compared to contemporary pop music. I'd be interested if you'd tell me, as someone who writes songs for the genre, what your musical influences are."

"Ah," replied Uri, weaving his long white fingers together before him. "I have many influences; the folk music from my country, a number of classical sources especially Bach, some of your English folk music, and some bands from the sixties and seventies, Curved Air, for instance, Genesis and Bowie. Then there's the literary and movie influences such as the Anne Rice books, *The Rocky Horror Picture Show*, any number of early Hammer Horror films that I watched during my youth; I suppose even *Buffy the Vampire Slayer* has had her influence." He laughed. "If you're interested in a genre you build up a kind of, would you say, *library* of images and ideas in your mind that you can draw upon for inspiration. You have already pointed out that the girls and I are steeped in this strange Goth culture, which eventually becomes an inspiration in itself."

The night moved on to a discussion of music and film and ended with Uri giving Moon a copy of Blood Velvet's latest CD, *Requiem for a Rose*. However, despite the superficial congeniality, Moon felt like he had spent most of the evening dancing at the edge of an abyss. The unspoken truth that Moon knew what Uri was, and his suspicions that Uri was fully aware of this, created an edge of tension that made relaxation impossible.

At ten o'clock Sonia whispered in Moon's ear, "Can we go now, I need to get my full eight hours for work tomorrow."

Moon nodded and turned to the vampires and said, "Sorry, guys we need to get off. Sonia has work in the morning."

"Sure, see you soon, Moon," said Uri with a strange promise lurking behind his eyes. "Remember that I can get you complimentary tickets to one of our gigs if you want them."

Charli and Roanne flashed two sets of pearly fangs as they smiled and wished them goodbye. Sonia smiled back, saying, "I like your fangs, I wish I'd brought my fangs too then we could have, you know... matched. Where did you get yours, off the Internet?"

"They were a present from Uri," replied Charli, grinning to show them off.

I bet they were, thought Moon grimly as he opened the bar door for Sonia and followed her into the night.

"Phew!" exclaimed Sonia when they were outside. "That was hard going. I've never spent so much time with Uri before. I mean, I like a bit of role-play as much as anyone but..."

"Sonia, that was *not* role-play," Moon interrupted emphatically.

"You mean you think... No!"

"Yes, I do. There's enough concentrated psychic fallout emanating from those three to rouse a thousand year old graveyard that's been concreted over and turned into a shopping mall."

"But they sat there and drank lager, for God's sake!" replied Sonia incredulously. "Roanne snaffled half my cheese and onion crisps."

"I don't care. Those three may have been human once but they aren't now, and I suspect they haven't been for a very long time. We may well have found our murderers."

Sonia shook her head. "But what about what Uri said about vampires not needing to kill to eat?"

"There are *three* of them, Sonia. Even if what Uri says is true they could drain someone in a couple of sittings and who's going to miss the odd Goth if the scene here's as changeable as you say it is?"

"Yeah, but Uri and the girls have been around for years; people have only been going missing for the last few months."

"You mean you've only noticed they've been going missing now. Perhaps they've become a bit careless and taken a few people that were less isolated and alone than the others. They could have been quietly disappearing people to their private larder for years. This could have been going on for a decade or more if they chose their victims well."

They were walking through St Augustine's Parade, which was surprisingly empty at that time of night, considering the rabble that would descend after throwing out time. Deciding not to risk walking along the Waterfront at night, they walked up to College Green, which separates the Cathedral from the bottom of Park Street with the 'Council House'; the City Council Offices making the third side of a rough triangle. They took a side street that ran between the Council House and some of the Bristol University Buildings towards Hotwells and the docks. Once past these imposing buildings, the grandeur quickly fell away. The road became a rather grubby back street until it reached the roundabout at the junction of Hotwell Road and Jacob's Wells Road. In the dingy lamplight, half a dozen tiny blue fireflies hovered along behind the lovers who, too caught up in each other's presence, failed to sense their purposeful pursuit.

The left side of the road had once been un-reclaimed dockland but the recent astronomic rise in property prices had resulted in blocks of luxury flats shooting up like mushrooms with selling prices in the £250,000 to £350,000 range. In a fit of devilment Moon had once phoned the developers and asked if he could view the 'affordable key-worker property' that the Government had promised would be included in any new housing development. The response had been short and obscene. He had barely resisted the temptation to sneak round and throw rocks through the windows in reply.

Sonia pulled her thin coat tighter around her body. "It gets windy around this bit where it's open to the harbour," she said.

Moon put his arm around her shoulders. "Here, is that better?"

"Yeah." She kissed him on the cheek. "You know, I really don't want to get home tonight. It means I won't be seeing you for a while. I've enjoyed the last two days so much despite Dominic dying and everything."

"Well, I could pop round tomorrow evening if you'd like. I'm not working until Tuesday night, then I'll be out of circulation until Friday, I'm afraid, but I can still call you."

"Why don't you come for tea tomorrow, then?" said Sonia. "It won't be much. Turkey burgers and chips, you know, that sort of thing. I'm afraid I'm not much of a cook."

"Turkey burgers will be fine," replied Jerry as they stopped on the steps of her building.

"Okay, get here for about six then. I'd ask you in but I really meant it about getting eight hours."

"That's okay, it's quite a walk back anyway." They kissed long and hard, desperate not to waste a moment of each other's company. "I'll need your phone number," he said, drawing out his mobile.

They spent a few more minutes programming each other's numbers into their mobile phones by the light of the porch lamp then Moon said, "Good night, love."

Sonia kissed him one more time before closing her front door. "Don't let the vampires bite, Jerry," she quipped.

"Damn! I left the garlic and crucifix in my other jacket!" As Sonia closed the door Moon wondered whether he might really need them.

Chapter 9

It might be a bit scary at night but the quickest way for Moon to get back to his flat was to climb straight up the hill from Hotwells, cut through St Andrew's Cemetery and then across Whiteladies Road and into Redland, where he lived. If he kept up a decent pace he should be home in just over half an hour. The climb out of Hotwells was steep, as it included the first part of the cliffs that rear up on either side of the Avon Gorge. However, Moon was reasonably fit. The way was paved and there were steps at the steeper parts, so the climb wasn't too much of an obstacle. He was only mildly breathless when he emerged at the top of the hill from a road junction near Bristol University's Monica Wills hall of residence, which lay just opposite a narrow pathway that led up to the entrance to the cemetery.

On the right side of the entrance, what used to be the church's front churchyard was shadowed by several mature trees, predominantly holly, oak and yew with some whitethorn filling in the gaps. There had once been a huge willow near the gate but all that marked its passing now was a wide shallow stump displaying the dark hollow of its diseased core. It had been felled to preserve the safety of passers-by, but Moon saluted it as he walked past, for he had been fond of the tree for its size and beauty. His sideways glance caught something pale flashing briefly in the shadows over the flattened tombstones that paved the frontage. He peered curiously into the gloom under the trees but nothing was there so he dismissed this as his imagination playing tricks after the creepy experience of talking to Uri.

The three-quarter moon was high as he crossed the open area where the church used to be, filling the rough quadrangle with pale light and sharply contrasting shadows. The entranceway to the path through the cemetery, however, was a forbidding dark tree covered cave under the moon's stark, grey light. Moon was surprised because Bird Cage Walk was usually fairly well lit at night but, chiding himself for being spooked by the dark, he stepped briskly into the shadows and opened his psyche to greet the healing presences that he had communed with in this place only the day before. However, no sooner had the words of welcome left his mind than he wished that he hadn't uttered them. Suddenly, he felt like a minnow that had unwittingly entered the territory of a patrolling shark and had just received the predator's full attention. Spider-like patterns of shadow crept together from underneath the trees and gravestones, pooling into an area of deeper darkness directly in front of him, which seemed to twist and turn like a nest of writhing snakes. He wasn't certain if anything was really there but he was sure as hell in no hurry to find out. There were other ways to get home that didn't involve braving that shadowy horror, he decided, and he turned to run. Unnoticed in his panic, his six tiny glowing companions flew past him at breakneck speed and scattered to hide themselves in the nearby flowerbeds.

He made all of two paces before the dreadful realisation dawned that his feet were frozen in place. Fighting a growing sense of panic, he looked down and, to his horror, saw that his lower legs were entangled in smoky tendrils of shadow: cold, paralysing and unbelievably solid shadow. He began to shiver uncontrollably as they crept up towards his thighs, like a stop-frame recording of climbing ivy, then they tightened like the coils of a dozen pythons and tugged backwards. He barely managed to extend his arms in time to prevent himself cracking his chin on the stone paving; instead the impact jarred his palms and elbows and winded him badly, leaving him gasping for breath as he writhed in the chilly grip of the strangling darkness.

Struggling to fill his lungs with air, he twisted to look down his body towards the source of his peril but all he could see was thick inky blackness filling the tunnel of trees and drowning out the lamps which usually lit the pathway from above. In its centre was a pit of blacker, apparently endless darkness, from which emanated an unearthly chill; above this floated the tiniest hint of two glittering black eyes, which radiated malevolence as they seemed to bore into his soul.

A high, persistent keening came from that open maw, piercing his brain with ice-hot needles as he was drawn towards its chilly emptiness. He tried to fight against the relentless pull, clawing his fingers and scrabbling against the paving stones only to leave them bruised and broken-nailed. Eventually, the darkness surrounded him; it felt like concentrated terror, clamping his heart in a frozen vice. It was sucking the life out of him and he realised with chilling certainty that he would die this night.

"Cease!" The deep baritone command penetrated the night like a thunderclap heralding a storm. "Let him go! Leave him I say!" Before him on the path a dark clad figure alighted, surrounded by a pale nimbus of glowing blue fire.

With grudging reluctance, the grip on Moon's heart withdrew and the surrounding darkness dispersed into the cemetery on either side. "Thanks, Uri," Moon managed to stutter as the vampire's flame dwindled to a mild shimmer that most normal mortals wouldn't notice. "What the hell was that? Usually this place is quite friendly, spiritually speaking."

"That, my friend," replied Uri, tidying his pale locks back from his face, "was a *haunt*, a *boggart*, a *goblin*. Or, to put it in more modern terms, a negative thought form; a shadow beast originally summoned into being by the locals' fear of this burial ground and sustained by the many decades of belief that the place is haunted. It was trying to kill you."

"You don't say?" asked Moon sarcastically, remembering the icy tendrils tightening around his heart.

"Oh, yes, indeed," Uri continued, oblivious to the sarcastic edge Moon had set to his comment. "It would have sucked out all your energy and in the morning some early rising jogger or dog-walker would have stumbled upon the pale-faced corpse of just another heart attack victim. Reports of this mysterious death would also, of course, add to the legend of this place and fuel the core of belief that provides that black parasite with its wretched existence."

"Talking of black parasites, what do you care? You're a vampire." Moon was aware that this probably wasn't a wise line of questioning but for some reason he felt that Uri was not inclined to harm him, for the moment at least.

Uri sighed wearily. "Certainly, Moon, I am a vampire; I shun daylight, sleep in a coffin, fly by moonlight and occasionally have to drink human blood but never from anyone who is unwilling. Charli, Roanne and I have a few close confidants who allow us to take from them what we need. We don't kill, never take by force and by doing so we attempt to be as 'good' as our condition allows. We also try to avoid making others like ourselves, no matter how much we might be entreated; an eternal life that is lived only in darkness is a very mixed blessing, I can assure you."

"I thought being irredeemably evil came as part of the vampire package?" Moon's natural inquisitiveness took over once he realised that he was no longer in danger.

"Is this to be another interview, Moon?" Uri replied archly. "Which of the dreadful rags you write for would publish an interview with a vampire? Besides, it has already been done, has it not? I think a certain author might sue you for pinching her ideas, no?"

Moon snorted a short laugh. Uri was as disarming as he had been earlier in the pub. Could he really trust this charming monster not to kill him, or worse? Finally, he decided to go with his gut instinct. "Look, I'm on my way home but I happen to be a late night type myself. I only live over in Angel Terrace, why don't you come back to my place and you can tell me what it really means to be a vampire over a coffee. Or don't you drink… coffee?"

Uri smiled knowingly, he must have seen *that* film too. Waving a long, pale finger he replied, "You're making fun of me, Moon. No, I don't drink coffee, but I do drink tea: strong and black with lots of sugar or jam, like they do in the old country. I think I will take you up on your offer. I'll give you a lift, why walk when you can fly, eh?"

Before Moon had a chance to refuse Uri gathered him up in the steely grip of his arms and leapt into the sky. This was no Hollywood special effects fuelled dream of flying; Moon was almost as terrified as he had been shortly before in the chilly grip of the graveyard 'boggart'. Just because Uri was immune to gravity this didn't mean the same for Moon, who felt its dreadful pull for the entire five-minute eternity it took from their take-off in the cemetery to when they alighted a few paces from his front door. "Are you all right, Moon?" Uri's face was a picture of concern. "You look a bit pale."

Moon took a second to regain his ability to speak. "V-vertigo," he eventually stammered. "I get dizzy stepping off tall kerbs."

"Oh dear! Sorry, Moon, the girls are always chiding me for being over enthusiastic. It'll be the death of me yet."

"If that's a sample of the way you carry on," observed Moon with chagrin, "I'm surprised it hasn't been the death of someone already! Oh well, come on up. My flat's on the second floor and no, I don't want a lift."

They climbed up the stairs to Moon's landing, Uri floating silently up the stairs beside him with a cat-like grace that made Moon feel leaden and clumsy in comparison. Then Uri halted, suddenly still like a cat that's seen a mouse. "Who is the little girl?" he asked, staring into the shadows around Mrs Foley's doorway.

Moon was startled that the vampire was able to see spirits. "Anna, she used to live upstairs early last century. Say hello to Uri, Anna."

"Hello, Mister Vampire," replied Anna. *"You're not going to eat Jerry are you? He's my only friend."*

Uri laughed gently. "No, Anna, I won't eat Moon if it's going to upset you."

"Good! Because I can be really scary if I want to. And I'd be my very scariest for you if you hurt Jerry!" and for a second Moon saw a glimpse of just how truly terrifying Anna could be if she set her mind to it: menacing Victorian china doll type scary. He hoped she would never, ever get mad enough with him to turn *that* scary.

Uri sat in one of the down-at-heel armchairs in Moon's flat while Moon prepared beverages in the kitchenette. "Nice, um... place, you have here Moon."

"No, it's not!" replied Moon. "It's a grotty overpriced hole but it's all I can afford on a nurse's salary now the house prices have gone ballistic and our so-called 'Labour' government haven't got the balls to step in and do something about it."

"Well, I didn't want to embarrass you," replied the vampire with a smile, shamelessly flashing a set of fangs that he most definitely hadn't got off the Internet.

"There you are." Moon set a mug of dark fluid in front of Uri. "I don't have any jam but I piled in the sugar like you said." He sat down in the other mismatched armchair, balancing a plate of chocolate digestive biscuits on one of the arms.

"I don't suppose you have any lemon to put in this?" Moon shook his head. "Well, then, could I trouble you for a couple of those wonderful biscuits instead?"

"I didn't think you'd want any." Moon proffered the plate towards Uri. "According to most of the stories I've heard vampires aren't meant to be able to stomach solid food."

"I can't see why not," replied Uri rather indistinctly through biscuit-coated fangs. "I still *have* a stomach after all and blood is a very boring diet, believe me."

"So, how long have you been…?" Moon sought in vain for a euphemism.

"…A 'blood sucking fiend'?" Uri completed the sentence for him brightly. "About a thousand years or so; it's amazing how the years roll by when you're undead. However, I always thought that was a very inaccurate description for people like myself. Okay, for your zombies: rotting lumbering corpses with worms for brains, 'undead' might just fit. Although 'annoyingly not dead' might be more accurate. But for someone so very much full of life as a vampire, no I don't think so."

Moon regarded Uri with horror. "You mean there actually *are* such things as zombies? You've met them?"

"Not socially, no. They lack the, what is the term? …Oh yes! They lack the communication skills and of course they smell very, very bad indeed. I have helped dispatch one or two though. They tend to be a great nuisance in some countries because they eat people, of course, and once you have one you usually end up with a whole graveyard full if you're not very vigilant. But they do exist. In my experience anything human beings believe in strongly enough for long enough will manifest itself eventually."

Moon paused to digest this titbit. It hinted at a more interesting but much more frightening world than he had previously thought possible. "And is that what you did? Did you 'manifest yourself'?"

"No, I was human once. And no, I wasn't bitten. It is a long story, which I don't care to tell at present. Enough to say that I fell victim to a sorcerer. It was my own fault of course; when I was younger I did many things that I am now ashamed of. I was a man of my time you see and a callous, violent time it was. The old man had his rightful vengeance for the way my companions and I treated his people, but I think now, if I met him again, I might thank him for giving me the last thousand years."

"But doesn't becoming a vampire mean that you're somehow infected with evil." Moon shrugged. "At least that's what all the books and movies say."

"Ah, yes. Black and white, white and black, that's the way I used to think it was. I was a vampire so I must be evil and therefore evil and terrible was how I behaved, which wasn't that much different from how I'd behaved as a human now I come to think of it. I was born to a noble family in eleventh century Russia and we were all what you would call 'bad sorts'.

"It was Roanne who taught me differently; sweet, infuriating Roanne, with her Celtic stubbornness and talent for asking bloody awkward questions. I stalked her for her beauty, you know, and turned her to the Blood. Then I expected her to behave like every bad little vampire should but she backed me into a corner one day demanding to know 'why. Why must we kill? Why must we terrify people?' Suddenly, 'because this is the way we are' became a less than satisfying answer. We're thinking beings, Moon, with the ability to sense the pain of others and put ourselves in their place. What a dreadful thing it must be for a person to be hunted and killed by a terror like me. That's what Roanne taught me. She taught the two of us: Charli and me. By refusing to take on the mantle of the monster she reawakened the humanity in us both. That was over five hundred years ago, shortly after I fled the burning craze in Europe with Charli hiding like a newly hatched fledgling under my wings."

"Are you talking about the Inquisition?" asked Moon, trying to dismiss visions of the Monty Python team in black robes and flying helmets.

"That and the witch burnings, yes. It was never as organised as history might suggest. Much of what occurred happened because the bastards in authority realised that they had discovered a legitimate way to steal property from those they accused. Did you know, in many places all the property owned by those found guilty was forfeited directly to the state? It was a terrible time and I feared that Charlotte and I would be hunted down and executed for being exactly what we were: vampires hiding on the edge of human society and preying on the weak and unwary."

"So you came to England?"

"Yes, where the Church itself was heretical and the madness was less widespread. Then we moved to Wales, where older ways still lingered and the Church was less powerful still."

Moon wished he could publish this; it was potential gold dust. "And you spent the next five hundred years in Wales being good little vampires? That's hard to believe."

"It took time, Moon. Once you've begun to think of people as cattle to be bled for food it's hard to teach yourself to believe differently. And I hadn't had a good start for that, even as a human, to begin with." He lifted his cup and found it empty. "Do you have any more tea?"

"I'll fix some," replied Moon, getting up and reaching for the cup. Unexpectedly, Uri seized his hand in a grip like cushioned steel and forced him to look him directly in the eye. The dancing red shimmer deep in his black on black pupils held Moon's gaze like a vice and teased a thread of terror from his soul. Had Uri just been playing with him, a game to add some flavour to the kill?

"What I am about to tell you could harm not only my ladies and myself but others who are as dear to us as family if it falls on the wrong ears, Moon. If I find that you have broken my confidence I will not be merciful. Do you understand?"

"I think so," replied Moon, sagging with relief as Uri relaxed his grip. For a moment there he had thought he was going to lose his hand. "You *could* trust me without having to resort to threats. But I suppose you don't know that, do you?" He took the cup and poured some fresh tea out of the pot, lacing it generously with sugar. *Hope this gives him cavities*, he thought, wringing his bruised fingers. "You were saying?"

"Ah, yes." Uri relaxed back in his chair, his charm returning, like a fleeting cloud vacating the face of the sun. "It wasn't easy but slowly and surely we began to build a circle of close friends around us; people who would let us have what we need out of love and not out of terror. We no longer had to kill our victims to hide what we are and, over several generations, we built a small enclave of trusted families around us. Two hundred years ago a small group from one of those families moved across the Severn from Wales to Bristol to expand their silversmith's business. We decided to come with them and we live here with their descendants still."

"So there's a family in Bristol who've harboured a trio of vampires for two centuries! And no one's let it slip or leaked it to the press? That story would be worth a king's ransom to the tabloids."

"Yes, but we are very secure nonetheless. Our relationship with our human friends is a mutually beneficial one. In return for their protection and the occasional donation of blood we offer them *our* protection. Also, we have invested wisely over the years and we supplement their income handsomely." Uri's red lips curved into a smile of candid affection. "And, of course, we are now family as well. They have all known us from their childhoods; I played with the oldest of them on my knee as a baby and she was ninety-three last birthday. For, it seems, while we no longer turn people to the Blood, something in our bite prolongs life and improves health. Our family members are seldom ill and tend to live to a ripe and healthy old age."

Moon pondered on what Uri had told him. This sounded far too good to be true. "It sounds delightful but are you sure you're not kidding yourselves? These people could merely be your 'ghouls', is that the word? Could they not just be slaves attending to your needs under the enthralling effect of your bite?"

An angry flash of offence passed through Uri's pale blue eyes. "That, you would have to ask them yourself but, believe me, we would never knowingly make slaves. Fate has turned us into parasites so the best we can aim for is some form of symbiosis but I think we manage to do this very well."

Moon nodded but he wasn't entirely convinced. "I respect your intentions to bring good out of your situation but there are still a couple of things I'd need to get straight before I'd be willing to take you on face value."

Uri made an expansive gesture that was unmistakably Russian in origin. "I will do my best to answer your questions." The accompanying reassuring smile was marred by the glint from his three centimetre fangs.

"Well, firstly, when you came into the *Rest* tonight every ghost in the place scattered like the devil was after them. That doesn't exactly gel with the 'Father Christmas' image you're trying to sell me, does it?"

"Hmm," Uri nodded. "Vampires are powerful predators, Moon, and we are vessels for great power. I suspect the ghosts detect that and avoid us. You witnessed the sheer force of the spiritual energy that one of us can release, tonight in the graveyard. Considering the depth of a vampire's potency, it is a tribute to your tiny Anna's love for you that she was willing to stand her ground before me."

"I suppose I'll have to take your word for it," replied Moon. "I never knew that vampires wield such power over ghosts."

"Not many do, except the ghosts of course and who are they going to tell, eh? No, sadly, a vampire is a monster to both the living and the dead. Did you have something else to ask me?"

Moon toyed with his empty teacup and studied the faded pattern in the carpet. "Why the music? You've already implied that you're independently wealthy and you say that you don't need to draw victims to you. By performing you regularly place yourselves in danger by flaunting your true nature in plain sight. What have you got to gain?"

"Ahh, Moon, there is some virtue to hiding in plain sight but it is also to do with something very important to our existence indeed, *belief*!" Uri's clasped fingers flew open in a starburst gesture and his eyes flew wide open as his eyebrows raised expressively.

"Belief?" Moon fingered his chin. "You mean you need people to believe in you? Why?"

"We may be flesh and blood, Moon, but we are also creatures of phantasm. I think I mentioned earlier that those things that people believe in over time somehow tend to manifest? That is also true with us. We discovered this when we moved away from Europe and began to live a more benevolent existence in Wales. Our powers slowly began to wane and, after a couple of centuries, we noticed that we'd begun to *fade*; there was a sort of thinness to us, nothing obvious but just a feeling. At first I thought we'd have to go back to hunting humans or choose to fade away to nothing. Then Roanne began to change."

"In what way, change?"

"She changed physically. It was almost imperceptible to begin with, but eventually her hair became greenish and lank and it grew at an alarming rate. Her fingernails turned claw-like, her beauty began to fade as her features grew sharper and her eyes became dark and piercing like a crow's. Even her normally gentle nature gave way to crabbiness and violent outbursts. The poor thing was so distraught at not being able to be herself. The most profound change however was that a small pair of bat-like wings began to grow from her shoulder blades. We thought at first that this was some strange vampiric mutation but Roanne herself was the one who eventually realised the truth. She began to be attracted to those who would soon die and have premonitions of death; 'Oh no!' she cried one day, as she was trying to do something with her poor hair in front of the mirror. 'I know what's happening; I'm turning into a *gwrach-y-rhibyn*!'"

"A what?" asked Moon. "I'm afraid I don't know any Welsh."

"The *gwrach-y-rhibyn* is a kind of Welsh banshee. She has crone-like features, bat's wings and a foul temperament. With some discussion we realised that because there is no vampire in Welsh folklore Roanne was acquiring the attributes of the nearest Welsh alternative. That was why we decided to leave Wales, for all our sakes. God knows what sort of goblin I would have eventually turned into if we had stayed and Charli had also discovered tiny black lumps growing from her shoulder blades."

"So your act helps to maintain the belief that you are vampires?"

"*Might be*, Moon; that we might possibly be vampires. It prevents us from drifting into other forms or fading. The current fad for seeing vampires as beautiful and sexy helps of course. I wasn't quite so pretty when we were performing stage adaptations of *Varney the Vampire* and *The Cabinet of Doctor Polidori* back in the eighteen-hundreds but they served their purpose." Uri paused as if wondering whether to say more then seemed to reach an inner decision. With a brief nod he continued, "There is more to our performing though, Moon, especially since we started making music together. Audiences produce a kind of energy that we are able to feed on. An audience becomes a huge group entity, which we can tap into without draining the individuals involved. We have had to feed physically much less since we started the band."

Moon nodded in understanding. "Some human performers seem to get energy from performing. Perhaps what you're describing is a more concentrated form of that energy. Maybe because you're vampires you're able to absorb it more efficiently."

"Perhaps you're right, Moon. As entities we span the physical and the supernatural further than humans do, which could explain our advantage in this area, and maybe our weaknesses in other ways."

"One last question," said Moon, "then I'll have to ask you to leave and let me get some sleep, okay?"

Uri nodded. "Okay, I need to get back to the girls soon anyway. They will worry."

"Why were you following me tonight?"

Moon studied Uri's face for signs of duplicity as he replied. "Moon, I know Dominic is dead. Very little happens around the *Rest* that we don't know about. We've suspected for a while that someone has been vanishing Goths from the community that gathers at the *Rest*, but we didn't want to risk exposing ourselves. You might provide us with an opportunity to help."

"Why me?"

"Because of your gifts, Moon." Uri stroked his chin then pointed at Moon. "I knew you had the Sight the moment we met tonight. I could tell that you knew what I am by the scent of fear you gave off when we were introduced. You also watch things that aren't there. It's a bad habit."

"Well, it's pretty hard to ignore them entirely, especially when they're as agitated as they were tonight. One of the old highwaymen was waving to me frantically over your shoulder and mouthing 'vampire' at one point in our conversation."

Uri laughed. "Was that what he was doing? He disappeared very rapidly when I turned round and glared at him while you were in the loo." Then he sobered, regarding Moon steadily over his steepled fingers. "Moon, Dominic belonged to one of our Welsh families. His death makes this business very personal to us so please help us to find this killer."

"Well, I suppose I can try but you and the girls would appear to be the prime suspects at present. You know he had bite marks on his neck?"

"No... no, I did not." Uri seemed to grow even paler if that were possible. "It would seem, Moon, that someone may be intending to implicate us in this murder, assuming they know of our presence here."

"Are you sure it's not another vampire?" asked Moon.

"Yes, I would know if one of my dark brothers entered Bristol and besides I think most, if not all of them have been destroyed. I don't think it's another supernatural being either. I haven't sensed anything unfamiliar entering our domain recently."

Moon shook his head at the idea *him* of chasing down a killer. "I am no detective."

Uri gave a short knowing laugh. "But I think you are as curious as the proverbial cat. You will not be able to leave this alone now you've started with it."

"Looks like you've got my measure," Moon laughed wryly. "Okay, I'll see if I can help."

"Good, I suggest you start with the local ghosts. They may have seen something."

Uri finished his tea then flew off into the night by way of Moon's main window, which had opened readily under the vampire's strength. It *had* been nailed shut and cemented in place by several decades' worth of paint. Moon hoped he could fix the splintered woodwork before his landlord discovered it. Uri may be a dark graceful creature of the night but he also seemed one of those doomed to go through life like a bull in a china shop.

Chapter 10

Moon was standing again, paralysed with fear, on the walkway through St Andrew's Cemetery. The Shadow Beast's tendrils constricted numbingly around his throat and he was gasping desperately for air. Suddenly, a swarm of tiny fireflies appeared out of the darkness. They buzzed around and around and then, somehow, through his head, leaving odd shaped retina burns as they flashed through the substance of his eyes. He awoke with a start and the 'Beast' transformed into part of his duvet cover wrapped around his neck. The fireflies were real though, the tiny ghostly lights he had seen a couple of days ago now danced above his face like damsel flies over a stream.

"What the hell...?" he croaked, waving his right hand to drive them off but instead his fingers passed through the nearest dancing glow. His mind filled with another's memory of the vile chemical taste of a cocktail of cider mixed with surgical spirit, swigged directly from a plastic bottle. The residual presence of the memory's owner resonated with a sense of malicious mischief. "Gordy?" he cried out with horrified recognition. "Is that you?" There was no reply but the name 'Gordy' seemed to echo on the air, resonating with the sound of his voice.

The tiny sphere settled on his hand, filling him with craving for alcohol and a sense of ingrained grubbiness, which made him yearn desperately for a shower. The remaining five also settled upon his recumbent form, stirring up a mixture of borrowed memories. Moon sat bolt upright, causing the minuscule glows to fly up and scatter across the ceiling. "That must be what you are! You're the remnants of ghosts!" He watched as the tiny, pitiful scraps of consciousness returned to him and bobbed excitedly before his face.

"How did you get like this?" he asked not expecting an answer but slowly, one by one, each radiant globe approached his right hand, dipping to touch it as they passed. The memory that each showed him was the same: a pair of hellishly red, glowing, eyes glowering out of a dark shadow and the feeling of his entire being draining down into that darkness like a doomed ship spiralling downward, into a whirlpool. "What the hell was that thing?" he queried, but his visitors made no move to answer, just hovered before him radiating a sense of bewilderment.

Some *thing* was draining the life, for want of a better word, out of the local ghosts and, despite his misgivings about his *gift*, he realised that this mattered to him. They had come to him because he was the only person they knew that could see them... that could possibly help them. He wanted to deny the responsibility but the sense of desperation radiating from those minute blue sparks cut him to the quick. "Okay, I'm not promising anything but I'll see what I can do," he muttered, not relishing taking on this 'ghost-eater' face to face. The ghost-balls danced ecstatically around his room in response to his half-hearted decision.

Moon rose about noon on a Monday in preparation for working at night the next day. He would stay up as late as possible tonight, sleep until one or two in the afternoon then go to work at nine, and from then to Friday afternoon he would be out of touch with the world outside of work. It was tough going for those three days but he liked the extra time it gave him.

He breakfasted then showered, gratefully washing away the memory of Gordy's grime as he did so. Once clean, fed and ready to face the day he decided to use the early part of the afternoon to type up his interview with Uri and the girls. As Uri's voice took him back to the previous night, he wondered how he should begin investigating Dominic's murder. Dominic himself had been unable to tell him much about what had occurred before he was dumped in the alley behind the *Rest*, but perhaps the other spirits there could help. Moon decided to pop down to the pub once he had finished drafting his article to see if any of the local spooks were feeling talkative.

When Moon walked into the *Hangman's Rest* a few minutes after two o'clock Kate was serving behind the bar. She was dressed less aggressively than she had been the first time he'd met her. The dark purple silk and lace blouse she was wearing combined with her subtle purple eye shadow emphasised the bright, liquid quality of her dark brown, almost black, eyes. *Less of the biker queen and more of the Goth princess today*, thought Moon. She looked at him askance and said archly, "You're the one who found Dominic, aren't you? Poor kid, never did any harm to anyone. The place has been swarming with cops for the last two days, very bad for business, Moon. Next time you go looking for corpses look somewhere else."

"Sorry?" Moon was shocked by Kate's irreverence and it must have shown.

"Oh, I'm sorry, Moon. This bloody awful business upsets me and I tend to cope with rotten problems by joking about them. What are you drinking? Ostrich isn't it?"

"Yeah, a pint please. What time do you stop serving lunch?"

"Kitchen's open all day."

"Okay, I'll order something later but for the moment I just want a quiet spot to sit and read a bit."

Kate pulled his pint of Ostrich and pointed to a corner at the front of the pub where the windows looked out on the street. "No-one should bother you over there."

Moon took his beer over to a single table near the window and sat down. Pulling out a battered paperback and resting it on the table as a kind of camouflage, he opened up his senses to see if *anyone* was nearby. It was harder to see ghosts in daylight so he had to rely more on the strange inner sense that allowed him to perceive them at all. Slowly, his eyes were drawn to a dark patch of shadows in the opposite corner, where the light from the window, caught in the dust motes and cigarette smoke obscured most of his view. The shape of the shadows resolved into the vague outline of a figure in a dark leather coat and wide brimmed hat. The brim lifted slightly revealing the impression of two hostile black eyes and a twisted hook of a nose peeking out from underneath. *"What you lookin' at, Sunshine?"* vibed the ghost. *"I've gutted men for less in the past."* Ghostly laughter susurated briefly through the ether. *"Not that I'm up to guttin' anything these days, eh?"*

"No, I suppose not," Moon vibed back, grinning uncertainly over the top of his paperback. *"I was wondering if anyone here might know something about a ghost that eats ghosts..."* He felt a bit guilty that he hadn't started by asking for information on Dominic's murder but this morning's experience had placed this foremost in his mind.

"Interestin'." Moon jumped in his seat as the dark figure suddenly materialised in the chair opposite him.

"Do you mind? You nearly scared me out of my boots!"

"Arr, but that be ol' Dick's job now, bain't it?" A pewter tankard materialised on the table and Dick took a deep swig of it: a useful trick given the price of beer these days.

"Well, have you heard anything about a monster that drains spirits until they're nothing more than this?" Moon indicated the tiny balls of iridescent blue mist, which were huddling in the darkness of the corner behind him. *They must not like the light*, he thought. He'd noticed that most spirits tended to steer clear of direct sunlight. Perhaps it was worse for the little ghost balls, he wondered, because they had so little of themselves left to hold onto.

Dick grinned. *"Is that what they be? Little ghost o' ghosts, I had wondered."* He shook his head. *"No, I ain't seen nothin' like that. Nor heard tell o' un either."*

"What about that murder a few days ago in the alley behind the pub?"

"Ah, y'mean young Dominic?"

Moon nodded. *"You know him?"*

"Know un now don' I. Now 'e's part o' our 'appy fam'ly an all. Weren't no murder in Gallows Alley either, 'is body were dumped there. Mus' o' bin shortly after 'is death too or 'e'd be 'auntin where 'e was killed." Dick took a deep pull from his phantom tankard.

"Did anyone see who did it?"

"Aye, Gulley Longshafts says he saw one o' they 'orseless carriages pull in by the Rest in the middle hours o' the night. A young cove got out an' opened the other door, dragged Dominic out, makin' out as if 'e were drunk until 'e got un into alley then 'e jus' drops un an scarpers.'

"Is this Gulley around so I could ask him about it?" asked Moon.

"Ye might catch un in poolroom if ye be lucky, next to yon flashy noisemaker. Poor ol' Gulley, 'as made a fine torment o' 'is afterlife that thing 'as."

"I'd better go and see if he's there then," replied Moon, picking up his finished glass to return it to the bar.

"Best o' luck mate. If I see yer ghost-eater I'll let ye know."

"Just beware of dark shadows with glowing eyes. I don't want any more blue glows following me around. I already feel like the Pied Piper." He got up to leave.

"Pied who?" asked Dick as he faded back to the corner where he had bled to death all over his favourite deck of marked cards two centuries before.

The pool room was upstairs just off the first floor landing next to the corridor to the toilets so Moon had a reasonable excuse to head up there. He visited the gents first, with some trepidation, because the plump and bawdy Georgian prostitute, who haunted the first floor, liked to jump out and scare male customers then laugh at them when they peed on their shoes. She did put in an appearance but merely popped her powdered and pockmarked face through the wall behind the urinal, looked him up and down appraisingly and said, *"Oh, it's you, Moon,"* then she faded, crestfallen back into the plaster.

"And good day to you too, Madam," replied Moon out loud. It seemed that the news that he didn't spook easily had done the rounds at the *Rest*.

Fortunately the pool room was empty. The lunchtime punters had rushed off unhappily to their office jobs and it was too early for the evening clientele to make an appearance. It was dingy, windowless and full of shadows. The only light shone down from the canopy hanging over the table, which highlighted a myriad of minor tears and threadbare patches left by hundreds of drunken contests. Two video game machines raved at each other on the wall across from the door next to Gulley's hated jukebox, which was mercifully silent at present. The ghost of Gulley Longshafts dangled in an advanced state of decay in the far corner just left of and above the jukebox. What remained of his desiccated features were twisted into an expression of extreme boredom. "It's okay, Gulley," said Moon cheerfully, "you don't have to put on the full show for me."

"Oh, 'ullo, it's Moon, innit?" Gulley gave Moon a ghastly grin and drifted down to floor level, his features rapidly returning to what they had looked like in life, which wasn't much of an improvement. Gulley had been a tall, gangling, cadaverous individual with a mouth full of yellowed tombstone teeth and a pronounced squint in his pale-blue right eye. *"It's me penance, y'know, for killing me wife. I 'as to walk the gallows path in the 'our before dawn and 'ang on the gallows when e're a soul may see to warn 'em o' the consequences o' murder."* He said this last word expressively, as if he were warning a child. Moon could tell that Gulley wasn't very bright. He'd come across similar situations before and as far as he could tell such 'penances' were not invoked by any higher power, except perhaps the penitent's greater soul. From what he'd encountered it was usually some fairly decent type's way of coping with something terrible they had done. He had encountered enough unrepentant monsters in the spirit world to know that this was not compulsory.

"Yeah, it's your walk along Gallows Alley that interests me, Gulley. Dick downstairs says you saw someone dump Dominic's body a few nights ago. I'm guessing that it would have been about an 'hour before dawn'; any idea what day it was?"

"I fink it were Thursday. Aye, Thursday, 'cause the beer lorry called that mornin'." Gulley grinned beatifically. *"I likes the beer lorry, lots o' nice fumes, it makes I 'appy."*

"So, Wednesday night to Thursday morning then. What about the person who dumped the body? Could you describe him?"

Gulley scratched his stubbly lantern jaw. *"Well, I was on the gallows walk, see, so I couldn't take much time to get a good look at he. 'Bout five feet 'n a half tall, pale faced lad, not too well favoured in the face, scrawny lookin', wore those faded blue pantaloons 'angin' half-way down 'is arse, like they do these days, baggy smock thing on top."*

"Jeans and T-shirt?" asked Moon, trying to marry an eighteenth century description with twenty-first century clothing.

"Aye, I fink that's what ye calls 'em," affirmed Gulley, frowning with concentration. *"'Ad some kind o' writin' on it. Never learnt to read meself. Knows me letters though, began wi' a big 'J' for jackdaw."*

"Any pictures on the T-shirt, Gulley? Anything you might recognise?"

"No, but I recognised 'im though."

Moon was startled. "You did?"

"Aye, many's the time I've 'ung 'ere o' an evenin' watchin' yon lad play wi' those long sticks an' shiny balls in this very room. 'E'd changed though, used to be one o' they young uns in black, now 'e'd cut 'is 'air an' it were goin' yellow at roots. I nearly didn't recognize 'im 'cause 'e looked so diff'rent."

This was more promising than Moon expected. "You don't know his name, do you?"

Gulley's face fell. *"Sorry, mate, can't 'ear a bloody fing for that soddin' jukebox most o' the time so I don't get t' 'ear their names often. I'm fairly certain 'is wasn't one o' those strange nicknames like some o' 'em 'ave, more one o' yer Tom, Dick or 'Arries, ye might say."*

"Oh, well," Moon grimaced, "I suppose that was too much to hope for. Thanks anyway, Gulley."

"Think naught o' it," replied Gulley, returning to his gallows-corpse phase. *"Murder is a terrible fing, I knows. Do you fink you could unplug the jukebox on your way out. They might fink it's broken."*

"Right you are," said Moon, removing the plug from its socket. *Can't be much of an afterlife*, he thought as he headed down the stairs.

Back downstairs, Moon ordered a sandwich at the bar. Kate looked at him strangely, "Did you enjoy your chats?" she asked as she pulled him a fresh pint of Ostrich.

Moon's eyes widened. "How did you know?"

"Well, I'm psychic enough myself to know when that presence in the window corner's active. But several minutes of close circuit TV footage from the camera in the pool room *did* confirm my suspicions. Either you're a gifted psychic or a raving nutter."

"The former, I hope, although some days I'm not so sure."

"Oh, yeah? Why did you unplug the jukebox then?"

"You've got a three-hundred year old gallows victim in there and the jukebox is just under where he hangs. I unplugged it to thank him for a favour and give him a chance at a little peace."

"Now I know you're on the level. Only a handful of people know that part of the pub was built directly over where the old gallows were sited before they relocated them to the crossroads. I'll see about moving the jukebox." Kate handed Moon his Ostrich.

"Thanks. Old Gulley will be well pleased."

"So you can actually see and hear these things?" Kate shook her head with awe. "All I get is a vague inkling that someone's there and sometimes the slight impression of words. You're really lucky you know."

"I'm not so sure about that. I'm beginning to learn it comes with a lot of responsibility."

"Doesn't everything?" replied Kate with a wink.

"I guess so." Moon picked up his drink and turned to find himself another seat as a middle-aged couple in biking leathers had taken the table by the window.

"Just out of interest…" Kate placed her hand on Moon's arm. "What exactly were you talking to our ghosts about?"

Moon didn't think he should mention Uri's interest in Dominic's murder at this time so he decided to tell Kate half the truth. "Something's hurting them, the spirits I mean. It drains them like a glass of wine and leaves only the tiniest dregs of existence behind; so they've come to me for help and, for the life of me, I couldn't turn them away."

"Sounds like you have a bit of a calling to me."

"Sonia told me something similar yesterday." Moon shook his head. "I wasn't sure back then, but I'm beginning to think I haven't got a choice."

Kate smiled a knowing smile. "Oh, there's always a choice. But those touched by the gods usually find out that it's much better to go with the flow than fight it after the first few attempts." She looked up the bar to where a group of men in overalls had congregated; one of them was waving a ten-pound note. "Damn, customers!" she said *sotto voce*. "We must talk about this again sometime when I'm not working behind the bar. See ya later, Moon."

Moon left the *Hangman's Rest* at about four o'clock. It was pointless for him to head back home if he was going to get to Sonia's for tea at six. So he decided to pop into the town centre to get some exercise and do some window-shopping. As he passed what he would now forever more think of as 'Gallows Alley' he gave in to a compulsion to take a few steps into the entrance and have a quick look. There was nothing to show that a corpse had lain there at all. The police had obviously been and gone, leaving not even a shred of incident tape to mark their passing. "Returning to the scene of the crime, Mr Moon?"

Moon turned towards the voice with a start. "Er, no, sorry, I just couldn't avoid thinking about what I saw here last time I passed, Inspector."

"No need to look so alarmed, Sir," replied Detective Inspector Whatley. For it was he, standing at the entrance of the alley wearing what appeared to be exactly the same shirt, tie and wrinkled suit he had worn on Saturday night. "You've a firm alibi for the time of the murder, which we've estimated happened some time between ten p.m. last Wednesday and two a.m. on Thursday morning. Mr Llewellyn's body was then taken from the place where he was murdered and deposited here in the alley some time in the early hours on Thursday. According to your statement, which we've verified with other members of staff at the hospital after you were busy saving lives in Casualty at the time." Whatley looked down at the cobbles of the empty alley. "Bloody strange case, this one, Mr Moon, could make a body start believing in fairy tales."

The ghost of Dominic materialised out of the shadows of the alleyway and floated indistinctly in the afternoon sunlight. *"Hi, Moon, is this what they've decided to put on my case? He looks a bit iffy to me."* Whatley shook his head as if he was being buzzed by an annoying insect.

"How do you mean, Inspector?" asked Moon, trying not to make eye contact with Dominic, who was flicking Whatley's right earlobe with a ghostly fingernail.

"Well, you remember you mentioned the lack of blood on the scene on Saturday night, Sir?" Whatley quickly put his hand to his ear and looked round.

Moon suppressed a grin and nodded. "When you've seen as many trauma cases as I have you know how much a wound like the one in Dominic's neck can bleed."

"Yes, the autopsy shows that the deceased's body was almost completely drained of blood. That bite wound on the neck is also very odd; it's not consistent with any known type of animal. We thought at first that it was probably rats but whatever made it was much larger and the bite pattern most closely resembles that of some kind of anthropoid, that's an ape to you and me." *Or possibly something closer to human, like a vampire*, thought Moon. "Bring that together with some of the rumours we've heard since we've started investigating Mr Llewellyn's death and it makes you start to wonder if there isn't something, well… supernatural about it all."

"Too damn right!" agreed Dominic, *"Me!"*

"Sorry, Mr Moon, did you say something?"

"What kind of rumours, Inspector?" asked Moon, as if repeating himself. He was fairly sure he knew but he wanted to hear it from Whatley's mouth. The detective was obviously more than a little disturbed by what he had discovered for him to reveal key evidence to a member of the public. Perhaps he thought Moon's journalistic research might throw more light on the matter, which it could, but Moon didn't think now was the time to reveal the truth about Uri and the girls.

"Well, there's some suggestion that there might be a vampire or vampires involved. The source is unfortunately not a very reliable one but I was thinking it doesn't have to be a real vampire, just some lunatic who thinks he is one. You might think it unlikely but there has been the occasional vampire-inspired murder in this country in the past. It's a very popular type of fiction and you only have to look on the Internet to find how many nutters there are out there who think they're the real McCoy. Have you encountered anyone like that in your journalistic endeavours, Mr Moon? I expect these Goth types would go in for that sort of thing."

"A vampire? I wish!" Dominic shook his head sadly and spread his vaporous arms out wide. *"Just look at me! And I'm stuck in this bloody alley until someone solves my murder."*

"I haven't met anyone who *thinks* they're a vampire since I started my research. There are plenty of Goths who like playing at being vampires, even Sonia, my girlfriend, has some fake fangs that she wears to concerts. I *have* heard the rumours you mentioned but I've established that they were started by one of the local Goth bands to add to their mystique."

"That would be Uri Kievich and his two lady friends? What do they call their group?"

"*Blood Velvet*," replied Moon. "I've heard one of their albums, they're very good."

"Uri? No, it wouldn't have been Uri. He's an old friend of the family," cried Dominic.

"So you're sure that's all it is, a publicity stunt?"

Moon wasn't happy lying to the police but if he told the truth at best he'd be drawn into this horrible business much more deeply than he wanted to be. If the worst happened, he could end up struggling to prove his own sanity. "Yes, I interviewed Uri last night and he told me all about the game they play with their fans. It's all just harmless fun."

"Nonetheless, I think I'll have to check up on this Mr Kievich. Do you know where he lives?" Whatley pulled a crumpled black notebook out of his jacket pocket.

"Not sure. Somewhere up by the Downs is all that I've heard." Moon was glad that was all he knew. He still remembered the steely grip of Uri's hand around his own. Friendly vampire or not, Uri was not someone he wanted to piss off. Perhaps he ought to try to get word to Uri that the police were investigating him; he'd been in Britain for 500 years so Moon doubted he had immigration papers.

"Damn!" Whatley pocketed his notebook. "That's all I've heard so far. He's ex-directory too so I guess the next stop is the electoral register."

"Why don't you ask inside the pub? They play there occasionally and have connections with some of the other bands who perform there as well. I'm sure the landlady could at least let you have Uri's phone number." *And maybe have the sense to tip Uri the wink once your gone*, he thought.

"I'll try that, thank you, Mr Moon." Whatley tilted his head to survey the rest of the alley. "I'll be glad to get out of this stinking alley. There's a nasty buzzing insect of some sort down here and it's giving me a headache."

Moon glanced sourly at Dominic, who was doubling up with ghostly laughter. "I'd do that, Inspector. Insects like that can be a real nuisance."

Moon sauntered through the Broadmead shopping centre amid the flow of homeward bound workers. A lot of the shops had closing down sales because there were plans to drastically remodel the area. One of these was *Ethnicity*, a store that sold South American, African and Indian clothing and jewellery, where he bought a very nice amber bracelet for Sonia for half price. He also purchased the matching pendant and earrings, which he thought would make good birthday presents.

He whiled away the next hour browsing bookshops and comic shops then headed across town towards Hotwells. The skies had darkened while he had been shopping and now the odd drop of rain was falling from the ragged grey sky. Moon considered catching a bus in the centre but quickly abandoned the idea when he saw the length of the evening bus queues. He would just have to hope it wasn't raining too badly by the time he got to Sonia's place. So he set off along the covered walkway by the Watershed building, which was crowded with post-work pub-goers, and by the time he reached the other end it was raining bucket loads. Frowning with disgust, he pulled a brown suede baseball cap out of his inside pocket and cramming it on his head he plunged into the rain. He decided to use the roadway, which ran behind the university and was marginally more sheltered than the quayside route. Pulling his collar up around his ears, he trudged through the worsening rain. This was one of the worst things about of living in Bristol, he thought: every now and then the skies would open in biblical proportions.

He arrived eventually at Sonia and Avril's door, sodden to the core and wondering if he was in danger of evolving webbed feet and gills. Avril opened the door in response to his ringing of the bell. "God, you're soaked. You'd best come inside quickly. Sonia, your beloved's here, and you'd better bring some towels!"

Avril ushered him into their kitchen where Sonia had briefly stopped cooking to take some towels down from one of the cupboards. "Shit, Jerry, you look like a drowned cat!"

"Don't you mean 'rat'?" replied Moon, conscious that he was dripping a sizeable pond onto the lino.

"No cat, definitely cat, cuter but more miserable when wet; we'd better get you out of those wet things. You know where the bathroom is and you can borrow my bathrobe, it's the dark purple one with the hood."

Chapter 11

It was fifteen minutes later and a much warmer and drier Moon was sitting at the kitchen table with a mug of tea in his hand. The mug, shaped like a dragon's head, glowered at him disapprovingly. He was wearing his boxer shorts and Sonia's purple bathrobe, which had a black furry trim around the hood and a bat on the pocket. He felt like the vampire Father Christmas. "You should have taken the bus," said Sonia in a motherly tone.

"They were full," replied Moon, "and it didn't start raining heavily until I was part of the way here. Sorry, I'm just not weather-wise I guess." Sonia shook her head while working busily at the cooker. "Didn't you say it was just going to be turkey burgers?" Moon commented as she threw diced courgettes into a frying pan.

"I thought I'd surprise you with my culinary expertise," answered Sonia with a hint of pride. "Garlic chicken stir-fry sound okay?"

"Wonderful," replied Moon, sipping his tea and enjoying watching Sonia fuss with her cooking. "You never said you could cook."

"Well, a girl has to keep some mystery in her relationships. Anyway, this is recipe number two in a huge repertoire of five, so enjoy the novelty while it lasts."

"I'll buy you a recipe book for your birthday," said Moon, cocking a mischievous eyebrow at Avril, who tried to hide a grin.

"You bloody well dare!" Sonia rounded on him with her spatula raised in killing position.

Moon laughed. "It's okay love. I've had to fend for myself long enough to have a few recipes of my own up my sleeve. Together we should be able to manage oh, ten at least."

Sonia bent to kiss him. "A couple more and we can open our own restaurant. Perhaps I'll buy *you* a cookbook then you can really be my ideal man."

Moon aimed a light slap at her rump. "You never told me you were into D and S."

"You never asked me, slave!" Avril, who was feeling a bit left out, coughed and pointed at the frying pan, from which the first thin wisps of smoke were rising. "Bloody hell!" Sonia grabbed a jug of water, which she had wisely left within handy reach on the counter top, and poured some into the sizzling pan before the contents could burn. "Just caught it! Any more of your lip, Jerry Moon, and it's burnt offerings for tea."

Moon decided not to mention what he had learned about Uri over tea or to discuss his visit to the *Hangman's Rest*. Partly because he didn't think Avril would take him seriously, but mainly because he thought it best to keep the matter of Uri's true nature between Sonia and himself. So the conversation over the meal, which turned out to be very tasty despite its earlier brush with incineration, was restricted to small talk and general banter. When the meal was finished Avril insisted that it was her turn to do the washing up so they retired quickly to Sonia's room with cups of tea.

They sat down on Sonia's bed. "You look really cute in that bathrobe, you know," said Sonia playfully tweaking Moon's left nipple, which was partly exposed by the gaping robe.

"Ouch! Do you think so? I was going more for the Grim Reaper option myself."

Sonia shook her head. "Too fluffy, anyway Death wears a black robe and I don't remember hearing anything about him wearing white boxers with red hearts on them; how romantic."

"They were a gift from my Mum," insisted an embarrassed Moon, covering them up with a fold of towelling. "I hadn't bargained on this amount of exposure for tonight."

"Well, I'm really glad you decided to walk then." She slipped her hands inside the robe and felt Moon's response to her touch through his romantic boxers. "Damn! I'll be glad when that week's over!"

"Me too!" replied Moon, kissing her deeply.

A passionate ten minutes later, Sonia pushed Moon gently away, "Okay, okay, I can see where this is heading and we need to calm down a bit. I'm still black and blue down there and we're not going to risk making it worse! Sorry."

"Damn!" Moon released his hold on parts of Sonia's anatomy, sat up and re-tied the bathrobe. "Sorry, I just got a bit carried away in the heat of the moment."

"You and me both." Sonia buttoned up her blouse and zipped up her jeans. "Okay." She cuddled back up to him primly. "Take our minds off you-know-what and tell me what you did today while I was fending off abusive phone-calls from unhappy customers." Sonia worked as a team leader for a telemarketing call centre.

"Actually, it's a long story," replied Moon and he told her about his encounter with Uri and the shadow beast.

"God, Jerry, you almost died! You've got to promise me you won't go wandering through graveyards on your own at night again."

"It's not something that I'm intending to take up as a pastime, you know." Moon was a bit taken aback by Sonia's protectiveness. "Anyway, that shortcut is definitely off the map for me in the evenings from now on."

"And Uri told you that the monster that attacked you exists just because people *believe* in it?"

Moon shrugged. "He seemed to imply that a *lot* of things exist just because people believe in them."

"Including vampires?"

"Yes, including vampires, but in their case you need to have a human being as well; to provide the raw materials, so to speak."

"And Uri really is a vampire?" Sonia shook her head.

"And Charli and Roanne too; I told you as much last night."

She looked up at him sheepishly. "Yes. But it's a lot to take in without harder evidence than your spook sense. You know this means that they really could have murdered Dominic…"

"Uri gave me some very good reasons to believe otherwise. Sonia, the guy saved my life, that's not something I'd expect from a cold-blooded killer. He also asked me to investigate Dominic's murder. That's what I was doing all afternoon. I talked to some of the resident spooks at the *Rest* about Dominic and, guess what, we have a description of the guy who dumped the body."

"Really?"

"Really. According to one of the ghosts until a few months ago he was one of the Goths who regularly hang out at the *Rest*. He spent a lot of time in the poolroom apparently. But he's changed now. He's cut his hair short and is growing out the black dye so his yellow roots are showing. Any ideas?"

"He's probably one of the other guys that have disappeared off the scene in the last few months, which narrows it down quite a lot. I don't know everyone who goes to the *Rest* but as far as I know there have been four blokes, including Dominic, and two girls. I didn't know any of them very well, so I couldn't give you names for all of them, but I can find out."

Moon shook his head. "It's a pity we can't tell all this to the police. And speaking of the police, on my way over here I also ran into our favourite sartorially challenged copper, Detective Inspector Whatley. He let me in on a few things about their progress with Dominic's case because he hoped I might be able to provide him with a lead. It's looking more and more like a vampire attack. Whatley thinks it's probably some loony who thinks he's a vampire. Apparently, there have been other murders in that 'genre' – is that the right word, can you have a *genre* for murder? – in the past, but we know that it *could* be the real thing."

"I thought Uri told you that he'd know if another vamp was in the area."

"Yeah, but he doesn't have to be in the area does he if he's got a flunky with a car to move the body for him. Anyway, I think Uri was right, dumping Dominic pretty much on Uri's doorstep looks like an attempt to frame him."

"So you think it's a rival vampire trying to 'out' Uri?"

"It looks like it." Moon thought for a second, "Look, do you have any way of contacting Uri? I think we need to warn him about this."

Under the pretence that Moon needed to ask Uri some questions to clarify a few things from the previous night's interview, they asked Avril to phone her boyfriend, Roger, who reluctantly let them have the number *Unquiet Grave* used to contact Uri. Back in Sonia's room Moon called the number from his mobile and was surprised when a cultured male voice answered, "The Maddocks' residence, who is calling?"

"Hello, I hope this isn't a wrong number, my name is Jerry Moon and it's very important that I speak with Uri." Moon hoped that, if this was the right number, he wasn't about to get the brush off from the vampires' butler or whoever *this* was.

"Ah, Mr Moon, Uri has mentioned you. It may be a little early to disturb him; I'll just go and see if he's up." Moon cursed and looked at his watch, it was shortly after eight-thirty, out of the window it was still daylight.

"What's up?" asked Sonia looking up from the magazine she had been flicking through.

"It's still daylight. Uri may not be out of his coffin yet."

Sonia chuckled, "Not something you normally have to worry about, is it?" She looked up thoughtfully from her magazine. "You know, their vulnerability to daylight is one of the things the literature's a bit unclear about. The main theory seems to be that the older they are the more they're able to stay active during daylight hours but direct sunlight can kill them. But then it's probably all invented by Hollywood. I don't think vampires were all that bothered by the sun before Christopher Lee played Dracula."

"If what Uri has to say is true they probably have to stick with the prevailing mythology, which, sad to say, is probably *Buffy the Vampire Slayer* at the moment... Ah! Uri?"

"Hello, Moon." Uri's voice was still as deep and resonant over the phone as it was in person. "How can I help you?"

"Hi, Uri, I was just wondering if I'd phoned too early for you to be awake."

"It is early, yes. But, like Stoker's Count Dracula, I can be active in the daytime if I choose. Now, what can I do for you so early in the evening?"

"It's more a matter of what I can do for you. First of all, the police want to talk with you. I suggested they might be able to contact you via Kate at the *Rest*. I hoped that she might be able to warn you before they got to you, because I was worried that it might cause problems, if they start looking into your background."

Uri laughed gently. "Thanks, Moon. But it's okay, my ladies and I all have birth certificates registered at Somerset House in case of such emergencies. It is one of the advantages of having doctors and lawyers 'in the family', as you say."

"Oh, right." Moon hadn't considered how widespread Uri's human family's influence might be after three hundred years. "The other thing I wanted to warn you about is that I met the policeman who's working on Dominic's case today and the evidence seems to be pointing towards some kind of vampiric attack. His body had been drained of blood and forensics are saying the bite on his neck looks like it was made by some kind of ape."

"...Or a human with fangs, perhaps? Well, perhaps one of my brethren is involved after all but I would have expected to have sensed him."

"Not if he was killed elsewhere and then driven to the *Rest* by an accomplice. I did some detective work myself today at the *Rest*, as you suggested. The ghosts there say that Dominic's body was deposited in the alley by someone who used to be a regular at the pub. The police also think he was killed somewhere else."

"This is very strange. If you wanted to hide a body you wouldn't just leave it in open view in the middle of a city. The only explanation I can think of is that someone is attempting to draw attention to Charli, Roanne and myself." Uri said a few words in rapid Russian. From his tone of voice Moon assumed he was swearing. "We have to find this lunatic, Moon, and stop him before he does anything else to expose us."

"I understand. From the description the ghosts gave me, the accomplice is one of the Goths that have recently left the scene around here, which narrows the search down to a handful of people. I hope you don't mind but I've let Sonia in on your secret and she's going to see if she can come up with some names."

"That was... unwise of you, Moon." Uri sounded edgy, "But if she can help us, it's... okay."

"Well, I let her know my suspicions before we met for the second time last night, so I didn't think telling her everything would make a lot of difference. You can trust me not to let the truth go any further and I believe you can trust Sonia as well."

"Thank you," whispered Sonia, kissing his cheek.

"Very well, Moon, I suppose I can't blame you for confiding in your girlfriend. Now, if there is nothing else I must let the family know what's happening and prepare them for a visit from the police."

"Well, there was one thing…" Moon explained about the being that was attacking the local ghosts. "Have you any idea what could be doing this?"

"You know, the way you describe it, it could almost be some kind of vampire." He gave a short laugh. "But no, that is too absurd, I have never heard of a vampire that feeds off ghosts."

"Well, anything's possible, I suppose. Thanks Uri, I'll keep you posted with any new developments. Please let me know how things go with the police." Moon gave Uri his mobile number and explained when he could be contacted over the next three days because he would be working nights.

"Okay, thank you, Moon. If nothing new happens I'll contact you in a few days' time."

The rest of the evening was uneventful. They ended up watching a movie from Avril's DVD collection called *Mr Vampire*. Avril collected Hong Kong Cinema horror films and assured Moon that this was a particularly good example; Moon hadn't seen anything like this before and found the combination of kung fu, weird Chinese humour, horror and naff special effects extremely unusual but strangely satisfying. As he rose from the couch after the end of the movie he again noticed the small trophy among the skulls on the mantelpiece. Intrigued, he picked it up and read out loud what was written on the small silver plaque on its base: "*All Out Winner – South and West Ladies Amateur Taekwondo Championship 2002.* Is this yours, Sonia?" Avril had left to pay a visit to the bathroom.

"No, it's Avril's, she's very proud of it. She's really into martial arts. Not just Taekwondo but Kung Fu and Karate as well. She runs training sessions in her spare time."

"I would have thought she's a bit, well, chubby to be any good at martial arts."

Sonia hit him in the shoulder. "Don't let her hear you call her that. But no, she's really very athletic despite her family's tendency to plumpness. And it's proved very useful on one or two occasions. She gave a couple of muggers a really hard time a few months ago when they thought they'd pick on a couple of Goth chicks, I can tell you that."

"Well, I'll have to try not to get on her bad side, won't I?" Moon unconsciously weighed the statue in his hand before returning it to the mantelpiece.

"You'll have to come over and watch more of Avril's collection," said Sonia, as she saw him to the door shortly after ten o'clock. "They're not all as good as *Mr Vampire* but most of them are good fun."

"I'll take you up on that invitation." Moon gave her a lingering kiss. "I'm sorry but I won't be around much for the next few days. I tend to get up about two and head off for work at about eight, so phone me tomorrow at six, and you can tell me all about your day."

"Yeah, okay. Avril and I are heading up to the *Rest* tomorrow night so I'll see what I can find out about the guys who've gone missing. Okay?"

"Great, I love you, you know." It was the first time he'd said it and he watched her face for her reaction.

She looked down for a second and he could almost see the ghosts of past disappointments flow behind her eyes, then she gazed back up at him. "Yeah, I guess I love you to, Jerry." They kissed again, long and hard. As they were parting Sonia reminded him, "Not through the cemetery tonight, Jerry, I want you in one piece when we get together on Friday. You know that ruddy week will be over by then." She winked at him suggestively as she closed the door.

Moon walked home elatedly but he made sure not to take the cemetery route and took the road round by the Monica Wills

Chapel instead. Although it avoided the cemetery itself, this route did take him past its gateway, and he glanced in towards the darkened path as he went past. He felt the cold aura of the Shadow Beast emanating from the place, even at this distance, and could see that something strange was happening on the path just by looking through the gateway. He hoped someone wasn't in trouble down there, because there was no way he was willing to risk pitting himself against that creature again, not without Uri for back-up. Shaking his head guiltily, he turned to follow the slightly longer path towards Whiteladies Road and home.

In the darkened graveyard a fierce battle raged. Tentacles of darkness thrashed soundlessly among the tombstones as two opponents, predator and prey, locked in deadly combat. Finally, a single long, ghostly scream shredded the night as the loser succumbed and was sucked into a cold, malignant vortex of spiritual oblivion. The lights over the pathway returned to their normal brightness as a sinister figure, cloaked in shadows, disappeared into the night, leaving in its wake a tiny red glowing ball that hovered angrily among the headstones like an enraged bee. This furious little spark of existence was all that remained of the Shadow Beast of St Andrew's Cemetery. It had fought the mysterious 'Ghost Eater' and had lost.

Chapter 12

The next day passed quickly for Moon, having stayed up until about four thirty a.m., reading and playing computer games, had gone to bed as the sun rose. It hit him as slightly ironic that being out of step with the normal flow of life was something he and Uri had in common. He woke before his alarm rang at one-thirty in the afternoon and spent the next few hours pottering around, watching some television and adding some extra touches to his article.

Moon found his off-duty time during the working part of his week slightly dissatisfying. This was because, if he intended to return to anything like a normal sleep pattern at the weekends, he had to fit his leisure time in before going to work, which meant it was always at the back of his mind that he had to start work in a few hours. It was the one unfortunate aspect of an otherwise ideal arrangement that got his breadwinning out of the way quickly in the middle of the week and allowed him to enjoy long weekends.

He ate his main meal at about five-thirty then, as he was washing up, the phone rang. It was Sonia calling as they'd arranged. They spent the next forty minutes chatting generally about their days and each other's lives, punctuated occasionally with gentle words and wishes that they didn't have to be apart for the next three nights. Then Sonia said, "Oh, by the way, I've a bit of info about our missing people. Two of them, Tonya and Jeff, aren't missing at all. They're both artists and they've been involved in some kind of communal art project down in Devon for the last few months. They didn't tell many people where they were going, but Roger knew about it. I asked Avril to see what she could find out about the guys who'd gone missing and he told her about them last night while they were romancing over the phone."

"So that leaves us with, how many, three blokes and one girl?"

"Yeah, that's right, Dominic, Animal…"

"'Animal?'" Moon laughed.

"Yes, 'Animal', he used to play drums for *Jumping Corpse*, one of the death metal bands; they called him Animal because he played like the crazy drummer from the Muppets. The other guy's called Andy and I think the girl's name is Lorraine. Now that I come to think of it, I think Animal and Andy were something of an item for a while before Andy dropped out of the scene."

"You mean they're gay?"

"Yes, or bi. Whichever they are, I'm fairly sure they were together for a while up until late last year. Andy stopped coming to the *Rest* regularly shortly after Christmas, or so Avril tells me."

"What about the girl?"

"Lorraine? She never came back after the Christmas break. She was a bit of a drifter so no one really took much notice when she disappeared. I remember her telling me that she was squatting in a disused office building down between the M32 access and Old Market with some other kids. The place was really disgusting so I guess everyone thought she'd got fed up with Bristol and either gone back to her parents or moved on elsewhere."

"So either Animal or Andy is the prime suspect for our killer."

"I guess so."

"We need to give this information to the police. Look, I'm going to have to get off to work soon. I hate to ask you but could you phone them."

"Sure, no trouble, it should sound less suspicious coming from me anyway because I'm a Goth myself. I'll phone them once we've got off the phone." There was a mischievous pause. "So, when do I get to see you in your nurse's uniform? I bet you look really sexy," Sonia giggled.

"Ah! Now I know why you're still going out with me. I've heard about women like you."

"Aw, c'mon, you love it really."

"More to the point, I love you, Sonia."

Sonia quietened on the other end of the line. "And I love you, Jerry. Sometimes too much, I think."

"You don't trust me, is that it?" Moon was concerned about the reluctance he'd sensed from Sonia when he'd tried to steer their relationship towards a deeper commitment. He knew how he felt about her but he was worryingly unsure if she felt the same way.

"You're a great guy, Jerry. It's just that Craig, my last boyfriend, turned out to be a real bastard. I've still got the scars to prove it."

"Scars? What happened?"

"He was really possessive and would beat me up if he thought I'd stepped out of line. It got so that he wouldn't allow me to go out on my own. Then one night we got into a row about me talking to one of his friends. He thought I'd been flirting with him and, when I denied it, he took a kitchen knife and stabbed me in the side. The neighbours took me to casualty and I ended up in hospital for a week. After that I decided I didn't want to see him ever again."

"I don't blame you."

"Yeah, well, getting away from him turned into something like a James Bond operation. I didn't let him know when I was being discharged from hospital, sneaked into our flat while he was at work, packed most of my stuff and took a taxi to my mum's. I'd only been there a few days when he came around and tried to kick the door down. It was then I realised that I'd never be free of him in Reading, so I put in for a transfer from work. Thankfully, they were able to move me to Bristol within the month. I found out later that he'd been having it off with a bunch of other women all the time we'd been together. Talk about double standards; I'm lucky the arsehole didn't give me AIDS."

"God, I'm surprised you didn't go off men altogether after that kind of experience."

"I have to confess there have been times that I've wished that I *was* gay. It would have made things so much easier, but I'm just not wired that way, I suppose. Anyway that was four years ago and you're the first bloke I've had more than a one-nighter with since. That's why I'm a bit wary of putting all my emotional eggs in one basket. You'll just have to give me some time, Jerry, okay?"

"Yes, sure. I didn't know that you had that kind of emotional of baggage to cope with. Just let me know if I'm getting too intense, yeah?"

He sensed her smile over the phone. "Yeah, okay."

They spent five minutes playing the normal lovers' game of trying not to be the one to put the phone down last, then Moon checked his watch. He needed to get a move on if he didn't want to be late. One of the Sisters on the ward where he was working that night wasn't too fond of him and it would be just his luck for her to be on duty. The last thing he needed was another complaint to the hospital's night managers.

Moon's night was generally uneventful. The night managers had scheduled him for the cardiology ward, where most of the patients, although not well, were reasonably stable. He did have to bleep the on call house officer once when a patient's vital signs went outside of safe limits and he had to monitor that patient hourly for the rest of the night but, apart from this, his biggest concern was staying awake, which was never easy on his first night of the week.

In the morning Moon gave his patient handover to the day staff then staggered wearily back to his flat. The first night tended to affect him like this but by Friday morning he'd have trouble getting to sleep. He smiled at Anna, who was grinning at him mischievously, as he trudged up to the first floor landing.

"Hi, Anna, I hope you haven't been upsetting Mrs Foley again. Remember how I told you that she's a nice lady and it's not kind to tease her like you do."

"Oh bother!" Anna's grin turned to a scowl. *"But she's so rude, Jerry, she won't play with me or talk with me or anything!"*

"That's because she can't see you, sweetheart." Moon wondered how to explain this to Anna. Past experience of trying to explain to ghosts that they were actually dead had, at best, resulted in fierce denial. The last thing he wanted was the four-year-old ghost throwing a poltergeist tantrum when he needed to sleep. He had a flash of inspiration. "You see she's very deaf and almost blind. You know how older people get, and it's not right for you to make fun of her just because she's so old, is it?" Julie Foley was a well preserved forty-eight year old with a passion for younger men but Moon was banking on the hope that to Anna anyone older than about twelve was probably over the hill.

"*Oh, right,*" replied Anna thoughtfully. Moon missed the strange little smile that played faintly on her lips. "*Is that why she has to feel those gentlemen callers she has all over, because she can't see them very well?*"

Moon felt himself going a bit red at the ears. "Yes, that's right Anna, and you're so very small she can't see you at all." He wasn't going anywhere near trying to explain the birds and the bees to a Victorian four-year-old.

"*Well, that's funny,*" snapped Anna, fixing him with a very adult look, her chubby hands rising to her hips. "*Because I thought they were making love, actually. They were certainly making enough noise about it.*"

Moon was shocked He had assumed that Anna was as blind to the present as most of the ghosts he had encountered, which was apparently not the case. This put a whole new complexion on Anna's situation and he sought desperately for the right response. "I'm sorry, Anna, I forgot that you've been around for a long time even though you're still a little girl."

"*And I've seen some things in these flats that a little girl really ought not to see, Jerry; even things that a big girl ought not to see, sometimes. You're my friend, Jerry Moon, and it's easy for me to be the fragile Victorian child for you, because that is what I am. It's what the Fates or whoever it is decides these things dictate I should be, for now at least. But please understand that is **not** all that I am. I'm one hundred and two next birthday and most of that time I've had nothing to do but watch the people who live here. Ever since my idiot father!*" She raised her voice to reach the upper landing, eliciting a small whimper from the object of her wrath. "*Ever since my father threw me down these stairs, in fact. So, I know all about people. About their sordid little acts of selfishness and their unsung acts of greatness, and the long, boring, normal bits which fit in* *between."* The smile she gave him seemed entirely out of place on her chubby, child's face. It was complex, ancient and wise: full of knowledge of all the massive contradictions that made up the human race. To Moon's surprise, it also contained a great deal of love. *"You don't need to protect **me** from anything, Jerry. The things I probably needed protecting from got to me years before you were born."*

"Sorry," replied Moon with chagrin.

"That's all right. How were you to know that some people are stuck on earth as ghosts for the benefit of others? The day that drunken fool upstairs finally catches on and faces his guilt, I should be able to move on as well."

"That still doesn't justify upsetting Mrs Foley," said Moon sternly.

"Oh well, perhaps you're right, maybe I should give the poor woman a rest. It's just that I get so bored haunting this floor with no-one to talk to." The little ghost looked up tearfully at Moon then gave a heavy sigh. *"You can't believe how hard it's been not being able to talk to someone about this for nearly a century, Jerry. I'm glad you came to live here."*

"It's good for me too, Anna. I haven't found anyone to help me since I began to discover my 'gift'. Perhaps it would be a good idea for us to talk about it sometime, but not now because I need to go to bed."

At that moment Mrs Foley opened her door and looked at Moon with bleary eyes. "Oh, hello Moon, it's you. Who were you talking to, I thought I heard voices?"

"Nobody, Julie," replied Moon, trying not to laugh at Anna, who was pulling faces behind Mrs Foley's back. "I was just talking to myself. You know; going through last night's shift in my head."

"Well, next time could you not do it on my landing, some of us don't have to get up until half past eight."

"Sorry, Julie, I sometimes forget how early it is when I come home after a shift."

"Well, you could do with keeping it down a bit generally. I know you're a night worker but the rest of us aren't. What on earth were you doing a couple of nights ago? There was an awful bang from your room at about three o'clock. I nearly jumped out of my skin."

"A pile of books fell off one of my shelves," Moon lied, remembering Uri's cack-handed abuse of his window. "I'll be more careful in future."

Mrs Foley paused to take in the sight of Moon with his nurse's uniform showing under his jacket. It clearly pleased her because she smoothed her hair and managed to inject a whisper of seductiveness into her next statement. "You'd just better be," she said with a suggestive smile as he headed up the stairs. Moon mentally shook his head, the woman was hopelessly incorrigible.

"I'll see you later, Jerry," vibed Anna.

"I will," Moon replied to both of them as he stumbled wearily off to his bed.

Chapter 13

After waking at about three o'clock the next afternoon, Moon lounged around the bedsit until it was time to phone Sonia in the evening. After they had discussed each other's work days and shared some general lovers' chat Moon asked Sonia how her visit to the pub had gone the night before. "I hope you behaved yourself while I was slaving away over a hot patient," chided Moon light-heartedly.

"Impeccably," she replied. "Anyway, I thought you weren't allowed to let the patients get hot. Isn't it bad for them or something?"

"Yeah, but it keeps the NHS heating bills low."

Sonia laughed. "I always wondered why hospitals are usually so warm. Anyway, it was a typical quiet Tuesday night at the pub. But it wasn't so quiet, because that idiot Moz was working behind the bar and he always insists on playing Death Metal over the pub system. I don't know why Kate puts up with him. You know, he must lose her more customers than he brings in with that mangy crowd of his. Anyway, I did manage to find out a bit about our suspects because Moz knows them both quite well. He told me that Animal went back up to Scotland in the middle of last December. It really pissed off the rest of the guys from *Jumping Corpse* because they had several gigs booked over Christmas and they had to hire a replacement drummer. Apparently Animal had a great job offer but had to move quickly. He used to work freelance in IT down here but a big programming firm based in Glasgow head-hunted him.

"As for Andy, Avril was right about him and Animal being a couple but they split up shortly before Animal left. The split seems to have hit Andy pretty hard at the time but now he's moved on to 'higher things'. Apparently, the reason why he fell out of sight is that he's become a born-again Christian."

"A Christian? Aren't they a bit against the whole gay thing?"

"Yeah, it does seem a bit odd, doesn't it? But Moz says he's joined up with a 'good ole' holy rolling fundamentalist church out in Nailsea."

"That seems to rule out our two main suspects, doesn't it? If Animal's writing software in Glasgow and Andy's joined the fundies."

There was a pause and Moon could almost feel Sonia thinking at the other end of the phone. "I guess so. But, Jerry, Andy's still in town. Just because he's got religion doesn't mean he isn't involved."

"Of course, I see what you mean! Nailsea isn't that far outside of Bristol and it's certainly close enough to come in to the centre by car. Do you know if Andy had any issues with Uri? Any reason why he might want to frame him for murder?"

"Not that I know of. He'd have known about the 'vampire' rumours of course, but that's all. But, murder though, Jerry? Andy was one of us and Dominic was, if not a close friend, at least one of his pool buddies. Do you really think he would be capable of killing him?" He heard her worried sigh brush across the receiver.

"Who knows, love? I'm no shrink, so I couldn't say. Anyway, you let the police have the new information from yesterday, so they'll probably have come to the same conclusion and hopefully they'll take the investigation from there. I don't think there's much more we can do about it."

"Yeah, they thanked me for the information but it would be much easier if we could just tell them what the ghosts told you."

Moon sighed. "It's frustrating for me too but what can I do. I know sometimes psychics help the police but I doubt it's that common. You'd need to find a sympathetic copper to begin with…"

"What about Whatley? You said yourself that he seems to think there's something supernatural about this case. Perhaps he'd be open-minded enough to consider what you have to say."

"He's more likely to arrest me for wasting police time. I don't know, Sonia, perhaps I can pass on the information some other way. I'll try to work something out."

"All right, I'll phone you when I get home tomorrow, okay?"

"Okay."

"I love you, Jerry." The statement had a ring of decisiveness about it.

Moon was happily surprised. "You sound like you mean it this time."

"Well, I've decided that perhaps it's time to let go of the past. You're the best, Jerry. Even if you do have a tendency to see and hear things that aren't there."

"Huh, look who's talking. You and your weird feelings; if we're lucky they'll let us share a padded cell between us." Their laughter turned into more tender words as they reluctantly drew their conversation to an end.

Moon's Wednesday shift was providing nursing cover for the overflow beds in the Day Surgery Unit. When there was a high demand for beds on the wards the night managers would allocate reasonably well patients, mostly those who were to be discharged the next day, to the five recovery beds used for Day Surgery patients during the daytime. This was a far from ideal arrangement. However, at times when there had been a real bed crisis in the past, Moon had seen all the beds and the theatre trolleys in Day Surgery occupied by inpatients. But tonight he and Claire, one of his colleagues from the night pool, only had five patients to look after and it was a very quiet night. There weren't even any spirits haunting the Unit to break up the monotony because it was situated in a relatively new part of the hospital. There had been very few deaths there to his knowledge and, apparently, none of those who had died there had any reason to stay.

Once all the patients were tucked up in bed there was little more to do but to keep an eye on them. So, having updated the patients' notes, he and Claire sat at the nurse station reading or chatting quietly into the middle of the night. At about two in the morning Claire went into a side room off the Unit to take her mid-shift break and Moon was left on his own to look after the patients. He always felt it was like the early hours of the morning existed in a slightly different reality. Even if you were used to being awake at that time, there was a slightly brittle edge to the senses, as if everything was somehow sharpened. It was the time that his supernatural senses were at their most acute, so he wasn't greatly surprised to suddenly find a spirit standing in front of him. On first glance she looked like a girl in her early teens wearing a sodden, tattered, mildew-stained shift, which may once have been white but was now a variety of shades of mottled green. Her face might have been pretty if she'd looked alive but her appearance was that of a drowned corpse. Her waterlogged skin had a sickly blue-grey tinge and her eyes were pearly white and glowed slightly like the eyes of the drowned underwater dead. Her hair was lank and colourless, except where it seemed to be composed of dark green pondweed and her teeth when she smiled, and she was grinning at Moon now, were a set of uneven motley green fangs. This wasn't a ghost, it was something else entirely; something dark enough and nasty enough to make Moon suddenly very concerned for the safety of his patients. *"What are you doing here? Are you out to cause trouble?"* he vibed defensively.

The creature produced a strange echoing, bubbling sound, as if it were laughing underwater. *"Worry not, Jeremy Moon. I come not for any of thy charges. I wouldst speak with thee, 'tis all."* Her voice was similar to her laugh, it sounded as if it was deadened by water.

"Who or what are you? And why do you want to talk to me?"

"Thou mayest call me Jenny Greenteeth, for that is both who and what I am." The spirit leered at him again.

Since he had discovered his Gift Moon had been forced to put up with some hideous sights in his life, but this thing was even beginning to put the wind up him. The name it gave him rang a bell but he couldn't place it. So he asked, *"And what does a Jenny Greenteeth do?"* He wished it would stop grinning like that; he could foresee nightmares in his imminent future.

"My sisters and I haunt the still waters. It is our task to make sure the drowning stay drowned. Those who fall into my embrace seldom leave it alive."

Ah! Moon remembered now. One of his old girlfriends had owned a book about the folklore of good and bad fairies and the Jenny Greenteeth had been in the 'bad' section. To Moon that the author had decided to call such monsters 'fairies' had always seemed a bit strange. *"If you're not here for my patients, Jenny, then why **are** you here?"* asked Moon. *And how do I get you to leave?* he thought to himself.

Then Jenny reached out a long-fingered hand with talons like hooks and snared one of his tiny ghostly companions. Cradling it in the cage of her fingers, she held it up before Moon. *"It is about these that I have come,"* she replied. She didn't look any better highlighted in the blue light of the minute ghost globe. *"A drunken fool fell in the canal and I rode back here with his corpse so that we could give you a warning."*

"We?"

"Aye, we; the Dark Ones. The villain who did this." She thrust the spirit globe forwards. *"Has started to prey on us. If thou doest not find the cure for this, it will go hard with thee from us."*

"Is that a threat?" Moon wondered what it was about him that made every supernatural beastie in Bristol think he could help sort out their problems for them. He was worried that he was going to end up on the hit list of every goblin from here to Bath.

"Thou mayest take it as such." Her grinning face hardened into a mask of malice. *"I wouldst afford it such import if I were thee."*

"But why do you think I can help?" Unintentionally, Moon said this aloud, eliciting groans and other disturbed noises from the nearby patients. He shook his head. *"Why do all the spirits in Bristol seem to think I can help with this?"* he asked again, mentally.

"Because thou hast the Gift, thou hast also the power," she replied.

Moon was confused. *"Power? I know that I have the gift to see creatures like you but I have no special power."*

"Then thou must learn to use the power that thou doest not think thou hast." She laughed, then her bloated face became serious. *"But learn quickly, Jeremy Moon, for the Dark ones have little patience."* There was the sound of a door opening as Claire returned to the Unit. *"I must go, Jeremy Moon, the still waters call to me, but thinkest thou on what I have told you...*

and act thee quickly for thine own sake." She disappeared in a greenish mist, leaving behind a small pool of greyish water.

"What? I thought I saw…" said Claire, staring at the place where the Jenny Greenteeth had vanished.

"Saw what?" asked Moon, hating himself for having to play innocent.

"Oh, I don't know, never mind. Anyway, what's that?" She pointed to the pool on the floor.

"I'm not sure, I think we might have a leak somewhere. It just appeared." Moon got up from his seat. "I'll find something to mop it up with."

Having cleared away the pool of water, which Moon was fairly sure analysis would prove to be identical to that in the canal, he went into the side room with a cup of tea for his break. Most nurses tried to sleep on their night breaks but Moon found that grabbing the odd forty-five minutes or so only made him more tired, so he would usually just put his feet up and read. Tonight, however, he had a phone call to make.

The side room they used for their breaks was a doctor's examination room. Moon sat himself at the desk, fished out his mobile phone from his back pocket and looked up Uri's number. Moon used the desk phone to call out, rather than risk causing interference with nearby vital signs monitors, because they were close to both the Cardiology and Emergency departments. A female voice answered the phone. "Hello, the Maddock residence." She sounded irritated but not tired and the slight Welsh lilt to her voice made Moon suspect it was Roanne.

"Hi, it's Moon, could I speak to Uri please."

There was a pause then Uri came on the line. "Moon, it's nearly three-thirty in the morning, my ladies and I may not be sleeping but the household is. I hope you have a good reason for calling me at this time."

"Sorry, Uri, this is the only number I have for you. I've had a bit of a scare and I need your help." Moon described his recent visitation and the ultimatum he had been given.

"So you would like me to help you develop your powers of spiritual self defence, is that it?"

"If I have any, that is."

"I'm sure you do, Moon. Anyone who has the ability to interact with the spiritual side of reality the way you do should have a powerful enough aura to inflict damage on that plane. What nights are you not working? We should arrange a time and place for your first lesson as soon as possible."

"Well, I'm off duty from Friday to Monday but I don't think Sonia will take too kindly to us not being together over the weekend." He had been looking forward to spending some very active nights with Sonia that weekend.

"Far be it from me to stand in the way of true love, Moon, but this could save your life. It should not only help you to protect yourself from this ghost taker but also these *domovoi*: these goblins that are threatening you."

"Okay, let's say Monday night for definite and I'll ask Sonia if she's happy for me to meet with you over the weekend. Erm, There's just one thing, you realise that she's likely to want to come along."

There was a slight pause as Uri considered this. "Well, I suppose there's no harm in her coming with you. You've already let her into our little secret. I have sensed, also, that perhaps she has some psychic 'talent' as well."

"It wouldn't surprise me. She definitely has some borderline psychic ability. You know, sensing atmospheres and that sort of thing."

"Hmm, in which case she might be able to provide you with some – what is the term? – back-up. Why don't you ring me once you have had a chance to discuss this with Sonia, then you can both come up to our place and I will give you a crash course in psychic self-defence? How does that sound?"

"Great," replied Moon guardedly, unsure that he fancied taking Sonia into the vampires' lair. Did he trust Uri that much? Strangely, now he thought about it, it seemed he did.

Uri gave him the address of the house that he and the girls shared with the Maddocks, along with directions and a mobile phone number. "If we are to meet late at night please call me on the phone and don't ring the bell. I would rather not disturb the family and I do not want them drawn into this business at all if we can help it. Part of our commitment to them is to keep them safe and that includes not letting them fall into danger. Even if they would willingly do so out of loyalty to my ladies and myself."

"You really think it's that dangerous? This thing hasn't harmed any humans so far as I know."

"I'm not sure, Moon. If it is dangerous enough to frighten the Dark Ones, well, we can't be too cautious when dealing with an entity that powerful."

"Okay, Uri, I'll call you once I've had a chance to talk to Sonia."

When he got back off break it was about four-thirty. Claire, sitting huddled at the nurse station, was looking ill at ease. "What's up?" asked Moon quietly, so as not to disturb the patients.

"Oh, thank God you're back, Moon. You know, I'm sure I saw a ghost when I came back onto the ward earlier. I've been scared witless the last hour worrying that it might come back." Her eyes were wide and liquid with fear as she turned them up to him.

"What did it look like?" asked Moon.

"Well, I didn't get a clear look because it vanished, but it looked a bit like a woman... only horrible. Are you sure you didn't see her? She was looking right at you."

"No, I didn't see anything." Moon hated lying but he couldn't think what else to say. "Are you sure you weren't still partly asleep? Your mind can play tricks on you when you're very tired."

"Well, I suppose this is my eighth shift in a row. Perhaps you're right Moon; it wouldn't be the first time I've come back off break a bit disorientated." Claire worked eight nights on and eight nights off, which she claimed suited her. Moon could see the attraction of the long breaks but thought the physical impact of regularly working eight consecutive nights must be pretty unhealthy.

Moon smiled. "That's why I don't sleep on my breaks; I feel worse if I do." Their conversation quickly devolved into to one of those hospital ghost story sharing sessions that hospital staff occasionally indulge in during their night shifts. Claire had enough personal anecdotes to convince Moon that she was possibly quite psychic herself. However, any gift she had seemed to be suppressed by her fear of the subject.

It began to get light around five o'clock and shortly afterwards the patients were stirring so Moon and Claire were quickly caught up in taking vital sign observations and the other minor preparations that led up to the arrival of the day staff. With so few patients the handover was short and Moon was on his way home by twenty past seven. As he walked back through Cotham, he replayed his encounter with the Jenny Greenteeth in his head. It seemed unbelievable that creatures out of folk-lore actually existed. But then, if someone had asked him if he believed in vampires a few days ago he would probably have laughed at them. The spirit world was turning into a much more 'interesting' place than he was certain he could handle.

Chapter 14

Needing to buy some essentials, Moon decided to go out that afternoon and wandered up to one of the rather tatty looking supermarkets on Gloucester Road. Later, he stopped for lunch at one of the cafés that ran alongside a boulevard-like stretch of the road where the pavement widened. The locals called this part of Gloucester Road 'The Prom' for no particularly obvious reason that Moon could see. It had probably been a more picturesque place to walk in the past, but now it was like just any other part of the busy city street.

Having bought his meal, he sat at a pavement-side table and tucked into his burger and chips. He was watching the pedestrians walking up and down the pavement, some browsing the shop windows, while others hurried on to whatever urgent destination called them, when he saw something that filled him with alarm. For some reason Bristol seemed to have more than its fair share of eccentrics, several of whom frequented the Gloucester Road. Among the more extreme of these unfortunates was a petite, ageing Afro-Caribbean lady who swathed herself in white and wore a veritable Fort Knox's worth of gold chains around her neck and arms. From each of these chains dangled at least one gold crucifix. It was her habit to stop people in the street and subject them to a fire and brimstone sermon for as long as they would put up with her. Moon realised with panic that this fiery harridan was currently making a beeline for his table.

"What you gonna do when the Master comes a' callin'?" She asked, pointing dramatically at Moon.

"Ask him for some form of identification then lodge a complaint about the shoddy way he's been running things for the last fifty million years," replied Moon, looking desperately for an escape route.

This would be prophetess wasn't going to be fobbed off with sarcasm, however. "You may mock! You may mock..."

"Thank you," replied Moon. "I will."

She didn't even pause in her flow, "But retribution is comin'. Comin', I tell you!"

"Yeah, well it's about time because the service has been terrible, we're long overdue for a change of management and a refund if you ask me... Look is there any point to this? Because my lunch is getting cold and I'd rather like to finish it before the 'Master' gets here."

"But He is here! He is here!" Her eyes opened wide enough for Moon to see the whites all around.

"What on earth do you mean? We've supposedly been waiting two thousand years; surely something as important as that would be on the news?"

"Ah, but now He comes 'like a T'ief in the Night'. He comes after dark with fiery eyes to terrify the unbeliever and to instruct the faithful in how to punish the infidel. Already He gathers his army of strong and righteous warriors and when it is complete then Armageddon will fall."

Something about 'like a thief in the night' and 'fiery eyes' had a familiar ring to Moon. He frowned and looked up at her quizzically. "You've seen this?"

She nodded fiercely. "Yes. Yes! The Master, He comes to me, wreathed in shadows with eyes of fire. He say the time is soon when the unbelievers will fall before the Judgement for he has placed His winnowing sword in the hands of the faithful."

There it was again; an allusion to a figure cloaked in shadows with burning eyes. The woman was obviously barking mad and it could just be coincidence but the description bore a strong similarity to the vision the ghost-globes had shown him of the 'Ghost Eater'. "Are you saying that he encourages his followers to cause violence? I thought he was supposed to be all sweetness and light."

"That was then, this is now!" she replied sharply. "The Lord said He would come with a sword to set fathers against children and husbands against wives. His sword is in my hand, unbeliever!"

The woman threw back a long fold of white cloth over her right shoulder and Moon realised abruptly that she was holding a rusty, twelve-inch kitchen knife in her hand. Suddenly, everything seemed to become unreal, slowing down to a fraction of normal speed as his adrenalin kicked in. Without thinking he leapt to his feet, knocking over his chair and spilling the remains of his meal to the floor as he did so. He grabbed the woman by the wrist of the hand holding the knife. The other café clientele and passers by watched in astonishment as he wrestled her to the floor and knocked her hand against the cobbled paving until she released her grip on the weapon. The woman screamed with frustrated rage as he pinned her against the ground and yelled, "Someone call the police!" Then after what seemed like an aeon of waiting in the stunned silence he added an urgent "Please!"

The police arrived on the scene a few minutes later. Moon and the woman were both sitting in the café manager's office when they arrived. The latter, guarded by two not-so-burly kitchen porters, had calmed down somewhat but was still muttering under her breath about the 'Master' and staring at Moon with unveiled hostility. Moon was just hoping that this wasn't going to drag on too long as there were a few things he needed to do before he went to work for the night. Luckily for Moon enough people had seen what had happened to back up his account of an unprovoked attack. The woman, whose name was Benjamina Jones, continued to rave on about the 'Master' and his winnowing sword, which added further credence to Moon's account of the event. "Do you intend to press charges, Mr Moon?" the older of the two police officers asked.

"Of course I do," replied Moon. "This poor woman needs psychiatric help. We can't let her back out on the streets in this state; the next victim might not be as lucky as I was."

"Then I'll have to ask you to accompany us back to the station so we can complete the appropriate documents."

So, for the second time in a week, Moon found himself taken by police car to Bridewell Police Station. As he was sitting in one of the interview rooms making his statement to the same police officer, Detective Inspector Whatley entered quietly and waited, sitting on a chair beside the door, until Moon and the constable had finished. "Afternoon, Mr Moon, we seem to be seeing quite a bit of each other recently. I wonder why."

"Pure coincidence I hope, Inspector. I've no intention of making a habit of frequenting police stations. Did you just pop in to say hello or can I help you with something?"

Whatley attempted to straighten his tie. It was the same one he had been wearing the last two times Moon had met him. However, the tortured knot refused to budge. He was wearing a dark blue suit today but it was just as creased as the grey crumpled rag he had worn on the last two occasions. Moon wondered if the inspector actually slept in his suits because it was the only reasonable explanation for their state of extreme wrinkledness. "Well, I was hoping you might be able to shed some light on what's going on at the moment. The attack on you this afternoon wasn't an isolated incident you see; it seems like every single nutcase in Bristol has suddenly gone more doolally than usual and we've got a string of minor and not so minor assaults to show for it. It's just pure luck that no-one's been killed so far." He paused to stretch some kinks out of his shoulders, "Bloody deskwork – I swear I spend more time these days filling out forms than solving crimes. Anyway, did your assailant say anything unusual, perhaps to justify attacking you?"

"Inspector. Nothing that Benjamina Jones said to me, could be considered 'usual'. But she did say that the 'Master' had come to her and told her to do it."

"The 'Master', eh? Did she give any description of this person?"

"Well, what she described sounded like something from a horror film: shadowy black cloak, red glowing eyes, that kind of thing."

Whatley regarded him sharply. "Really? That's very interesting, Mr Moon, very interesting indeed. You see all the suspects so far have claimed that they were either coerced or bullied into acts of violence by an individual of a similar description to the one you've just given me. I have to confess I'm a bit flummoxed by this one. At the moment the only theory that comes close to fitting the facts is that some madman is using make-up and special effects, possibly combined with a hallucinogenic drug, to incite the less sane element of our community to commit random acts of violence. Which, even as a theory, is far from satisfying. How did this individual gain access to his accomplices' homes, for instance?"

Moon wondered how to respond to this and must have been lost in thought long enough for Whatley to be concerned. "Mr Moon?"

"Oh, sorry Inspector, I was thinking that I might be able to give you a better answer but you'd probably think I was barmy."

A connection seemed to click behind Whatley's eyes. "Is this something to do with your friend Mr Kievitch's suggestion that you may have what he referred to as 'special talents'?"

"Why? What has Uri been saying about me?" What *had* Uri told Whatley about him? Had he made a mistake in trusting the vampire?

"I interviewed Mr Kievitch at his home on Tuesday and it turns out he is, as you suggested, a rather eccentric but harmless musical entertainer. However, before I left he made a point of saying that you might be able to help me further with the case. It was his opinion that you are a very gifted psychic medium."

Great! Thanks a bundle Uri! Thought Moon. The vampire's anachronistic lack of understanding of what one could safely mention to the authorities in this age of scientific discovery, had probably just landed him in a pile of trouble. "Did he, Inspector? I wonder what might have given him that idea."

Whatley must have seen the panic flash behind Moon's eyes. "Don't worry, Mr Moon, I'm not about to write you off as a loony. The 'Sight' is in my family, you might say. My maternal grandmother was like you: talked to the spirits and that sort of thing. Even though my Dad used to call her 'that crazy old bat', we kids knew that Granny Huddlestone was as sharp as a knife… enough inexplicable things used to happen when she was around for us to be sure she wasn't fantasising about her powers. For instance, she used to know what we were doing even when we were out of her sight. Every now and then she'd tell one of us off for something we'd done when she hadn't been around to see it and we'd say: 'How did you know, Nan?' and she'd reply: 'Granddad Jack told me'. Granddad Jack was *her* father, Jack Huddlestone, who died ten years before even Tom, my older brother, was born. She told us that Granddad Jack had stayed around to watch over his children and grandchildren and make sure we kept out of trouble. Some people might say I have a touch of it myself; I certainly have a good gut when it comes to solving crimes. But that's the problem with this case we're working on at present, something about it doesn't sit right with my gut."

Moon eyed the organ in question. *It certainly looks well developed*, he thought. "Well, Inspector, if you're willing to entertain the possibility that I am actually in touch with the 'Other Side', I'll tell you what I know." Moon explained what he had discovered about Dominic's murder and his suspicions regarding today's attack on himself, without going too deeply into how he had gained the information.

When Moon had finished, Whatley regarded him levelly. "So you think that Andrew Gibbons is the most likely suspect, as an accomplice at least?"

"I suppose so but what about 'Animal'?"

"You mean Francis Walters, the lad who's supposed to be in Glasgow? We have nothing so far to indicate that he went there. His parents knew nothing about the move and haven't heard from him since before Christmas. We're just waiting for the results of the Glasgow Met's enquiries with the various software companies in their area before we decide that he's officially missing." Whatley thought for a moment then seemed to come to a decision, with a small nod he said, "I'll let you in on a little secret, Mr Moon, seeing as you've been so helpful. Since we last met there has been another murder victim found in the same vicinity, a young woman called Lorraine Newton. I think your girlfriend mentioned her to us when she called us."

"Yes, Sonia did mention a girl called Lorraine to me when we were discussing the missing Goths from the *Hangman's Rest*. It was me who suggested she should pass the information on to the police."

"God, the *Hangman's Rest*," Whatley grimaced. "Where did they come up with such a bloody awful name for a pub? It even sounds like trouble waiting to happen."

"It's traditional, apparently the old Bristol gallows used to be near there."

"I can bloody well believe it. I guess that's always been a bit of a problem area." Moon knew the part of town around the

Rest had actually been quite prosperous at times in the past but he felt now was not the best time to mention it. "Anyway, Miss Newton's body was wrapped in bin-liners and left in a dark corner in one of the back alleys, a short walk up the road from the pub. It must have lain there for several months but no one noticed it, probably because there's so much rubbish piled up back there. You know what Stoke's Croft is like, with all those dodgy take-aways, some of the garbage piled around her smelt worse than the body. One of our scene-of-crime officers found her while they were searching the area for clues."

"So, was there anything to connect her to the other murder?" asked Moon.

"Well, as you can guess, the body wasn't in the best of conditions after so long out in the open, but the autopsy suggests a similar *modus operandi*, right down to the bite on the neck. We're very keen to get this one solved as quickly as possible, Mr Moon, before it turns into a serial killing spree. In my case even to the point of accepting some supernatural help if it's offered; so why don't you keep your radar on alert and give me regular updates on what your friends on the other side have to say? I can treat you as an anonymous informant, if you like. So there's no need to mention psychic powers or draw attention to you in any way... what do you think?"

"Well, I want to see an end to these killings as much as you do, Inspector, so as long as I can rely on you to keep things confidential... I don't see why we can't come to some arrangement."

"Wonderful, it'll be easier from my point of view as well if we can keep the whole supernatural angle hidden. Looks dreadful in the paperwork and tends to interfere with one's promotion prospects." Whatley winked one bright blue eye at Moon.

"If you don't mind I'll be going now, Inspector Whatley," said Moon looking at his watch. "It's four thirty already and I need to catch up on a few things before I head off to work at eight o'clock."

"Fine, Mr Moon, but keep in touch and I'll let you know any fresh developments from our end." Whatley opened the interview room door for him. "Goodbye for now."

Walking back home, Moon wondered about this new development. He was amazed that a policeman like Whatley seemed to be willing to accept the idea of contacting the dead, when he, himself, had so much trouble accepting his own gift to begin with. It would certainly make helping to solve Dominic's murder less difficult. However, he thought he might find it hard to protect the secret of Uri's true nature from the detective. It was likely that the vampire had used his glamour to cloud Whatley's mind, the way he had done with Moon the first time he had seen him. He certainly seemed convinced that Uri and the girls were human, which was fine as far as it went, but Moon suspected that a mind like a vice lurked behind Whatley's scruffy exterior. You didn't get to be a detective inspector without having a certain capacity for winkling out the truth. Moon was certain that if Whatley developed an inkling that he had been deceived in some way, he would probably decide to subject Uri to much closer scrutiny.

The news that the shadowy figure that Moon had christened to himself the 'Ghost Eater' had progressed from attacking spirits to inciting attacks on living people was also worrying. Moon wondered what it could possibly hope to gain from this. From what Benjamina Jones was raving about before she attacked him it seemed that the evil creature somehow intended to appropriate material power. The Ghost Eater seemed to be just another kind of ghost, so how could it have power over the living... and what could it possibly gain from it? He thought his discussion with Uri about the power of belief may have given him the beginnings of an answer but it was patently absurd. The thing couldn't have been gathering followers, could it? Or perhaps it believed it could draw others to it once it began to organise the core of unstable individuals it already had under its influence.

Moon got back to his flat at about ten past five. Feeling the effects of his interrupted lunch, he fixed himself a Spanish omelette, which he ate in front of the television before having a quick shower. He was sitting on his bed in his bathrobe drying his hair when the phone rang. Throwing the damp towel on the floor, he quickly grabbed the receiver. "Moon," he said brusquely, knowing this would sound unusual if the caller didn't know him. He had decided long ago that most unknown callers were probably trying to sell him something so if he could catch them wrong-footed at the start it was all for the best.

"Hi, Jerry," said Sonia's voice from the receiver. "You know you could really do with brushing up your telephone manner."

"Thus spake the telesales rep," replied Moon, grinning.

"Well, everyone's got to make a living, we can't all be trained professionals like you."

"'Semi-professional', please," replied Moon, shaking his head even though Sonia couldn't see him. "That's the special term the Government invented specially for nurses, so they don't have to pay us professional rates."

"My heart bleeds for you. So what kind of afternoon have you had, mister gets-up-at-two-o'clock?"

"Well, apart from the attempted stabbing, most of it was okay."

"Someone tried to *stab* you?" Sonia's voice raised two octaves with outraged disbelief.

"Yes, because 'the Master' told her to." Moon described his afternoon's encounters to Sonia, including his meeting with Whatley.

"So now you're what, some kind of supernatural snitch?"

"I suppose so."

"Does that mean you'll have to start wearing a scruffy Mac and a tweed cap, smoke dog-ends and talk in a miserable cockney accent?"

"Not all police informants are socially inadequate. Anyway, I see myself more as a civilian specialist who helps the police with unsolvable cases out of the goodness of my heart."

"How philanthropic of you," Sonia chuckled. "It's good news though, isn't it? Now you can let the police in on everything you know and they'll be able to catch the killer so we can stop having to worry about the safety of the local ghoulies and ghosties and have more time for making mad, passionate love."

"I don't know. I'm a bit worried about possibly outing Uri as a vampire. Also, there's something about this other thing, the creature that's attacking the ghosts, that makes me think that it might be connected to the murders in some way. Uri seems to be the focus of all this somehow. He's managed to convince Whatley that he's not a vampire but if Whatley turns over enough stones..." Moon left the consequence hanging and decided to change the subject. "Anyway, speaking of mad passionate love how's the old...?"

"Oh, much better thanks. I hope you've nothing planned for tomorrow night because I intend to ravish you repeatedly."

"I'll have to see if I've got a window. Oh damn! I meant to ask you. Uri's agreed to teach me the noble art of psychic self-defence. We'll be getting together on Monday night but he suggested it would be better to start some time over the weekend. Do you mind if I spend part of Saturday night learning how to zap nasties?"

"Not if I can come along. I've been dying to have a nose around Uri's place."

"Okay, I *thought* you might want to tag along and Uri's cool with it. It's likely to run late though, Uri and I are both night owls, or should that be 'bats'?"

Sonia laughed. "Don't worry; if it gets too late I'll just curl up in a corner and go to sleep." Moon could hear a faint popping on the other end of the phone for a few seconds and knew it was Sonia tapping the receiver with a fingernail. It was a little habit she had when she was thinking hard about something. "But what do you think this ghost eater of yours is up to? Bullying the local oddballs into assaulting people seems an odd pastime even for a spook."

"I don't know," Moon confessed, sitting forward on the bed. "I wondered if it might be trying to establish some sort of powerbase in the 'real' world. I'm not sure how it could do that. Bristol may have its fair share of weird characters but I can't see how making them attack people can further its cause. Can you?"

"Not unless it gets something out of the attacks themselves... who knows, perhaps it's doing all these horrible things out of pure sadism." Moon could sense Sonia's concern at the other end of the phone. "You just be careful, Jerry, this thing sounds dangerous."

"I'll do my best to take care of myself. Hopefully, these sessions with Uri will help me learn how." Moon realised that he was more anxious about this than he had thought. "I've never worried about contacting spirits before now, you know. I've always thought of them as just people without their bodies and it's never once crossed my mind that they might be able to hurt anyone. Though I've met some pretty nasty things in the last couple of days that have made me reconsider. Let's hope that Uri really can help."

"Yes, let's." Moon could hear the worry in Sonia's voice.

"I'm sure he will, he's very impressive in action, I can vouch for that." Their conversation then drifted away from Uri and the murders and before they finally said their goodnights they arranged to meet up at the *Hangman's Rest* around seven-thirty the next evening.

Moon was back on the Cardiology ward that night, covering for one of the night staff, who was on holiday. None of the patients tonight were particularly unwell, although the condition of the lady who had been experiencing problems two nights before was still considered a bit 'brittle' so she was on continuous oxygen therapy.

When they had finished the late drug round and settled the patients into bed, Moon and the rest of the nursing staff sat at the nurses' station with cups of tea or coffee while he and Svetlana, one of the permanent Cardiology nurses updated the patients' notes. Later they chatted quietly for a while as they worked on some less demanding paperwork to prepare for the next shift.

About two in the morning Svetlana had gone off the ward to take her mid-shift break. Jenny one of the healthcare assistants had popped outside for one of her frequent cigarette breaks and the other healthcare assistant, Juni, was recording the two o'clock vital signs observations for those who needed them. Moon was sitting alone at the nurses' station, making a few notes for his article on his palmtop organiser, when his attention was abruptly drawn to his retinue of ghost globes. He had grown quite used to the tiny blue lights following him and had begun to ignore them but something was definitely bothering them. They had been drifting gently around the ward, flitting inquisitively in and out of corners and, he supposed, getting the feel of the place. But now they were huddling together under the resuscitation trolley as if they were frightened of something. Reaching out with his ghost sense, Moon tried to pinpoint what was upsetting them and, after a second's worth of feeling around, he was drawn to the side cubicle belonging to Mrs Brent, their 'poorly' patient.

Moon crept quietly up to the entrance of the cubicle and peered through the open door. There was a spirit inside but quite an ordinary one and nothing that should have frightened the ghost globes, even if it didn't bode well for Mrs Brent. It was a ghost that the regular staff had given the unoriginal nickname 'the Grey Lady' and who seemed to think it was her job to visit dying female patients, perhaps in hope of offering comfort as they passed over. Moon had attempted to communicate with her on their first encounter but had only been greeted with a haughty silence; whoever she was she certainly didn't think much of men. As he watched her hover by the bed, her face composed into a sad expression reminiscent of one of those stone angels that occasionally guarded Victorian tombs; he noticed that the collection of shadows in the corner behind her was slowly becoming darker and growing larger. It swirled oddly, like disturbed mist and then two fiery eyes with slitted pupils like a cat's blinked open in the middle of that roiling cloud of darkness. *"It's no good hiding behind the door, seer, I know that you are there,"* hissed the Ghost Eater in Moon's mind.

Moon tried to think of a proper response. 'So we meet at last!' seemed a bit corny so he settled for: *"If you harm my patient you'll pay for it."*

"Later," replied the Eater looking down at Mrs Brent mockingly. *"At present neither of us has the power to harm the other. Moon, is it? You disappoint me with your hollow threats."* It pounced and wrapped shadowy arms around the Grey Lady, who started keening piteously. *"But for now, I feel like a snack!"*

"Don't!" vibed Moon, almost yelling out loud as the monster consumed the wailing ghost in seconds, leaving nothing but a tiny glowing blue speck.

It reached up and caught the new ghost globe between its pitch black thumb and forefinger. *"Give my regards to that weakling Uri. Tell him that Prince Rurik has chosen to take this city for his own. He will understand."* The red eyes flared nearly yellow with profound hatred. *"Before I destroy him... he will understand!"* Rurik, the Ghost Eater, flicked what remained of his victim up through the ceiling then vanished in a dwindling whirlwind of blackness. Before Moon could consider what to do next the heart monitor alarm suddenly started blaring. Mrs Brent had gone into ventricular fibrillation, which usually precedes a full cardiac arrest, so without pausing to think about what he had just heard, Moon hit the 'call for assist' button then began administering CPR. Juni poked her head through the open doorjamb. "Call the Crash Team then bring the resus trolley!" yelled Moon urgently in mid thoracic compression.

The Crash Team reached the ward very quickly due to its proximity to Coronary Care and they managed to save Mrs Brent, who was later transferred to the Coronary Care Unit for more intensive monitoring. The rest of Moon's shift was taken up with the transfer and with receiving a new patient from CCU to fill the vacated bed space. By the morning handover he was exhausted, having spent his break period filling out the relevant paperwork, but he managed to give a reasonably coherent report to the day staff before heading home in a daze.

As the morning air revived him a little he wondered whether Mrs Brent's cardiac arrest had been a coincidence or if this... 'Rurik' had caused it. It would be a terrifying new development if the Ghost Eater could intentionally provoke heart attacks, even if it was only in people with an existing heart condition.

Moon went straight to bed when he got home. Often on Fridays he would either attempt to stay awake, just taking it easy through the day, or would get by with only an hour or two's sleep. This made the transition to a more normal waking pattern easier for the weekend. Today, however, his only concession to this was setting his alarm for twelve instead of two. Having done this, he simply stripped off his trousers and tunic and threw himself into bed and was virtually unconscious the moment his head hit the pillow.

Chapter 15

Moon's alarm clock started trilling quietly then, when its owner failed to silence it, began to build up to an unpleasant warbling crescendo. He awoke grudgingly, turning over to stop the hellish noise with a push of a button. The room seemed unusually dark for early afternoon until a bright flash threw everything into stark relief for an instant, followed a few seconds later by a rumbling crash. Bleary eyed, Moon pulled aside a corner of one of his curtains, as he had suspected a heavy electrical storm was raging outside.

As he soaped himself down in the shower Moon recalled the events of the previous night. He ought to contact Uri to warn him about Rurik but he wouldn't be able to get hold of him until the early evening. It was intriguing that the Ghost Eater knew the vampire and he wondered where the two had met before; wherever and whenever it was, he would happily bet his pension that they had been more than passing acquaintances. Only a deep relationship would fire the sort of extreme hatred that had burned in Rurik's eyes last night.

His shower finished, he wrapped himself in a towelling bathrobe, lay back on his bed and switched on the television just towards the end of the BBC news. He caught the last couple of minutes of a report from America covering President Bush's proposal to invade Iraq. Moon wondered when the post 9/11 backlash was going to stop. Were the Americans and their allies going to invade every Islamic country with suspected terrorist connections like some modern day continuation of the Crusades? Moon was jogged out of his unhappy train of thought by the tag line for the first item on the local news, which came up after the final credits of the national programme. "Three dead in Bristol as a wave of violent attacks sweeps the city…" Moon turned up the volume, he didn't like the sound of this at all. Two more tag lines followed over the opening sequence then the regular newsreader came into view. As the camera zoomed in he said,

"Three people were killed yesterday evening and ten others were hospitalised following a rash of, apparently unconnected, violent assaults, which broke out in several different areas of the city." Looking into the camera with a grave expression, he continued, "The attacks took place in the City Centre, North Street in Bedminster, City Road in Saint Paul's and the Stokes Croft and Knowle West areas. The three dead include a twenty-four year old mother of two and two men in their late twenties, one of whom died while attempting to prevent an unprovoked attack upon another victim. There were several other victims, two of whom suffered serious injuries and are now in intensive care. The police have not released details of the victims at this time and are treating the current total of seventeen attacks as unrelated incidents. Further details are expected to be released later in the day. Julie Gates is on the scene in Knowle West…"

The programme cut to the inside of a local community centre where, against a backdrop of rain pouring down the building's windows, the roving reporter questioned a police representative who confirmed that all the attacks seemed to be random and motiveless. "We don't know why so many serious assaults or attempted assaults occurred within such a short period of time," he said. "There doesn't appear to have been any shared motive or indeed anything that linked the perpetrators at all…"

"Except that they were all a bit mentally unstable and had nocturnal visits from a dark figure with glowing eyes, I'll bet," Moon said to the screen. "I wish I knew what Rurik was up to with this."

"Who is Rurik?" asked a small voice behind him.

Moon turned to find Anna sitting in the gloom at the corner of his bed farthest from the windows. "Oh hi, Anna," he was surprised because he had assumed that Anna was confined to haunting the floor below. "I didn't know you could come up this far."

"It takes some effort," she replied, drawing her knees up to her chest under her flowery striped cotton dress, *"but I thought you might like to talk a while, like you suggested on Wednesday. Now, who's this Rurik?"*

"Rurick is the creature who's been attacking the local ghosts and turning them into these." He pointed to one of the blue globes, which was orbiting Anna and himself like a tiny moon. He couldn't be certain but some of them seemed a little bigger and brighter than when he had first seen them. Perhaps they were recovering slowly from whatever Rurik had done to them. "I think he's also responsible for the attacks and murders that happened last night."

"There were murders committed last night?" Anna seemed puzzled. *"Here, in Bristol? But I didn't sense them."* Anna shook her head. *"If anyone dies in this city I feel it, especially if their death is a violent one. I either feel the tremors in the spirit world as they pass on to the other side or a new presence if they become an earth-bound spirit. If they died and I didn't sense it then something very odd and unpleasant happened to them."*

"But what could that be?" asked Moon, half to himself. "I've met this Rurik and I don't believe he would do anything without a motive. These killings must play some part in his plan."

"Do you have any idea what that plan might be?" Moon was having trouble getting used to this more mature version of Anna. The problem was that, while she talked like a woman with a century's worth of experience, she still looked like, sounded like and had the *feel* of a four-year-old girl.

"I think he wants to create some kind of powerbase outside of the spiritual world here, in Bristol. But how could he do that?"

"There may be ways," replied Anna looking thoughtful. *"Even a ghost can influence the material world. It would just be a matter of gathering enough power. It's difficult, which is why most of us don't bother trying, but that's probably what this Rurik's plan involves; collecting enough spiritual energy to influence the world of the living."*

"Oh? And these killings are helping him to do this?"

"Possibly, I don't know that much about it and I wouldn't know who you'd ask. Anything which would know more than a little about that kind of thing is likely to be something you wouldn't want to get close to, let alone talk to."

Moon nodded, thinking of a certain reformed vampire. "Perhaps Uri could help me; we're meeting for some psychic self-defence lessons this weekend."

"I might be able to help you with that myself," said Anna, rolling up the sleeves of her little pink cardigan. *"You could do with learning a few tricks as soon as possible if this Rurik thinks you are enough of a threat to want to hurt you."*

Moon barely suppressed the laughter he felt welling up within him at the look of fierce determination on Anna's chubby features. "Do you mind if I get dressed first?" he asked, getting up off the bed.

"Of course, go ahead," replied Anna, sitting up cross-legged on the bed and giving him her full attention.

"Well, I'd rather do it in private," replied Moon bashfully, not happy with the idea of disrobing in front of a four-year-old, regardless of how long she had been a ghost.

"Oh, come on, Jerry!" she moaned as he picked up a pile of clothes off the end of his bed and headed for the bathroom. *"I've seen it all before, you know. You've a big mole at the top of your back and you've got a hairy chest, **and** bum and..."* Moon slammed the bathroom door and blocked out her voice with his mind then threw on a pair of briefs, some jeans and a T-shirt. When he came back into the room Anna was still listing his physical attributes: *"...And a scar on the right side of your tummy, and a freckle right on the end of your..."*

"That's *enough*!" growled Moon. "You pint-sized peeping Tom, have you nothing better to do than watch people get undressed?"

"...Nose! I was going to say 'nose'," complained Anna giving him a wounded look. *"And, to answer your question, no I don't have anything better to do than watch the living. I'm a ghost, Jerry. At least these days people have televisions. In the old days there was absolutely nothing to do but hover around the boundaries of my haunting and watch. Have you any idea how tedious it is to watch someone sleep for hours on end? It is horribly, **horribly** boring. So, yes I did sneak a look at you once or twice when you first arrived, partly out of curiosity but mainly for a change of scenery. And I wouldn't call it 'peeping' because I'm too young to get any pleasure out of it. To be honest, from*

what I've seen of 'it', I don't see what the fuss is about. How anyone gets any fun out of all that writhing and moaning is beyond me, it looks like a total waste of time and effort."

Moon smiled. "You'd be surprised. Anyway, you were going to teach me something."

"Oh, right, yes. To start off with, touch my arm."

"But I can't, you're a ghost." Moon shrugged.

"And you've got a ghost living in you," she replied, grinning mischievously. *"That's what a living person is, a ghost in a body."* She thought for an instant, head on one side with her ringlets dangling, then smiled as an idea dawned in her eyes and said, *"How is it that you can see me when most other people can't?"*

"I don't know, I always thought that it was a gift."

"I suppose you could look at it that way, but what's really happened is that you've somehow learnt to use your ghost's eyes to see with. What else can you do?"

"I can hear spirits and talk to them telepathically... Oh yes, and I also have a sort of spiritual sixth sense that lets me feel their presence when I can't see them."

"That's the thing you need to learn to use, your ghost sense, it's an extension of your spiritual body, what I've heard some people on the telly call your aura. Now, try to touch me by focusing your ghost sense. Try to feel me even though you can see me."

Moon closed his eyes and composed himself and tried to sense Anna, reaching out with his mind. Once he had pinpointed her presence, he opened his eyes and reached out his hand while still holding onto the sense of her in his mind. As his fingers contacted the boundary of her image he felt a tiny resistance, like thick icy cobwebs, and a tingling in his fingertips. *"That's fine, Jerry, but don't push so hard you're hurting me a little."*

"Sorry, Anna," said Moon, drawing his hand back until he was only touching the skin of her arm. A fine glow of brightness rimmed his fingertips as he touched her. "Is that meant to happen?"

"I think so. It would be the mingling of our energies. Our spirits are much stronger when they're inside of bodies so when a living human touches a ghost there's a small transfer of

energy. That's often what happens when a person says they feel like someone has walked over their grave. Its quite likely that a passing spirit has tapped them for a bit of a boost."

"We've talked a lot about energy this afternoon," said Moon thoughtfully. "Is it really that important to ghosts and other spirits?"

"Well, I think it might be a little different for non-human spirits. You know, those who're naturally part of the spirit world. It's my guess that they have natural ways of replenishing their energy. But, we ghosts seem to diminish down to a lower energy level than when we were alive, so even the tiny boost that we get from touching a human can be very refreshing."

"So how do I use this to fight?"

"You're keen!" Anna laughed.

"No, I'm just eager to preserve my hide."

"Right, well all I can give you is theory because I haven't had to put this into practice but the way I would use it to fight is to turn it into a weapon. Instead of reaching out tentatively I would strike out hard with my ghost sense, using it like a whiplash to snap energy away from your target. Like this!"

Moon saw a vague tendril of blue fire strike forth from the tiny ghost's forehead and slash across his extended hand. It felt like a blade of ice cutting through the top layer of his skin. "Ouch! That stung."

Anna looked as surprised as Moon felt. *"It actually worked? That's wonderful!"* she yelped.

"I thought you were supposed to know something about this sort of thing," complained Moon.

"Only what I've managed to work out for myself over the years but I was right, wasn't I?"

"Only by accident," replied Moon sarcastically.

"No, by a work of careful deduction," replied Anna firmly. *"Why don't you try to do it to me now?"*

"Okay," agreed Moon, attempting to narrow his ghost sense into a fine whip the way Anna had. The first attempt merely resulted in mocking giggles as his effort dispersed harmlessly before reaching the ghost but the second, driven by Moon's frustration, brought forth a keening wail from his target.

"You hurt me," sobbed Anna accusingly, her face crumpling into a tearful mask of resentment.

"But you told me to!" replied Moon defensively.

"I didn't mean you should do it so hard." Anna rubbed her left hand over her right forearm, which was haemorrhaging a cloud of bluish energy as a result of Moon's attack.

"I'm sorry Anna; I guess I don't know my own strength." Having just begun to get used to the new mature Anna this sudden reversion to the four-year-old had caught him off guard. Concentrating the way she had taught him, he reached out his hand and gently stroked her hair.

Anna composed herself, drying her eyes with her small fists. She looked up at him. *"It's alright, Jerry. I just wasn't prepared for such a powerful attack so I reverted to type for a moment there. It's so difficult to keep focused on being adult when your soul's trapped in childhood."* She rubbed her small head against his hand. *"This is the first time someone has touched me for nearly a century, Jerry. Thanks, it's nice."*

She crawled up onto his lap and he cradled her to him. "A hundred years is a hell of a long time to go without a cuddle, isn't it?" he replied with tears forming in his eyes.

At about six o'clock, Moon decided to phone to see if Uri was available. He wasn't sure just how early the vampire would be able to rise during daylight hours. Uri had said that he was like Count Dracula in this respect and, from what he remembered of Bram Stoker's creation, Count Dracula was able to move around in daylight like any other nocturnal creature. So perhaps Uri was like a human, having to 'sleep' a number of hours to regenerate but able to wake if necessary. He phoned the mobile number that Uri had given him and a female voice on the other end of the line said, "Hi, Uri's phone, who's speaking?"

Moon detected a slight Spanish accent. "Hi, Charli isn't it? It's Moon here, I'd like to speak to Uri if that's possible."

"Hi, Moon," replied Charli brightly, "he's in the shower at the moment, can I get him to call you back?"

"Okay, but please tell him it's quite important that I speak to him."

"I will do. Something to do with our poor Dominic is it?"

"I think it's connected, yes."

"I'll get him to phone you right back; does he have your number?" Moon gave her both his home and mobile numbers then hung up.

Five minutes later the phone rang. It was Uri. "Hi, Moon, Charli says you might have a lead?"

"Yes, I have a name for our Ghost Eater. His name's Rurik and he sends you his regards."

"Rurik? My God, it can't be, he's dead. I killed him centuries ago."

"Well, that explains why he doesn't seem to like you very much. He must be some kind of ghost then. I thought he might be a generic supernatural, like the boggart."

"That is the only explanation that could fit. It *must* be Rurik's ghost. This is terrible! Rurik is the most ruthlessly evil creature I have ever known. Does this mean that you've actually encountered him?"

"I met him last night..." Moon recounted the tale of his previous night's experiences to Uri.

"Ah, so it seems Rurik's spirit is looking for revenge. It's all beginning to make a strange kind of sense now. You see Rurik was a vampire when he was alive, a very evil and powerful vampire who held others of our kind, including myself, in thrall. It would seem that the ghost of a vampire can suck the life force from ghosts like a living vampire is able to draw blood from the living." There was a slight pause at the other end of the phone. "Moon, I need to consider this new development further. Could we meet later so I can let you know any fresh notions that might have come to my mind?"

"I'm meant to be spending the evening with Sonia, Uri," replied Moon unhappily.

"This is important, Moon. If Rurik is involved we need to consider a plan of action. People... many people, will be in danger."

Moon thought of the victims of the last night's storm of madness. Was Uri suggesting that this would escalate? "Okay, we're meeting at the *Rest* in just over an hour, I'll try to explain to Sonia why we can't just have a fun evening together."

They said their goodbyes then Moon readied himself to go out. He had a new dark blue, velvety textured, long-sleeved shirt, which brought out the darker colours in his eyes to good effect and he had decided that this would be a good occasion to try it out on Sonia. He also chose a pair of black dress trousers, tooled black slip-on shoes and a mid length black coat. "Not so bad," he said as he winked at his reflection in the full-length mirror on the back of his wardrobe door. "Looks quite Gothy too so I shouldn't be such an obvious outsider tonight." He wondered if he should grow his hair. Sonia would probably like it but past experience had taught him that he hated it at medium length. It tended to stay at that stage so long he usually gave up and had it shorn to within an inch of its life out of sheer frustration.

Chapter 16

To avoid the foul weather, Moon took a taxi into the town centre. Fifteen minutes later he was dodging king sized raindrops as he dashed the ten metres or so across the *Hangman's Rest*'s courtyard to the door. By the time he entered the bar his hair was plastered flat to his skull and the shoulders of his coat were soaked through. The bar was very quiet even for this early on a Friday evening because of the rain. It took no time to locate Sonia, looking very bedraggled, sitting on her own at a table near to one of the ancient radiators, which had various bits of steaming clothing, including Sonia's black trench coat, hanging over it to dry. "Hi, love, how're you doing?" Moon hung his own coat over the back of a vacant chair.

Sonia looked up and smiled. "Hi, Jerry! I've had a good soaking, but I'm fine otherwise. Like the shirt," she reached up to stroke its soft folds, "it goes well with your eyes."

Moon grinned then bent down to kiss her. "That was the idea. Can I get you a drink?"

Sonia pointed to her full glass. "I'm fine for the moment, thanks."

At the bar Moon bought himself a pint of Ostrich. He didn't recognize either of the on-duty bar staff but raised his glass to Kate, sitting at the other end of the bar chatting with friends, who waved back cheerily. When he got back to their table he told Sonia, "I'm sorry but we're not going to have this evening to ourselves. Something important has come up and Uri's coming in to see me later."

Sonia frowned and he could almost see the fires building behind her eyes. "What! But, Jerry, this was going to be our special night."

"And it still can be... later," replied Moon with a calming gesture. "I wouldn't have let Uri butt in on us at all, except that he insists that it's very important. If it isn't I'll be standing by to hand you the stake."

"So what's so all fired important that he thinks he can spoil our night out?" asked the less than mollified Sonia.

"I came face to face with the Ghost Eater last night and it seems he and Uri are old acquaintances."

"You've seen the Ghost Eater?" Sonia's eyes went wide with surprise. "When?"

"Last night during my shift. It gobbled up one of the hospital's resident ghosts right in front of me then told me to give its regards to Uri. When I phoned Uri and told him that its name is Rurik he sounded really terrified over the phone. According to Uri, Rurik was some kind of master vampire that he killed a long time ago. He thinks that the Ghost Eater could be Rurik's spirit come back for revenge."

Sonia frowned with concern. "Oh, Jerry, I don't like this. This whole thing is beginning to scare me. I've only just met you and I don't want to lose you to some... invisible monster."

Moon shook his head. "I can't back out of this, love. The thing thinks that I'm a threat to its plans, so if I did try to ignore it all it would do is track me down and try to kill me. I think my best plan of action is to learn all I can from Uri about how to get rid of it, assuming he does know how to fight it, that is."

"I guess so." Sonia looked towards the door. "Speak of the devil, here he comes now."

Uri strode through the door like a gothic fashion model. He threw back the hood of his long black leather coat and his long white-blond hair streamed back from his finely chiselled masculine features. Peeking through the open front of his coat, his hard, well defined torso rippled under the highlights of his black silk shirt. Moon noticed that most of the female eyes in the pub, and one or two pairs of male eyes as well, turned to appreciate his graceful walk up to the bar. The petite Kiddy Goth who was serving nearly fell over herself in her eagerness to get his order. Say what you will about Uri you could never fault him on his sense of style. Having acquired a large glass of vodka Uri made his way directly to Moon and Sonia's table; Moon noticed that there was not a drop of moisture on him despite the storm, which still raged heavily outside. "Hello, Moon," he said in his chocolaty baritone, "and Sonia," he continued, bowing to kiss Sonia's hand. Moon thought this was over the top but Sonia clearly found this display of old world charm beguiling, judging by the dark flush of pink that now crept up from her cleavage, betraying the hidden ginger nature under all that Gothic black.

Moon gave up his chair to Uri and sat down on the leather covered bench next to Sonia. The vampire's larger than life presence making their small round table seem a little crowded. "I apologise for interrupting your evening," he said to Sonia. "Has Moon explained why I must be such a boor?"

"He says that you've had dealings with the Ghost Eater in the past and that you think he's a bigger danger than we originally thought," summed up Sonia.

"My dear, that is an understatement of enormous magnitude." Uri took a deep sip of his vodka. "Has Moon told you anything about my origins?"

Sonia looked over at Moon. "A bit," she replied.

"Only what little you told me," Moon explained. "That you were born into the Russian nobility nearly a thousand years ago and were changed into a vampire by a sorcerer in revenge for some atrocity you and others committed."

"Brief but correct." Uri smiled sadly. "Of course there's much more to it than that. I was born in Byelorussia, a day's journey northwest of Kiev in 1028, a descendent of the brothers Rus themselves and of almost pure Norse blood. Did you know that Russia was founded by Vikings?"

"Yes," replied Moon, who was a bit of a history buff. "So you were a Viking?"

"We weren't called that by then, we were the *Varangians,* merchant warriors who used the Dnepr and Volga rivers as our highways to the Black Sea and beyond there to Constantinople where we traded furs and honey for silk, spices and works of art."

"There was a programme about that on the History Channel a while back," interjected Sonia. "Wasn't there a lot of internal strife in Russia at the time; lots of little princedoms that didn't get along?" Moon shot Sonia a surprised glance; he hadn't realised she had any interest at all in history.

Uri nodded. "The history of Russia has always been, shall we say, interesting. There was no strict convention for establishing succession back then so a local ruler would usually be replaced by the most powerful of his relatives when he died. This meant they would often leave several disgruntled offspring who felt entitled to lands of their own. The customary way to prevent internal family feuds was to send them off to invade unclaimed territory, terrorise the locals and establish rights of princedom. Pretty much the same winning formula the Vikings or their descendants have continued to use over the last thousand years."

Moon nodded, thinking back to the Norman Conquest and the history of European empire-building. "I suppose you're right."

"Anyway, to continue my story, I was born into the midst of this civil turmoil. My father was a successful merchant and cousin to the local prince but, having been weaned on the old tales of conquest, I was not content to devote my life to the boring business of trade and I was determined to distinguish myself in the field of battle. I trained hard from the moment I could pick up a sword and by my late teens I considered myself a formidable warrior. Rurik was the eldest son of a prince from a southwestern principality and a remote kinsman of mine but his family's lands had been transferred to his uncle when his father died and I'd heard rumours that he was putting together an expedition to claim lands of his own elsewhere. Seeing this as my chance to prove myself, I sought him out and signed on as a member of his *'drujina'*: his war band. Because most of the lands near the boundaries of our homeland were already spoken for we ventured south and west into the region bordering Poland, seeking wealth and conquest.

"We were nearly a hundred fighting men, all well trained and riding on horseback, and we fell upon those unprotected pagan villages like the wrath of our new God. Where we struck we killed those who fought back, took anything worth having and had our way with any of the wenches we found fair. Any male prisoners of fighting age were killed painfully and messily before the eyes of what was left of their village as a hard lesson in what awaited anyone who thought to oppose us." He met Moon and Sonia's disapproving eyes with a steady blue gaze. "Yes it was wicked, bloody work, my friends. But you must understand that this was the way we were taught to behave in that time and it would remain the normal way of things up until nearly the present day. I did nothing that the members of my culture would consider evil and it has taken me centuries to learn to think otherwise."

"Sonia shook her head. But how could you be so callous? Didn't you feel guilty about what you had done?"

"About some things, yes, I did. One cannot harm and use others, especially women, the way that I did then without eventually feeling remorse. Not if one possesses any shred of humanity anyway. I quickly tired of that kind of sport, regardless of how lustily my comrades pursued it, and it was that pursuit that eventually brought about our downfall." Pinkish tears formed in Uri's eyes as he drained his glass. "This tale calls for more lubrication, my friends, may I get them in?"

As Uri headed for the bar to replenish their drinks Sonia turned her angry gaze to Moon. "The man's a monster. How can we dare trust him after hearing about the terrible things he's done?"

Moon thought it ironic that Sonia could accept Uri as a vampire, but that when he confessed to his ancient human cruelties he suddenly became a 'real' monster. "He's in good company," he replied with wry a smile. "Most of the heroes of British history would probably be considered war criminals or worse if they did what they became famous for today. I've read enough history to understand that Uri was just a man of his time." He put down his glass and touched Sonia's hand, looking deeply into her still hard eyes. "Try to cool it a bit about what he's done in the past, love, and have a good look at how it affects him now. Even after nearly a thousand years it still torments him to think about it."

Sonia sighed and grimaced at Moon. "I suppose he might have changed. It just sounds so horrible, Jerry."

Uri returned with a tray of drinks including, Moon noticed, another large vodka for himself, and noticing their expressions said, "So, you are wondering whether you can trust this evil beast?" A deep shadow passed behind his eyes. "I can't say I blame you. Even I have trouble coming to terms with it sometimes, and I have had a long time to do so, but I assure you that I am no longer the person I was in my teens and twenties.

Even then I was not truly the person I was trying to be; ruthlessness and cruelty were considered admirable traits in a warrior back then."

Sonia nodded. "I guess we'll just have to take you at your word for that, for now. You were telling us how your partiality for rape got you into trouble." Sonia did not bother to hide her disgust as she said the word 'rape'.

"Actually, I had no active involvement in that part of it," Uri replied defensively. "My crime was simply being a member of the *drujina* band which conquered a largish village just to the north of the Carpathian Mountains." Uri's eyes took on a misty look as he focused again on the past. "We had decided it was time to build ourselves a base of operations. Having discovered an excellent site for a fortification on a craggy foothill above a small lake, we bullied the men folk from the village into felling trees, hauling rocks, digging and building until we had the beginnings of a decently fortified keep. It overlooked the lakeside village and had a tall palisade surrounding it on three sides with a sheer cliff at the rear.

"The work was nearing completion on the day that Rurik decided to ride out to supervise the building work on horseback. As he was riding along the makeshift dirt road from the keep, a peasant suddenly lost his footing in the mud and tipped a handcart full of rocks in the path of his horse. This made it rear and stumble, breaking its right fetlock. Rurik was furious and demanded payment for his horse, which of course the peasant, a fisherman named Gern, was unable to provide. Rurik then slyly asked Gern if he had any children. The old man replied that he had two daughters and a son. Rurik laughed and declared that he would take Gern's two daughters as 'mares' in payment for the stallion that he would have to put down that day. The poor man was deeply distraught about this and begged repeatedly for mercy but Rurik was determined to have his revenge. He had the two girls brought up to the keep where he commanded that they should be used by the entire *drujina* as and how they wished, which of course meant that those poor maidens would be subjected to a continuous ordeal of rape and abuse until he saw fit to release them."

"Poor kids," said Sonia, obviously thinking back to her own not too distant past.

"Yes, indeed, 'poor kids'," agreed Uri, nodding sadly. "One evening, about a week later, Horvar, a huge Turkish mercenary, who was feared even among our band for his inventiveness at cruelty, had taken both girls to his tent. We thought nothing of this except that some of the men grumbled that the bastard had taken more than his fair share and that the girls would be no use for days after he had finished with them. A short time later, however, our night was suddenly disturbed by a man's outraged roars of pain accompanied by women's laughter, which quickly turned to screams. We followed the sounds to Horvar's tent in the compound, where we found him sitting crouched over on his blood soaked pallet groaning in agony with the broken corpses of Gern's daughters lying pale and naked on the ground beside him. Horvar told us that when he had made the older of the girls, Neela, remove her shift she had drawn a hidden knife from under it and plunged it deeply into his groin. In his anger at the unexpected attack he had slaughtered both of the girls with his bare hands. Horvar's own wound was deep and the knife had severed an artery so the Turk himself didn't last the rest of that night. Considering the consequences of his actions, he was probably the most fortunate of us." Uri paused and took a large sip of vodka, his unnaturally blue eyes clouded with dark memories.

"So what happened?" asked Sonia, obviously fascinated by Uri's recollections of the ancient past.

"Vengeance happened, Sonia: dark and dreadful vengeance. The girls' bodies were returned to their parents. When they saw how cruelly they had been used and how brutally they had died, they described the pitiful state of the corpses to the other villagers who conspired to put an end to our plans of conquest once and for all.

"One of their elders was a shaman: a tiny, wizened monkey of a man by the name of Korj. He seemed so insignificant that we had paid him little notice when we took over their village but, despite his humble appearance, he was a powerful sorcerer. This final outrage had stirred his anger against us enough for him to risk casting a dangerous and costly spell. I don't know the full details of course, but on the night after the girls' funeral the whole village gathered in the market place around a large bonfire. We thought they were just performing some kind of death ritual but more sentries, including myself, were posted along the palisade just in case they were planning something. All that happened, however, was that the villagers started a low rising and falling chant as they circled the fire. I remember joking with one of my companions that there was no end to the strange things these heathens would get up to. As we laughed their chant ended abruptly in a great yell: *'Upiri!'* which seemed to crash over our palisade like a great wave. The entire *drujina* was suddenly swept into a deep and dreamless sleep.

"How long we slept I do not know but it must have been at least three days as that is the time it takes to travel by cart from that village to the foothills of the Eastern Carpathians where we awoke. We didn't understand what had happened at first. I thought I must have been drinking and had passed out but a bleary-eyed examination of my surroundings was enough to make me realize that it was more serious than that. I was lying on the rocky floor of a large cave with Georgi, one of my companions, sprawled on top of me. We were at the edge of a pile of sleeping warriors who had been dumped unceremoniously on top of each other like corpses after a battle. As they began to wake up there was a barrage of growls and complaints accompanied by the sound of the occasional blow as those on the lower levels of the pile fought their way to the surface. Finally, when we were all pretty much on our feet, a bright blue globe of light appeared at the centre of the cave with the sorcerer, Korj, standing at its centre. He seemed somehow taller and more authoritative than the little old man we had encountered in the village, and around him I could sense an unmistakable aura of power. He laughed at us and told us of our fate. Because we had acted like *'upiri lichy'*, which means 'cruel vampires', that is what we would be for the rest of our lives. We would guard the entrance to their lands from other Russian invaders and visit vengeance on our countrymen throughout eternity. Then he laughed and exited swiftly through the cave mouth. Many of us tried to follow but quickly found we couldn't bear the direct rays of the early morning sun so we had to shelter in the cave until nightfall, all of us falling into a death-like sleep as the day progressed."

"So you were somehow bound to the area where you were left by the villagers, am I right?" asked Sonia.

"That's correct," Uri nodded.

"Then how come you're here now?" she demanded, sipping her *Green Fairy*.

"It's a long story. Korj had bound us to Rurik, but Rurik he had bound to the land itself. I don't know why he did it that way but perhaps he drew upon our existing loyalties to work his magic. I've learned over the years that those who use magic tend to opt for methods that are least expensive, in terms of power, to fulfil their purposes. A sorcerer's energy comes at least partly from himself so he tries to minimize the drain that his spells place upon his personal resources. We did not know that the spell worked this way, however, until Rurik died.

"You see, Rurik didn't change in the same way we did. We all grew fangs and developed the terrible hunger for blood and extreme sensitivity to sunlight but we remained essentially human in appearance, while compared even to us Rurik was a horror. Already a tall man, Korj's curse turned him into a giant nearly three metres tall, his features became an obscene mating between those of a human and a vampire bat, with a squashed back, fringed snout, tiny black eyes and huge pointed ears." Uri opened his arms expansively. "He had wings, you know. Huge bat-like things, with a spread of over thirty metres, that sprouted from his back and a leathery membrane grew down between his legs, divided by a long, muscular tail with a leaf-like vane at the end. While most normal vampires have the ability to levitate, Rurik could actually fly. He was also incredibly strong, much stronger than me and the rest of our brethren. Korj must have thought that making Rurik so much more powerful than us would make it easier for him to rule over us. The wizard obviously believed that Rurik's innate cruelty would guarantee that we would become the curse upon our own countrymen he intended us to be and this worked, for a few centuries at least."

"I don't get this," interjected Moon shaking his head. "This Korj didn't like the way you treated his people so, what? He turned you loose to do worse to the Russians? It doesn't make sense."

"Perhaps not to modern thinking, Moon." Uri's mouth pulled up into a humourless smile. "But people usually didn't think far beyond their own boundaries in those days. Korj was no altruist; the only people who mattered to him were his own villagers. We Russians had a terrible reputation at the time because of our ruthless expansionism, so the whole of Russia was the enemy as far as he was concerned. He couldn't care less what happened to the Russian peasants he had unleashed us upon, just as long as our presence prevented other *drujina* from invading his people's lands. We turned out to be very effective at doing just that once we had established ourselves.

"Under Rurik's pitiless leadership we carved out a kingdom of terror in the foothills of the Carpathians. At the start we just sallied out from the cave at night and attacked a few of the outlying farms but as we grew bolder and more confident in our powers we overthrew the local prince and took his castle. Some time later we discovered that we could enchant humans into becoming our servants so we had someone to watch over us as we slept. We created an army of these 'ghouls' with which we drove out or killed the nearby aristocracy until we ruled an area of countryside which spread over thirty kilometres." Uri gestured expressively with his arms, making Moon wonder if he wasn't getting a bit drunk. "We made more of our kind so the land was crawling with vampires and half-vampiric ghouls who preyed on any unwary travellers until eventually no-one sane would attempt to pass through our lands, be it for trade or conquest."

"Sounds horrible," commented Sonia, sipping her drink.

"Worse than horrible," replied Uri. "Rurik's presence seemed to blight the land itself, turning it into a place of treacherous swamps full of twisted growth and haunted mists. From the centre of this Rurik reigned like a great diseased spider in its web. I don't know whether his transformation went more than skin deep or it simply unlocked a hidden store of darkness within him, but he seemed to develop an unlimited capacity for evil and depravity. Once he was simply given to random cruelty when the opportunity occurred, now he went out of his way to indulge every wicked whim and dreadful imagining. Because Korj had made us all his slaves, he dragged us down into the darkness with him. It didn't help that we all believed that we *must* be irredeemably evil because we were vampires but even that spurious belief did not prevent the impact it had on our minds. Several of us actually went mad because of the depravities he expected us to witness or partake in, and I believed that I would eventually go that way too if I could not stop him."

The horror of those times turned Uri's eyes into bleak pits. He didn't describe what Rurik had forced him to do but their silent eloquence was enough to stir the darkest visions in Moon and Sonia's minds. Forgetting her earlier distrust, Sonia reached across and touched Uri's hand. "It's okay, Uri," she reassured him, "it's not as if you had the choice."

Uri looked up at her, shaking his head. "That's the problem, Sonia. I don't know. I just don't know if part of me was willing; if I gave in too easily to doing those dreadful things…"

"The very fact that you have those doubts and they trouble you so much convinces me that you would never have given in willingly," comforted Moon. "Everything I've seen of you since we first met suggests someone who has struggled to rise above the moral limitations of the society he was born into. I don't care about what you've done in the past, be it because of the time you grew up in or living under the domination of a mad vampire lord, you've done your best with the hand you were dealt as far as I can see."

Uri looked hesitantly over at Moon. "Thank you, my friend. But you see now why Rurik must be stopped at all costs. I am certain that he wants to turn Bristol, maybe the whole of Britain, into the same kind of nightmare kingdom that we built in Russia."

Moon nodded. "It looks like it. How did you kill him back then? It might provide us with a clue how to fight him."

"I don't think it will help much but I'll tell you. I wasn't particularly high up in our pecking order, possibly because he sensed my disgust at what we had become and my revulsion for his filthy 'amusements'. However, I was at least part of the inner circle because I was of noble blood and a member of the original *drujina*, so I did have access to his inner sanctum. Even so it was nearly three hundred years before the opportunity arose to kill him. I had to work alone, you see, because I didn't know which of my comrades felt like I did or who amongst them actually rejoiced in our transformation as some seemed to. There was no possibility of trust between us. Then one day I finally found myself armed and alone with him in his chamber.

"You see by then we had begun to cultivate our peasants rather like cattle. Blood was a limited resource so, rather than kill them, we kept a number of humans at our main strongholds and we would drink from them on a rotational basis, allowing them to regain their strength and replenish their blood in between feeds. It had become a necessity, you see, after the flow of travellers through our countryside had dried up. But Rurik was the exception to this; he claimed that his larger frame required a kill for each feed so we established a tithing system. This meant that each village within our thrall would surrender a number of their daughters on a staggered three-yearly basis. Rurik insisted it should be girls because he liked to satisfy his lust with them before draining them of blood."

"Ugh!" said Sonia, pulling a face and snuggling closer to Moon. "I'm liking this bugger Rurik less and less."

"Yes, Rurik was far from nice as a human but as a vampire he was a fiend from hell. But, as I was saying, this is where my chance came in. Normally, there would be two of us to take Rurik's nightly victim to his chamber but on this night his 'meal' was such a tiny young thing that the warrior who would normally have accompanied me suggested that I should take her up on my own, while he finished a game of chance he was playing with some of his cronies. I leapt at the chance, hoping that I might at last have an opportunity to end my thralldom, and I escorted the girl to Rurik's room in the main tower of the keep by myself. Similar opportunities had occurred in the past but I had hesitated because taking on Rurik face to face wasn't an easy prospect; I needed some way to surprise him, which was unlikely as he didn't fully trust me. However, this night I had a stroke of luck.

When I brought the girl through the door and she got her first sight of Rurik she screamed and broke free of me. She bolted towards the great open window that Rurik had installed as an exit for his nocturnal flights and which was the only other exit from the room. Since his transformation Rurik had instincts like a cat so he couldn't help but pounce after the girl, snatching her up in his mighty talons. This was all the opportunity I needed; my sword was already in my hand as I had drawn it to escort the girl so I went in swiftly for a two-handed side blow and struck his ugly head from his shoulders. The resulting shock as I was released from his power stunned me for several seconds, and I came round to the sound of footsteps on the stairs outside. Not sure whether my brethren would want to thank me or kill me for what I'd done, I barred the door from the inside. Then I quickly checked on Rurik and the girl, who were both dead, Rurik by my sword and the girl with her neck broken from Rurik's attack. Thinking quickly, I sheathed my sword and, making a makeshift sack from my cloak, I took Rurik's head and levitated out through the window into the night. I flew that way for several hours, heading westward towards Poland and travelling well outside of the boundaries Korj had set for us.

A couple of hours before dawn, I sought out a small cave high up in a rock face where I could hide myself throughout the day. Settling on a shallow rock shelf, I was alarmed to feel movement within my cloak and when I opened it I was horrified to see that Rurik's head was still partly alive, glaring at me with utter hatred, spitting and mouthing obscenities. I was afraid that if his head was reunited with his body all of my night's work would have been in vain so I risked detection by taking the foul thing down to the base of the cliff and burning it. Once the flesh was completely burned away I smashed up the ashes with the hilt of my sword and scattered them over an area of several kilometres. As far as I knew that was the end of Rurik until you phoned me last night with his name on your lips, my friend."

"So what happened to the other vampires?" asked Sonia.

"I never returned to that area but I suppose they spread out through that part of the continent, some establishing their own little princedoms while others fell to various fates. I'm sure that most of the vampire legends from those parts can be traced back to them, but somewhere along the way people learned how to kill them and I suspect most of them were either despatched by their intended victims or fell at the mercy of the Inquisition. I know I haven't heard many rumours of vampires from that area in the last couple of centuries, although some may still survive in isolation."

"Have you any idea what Rurik's up to?" asked Moon. "There must be some kind of plan behind his attacks on the ghosts, and the way he's manipulating people into acts of violence, but it doesn't seem to make a lot of sense as it stands."

"He's most likely storing up energy. You know I was telling you about the energy the girls and I receive from the audience when we perform?" Moon nodded. "Yes, well that's not the only form of spiritual energy that humans produce. Fear and violence do just as well as enjoyment. So by making these unstable individuals attack people, Rurik may well be creating an environment in which he can thrive."

"I hadn't thought of that," pondered Moon. "But I was wondering about another possibility. I spoke with Anna, the little ghost you met on the stairs at my place. She says that she didn't feel the people who died last night passing over."

Uri's eyes widened. "You don't mean?"

"Yes, I think that Rurik consumed all their energy at the point of death. Anna was telling me that humans work on a higher energy level than ghosts…"

"So if he drains them as they're about to pass over he gets a lot more power? That makes sense."

"That's awful!" exclaimed Sonia. "Doesn't that mean they'll not be able to move on to wherever they're meant to go?"

"I should think so," replied Uri unhappily. "There wouldn't be anything left of them but little ghost globes, like the ones that follow Moon around like lost sheep." He fixed his desperate eyes on Moon. "I don't know exactly what the bastard's up to but we have to stop him as quickly as possible. The list of casualties is already far too high."

"There goes our evening!" muttered Sonia ruefully. "I suppose you want us to come back to your place and get down to this spiritual warfare training straight away."

"Actually, no," replied Uri. "I think we're safe from further assaults tonight. This storm isn't forecast to clear up until two or three o'clock in the morning so most people won't be outside for any longer than they can help it. It'll be better if you both get some rest after your week's work so you can start the training refreshed in body, mind and spirit tomorrow night. How about if you two come over to my place at about seven in the evening. You can have tea with us. It's Charli's turn to make it and she's an excellent cook. Then once we've eaten we can get down to training."

Sonia sighed with relief as Moon agreed. "Okay, let's do it that way."

"Fine," replied Uri rising a little unsteadily from his chair. "Now you guys enjoy what's left of your evening and I'll wrack my memories for anything that might be useful against Rurik."

They said their farewells and as they watched Uri make his way unsteadily to the door. Sonia frowned, "Is he a bit tipsy or what?"

"Well, he has just sunk at least three hundred-proof double vodkas in less than an hour so I guess he might be heading that way," replied Moon. "This Rurik business must be upsetting him more than he's willing to let on."

"A drunken vampire, whatever next?" Sonia giggled.

"Well hopefully, if you're ready to blow this joint..." I hinted Moon, with a suggestive arch of the eyebrow.

"Oh, yes. Yes indeed!" replied Sonia enthusiastically, finishing her drink. They quickly gathered their belongings and left. A short taxi ride and a frantic race up the staircase later and they were soon happily naked in Sonia's bed.

Chapter 17

Moon woke at about nine the next day to the sound of two chaffinches squabbling outside the window. The storm had spent itself during the night and it looked like a lovely morning outside. Sonia was still asleep and he pulled himself up on his pillows so he could watch her as she snored gently, tangled half in and half out of the bedclothes. She looked like a teenager, with her face softened by sleep and the gentle sunlight muted by the red of her curtains. It had been quite a night, he remembered. They had made love several times, having both removed their piercings for safety's sake, and everything had been beautiful. As he lay there he felt a hand creep in and fondle a certain part of his anatomy. "Sonia!" he said with mock firmness.

Sonia's face transformed from feigned sleep to a sly grin. "Well, if you're not interested..."

"Who said I'm not interested?" replied Moon, faking prudishness. "It's just that I think these things should be handled with the correct decorum."

"Oh, very well," replied Sonia in a mock Victorian upper class accent. "One would be terribly obliged if you would fuck one, Sir."

Moon twiddled an imaginary handlebar moustache. "Indeed, Madam, one would be only too glad to oblige."

Twenty minutes of wild sex followed, which was sadly abbreviated just short of climax when Avril banged on Sonia's door and yelled, "Do you two perverts mind keeping the noise down in there, I've got a pounding migraine!"

"Sorry, Avril," replied Sonia, who had been responsible for most of the noise, swiping Moon round the head for sniggering. They finished off more quietly, Sonia obviously straining to contain her normal shrieks of ecstasy to muted moans and whimpers.

As they lay basking in the afterglow Moon said, "So what do you want to do today?"

"Don't you remember? We were going to look at Goth stuff in the market, if you're still up for it."

Moon hit his forehead with the palm of his hand. "Of course! I'd forgotten with all that's been happening. I haven't done much writing for my article over the last couple of days either."

"Well, this is your chance to do a bit more research for it and you can help me replace that stud you ruined at the same time."

They showered, dressed and went downstairs. Breakfast was spoiled slightly by Avril, who sat gloomily over her cornflakes, wearing dark glasses and holding her head. "Why don't you just go to bed, love?" suggested Sonia sympathetically.

"Because it's my sodding day off and I don't intend to lose it all to a bloody headache!"

Moon regarded her with concern. "Have you had any painkillers yet?" he asked.

"No, I hate taking pills," she replied with a grimace.

"Yeah, but they help a lot when you're feeling like crap. What have you got in the house?"

"Just some paracetamols."

"Well, that's a start. But why don't you try some ibuprofen as well." He pulled an antique enamelled pill box, which had belonged to his maternal grandmother, from his pocket. I've a couple of four hundred mils here. If you take one now it should kick in over the next twenty minutes then in about two hours take a couple of paracetamols. If you feel you need it you can take the other ibuprofen two hours after that and another couple of paracetamols two hours later. Okay?"

Avril nodded. "Thanks, Nursey."

"Good. Pills are fine as long as you keep to the rules so keep the paracetamol four hours apart and the same for the ibuprofen. Oh, and try to have something to eat when you take the ibuprofen; it can be a bit harsh on an empty stomach."

"God, Moon, you don't half get bossy when you've got your nurse hat on." Avril grimaced, taking one of the little pink pills and washing it down with tea.

"Comes with the job," replied Moon with a grin. "I'd try to grab at least an hour in a darkened room before you go out if I were you. It should help you to get over the migraine more quickly."

"I guess I can spare an hour out of my day off," Avril smiled wanly behind her glasses. "No more shenanigans while I'm trying to get some rest, okay."

Sonia blushed a little. "Well, actually, we're off out to the market to look in on *Dusk 'til Dawn* and a few other stalls."

"Great! It's about time Moon got some duds to go with yours. People were beginning to call you the 'odd couple' behind your backs."

"Ah, I wasn't thinking of buying anything," replied Moon, "just having a look for my article."

Sonia smiled knowingly at Avril as she steered Moon out of the door, "We'll see what I can talk him into," she whispered over her shoulder.

"What?" said Moon, who had half heard the comment.

"Nothing darling," replied Sonia, smiling sweetly.

The St Nicholas Market in the old Bristol Corn exchange contained a quirky mixture of stalls, ranging from common bric-a-brac to specialist dealers in such things as model making and memorabilia. There were also several stalls selling an interesting selection of clothing and jewellery. It being Saturday, the place was a-bustle with both the living and the dead and Moon was having his usual problem with sorting out the one from the other. Many of the stalls seemed to have at least two proprietors as the previous tenants clung on to the job they had loved in life, while long dead merchants in a variety of different historical garbs roamed through the crowd.

Sonia first took Moon to see some of the jewellery stalls, which were situated in the main hall of the Corn Exchange itself. Moon was fascinated by the variety of novelty rings, earrings and pendants on sale and, with a bit of gentle persuasion from Sonia, he bought a silver ring with a lifelike wolf's face on it.

Moon was fond of wolves, probably because for him they represented the wilderness and untamed Nature. As a boy he had spent a couple of summers staying with one of his aunts and his cousins, who lived in a remote part of the Lake District, and he had developed a deep fondness for roaming the forests and mountains in that area. Something about wolves reminded him of that wild feeling of freedom. Sonia broke his reverie, as he regarded the ring on his left middle finger. "Well, that's a start. We need to get you three or four more for you to pass as a Goth."

"Yeah, I'd noticed that they seem to wear a lot of rings and other jewellery for some reason..."

"Yeah, *we* do, don't *we*?" replied Sonia with a grin. "I guess it's just another way to create an impression, like the clothes. Plus jewellery's a very personal thing, isn't it?"

"So it's a way of stating your individuality among a group of people who dress alike?"

"I suppose so but less of the 'alike' thank you. I'd have thought you'd have realised by now that most of us go out of our way to try to look different within the general Goth theme."

"Okay, I guess you do, especially for concerts and going out, but you have to admit there's a lot of similarity as well. A lot of you seem to go in for black or purple hair, black leather trench coats, silver jewellery, crosses and pentacles and all that kind of thing."

"Yeah, but you could say the same about any other identifiable modern subculture from the Mormons to the Mothers' Union. Compared to people like that I'd say we're *much* more distinctive and creative in the way we vary the 'uniform' to fit our individual character."

"I think you've got me there," replied Moon. "And that's a valid point for my article. I'd say that from what I've seen there *is* a lot more individual creativity among Goths than is evident in the more conformist subcultures."

"Glad to be of help."

"Right," said Moon, "have you seen anything here that might replace that tiny skull of yours?"

"What do you mean – I've got a tiny skull?" Sonia deliberately misinterpreted Moon's question.

"You know what I mean; that item of jewellery that got broken a week ago."

"Oh, you mean my clit ring?" replied Sonia out loud; enjoying the obvious embarrassment her frankness caused Moon. "Did you know the tips of your ears go red when you're embarrassed? It's sort of cute." She grinned mischievously then shook her head. "No, I want something special to replace that. I'll probably see something I like at *Dusk 'til Dawn*."

Dusk 'til Dawn Fashions was situated in the covered market behind the main Exchange building and it supplied the kind of clothing Moon had learnt to equate with 'on duty' Goths. The wares displayed in the store's tiny windows were heavy on the use of velvet, satin, lace and leather, mainly in shades of black, dark purple and blood red. There were also some interesting accessories in black latex. "God!" said Moon. "It looks like Lilly Munster, Morticia Addams and Elvira got together and opened a charity shop!"

"Yeah, except for the prices," replied Sonia, pointing to a three figure price tag. Most people only splash out occasionally for the odd item from here and make up the rest of their wardrobe buying stuff off the high street, from real charity shops and off the web. There's even a bit of a cross over with the high street sex shops because they do the odd nice line in corsetry. And, of course, some people make their own costumes. Avril's a dab hand with a sewing machine, which is good because I can't sew a button on straight."

Moon had slipped a small notepad out of his pocket and scribbled a few notes. "That's something else for the article," he said appreciatively.

"Looks like I'm writing it for you; do I get a cut?"

"Only if you'll take it in kind," replied Moon with a wolfish grin.

"Down boy! We can come to some arrangement about that later." Sonia glanced at the small items of jewellery arranged on red satin at the bottom of the window but nothing seemed to meet her fancy. "They've got a bigger jewellery display inside, let's have a look."

The inside of the shop was dark and cramped. Most of the permanent stalls in the covered market were quite small but this one was tiny, presumably to reduce the overheads. There were two more customers in the shop, both of whom Moon recognised from the band festival at the *Hangman's Rest*. With Sonia and Moon and the girl behind the counter there as well the place was crowded. While Sonia browsed the jewellery in a glass topped display, Moon took the opportunity to talk to the assistant. "Hi, I'm doing an article on the local Goth culture for *Venue*, do you mind answering a few questions?"

"Of course not, if it means free advertising," replied the girl, who was wearing a pleasant ensemble of her own wares. Moon found the plunging neckline of her corseted dress most alluring.

Closer examination suggested that the epithet 'girl' was a bit inappropriate; she must be at least in her late thirties. "Are you the owner?" asked Moon.

"Yes, along with Graham, my partner. We take it in turns to work the counter."

"And do you get a good trade here?"

"Well, it's enough to make ends meet and with the Internet sales we do quite well."

"So you have an online store as well?"

"Yes. It's quite a competitive business but we have the advantage that we make a lot of our own stuff so we have something different to offer."

"Really?"

"Yes, Graham makes a lot of the jewellery and I make the dresses. We do buy in some stuff like the leather gear but not having to rely on external suppliers helps to bring the costs down. Some of the stuff here might seem quite pricey but it's quite reasonable compared to other places."

"I suppose that's what comes from being part of a minority customer base," observed Moon.

"Yes, but most of our customers wouldn't think of it that way; appearance is a big part of being a Goth."

"Jerry, what about this one?" asked Sonia, pointing to a small silver bat-shaped stud.

"Don't you think it's a bit spiky? Anyway, with your lower topiary I'd have thought you'd go for something with a bit of green in it."

"Damn, I guess so. Pity I'm too sensitive down there to dye it."

"Are you talking about what I think you're talking about?" asked the proprietor with a laugh.

"Yes, Kalysta. This is Jerry by the way. He's my latest squeeze. Likes other people to call him Moon."

"Hi, Moon," said Kalysta. "So someone's finally hooked our Sonia, and you seem like a nice guy too, if a trifle ordinary." She suddenly looked like she had an idea. "Sonia, if you can't dye your pubes why don't you have a 'Hollywood' instead."

"Uh-uh, no way," replied Sonia, "I'm not using anything sharp down there and I'm definitely *not* having it waxed, not after some of the horror stories I've heard. Anyway I'd probably get a rash. Some of the horrible things I've seen in the showers at the gym would put anyone off."

Moon grinned. "I have to agree, plus 'Hollywoods' remind me too much of plucked chickens, I like a bit of bush."

Sonia hit Moon on the shoulder. "This is my *privates* you're discussing in public!"

Moon laughed. "Well you started it! Anyway, Kalysta, what would you suggest to go with a redhead, if that's the right term."

Well, there's this," replied Kalysta, pointing to a tiny green and gold enamelled dragon's head. "It's one of Graham's favourite designs."

Kalysta opened the cabinet and handed the stud to Sonia. "I like it," she nodded. "Don't you, Jerry?"

"I think he'll look great," replied Moon, "and kind of appropriate when you think of all those fiery curls down there."

Sonia shook her head. "You're incorrigible!" she complained. "We'll take it, Kal."

Moon handed over the asking price of twenty-five pounds. It seemed rather steep for something that would spend most of the time tucked away out of sight, but it was worth it for the smile Sonia gave him. "Now, let's see if there's anything here for you," she said, whirling him towards the racks of clothing.

Moon ended up paying ninety-five pounds for a dark blue, high collared satin jacket with black lace on the cuffs and black brocade down the front and around the collar and he forked out another thirty-five for a set of black, bat shaped shirt studs with matching cufflinks. "We can get a second-hand antique shirt to go with them up on Gloucester Road, then you'll really look the biz."

Moon thought he'd got off lightly as Sonia had been egging him on to buy a pair of leather trousers with thong ties down the outside seams for over two hundred. "I'm sure I will," he replied uncertainly.

"Yeah, we've got to get you kitted out for the next band night," enthused Sonia. "What I think we should do is lighten your hair, bringing out the natural blond and you can have it cut in a close crop. That'll look better on you than black and it'll emphasise the dark blue of your eyes. Luckily, you're already quite pale because you work nights, so a bit of pale slap and a touch of eye make-up and you should look really otherworldly."

"I can't wait," replied Moon, trying not to sound as unenthusiastic as he felt.

On the way out they stopped for a cup of tea and a cake at a vegetarian café in the glass-roofed area between the covered market and the main hall. Moon was tucking into his date and walnut slice when a familiar voice from behind said, "Hullo, Mr Moon, Miss Crest, fancy meeting you here." Detective Inspector Whatley stood framed in the doorway to the main hall, several overflowing carrier bags in one hand and the hand of a small girl wearing a pink, hooded fleece and jeans in the other. A rather horse-faced woman in a T-shirt and jeans stood next to him holding onto a pushchair bearing a bawling toddler of indiscriminate sex. "Sorry, Annie," said Whatley, handing the small girl over to her mother. "Do you mind if I have a quick professional word with my friends here?"

"Okay," replied Annie with the hint of a sigh. "What do you want with your tea?"

"A scone and jam, thanks, love," said Whatley, handing her a ten pound note.

"Hello, Inspector," said Moon as Whatley took a chair at their table. Moon was surprised to see that his jeans and shirt looked like they had been put on crisp and freshly ironed that morning, even the leather jacket he wore looked new and smart. It seemed that Whatley's scruffy persona was reserved for work.

"I'm off duty, Mr Moon, call me Art," said Whatley with a grin.

"You'd better call me Moon then and you know that this is Sonia." Sonia smiled through a mouthful of cake. "Any developments with the murders?" asked Moon.

Whatley nodded. "Well, nothing on those fatal attacks a couple of nights ago but we've arrested Andrew Gibbons for the murders of Dominic Llewellyn, Francis Walters and Lorraine Newton."

"Andy killed them?" asked Sonia. "Why!"

"Well, Mr Walters was a crime of passion as the French say. He and Mr Gibbons were lovers and Mr Gibbons killed him because he had accepted a job in Scotland but wanted to go up there alone. We found Mr Walters' body in a chest freezer at Mr Gibbons' address. Apparently, he couldn't bear to be parted from him even in death."

"But what about the others?" asked Moon. "Surely, that wasn't enough to start him on a killing spree."

"You'd be surprised," replied Whatley sagaciously. "But this is the part which might interest you. Shortly after killing Mr Walters, Andy Gibbons became involved with a local evangelical church, probably because he couldn't cope with the guilt of what he had done, and, here's the odd part, he says that the Lord told him to kill them."

Moon's eyes widened with surprise. "Ah, this is beginning to sound familiar."

"Isn't it just?" At that moment Annie arrived at the table with a tray and stuck a mug of tea and a small plate bearing a scone and individual portions of butter and jam under Whatley's nose. "Thanks, love. This is Annie, my wife and, Annie, this is Moon and Sonia; Moon's been helping me with a difficult case."

"Pleased to meet you," said Annie with a sour smile. She gave Whatley a warning look. "We'll be over there on the next table but one, I'm not having the children exposed to the foul details of one of your cases, and don't be too long, we've got Debenham's to do before we go home and that place is murder on a Saturday," she said sternly before she bustled off back to her table where the children waited. The toddler had stopped bawling and was attempting to cover its entire head and torso with freshly pulped banana, while its sister nibbled daintily on a slice of carrot cake.

Whatley pulled a face. "Lovely woman most of the time but she hates shopping. Well, I can't take too long then. Where was I?"

"Andy Gibbons getting divine revelations," prompted Sonia.

"Oh, yes. He said the 'Lord' came to him at night wearing a hooded cloak and told him to kill one of the Goths who frequent the *Hangman's Rest*. Who he killed didn't matter, what was important was that their body must be found and it must look like they'd been killed by a vampire. He had this special contraption he'd made out of a mole clamp and some plastic fangs; you can…"

"…Get them off the Internet. Yes, I know," interrupted Moon, nodding his head resignedly. "But why did it have to look like a vampire attack?"

"The 'Lord' apparently convinced him that your friend Mr Kievitch is a vampire in more than just pretence and that he was the one truly responsible for Mr Walters' death. It wasn't poor innocent Andy's fault. Oh no. The evil 'vampire' had put the 'fluence on him and made him murder the love of his life. The plan was that he would draw attention to this 'vampire' by leaving fresh kills around the places that he frequents, which would implicate him, leading Mr Kievitch's 'true nature' being exposed so he could be dealt with in the traditional manner; certifiably crazy or what?"

"So it was okay to kill other people to do this? It doesn't seem to make a lot of sense," said Sonia.

"Oh, the 'Lord' assured him that anyone he killed would never be 'saved' so it was okay to bump them off because their lives were worthless anyway. 'Give me that ol' time religion,' eh? Unfortunately, he hid the first body too well so he had to kill again, this time making sure the body was more easily found." Whatley regarded Moon seriously. "Now, this would all look like a classic case of guilt driven delusion, except that over the last three days there have been a large number of seemingly random, fatal and non-fatal attacks where each perpetrator has told almost exactly the same tale with minor variations. So either this is some kind of weird lunatic's conspiracy or something very odd is going on."

"Well, Art," said Moon thoughtfully. "We think we have some leads but I don't think it's anything that would go down too well on a police report sheet."

Annie Whatley, who was getting up from her table and gathering her children and carrier bags, yelled firmly, "Art!"

"Just so long as we can find a way to stop it, sunshine," said Whatley, grimly as he rose from his chair. "Must be off, it seems," he continued, winking at Sonia. "Keep me posted on anything you get from your 'contacts'. I dread to think what's been happening today now there's no rain to keep the loonies off the streets. Let's get this madness over quickly, eh?"

"I'll do all I can, Art," replied Moon sincerely as he shook Whatley's hand.

"Just one thing, Moon." Whatley waved to his beckoning wife to say he was coming and turned his knowing gaze back to Moon. "Your mate, Uri, he really is a vampire, isn't he?"

"I can't say, Inspector," replied Moon as truthfully as he could.

"Thought so," Whatley's face was a mask of shrewdness. "Well, as long as he keeps his nose clean on my beat he can expect no trouble from me, tell him."

"I'll do that," said Moon to Whatley's retreating back.

"Well, well, DI Whatley, the hen-pecked husband," observed Sonia. "I wonder if his wife knows what he wears to work."

"I reckon it's his little bit of rebellion," replied Moon with a wink. "He hasn't a chance to be scruffy at home so he makes up for it at work; he's probably got a pristine suit in his locker that he puts on just before he goes home." They both laughed.

"Whatley's right though," said Sonia. "There could be attacks happening even now. Do you think we should have gone back to Uri's last night after all?"

"I don't think Uri was in a fit state." Moon shook his head. "Rurik's return seems to have really shaken him up."

"Is there anything we can do on our own, do you think?"

"I don't think we can do anything to stop the attacks that might happen today but there could be something we can do to prepare for this evening."

"What's that?" asked Sonia, eyes brightening with interest.

"I think it's time for you to meet a very special little girl," replied Moon cryptically.

Chapter 18

Moon and Sonia caught the bus from the city centre then walked the three hundred metres to Moon's flat. "I want to see you in that gear when we get up there," said Sonia with a predatory smile.

"It may have to wait for a while," replied Moon as he fumbled for his door keys. "I apologise for the state of the place, I'm not much of a housekeeper."

"Not too many men are in my experience," replied Sonia.

As they approached the second floor landing Anna popped into view. *"Hello, Jerry,"* she vibed. *"Who's this?"*

"Hi, Anna, this is Sonia, my new girlfriend."

"Is there someone there?" said Sonia, her eyes peering into the patch of thin air that Moon seemed to be speaking to. "You know, I can almost see something; is it a little girl?"

"She can see me?" vibed Anna in surprise.

"Yes, I thought she might," Moon vibed back silently. Aloud he said, "I thought you might be able to see her, with a little effort. Those spooky feelings of yours set me thinking that you might be a latent psychic."

"Why's she dressed like an extra from a sixties' vampire film?"

"You watch too much television," teased Moon. *"It's because she's what's called a Goth. I'll explain later."*

"Did she speak to you just then?" asked Sonia.

"Yes, she was asking about the way you dress."

"I thought that was what she said; something about vampire movies? And you actually replied to her without speaking?"

"Yes, I call it vibing; sometimes it's more convenient when there are living people around and I need to speak to a spirit. Anyway, I'd better introduce you so we can get off the stairs. Sonia, this is Anna, she died here nearly a hundred years ago when she was four years old."

Anna curtseyed and said, *"Hello, Sonia."*

Sonia laughed incredulously. "I actually heard that! Hello, Anna."

"Anna," said Moon, "I was wondering if you'd be willing to teach Sonia what you taught me yesterday. I want to get her as familiar as possible with her own psychic abilities before this evening when Uri's going to train us to fight spirits. It looks like there's some real trouble coming and I want Sonia to be able to protect herself."

"Fine, Jerry, I'll meet you upstairs." She eyed Sonia for a second. *"Although I don't know what you're worried about; in that get up she'll frighten away anything that wants to attack you."*

"You should see her with fangs," Moon vibed back with a grin.

"Hey, hang on…!" complained Sonia, but Anna had already vanished upstairs. "She's got a smart mouth for a four-year-old."

"Yeah, well she's had ten decades to perfect it," replied Moon as they climbed the stairs. "Don't take it to heart, she's just terminally bored and not used to company."

"And has a crush on you the size of the Atlantic, or hadn't you noticed. She's jealous, Jerry!"

"Oh?" Moon hadn't noticed. "I hadn't thought of that. I mean she's so young."

"Four; going on a hundred? Anyway, little girls get crushes just like big girls do; poor thing it must be so confusing for her being stuck like that. Not to say frustrating."

"Well, she goes in for a little poltergeist activity to vent the latter. Perhaps we'd better not make love here to spare her feelings." He opened the door to his flat.

"I think that might be for the best," replied Sonia. "Oh God, Jerry, this is squalid," she continued as she saw the inside of his bed-sit.

"It's okay," said Moon defensively, "*and* I'm not forking out five to six hundred a month to pay someone else's mortgage."

"I suppose so," replied Sonia eyeing a damp patch on the wall.

"I'm here, Jerry," vibed Anna from the sitting area.

"Hi, Anna," replied Moon. "Let's get started shall we?"

Sonia tilted her head as if she was trying to pinpoint a small noise. "She's over there by the settee, is that right?"

"Yes, that's right." Anna, jumped up and down.

"Thanks, Anna, I can hear you better than I can see you." Sonia sat down on the shabby green settee.

"Describe how you see and hear me," said Anna. *"It's important."*

"I sort of see you here," explained Sonia, pointing to the centre of her forehead. "And I hear you a bit behind that. It's almost like imagining, but not quite."

"That's called 'clairsentience'," explained Moon. "Where you don't exactly see or hear the Spiritual but sense it instead. Whereas I'm fully clairvoyant, meaning that I see the Spiritual pretty much as if it's part of normality, although I hear it more like a clairsentient medium, in my head."

"I call it 'ghost sense'," interjected Anna. *"If you can sense with it then theoretically you should be able to fight with it as well."*

Anna proceeded to teach Sonia how to extend her ghost sense to touch and harm spirits in the same way she had taught Moon. It took a little longer because of Sonia's more limited abilities but having the two of them learning together helped them both to refine their technique. Eventually, each was able to snap hard at the other's inner ghost with a psychic extension, causing pain and, Anna assured them, spiritual drainage. *"Now, don't over exert yourselves,"* she cautioned. *"You both need to be fresh if Uri's going to put you through your paces tonight."*

"Okay," said Moon, turning on the television. "It's time for the evening news; let's see what extra damage Rurik's crazies have done today." But surprisingly, although they watched through the entire national and local news programme, there was no mention of further attacks.

"That's odd," said Sonia. "Whatley was sure there'd be more today."

"So was I," said Moon. "I wonder what's going on?"

"I hadn't wanted to mention this," vibed Anna, *"but something huge has been making waves in the Spiritual for the*

last couple of days. Perhaps this Rurik has accumulated enough power not to need any more killings."

"Possibly," replied Moon. "Or perhaps the police have decided to stop the media reporting any more assaults in order to avoid a panic. I think I'd better phone Detective Inspector Whatley as soon as possible and ask him about this. I wonder if he's got a shift on Sunday."

"We need to get going if we're walking it to Uri's," said Sonia. It's on the other side of the Downs, isn't it?"

"Yes, you're right," answered Moon, grabbing his jacket. "Sorry, Anna, we're going to have to love you and leave you, I'm afraid."

"That's all right, Jerry. I've enjoyed the company; this is more people than I've had a chance to talk to in nearly a century." She placed a phantom kiss on Moon's cheek then ran over to Sonia and did the same.

"We'll have to do it again sometime under less difficult circumstances," promised Sonia. "Thanks for the teaching session; I'm sure it'll be useful against Rurik."

"If I wasn't tied to this place I'd help you myself," replied the little ghost pugnaciously.

They left the house and made their way up to the Downs via the middle class neighbourhoods of Cotham and Whiteladies Road. The Downs are a large area of parkland on the northeast side of Bristol. On the City side they border onto the prosperous areas of Westbury, Redland and Clifton. Uri lived on the northwest side of the Downs near the Avon Gorge, where Brunel's famous suspension bridge spans the river. It was a forty minute walk from where Moon lived, but both he and Sonia were reasonably fit and it was less trouble to walk there than to try to cross an outlying part of the city by bus. Uri's home turned out to be an impressive looking, three-storey, detached Georgian town house with a large and immaculately tended front garden. "It's a bit of a far cry from a crumbling gothic castle, isn't it?" commented Sonia with a hint of disappointment.

"Well, what did you expect? Gloomy turrets and a sign saying 'beware of the bat'?"

"I'm not sure what I expected but this isn't it," replied Sonia, ringing the doorbell.

A tall, elegantly dressed woman, who looked to be in her mid-fifties, answered the door. "Good evening," she said with a smile. "I take it that you are the guests that Uri is expecting."

"Yes, that's us; I'm Moon and this is Sonia."

"And my name is Karen Maddocks. I assume Uri has told you about his long standing relationship with our family."

"He has indeed," replied Moon, stepping through the door into a spacious hallway, well lit by the multicoloured beams of light that poured through stained glass windows above and on either side of the ornate oak and wrought iron front door.

"He would have liked to have greeted you himself but he has a problem with the evening sunlight at this time of the year."

"I suppose he would," commented Sonia. "Pardon my curiosity but just how big a problem does he have with the sun? I'm a bit of a gothic horror junkie and it's one thing a lot of the stories don't agree on."

"Well, it's like extremely bad sunburn so it's not as pyrotechnically dramatic as Hollywood sometimes makes it out to be, but an hour or so out in direct sunlight would probably kill them. Uri says that exposure to full sunlight is like standing in front of an open furnace."

"Exactly," said Uri's rich baritone as he pulled open a door at the end of the hallway, which lay beyond the reach of the sun's penetrating beams. "Here, in the shadows or at twilight, it is actually pleasant but full daylight is quite deadly. Welcome, my friends, to our home. If you would come through here to the dining room, dinner is almost ready."

Uri ushered them into an impressive room, which had at its centre a long, dark oak dining table of Moroccan design with ornate metal fixtures at the top of the legs and a complex marquetry mosaic of various woods inlaid in the centre. Matching chairs surrounded it and the accessories and wall decorations continued the Moorish theme. "This is beautiful," said Sonia, running her fingers over the ornately carved back of a chair.

"Yes, Karen is a wonder when it comes to home design."

"Well, Charli helped me out," said Karen Maddocks modestly. "She comes originally from Andalusia, you know, and the Moorish influence was much stronger when she lived there."

Moon noticed that the room had a northeast facing window, which would allow the vampires to dine here in the evenings in relative comfort for most of the year. Karen took their coats and Uri motioned for them to take their seats, drawing back Sonia's chair for her. "The rest of the family will be down shortly," he said. "They're waiting for the dinner gong."

"Getting back to our earlier subject," said Sonia. "Why don't you use sun block?"

"It doesn't work," said Roanne, who had entered the room like a ghost. "It isn't ultra violet that's the problem, it's the more spiritual influence of the sun; it's been a potent symbol of the power of Light for millennia and, whatever else we might be, we are creatures of Darkness." She took a seat beside Moon. "Fortunately, Darkness isn't necessarily evil any more than Light is necessarily good. They both have their place in the balance of things, which is one thing my people have never forgotten, despite the incursions of Christianity."

"By your people you mean the Welsh?" asked Moon.

"By my people I mean the British Celts," replied Roanne proudly. "'Welsh' is a name that was forced on us in cruel jest by the Saxons. It means 'slaves'. Memories of older wisdom and older truths linger on in all the Celtic fringes of Britain, where wave after wave of invaders have failed to stamp them out."

"Roanne, don't preach," admonished Uri. "You must forgive Roanne, my friends. She was born in a time when the animosity between the Welsh and the English was much stronger than it is now."

Moon smiled. "From what I've heard of those times I can understand your feelings, Roanne. I hate to think what it must have been like to be Welsh in the fifteen hundreds."

"Far from pleasant, I can tell you," replied Roanne.

Uri leaned forward in his chair. "You had an important question for Karen, Moon, didn't you?" he prompted with a nod. "I think it's best to ask her now, before the children come down."

"What?" said Moon. Then he remembered their discussion of a few days ago. "Oh that." He paused trying to think how to phrase the delicate question then decided the best he could do was ask bluntly. "Mrs Maddocks, are you free or are you and your family somehow enslaved by Uri, Charli and Roanne?"

"Call me 'Karen', please, Moon," replied Karen with a laugh. "And it's a good thing Uri warned me you might ask this or it would have been a bad enough insult for me to insist that you leave. Am I a slave, labouring under the power of evil vampires? You'll have to judge for yourself whether I'm telling the truth or doing my masters' bidding, but no, I am not a slave. Am I 'free'? That is a harder question. I would have to answer no; my family is not free and nor are Uri and the girls for we are all bound by ties of love and family loyalty that go back generations. Does that answer your question?"

"Very well," replied Moon. "I'm sorry if I caused any offence, I just had to be sure. Choosing whether or not to trust a vampire is a big decision."

"I understand," replied Karen. "Uri is honest, trustworthy and honourable. Twenty generations of Maddocks' and Llewellyn's can testify to that."

"I'm glad to hear it. Sonia and I may well be staking our lives on Uri's reliability very soon."

"Ah, yes. Uri has told us about this villain, Rurik, and the situation sounds like it could get very dangerous indeed. All I can say is that, while life holds no certainties, Uri has been our families' protector for nearly five centuries and he hasn't failed us yet, even against supernatural threats like the one you're facing now."

"I'd like to hear about those threats sometime," commented Moon.

"I'm sure we could arrange that if you'd like. You wouldn't be disappointed. Some of our family legends are quite spectacular," replied Karen, smiling and raising her eyebrows.

At that moment Charli poked her head around the door to the kitchen and said, "It's ready, could someone bang the gong." Roanne got up from her seat and beat a rapid summons on a small silver gong, which hung on an ornate oriental style stand on an occasional table by the door. Within seconds members of the Maddocks clan began to appear, starting with a small boy who entered at full pelt and jumped into Uri's lap with a joyful, "Hello Unkie Uri! Mam got me a Hahyie Pott, look!" he waved the stuffed Harry Potter toy under Uri's nose.

"Isn't that wonderful, Corwin?" replied Uri, taking the proffered toy and making him swoop through the air on his broomstick.

"Yes, and Mam says I can have a Hag'id if I'm a good boy."

"Well, you'd better be very good then, hadn't you," said Uri, handing the toy back to the child.

"Yes, ve'y good," said Corwin seriously, taking the doll and running off to find his mother.

There were five generations of Maddocks living in the house: from Karen's ninety-three year old mother-in-law, Sarah, who could easily have passed for someone two decades younger, to Karen's great grandson, Corwin, who was three. The Maddocks men were represented by Karen's husband, Bedyw, patriarch of the family, and their youngest son, Owen, who at twenty was studying law at Bristol University. As well as Corwin two other children were present: Bridget, Corwin's aunt, who was fourteen, and his big sister Poppy, who was eight. Corwin's mother, Gwynneth was in her mid-twenties and was taking time off from her job as administrator for the family's jewellry business to be a stay at home mother. Her husband, Griffin, was away on business in London. Moon was forced to change his estimate of Karen's age. He doubted teenage pregnancies were common in this family so she must be in her early to mid sixties. Uri's comment about the vampires' bites keeping the family young must be true. "This is just part of the clan," said Karen, who had been explaining who was who to Moon and Sonia. "There are nearly two hundred of us now, including the Llewellyns and the few Maddocks who stayed in Wales. Most of us are in the South West and Wales but there's quite an enclave in London because of the stores we opened there in the thirties. But we're not all involved in the jewellery trade any more, there are Maddocks and Llewellyns in most of the professions."

With the help of the older children Charli brought in the serving dishes, which were terracotta with a glazed Moorish design. The meal was very Andalusian, starting with gazpacho soup, followed by Madhûna chicken with spiced couscous and sultanas, accompanied with a salad of endives, tomato, chopped boiled egg, tuna and tarragon. For sweet they had khushkananaj, bread-like rolls filled with a sugar and almond paste, a bit like small Danish pastries. Charli broke tradition with these by serving them with custard.

"Is all this authentic medieval Spanish," asked Sonia, after tasting the chicken.

"With a modern twist," affirmed Charli, waving a hand to indicate the table. "Some ingredients are hard to find now and I've changed a few of them for convenience sake. For instance we used to use a fermented barley sauce called murri naqî in just about everything. It was horrible to make and when I discovered that soy sauce tasted virtually the same I gave up having bowls of rotting barley cakes in the pantry for good."

"Yuck!" observed Sonia with disgust. "How on earth does someone decide to try something like that for the first time?"

"I'm not sure," replied Charli. "Perhaps they were trying to make a new kind of beer."

"Sounds feasible," chipped in Moon. "But then you have to answer the question of why they first made beer. I don't think it's an obvious thing to do to ferment grains and drink the results. This sort of thing always gives me visions of some prehistoric pioneer who went around sampling various disgusting concoctions to see what they did to him and making a list of the results."

"Yeah," joked Uri, "and the last one he tried killed him." They all laughed.

After the younger children had been taken up to bed, Uri looked outside into the deepening twilight and said, "Well, my friends, I think it's time we got down to business. Karen, Bedyw, we must take our leave of you and the rest of the family." He rose from his chair and addressed Moon and Sonia. "We need to go outside to practise our fighting skills. There's a place not far from the Downs where we should be safe from prying eyes and we might find a suitable subject for our practice."

"A subject?" asked Moon, surprised. "But I thought we would be practising on each other."

"Some things can only be learnt in action," replied Uri. "Besides, this way we can – what is the expression? – kill two birds with one stone. I've heard rumours that there's a rather annoying little goblin haunting part of Leigh Woods that I've been meaning to do something about for a while."

Moon's blood ran cold. The memories of his recent encounter with the Shadow Beast were still very fresh in his mind. "Is it safe?" he asked.

"Safe? Of course it's not safe," Roanne sneered. "What's the point of hunting something if it's safe?"

"Gently, Roanne," interjected Uri, "remember, Moon was attacked by a particularly nasty graveyard haunt earlier in the week."

"Oh, sorry, Moon, I'd forgotten," Roanne apologised. "That's enough to make anyone wary of rushing into another supernatural battle."

Uri placed a long fingered hand on Moon's shoulder. "Moon, the thing in Leigh Woods is a *frightener*; a goblin that lives off fear, so the greatest danger it poses is that it might scare someone to death. It's nowhere near as powerful as that shadow creature we encountered but it will fight when it's cornered so prepare yourself for scary noises and visions and remember there are five of us and three of us are vampires, so it has every reason to be afraid of *us*."

"Well, if you say so," said Moon, not too reassured. The prospect of fighting any kind of supernatural beastie had not even occurred to him when he had considered tonight's possible activities. "Let's go then."

Chapter 19

It was nearly an hour's walk from the vampires' home to Leigh Woods. Moon had declined the offer of a lift from Uri and the girls. While it would have been quicker to fly, the thought of traversing the Avon Gorge at nearly three hundred feet supported only by someone else's arms, no matter how supernaturally strong they were, was enough to put him off flying for life. However, the prospect of crossing the Clifton Suspension Bridge in the dark almost made him consider changing his mind. Over a thousand people had committed suicide by jumping off the bridge since its completion in 1864 until the late 1980s, when the installation of a safety net had served to discourage all but the most determined jumpers. The spiritual atmosphere surrounding it resonated with generations of anger and despair. "What's wrong with this place, Jerry?" whispered Sonia, gripping his arm as they walked past the toll booth. "It feels horrible."

"The echoes of suicides," answered Moon, "hundreds of them." He put his arm around her for comfort. "It's just the impact of all that negative emotion on the atmosphere, love. Most suicides pass on just like anyone else. From my experience there aren't too many ghosts here and I don't think I've ever met anyone here that had actually taken their own life."

"Jerry Moon," said Sonia reproachfully, "what have you let me in for? Am I going to spend the rest of my life experiencing horrible things like this?"

"You get used to it," replied Moon consolingly. "And it's really not too bad as long as you steer clear of places where people die regularly, like hospital casualty departments. And, of course, places like this, where people kill themselves."

"I didn't kill meself," whispered a malicious ghost voice in Moon's inner ear. *"Good place fer dumpin' bodies, this. Not so many questions asked when they fishes them from the drink."* The voice's owner, a hulking brute in shabby Victorian

workman's clothes, materialised beside them and continued chattily, *"'Course I fell off one day, didn't I, gettin' rid of this old bird I robbed. Weighed a ton she did... I 'ad an awful time gettin' 'er over the railings, then I got tangled up in 'er skirts an' she dragged me down like the proverbial millstone. So now I 'aunts this place. It's not too bad, decent view like but there ain't too many people to chat wif, if yer know what I mean."*

The oppressive atmosphere on the bridge was already putting Sonia on edge and this fresh intrusion was the last straw. "Bugger off!" she said sharply, snapping out a line of ghost energy and catching the over-friendly murderer across the face with an edge of blue fire.

"'Old 'ard, lady, there's no call for that kind o' thing. I was only tryin' to be friendly like."

"I'm no friend of yours and there's more where that came from, so, piss off, you murdering scum!"

The footpad's ghost dematerialised with an air of injured virtue muttering, *"Bloody Livin', just 'cause I wanted to pass the time of day. I'd give yer wot for if I was alive."*

"So... you seem to have already learnt a little about how to use your spiritual powers," observed Uri with surprise.

"Anna's given Sonia and me some lessons."

"Anna? Ah, your little ghost friend. I wouldn't have thought she'd be that capable."

"There's more to her than meets the eye," replied Moon. "She's bound here to help work out someone else's unfinished business, not going through her own so she's more aware of the world of the living than most ghosts."

"Interesting, her contribution should make this night's work a lot easier."

They neared the end of the bridge feeling like they had run an emotional gauntlet. "Who's the guy in the topper?" asked Sonia pointing to a lone figure that she sensed was standing in the mist rising from the River Severn which swirled around the entrance to the bridge.

"It's old Izzy himself," whispered Moon, "Isambard Kingdom Brunel, no less. I've seen him a few times around Bristol, visiting his past triumphs like the railway station and the Great Western but he's supposed to like it here the best. You could say it's his 'unfinished business' because he died five years before it was completed."

"Evening, Mr Brunel," said Sonia with a wave. "Nice bridge."

"Most gratified," replied the great engineer, removing a half-smoked cigar from his mouth with one hand while doffing his famous stovepipe hat with the other. *"And a very good evening to you too."*

"Now, it is only safe to assume that the creature we're hunting is ancient and very cunning," warned Uri, as they walked towards the A369 and the entrance to the Ashton Court Estate. "So we need to be alert for tricks. It'll probably try to either frighten or lure us into danger so it's very important that we stay together and keep a close rein on our instinct to run. I don't want any broken legs or necks tonight. It is possible that our quarry could be connected to Stonleigh Camp, the old hill fort that's situated on the ridge over there to our right. It may even have been bound here by the local tribe to prevent their enemies from attacking by the lower slope to the west. The old Celts were quite well versed in the art of sorcery. If that is the case it is likely that they have planted one or two more spooky surprises in reserve against the possibility of their guard dog being muzzled. So we need to be prepared for the worst. If it looks like things are about to get nasty I'll yell: 'To Me!' and I want you two to close in behind us." He indicated Charli and Roanne. "We have the experience in dealing with the big supernatural nasties, so your job is to stay out of trouble and let us handle it, okay?"

"Okay." Moon and Sonia nodded in unison.

They took a right turn up a side road. The street sign read 'Church Road' and Moon recognised the neighbourhood; he and his friends had parked their cars up here on their visits to the Ashton Court music festival in previous years. As they walked past the high value properties on either side of the narrow wood-lined road Uri briefed them further. "Your friend Anna seems to have given you a good basis in how to reach out with your spirit and deal minor damage to supernatural beings but I need to teach you how to take this a step further so you are able to do real harm. To do this you don't just strike at the surface but reach deep inside your target, seizing the very heart of its being, and literally tear its life out. That way you can neutralise a supernatural foe like our goblin. You won't be able to kill it but you can deplete it enough to prevent it from doing harm for a very long time."

"So, how do we do that?" asked Sonia.

They had now reached the junction of Church Road and North Road, which ran along the southern edge of the woods. "The entrance to the woods is just a few yards down on the right," replied Uri. "We'll stop when we get there and I'll show you how. It is much easier to demonstrate than to explain."

It only took a couple of minutes for them to walk to the gateway that allowed access to the main footpath through the woods. "I don't fancy going into that," commented Moon, regarding the thick darkness under the trees with suspicion. It reminded him all too clearly of the Shadow Beast on Bird Cage Walk.

"None of us do," Uri answered grimly, "but nevertheless we will. Now, to business." He looked around then gestured to a small pile of rocks at the side of the path. "These should do."

"What're we going to do? Throw them at the goblin?" asked Sonia, incredulously.

"No, we will use them for target practice. You see everything has its own spiritual field or aura, even things which aren't actually alive like these rocks. A thing's aura helps maintain its presence in the material world, which makes it physically vulnerable to psychic attack. Watch…"

Moon saw a faint line of blue fire thrust forward from Uri's forehead and strike the topmost rock. The rock seemed to glow slightly for an instant then the line snapped away, dragging something faint and vaguely rock-shaped with it and the rock itself vanished in a puff of dust. "Jesus!" whispered Moon in awe.

"Did he just do what I think I saw him do?" asked Sonia, gazing at the slightly diminished pile of rocks with a shocked expression.

"What I did was remove the rock's spiritual substance," explained Uri. "Without which it could no longer exist. Well, not as a rock, anyway."

"Could you do that to a person?" asked Moon, horrified at the possibility.

"Theoretically, yes, but it would require more energy than a vampire or a human possesses. However, using a moderate amount of power one could affect their internal organs, which would hurt them or even possibly kill them if the attacker focused... on their heart, for example."

"I feel like you've just thrust a loaded gun into my hands and I need to be extremely careful where I point it." Moon shook his head.

"Power and responsibility are old bedfellows, my friend." Uri nodded at the rocks. "Now it is your turn."

Moon concentrated on a smallish stone near the top of the pile and snapped out at it with a psychic tendril like Anna had taught them. The stone wobbled slightly but was otherwise unharmed. "That was pretty pathetic, wasn't it?" he commented, crestfallen.

"Not bad for a start but you need to build upon what your little poltergeist friend has shown you. You need to reach out with your spirit inside of the rock, grasp its very essence, then take a firm hold on it and yank it out."

"Like this?" asked Sonia, a strand of glowing blue leapt from her brows into the centre of a medium sized rock in the pile then snapped back and the rock crumbled into a pile of sand and gravel.

"Yay!" said Roanne, slapping Sonia on the back. "Chalk one up for the girls, Charli."

Moon's confidence went down another notch. "Ignore them, Moon. I know you have it in you," encouraged Uri. "Give it another go. Try that big one on the top."

"Are you sure?" asked Moon, eyeing the two kilogram rock with trepidation.

"Sure, I'm sure," Uri grinned at Moon. "It's not a matter of size, just application. You could do it to one of the rocks from Stonehenge if you wanted to."

"Okay," said Moon uncertainly. "Here goes." He reached out with his ghost sense, feeling the size and weight and density of the rock and sensing faintly the gently pulsing energy that was its life force. Grabbing that luminous core with all his spiritual might, he wrenched it out of the rock itself and watched in astonishment as the rock collapsed in on itself and vanished entirely. He suddenly felt utterly wretched... what he had done was *wrong*. It may have been *only* a rock but he somehow *knew* he had just abused the entire matrix of life, leaving it missing a small but irreplaceable piece. "That was horrible," he muttered, covering his face with both hands.

"I'm sorry, Moon. I should have warned you but I was worried that if I did you wouldn't want to practise. This is the only way I know that does such little damage."

"What's up?" asked Sonia, staring at Moon with concern.

"You only took part of the life force from your rock, Sonia, so most of it still exists as sand and debris. Moon, however, completely destroyed his so he has to cope with the spiritual impact of having altered the web of nature. Such destruction, no matter how small or insignificant it seems, harms Gaia, the great Spirit of the Earth, to whom we're all connected."

"Will it be like this when we take on the goblin?" asked Moon. "If it does I don't think I can go ahead with this."

"No, it won't." Uri's white-blond hair whirled around his head as he shook it emphatically. "You can't destroy a spirit the way you destroyed the rock; all you can do is injure it enough to prevent it from doing more harm. Don't be fearful on that count my friend."

Sonia insisted on trying another rock to make sure she could do it properly, despite Moon's protestations, and then really wished that she hadn't when she managed to eradicate it and the inevitable impact hit her. "Ooh, that's *bad*!" she complained.

"I warned you," commented Moon, shaking his head with pity.

"Right," said Uri, "I think we're as ready as we'll ever be, so let's get going. We need to take the path to the right, which goes along the rim of the valley and then on up to the ridge of the old hill fort. It shouldn't take long to find what we're looking for. Now, whatever happens, stick together. This thing will try to separate us so it can attack each of us alone."

The path was easy to make out in the moonlight, distinct and quite well worn. Nightingale Valley, as the stretch of woodland below the hill fort is called, was a favourite haunt of mountain bikers during the day and the earth of the pathways through the woods was criss-crossed with their tracks. This created a difficult and uneven surface to negotiate in the dark. They were roughly a third of the way to the top, when Moon stumbled over one very deep tyre ridge. Sonia caught him, just in time to prevent him tumbling over the side of the path into the steep fall to the valley below, and Charli and Roanne rushed to help. They quickly got Moon onto safer ground and, as Sonia was helping him dust mud off the bottom of his coat, they heard Uri say, "Charli and Roanne, I think you two should scout ahead, I'll stay with the humans and make sure they're safe."

As the girls floated off into the darkness of the woods Sonia turned to Uri. "What happened to sticking together?" she asked.

"They can look after themselves and I wish to take you by a safer route," he replied, leading them off along a less well-trodden path which branched away from the main one.

A few minutes later, Moon could hardly see his hand in front of his face. "Are you sure this is the right path?" he asked Uri, who was walking as silently as ever at his left.

"Oh, yesss!" hissed the vampire, turning a face of hideously distorted evil on Moon. His yellow eyes were glowing slits of malevolence under heavy serrated brows, which met over a dripping hole in place of a nose. Underneath this grinned a mouth full of far too many sharp and uneven teeth.

Moon took an involuntary step backwards and felt himself begin to plummet feet first down a hidden shaft. "Jerry!" screamed Sonia, lunging in futility to catch him. Moon felt certain that he was plummeting to his death, but suddenly felt all the wind expelled from his lungs as another body cannonballed into him, knocking him to safety. It was Uri, the *real* Uri, who cradled Moon gently onto the ground and paused for an instant to check he was alright, before leaping up to do battle with his own doppelganger.

"It's not me!" he cried to Sonia. "It's the goblin pretending to be me!"

Sonia, who had already decided to act against their attacker, whether it was Uri or not, struck out with her ghost sense, ripping a chunk out of the creature's face. "Damn!" she spat when she realised that she hadn't done enough damage to disable it.

Turning what was left of its ruined countenance towards them, its remaining eye shimmering with furious malice, the goblin snarled and doubled in size, shape-shifting into an ogre-like form with long apelike arms, each ending in three scythe-like claws. "Don't be fooled," said Uri, "it can't harm us, it's all bluff." Then he launched his own attack on the creature, leaving a gaping hole in its chest, which leaked reddish ectoplasm like a mist of blood.

"Mine!" shouted Moon, who had finally regained his breath. He climbed purposefully to his feet. Adopting a defiant posture with his feet planted well apart, he raised his arms and a lance of pure light poured out of him into the body of the wounded beast, ripping away what was left of its substance. Very quickly, nothing was left but a single tiny red pinpoint that sped away into the darkness of the trees. "Bloody thing damn near killed me!" he said, the fury dying slowly from his eyes.

"Well, you really gave it what for, darling," Sonia commented with amusement playing around her lips.

"We all did," said Uri with a grin.

"What happened to you?" asked Moon.

"It was wilier and more powerful than I expected." Uri shook his head at his own lack of vigilance. "It waited until everyone else was distracted then trapped me with a tangling spell. It took me nearly ten minutes to break out of it and stop wandering in circles…" Uri might have explained further but a frantic ululating cry pierced the woods from the direction of the hill fort. "That's Charli," he said urgently, pointing up the hill. "There must be more evil at work in these woods. Come on, they need our help."

They followed the path to a wider clearing in the woods near the top of the hill fort, where Roanne and Charli were battling fiercely in the darkness with something Moon couldn't quite make out in the shadows.

"Bugger!" swore Uri, whose vampiric senses were more acute than a human's. "Skeletons, lots of them! We're in real trouble now!"

"Why?" asked Moon naively. "I've fought hundreds of these things in computer games. They just fly apart if you hit them hard enough."

"That may be true for your games," explained Uri with exasperation. "In real life they just fly back together again." He looked around. "They'll be animated by some kind of magical power source, which should be somewhere nearby. We need to find *that* quickly and destroy it."

One of the ancient warriors approached at a run, waving a rusty iron-tipped spear, a strangled, bird-like screech issuing from its lipless mouth. Uri punched its head into the trees then made a sweeping, kung-fu like kick to its thorax, scattering ribs and vertebrae over a wide distance. "Look, Moon, I'll keep them at bay while you and Sonia search for their power source. It should be quite obvious to someone with your talents." The pieces of the shattered warrior were quickly drawing together. His body was already almost complete and Moon caught glimpses of the skull rushing through the undergrowth. The way its teeth were snapping reminded him obscenely of an angry Yorkshire terrier.

"To me!" cried Uri, ripping a branch from a nearby tree to use as a weapon.

The two vampire girls flew through the air, landing on either side of him. "Where the hell did you get to?" asked Roanne angrily.

"I'll explain later," replied Uri, swiping at the reformed skeleton with his makeshift club. "There's no time now. We need to protect Moon and Sonia while they look for whatever's controlling these things."

The vampires formed a protective triangle around the two humans, who huddled together in the centre and tried to ignore the battle going on around them as they concentrated on pinpointing the skeleton warriors' power source.

There were nearly twenty of the skeletons, each wearing the tattered remnants of Iron Age armour and the occasional piece of jewellery, like a ring or torc. His senses sharpened with adrenaline, Moon was distracted to observe that these items seemed to hover over the bones as if supported by invisible flesh. Probably just another characteristic of the spell that animated them he supposed. He seriously doubted that there had been twenty complete skeletons lying in the soil of the mound, the magic must have somehow gathered them together from dust and fragments.

"Jerry," whispered Sonia, who had been concentrating more on the task Uri had given them. "I may be wrong but are there sort of *strings* attached to each of the skeletons?"

Moon quickly ducked a wildly thrown axe then focused his concentration on their attackers. "I see what you mean," he said with surprise. It was very faint but each skeleton had a misty tendril running from it and they all seemed to run towards the centre of the hill fort. "Uri, I think we've found what we're looking for."

Uri turned to Moon. He was holding a skeletal arm in each hand, which continued to claw at him with their sharp, bony talons, despite their removal from their owner. "Where?" he asked, flinging his grisly burdens far into the forest.

"Over there," Moon pointed.

"Right, Charli, Roanne!" he shouted to his embattled lovers. "We need to head for the centre of the fort, over there."

"But we'll have to go straight through the middle of them," complained Charli.

"Then that is what we must do," replied Uri firmly. "We can't leave these things wandering around or the woods won't be safe night *or* day."

Trying to maintain their protective formation, the five of them, started moving towards the centre of what would have been the old fort's main enclosure. It was dangerous work for the humans because their ancient foes were armed with solid weapons and seemed to have retained the skill to use them. The vampires were in less peril, as long as they kept their heads on their shoulders and prevented any of their opponents' wooden shafts from piercing their hearts, but they were finding it a struggle to protect their more vulnerable friends from harm.

"I've had enough of this," muttered Moon under his breath as an ancient spear shaft grazed his leg. He grabbed the spear before its owner could retract it and struck the nearest grinning skull between the eyes with the butt of the shaft, knocking it into the undergrowth. He then smashed his borrowed weapon down on the decapitated warrior's breast bone, scattering ribs everywhere. When the rest of it continued attacking he desperately smacked the spear's butt into the middle of its spine, effectively snapping the skeleton in two.

"Sweeping strokes," said Uri, snatching up the warrior's sword from its searching fingers and tossing it to Sonia, "and try to scatter the bones as far apart as possible, especially the skulls." As if to demonstrate this he made a high, sweeping kick at his nearest oncoming assailant, knocking its helmeted skull into the woods.

Moon whirled his spear at another skeleton, catching it in mid thorax and dispersing bits of bone over a twenty metre area. "How come all modern vampires seem to know kung-fu?" he asked.

"This isn't kung-fu," replied Uri, effortlessly kicking through his headless assailant's rib cage and spine. "It's called *Thor's Hammer*. It's an ancient Viking combat technique I learned in Kiev. Not all martial arts come from the East you know."

Sonia screamed, bringing Moon quickly to her side. He could see that she had been wounded but didn't have time to investigate further because her assailant was pressing in for the kill. Fuming with anger and worry, he stuck his spear between its legs, tipped it over then delivered a devastating kick to its head, sending its skull curving up and out over the ridge and down into Nightingale Valley, then he jumped on its ribcage, pounding the brittle bones into pieces and kicking them around. "I think you can stop now, Moon," said Uri, surveying their battlefield where nothing but fragments of skeletons twitched and writhed, struggling to reform. "We seem to have a respite. Moon, do what you can for Sonia, quickly! Then we need to break for the source of these horrors before they can reform themselves."

Moon, approached Sonia, who looked very pale and faint. "Let's see," he said.

Sonia took her arm out of her right coat sleeve and displayed her wound to Moon. "I feel a bit sick and wobbly."

"Sit down on the ground and try taking a few deep breaths." He crouched down with her and examined the wound as best he could in the dark. The skeleton's blade had sliced lengthwise down through the muscle of Sonia's bicep. The wound was quite deep and obviously painful, but thankfully it hadn't hit any major blood vessels. "I need something clean to bind this with," he said, looking up at their companions.

Charli tore a strip of white lace off one of her cuffs. "Will this do?"

"Sure, thanks," said Moon taking the material.

"Moon, we need to hurry," urged Uri, indicating around them where several of the skeletons were nearly complete. Some of them were beginning to struggle to get up, despite missing parts of limbs.

Moon quickly bound Sonia's arm. "You'll live but we need to go to Casualty later to get this cleaned up and stitched."

"Casualty, again? You really know how to give a girl a good time, don't you?" Sonia grinned weakly.

"That won't be necessary, we have what's needed at home," hissed Uri urgently. "But right now we need to *move!*"

They rushed past the struggling skeletons, one of which grabbed at Moon's foot, digging its talons into his flesh. Pausing for an instant, he drove his other foot down, crushing the thing's bony forearm, then continued to run forward with the skeletal hand still attached painfully to his ankle. As they neared the source of the magic they saw the slight figure of an old man glowing softly against the darkened undergrowth. "Who the hell is he?" asked Moon.

"My guess is that it's the ghost of the sorcerer who conjured up the goblin," replied Uri. "He must have bound himself to this place to provide added protection for his tribe."

"Curse you, Romans!" The ghost glowered at them. *"You have invaded the home of the Dobuni and for that you must die."*

Moon was experiencing something he had come across before when he had encountered spirits whose native tongue wasn't English. Within his head, the ghost's words were being translated into English but, like an echo behind the words, he could just hear the ancient wizard's voice speaking in something which sounded like Welsh. "Romans, why does he think we're Romans?" asked Sonia.

"They were probably invading Britain at the time he died," replied Uri.

Roanne stepped forward and said something in Welsh. *"Not Romans then?"* Surprise filled the ghost's face. *"But your use of the Tongue is awkward and strange. Where were your born, child?"* He frowned with suspicion. Roanne spoke again. *"Ah, then you are of the Silures tribe,"* said the wizard when she had finished. *"They are great warriors. Not always our friends but fierce opponents of the Romans."*

There was a rattle from behind them and Moon looked back, realising they were surrounded by skeletal warriors, standing motionless as if awaiting instruction. "Erm, Uri…" he whispered, gesturing with his eyes.

"I know," Uri frowned, "but our best bet here is to try to convince this gentleman that we are friends, not foes."

"But what of these?" asked the sorcerer, indicating Moon and the others.

"They are my friends," replied Roanne, reverting to English.

The ghost cocked an eyebrow. *"Friends? They use a very strange tongue, and three of you bear the reek of a kind of magic that I have not met before."* He tilted his head like an ancient crow. *"Hmm, yes; death magic and life magic intertwined. It took a very clever Druid to do this. But how could that be? I felt most of my brethren die on Mona when the Romans came…"*

Moon caught Roanne's eye. "Mona?" he whispered.

"Anglesey," she replied. "It was a holy place once and the Romans slaughtered all the Druids while they were gathered there. But we don't have time for history lessons at the moment, Moon."

The ghost's eyes refocused on Roanne. *"Yes, killed them all they did. So who wove this magic that keeps these three forever young?"*

At this point Uri displayed how utterly green he was when dealing with ghosts. "The magic was woven long after you and your people's time, old man, by a sorcerer from a land far east of this island."

Bugger! thought Moon, Uri had just broken the cardinal rule of ghostly diplomacy; 'never tell them they're dead'.

"After our time? What mean you, after our time?" the old man's eyes glowed an angry blue. *"The Dobuni are great warriors, their battle prowess unsurpassed, high the hill of skulls they raise in battle, loud the laments of their foes. Even now they wage war upon the Romans and I but await their return. What cowardly trick is this you try to trap me by? You pretty, woman-haired, Roman bed toy!"* There was a menacing rattle as the ancient warriors raised their weapons all around them.

"I'm sorry, Sir, I meant no offence," replied Uri in confusion.

Too late for that, thought Moon, striking out desperately to stop the Druid before the weapons found their mark. Twenty ancient skeletons clattered noisily to the ground as he ripped the essence out of the angry ghost and dispersed it into the night, leaving nothing but a tiny blue globe hovering where he once stood. Watching it spiral aimlessly, Moon felt sick at heart. Had he descended to the level of their adversary?

"You didn't have to do that." Uri glared accusingly at Moon.

"Yes, I did," he replied sadly. "You don't know the spirits of the dead the way I do, Uri. The one thing you never do if you don't want to upset them is confront them with their own death. He was probably killed during a Roman attack so as far as he knew he had only been there a short time minding the fort. Given enough time we might have been able to convince him otherwise, but we didn't have that convenience. If I had hesitated… Sonia and I at least would be dead. I'm sad I had to do what I did and I hope that by the time he recovers he will be free to move on but I won't let you pour guilt on me for something I had to do."

Uri stood silently for a moment, his eyes darting in their sockets as he thought through what Moon had said. "I guess you're right, my friend," he said at last. "I don't know the dead like you do. I'm sorry."

"Thanks," replied Moon with a short nod. "Now let's get back to your place and get Sonia stitched up. Although, I have to warn you, I've not been trained to suture."

"But I have," replied Uri. "You have to be something of a field medic when you ride with a Russian war band."

"Oh God!" moaned Sonia. "I think I'd rather go to hospital, even if it does mean a two-hour wait."

Chapter 20

In the end Sonia agreed to go back to Uri's house, where Moon helped as the vampire made a very competent job of cleaning and stitching Sonia's wound while his patient relaxed on an antique, velvet-upholstered chaise longue in his basement apartment, sipping rum and coke from a cut glass tumbler. With Sonia patched up and one or two other minor wounds treated, the friends spent an hour or so talking through the night's adventure and discussing their strategy against Rurik. Hoping that he would stick to his current method of working, despite the recent lack of incidents, they planned to track him down through the outbreaks of violence he orchestrated over the next few days. They could then, hopefully, corner him and incapacitate him, the same way they had done with the Stoneleigh druid, before he was able to grow too powerful for them to handle. But as time passed there *were* no outbreaks of violence; no more of the little ghost globes turned up to join Moon's tiny entourage and Moon received no further contact from Inspector Whatley. It would have been easy to assume that Rurik had simply left the city, if it had not been for continued reports from Anna that she could still feel a malevolent presence growing in the ghostly realm. Moon thought he could sense it too; a nexus of sentient evil, the influence of which seemed to permeate the atmosphere of Bristol rendering the whole populace tense and edgy.

A month passed and summer came in hot and humid, transforming Moon's stuffy little flat into an intolerable oven and forcing him to buy no less than four large electric fans to circulate the torpid air. Moon and Sonia's romance now began to transform into something less intense but more comfortable. They became an established couple and Moon spent most of his weekends at Sonia's place. He also became a regular at the *Hangman's Rest* and, under Sonia and Avril's combined influence, began to accrue a complete Goth wardrobe. He still didn't think of himself as a Goth but he now stood out less from the *Rest's* regular crowd and any outsider would be hard pressed to tell the difference. Moon's article on Goth culture was published in the June edition of *Venue* Magazine and they were impressed enough to offer him a regular two-monthly slot, which he accepted eagerly and he had already started the research for his next assignment –a two pager about Bristol's blues-folk guitarist community.

Following the battle at Stoneleigh Camp, Moon and Sonia met regularly with Uri, Charli and Roanne to discuss any local developments which might hold some hint of Rurik's involvement. They also met just for friendship's sake, as the shared experiences of that perilous night had created a lasting bond between them. Unfortunately, there seemed to be little enemy activity to report from either side and they were at a loss to come up with any kind of plan. Then, one Monday morning in early July, Moon was woken unexpectedly by the sound of his mobile phone playing the William Tell Overture. He answered and was greeted by the deep Yorkshire tones of Inspector Whatley. "Hi, Moon, Art Whatley here. I was wondering if you could help me out with something."

"Oh, hello, Inspector." Moon yawned and wiped the sleep from his eyes; nine-thirty was a bit early for him.

"Oh, did I wake you? Sorry, I forgot you're a night worker."

"That's okay, I'm not in hospital until tomorrow night. What can I do for you?"

"How are you at finding missing persons?"

"I'm not sure if I could be much help. I'm a medium, not a psychic, so it would all depend on whether the local spirits had seen the person you're looking for. Unless they happened to be dead, perish the thought, then I might be able to speak to them directly."

"Oh?" Whatley seemed to be thinking for a second or two on the other end of the phone. "Well, it could be worth a try anyway. We've had four young women go missing from the Stapleton Road to Fishponds Road area in the last month. Three of them were known prostitutes but the most recent was a student at the University of the West of England. We think she just happened to be in the wrong place at the wrong time. There are no bodies but we think that someone is preying on prostitutes, probably thinking that they won't be missed. It's possible that more than these four have gone missing because, as you can imagine, 'working girls' tend to be a little tardy in running to the police. We could really do with some help here, Moon. The last thing we need is a serial killer hacking his way through the female populace." Moon could hear the edge of tension in Whatley's voice. He hadn't mentioned the obvious but 'Bristol Ripper' headlines were probably featuring prominently in his recent nightmares.

"I suppose I could pay a visit to the area and ask any local ghosts if they know anything. Is there anywhere specific you want me to try?"

"Not really. The prostitutes all had their own 'patches' on Stapleton Road, a bit up past the railway arches near the *Black Swan* pub. The student went missing in the same area after a night out at the *Three Blackbirds*."

Moon paused then replied reluctantly, "Well, I could pop over there this afternoon and have a poke around. I can't guarantee anything because it's easier to contact spirits at night. But I'm going out with Sonia this evening and after that I'm working until Friday, so I'd have to do the best I can in daylight." He wasn't too keen on wasting his afternoon searching for spooks in the sunshine but if it might save lives he'd give it a try.

"Oh?" Whatley could obviously sense Moon's lack of enthusiasm. "Well, there's no great hurry. Whoever's doing this seems to be leaving a gap of at least a week between hits, so perhaps we could do it on Friday night instead? I'm working a late shift that day so I can accompany you. We can't have you wandering around such a dodgy part of Bristol alone after dark. Don't want *you* going missing as well, do we?"

Moon sighed with relief. "Okay, Inspector, if you're sure it'll keep, but it'll be fairly late in the evening. I don't know exactly what time the sun sets at this time of year but it must be after eight."

"Hang on," replied Whatley followed by a small grunt and the sound of other activity. "About eight-twenty according to my diary. Could you meet me by the railway arches at about half-eight?"

"Yeah, sure. It's likely Sonia will be there too, she's bound to insist on coming, and she could prove very helpful. She's got quite a 'gift' of her own, you know."

"If you think it'll help having her there, by all means. So I'll see you on Friday then. Take care."

"You too, Inspector." Moon suddenly thought of something; "Oh, is there anything to indicate this might be connected with our earlier trouble?" he asked before Whatley could hang up.

"Nothing, I'm afraid, Moon. We've had to write those random attacks off as some kind of crazy coincidence, regardless of what you and I suspect to the contrary. Your phantom nuisance seems to have gone underground."

"I have to agree with you. I just hope we can avoid another body count when he finally surfaces. Bye, Inspector."

The only thing Moon had planned for the rest of the week was a trip a semi-working trip to an 'open mike night' at the *Nova Scotia* Pub, which wasn't far from Sonia's flat. He hoped this would provide an opportunity to make a few contacts among the local guitar players. Apart from this, the rest of Moon's week was his normal run of working and sleeping with a few hours relaxation in the afternoons. Sonia hated this because it meant that they couldn't share a bed for three nights a week but Moon thought that the advantage of his long weekends and getting all his work out of the way at once compensated a lot for the inconvenience.

On the Friday morning Moon returned to his own flat, changed into lounge-around clothes and lay on his bed and dozed until eleven-thirty when his alarm went off. He then pottered around for the rest of the afternoon. He always tried to take it easy on his turnaround day because the lack of sleep made him dog-tired. At about half past four he slipped into his street clothes and set off to Sonia's for tea.

Moon was beginning to appreciate that Sonia was a better cook than she was willing to confess. She was much better than he was anyway, so he had started to chip in to Sonia and Avril's food kitty and had supper with them two or three times a week. Tonight Sonia was making chicken kebabs with satay sauce, which was one of his favourites. As he was leaving the flat Anna materialised in front of him. She levitated herself to the right level for eye contact. *"Something's happening, Jerry,"* she said in what he thought of as her 'big girl' voice, as opposed to the slightly lisping four-year-old singsong she still lapsed into occasionally. *"I've been sensing odd ripples in the Spiritual; almost like the tiny vibrations I feel just before someone passes over but without that bright burst that follows as they leave. They've been coming once or twice a week. I didn't notice them at first because they're so small, but I'm wondering if they may be connected with Rurik."*

"What do you think they are, Anna?"

"You know a few weeks back when you told me that people had died and I said that I hadn't felt them pass over or become ghosts..."

"Yes?" Moon didn't like where this was going one bit.

"Well, I think I felt this back then but didn't know what it was."

"Are you saying you think people are dying but you can't feel what happens to them next?"

"Yes. And, as all those earlier deaths you told me about were somehow caused by the ghost of a master vampire, it's not too big a leap to assume there's some kind of connection."

"Any idea where this is happening?"

Anna shook her head. *"No, not really. Physical directions don't mean a lot in the Spiritual; it's more governed by emotions and intuition than anything else."*

"Damn! We could really do with a lead right now." Moon gazed deeply into the small spirit's fathomless eyes in desperation. "No ideas at all?"

"You don't have to do much to hide if you're a ghost," Anna shrugged noncommittally.

"Hmm, I suppose you have a point there. Still, Rurik doesn't seem to be able to kill people without human help."

"I hope he still has that limitation," replied Anna, her tiny face a mask of concern. *"He may have grown strong enough to do his own dirty work. Look, I've heard that Bristol's full of*

hiding holes of one sort or another: mines and quarries and smugglers' caves. Perhaps he's using something like that."

"That may be worth looking into," said Moon thoughtfully. "I don't think he's started killing people on his own though. If Uri's description of him is at all accurate he probably wouldn't restrict himself to one or two a week. It's not as if he needs to worry about the police, is it?"

"I suppose not. But he might not want to come up against you and your vampire friends until he's strong enough to face you."

"I doubt that he sees us as much of a threat to be honest. I didn't come off well in my only encounter with him and he probably still thinks of Uri as the weakling who bested him by chance several centuries ago. There's no way he could suspect how much of an expert Uri has become in spiritual combat since then." Moon paused for thought then shook his head. "No, he's using humans, I'm sure of it. Everything Uri's said about him suggests that he'd rather work through minions if he can avoid acting himself and the way he's acted since he got here backs that up. We also need to remember that he's not just here on a killing spree. We know he's set his heart on building some sort of power base in this city and that's going to require allies."

"Oh, Jerry," Anna sighed. *"I wish I could be more helpful rather than just sitting here reporting what's happening in the Spiritual. It's so frustrating!"*

Moon summoned up his ghost sense and stroked Anna's hair then kissed her on the forehead. "What you're doing is great, sweetheart. You've been loads of help and I'm glad you're not able to go out there and fight. It's not because I don't think you're up to it but because I don't know what I'd do without you if you were turned into one of these little blue blobs." He indicated his host of ghost globes, which had drawn in around them, seeming to feed on the intensity of their emotions.

At that moment, there was a thunder of footsteps coming down the stairs and Moon barely had time to bend down and pretend to tie his shoelace as Theresa, one of the two girl students who shared the upstairs flat, rushed onto the landing and barely saved herself from colliding with him. "Oh hi,

Moon," she said when she had recovered. "What're you doing clogging up the stairs?"

"Shoelace came undone," he replied sheepishly by means of explanation, hoping she didn't notice that he was wearing slip-ons. *"See you later, Anna,"* he vibed to his ghostly friend.

"Oh, Moon!" she vibed back, giggling. *"You must be the world's most unconvincing liar."*

Theresa, who was one of those individuals that barge happily through life without taking much notice of their surroundings, simply said, "Okay, see-yah," then stamped off down the stairs. Moon winked at Anna then continued more sedately in her wake.

Moon had intended to walk to Sonia's place but the conversation with Anna had taken up too much time so he decided to catch a bus to the bottom of Park Street and walk from there, which should shave about twenty minutes off his journey. He did have a driving licence but owning a car was an expensive luxury if you lived near the centre of Bristol; most necessities were in easy walking distance and he liked to walk when he could. Not being an athletic type, this was a convenient form of exercise so he walked or cycled most of the time and used public transport if necessary. He arrived promptly at Sonia's at around half past five, just as Avril was letting herself in through the front door, so he called out to her and jogged the last few yards so they could enter together. Avril worked as a clerk for the Department of Transport, which had offices east of the city centre. The work was mainly number crunching and she hated every minute of it so she was always a bit grumpy when she got home from work. A half-hearted, "Hello, Moon," was all that she could manage as she let him through the door.

The air in the hallway was pungent with the smell of freshly squeezed limes with undertones of curry and peanut butter. Sonia popped her head out of the door of the kitchen-diner. "Hi Avril…" she started. "Oh, hi Jerry," she finished when she saw him. "Come on in and make yourself a cup of tea, supper's well on its way."

"Smells great," observed Moon, kissing her briefly on the lips as he entered the room. He took off his jacket and started to fill the kettle at the sink. "All set for tonight?" he asked over the sound of Avril stomping upstairs to her bedroom.

"I suppose so," Sonia nodded unconvincingly. "I'm just not sure how much help I'm likely to be."

"Don't put yourself down. At the very least you'll be an extra set of 'eyes'. Anyway, dealing with spirits isn't just a matter of having the Sight; there are also emotions, affinities and aversions to take into account. Over on Stapleton Road it's fairly likely that we'll be dealing with the ghosts of prostitutes."

"Well, won't they be more likely to talk to you, seeing as you're a man?" asked Sonia.

"A 'client', you mean?" Moon shook his head. "No, they might approach me, but I doubt they've got much respect for men. They'll be more likely to confide in you."

"Hmm, I suppose you're right," Sonia brightened. "So maybe you do need me after all." She kissed him.

A few minutes later tea was ready and a call from Sonia brought a slightly less grumpy Avril downstairs. "Thank God it's Friday," she muttered as she plonked herself down in one of the mismatched kitchen chairs. "Not only do I have to input MOT results until I'm bleeding from the ears with boredom but I'm accosted at the bus stop, by a handful of nutters in robes banging on about their 'Returned Master' or some such gumph."

Sonia paused while serving out the kebabs and asked with a puzzled frown, "Hari Krishnas?"

Avril shook her head irritably. "I don't think so. You don't often see Hari Krishnas in robes nowadays and these guys were wearing cotton robes: a bit like the Hari Krishna ones but these were darkish grey and purple. They shave their heads down the sides as well, you know like some kind of tonsure. Whatever they were, they gave me the creeps. I just ignored them and jumped onto the bus as soon as it arrived."

"Maybe you should try to look less miserable coming home from work," Moon teased. "I'm not surprised people think you need converting if you make habit of wearing a face like the one you greeted me with earlier…"

"Jerry…!" Sonia whacked him with the edge of the teacloth she was holding.

"Oh, sod you, Moon." Avril scowled at him. "Not all of us have the luxury of a fulfilling job you know; I consider it my right when I come home at the end of another God-awful week collating MOT statistics to look as miserable as I feel."

Moon relented. "Sorry, Avril. I know I can overdo it with the teasing sometimes. First round's on me when we're next at the *Rest*, eh?"

Avril gave the first hint of a smile they'd seen since she came in. "Okay, but mine's a double."

Moon grinned. "Sure, make it a triple if you like."

"No, a double will do but you can pay for the snacks as well."

"Done!" Moon held out his hand and they shook on it, both grinning.

"Well, if you two have made up can we start tea," said Sonia with mock primness.

Getting from Hotwell Road to Stapleton Road was a two bus trip, so Moon and Sonia set off at about six-thirty to give themselves plenty of time. They caught one of the out of town buses from outside the picturesque Trinity Chapel, which was a few yards down the hill from Sonia's flat. This took them to the city centre, then after short walk and a few minutes wait they hopped onto the number 5 which took them to Stapleton Road. "I used to take this route a lot when I worked out at Frenchay Hospital," Moon told Sonia. "There seemed to be a prostitute on every corner, even quite early in the morning, trying to catch the office guys on their way to work I guess. Who's going to notice you've come in a bit later when you work flexi time, eh? Not a very safe profession though; a friend of mine who used to live around here said that there are several prostitutes murdered every year in this small area."

"Shit!" Sonia shook her head. "I wish we could get away from these stupid Victorian values and create a legal framework for prostitution. Then these poor women could work in a safer environment. I mean it's not something that's going to go away as long as men are willing to pay for sex, so why sweep it under the carpet and leave so many people vulnerable?"

"It's not a vote winner I guess," replied Moon philosophically. "While your middle-class conservative types might be quite willing to pay for sex, they're not too keen to admit it."

"Well, it stinks!" said Sonia, loud enough to turn a few heads and elicit an approving "Right on girl!" in reply from a matronly black woman wearing a colourful, ethnically patterned cotton dress and turban, sitting a couple of seats behind them, who must have been listening in on their conversation.

Moon looked up as the bus passed under a railway track. "Our stop's next," he said, pressing the request button.

The bus stopped a short walk up the road from the railway bridge next to which Moon had arranged to meet Inspector Whatley. As they strolled down the road arm in arm they noticed a number of provocatively dressed women and girls, at fairly even distances on either side of the road, who looked like they were waiting for someone. "God!" exclaimed Sonia. "I didn't expect there to be so many of them."

Moon shook his head. "I guess it's a matter of supply and demand. Bristol's a big city." He pointed ahead to where the silhouette of a burly figure was outlined in the harsh glow of a streetlight against the misted windows of a dark coloured Mercedes, which was parked just off the main road on the path that ran up one side of the railway bridge to Stapleton Road Station. "That looks like our man over there."

As they approached, Whatley stepped out of his car. "You took your sweet time," he said. "Pity I'm not working vice; I've been propositioned three times in the last half hour."

"Hi Inspector," replied Moon. "Do you think we could get on with it? The atmosphere around here isn't too pleasant."

Sonia looked up sharply at Moon. "Is that what I'm feeling?"

Moon sighed. "Yeah, decades worth of too much human nastiness around here. Eventually, it kind of seeps into the spiritual pores of a place so, psychically speaking, it's a bit like standing next to a sewer." He looked quizzically at Whatley, "Okay, Inspector, where do you want to start?"

"Well, most of the victims have gone missing in the area of the *Three Blackbirds*, so it would seem logical to head up past there and work our way down. Hop in the car and I'll drive us up there."

Moon and Sonia climbed into the back of Whatley's car and he drove up the road, parking just off the main road near the corner of Boswell Street, which was a few hundred metres uphill from the *Three Blackbirds Tavern*. As they strolled down the road, trying not to look like an incongruous trio of two Goths and a plain clothes policeman, Moon felt Sonia opening up her extra senses. "What feels weird?" she asked looking warily up and down the road.

Moon focused on what was going on around them. It had been dusk when they arrived and too light for ghosts to easily manifest but now, with the growing dark, shadowy figures were beginning to appear around the obvious prostitutes who lingered on the pavements on either side of the road. Every street corner seemed to have at least one ghostly female silhouette hovering under a street light in what would have been considered risqué attire for her particular period. Judging by the range of clothing there had been ladies of the night working along here for at least four centuries. "The ghosts of prostitutes," he whispered to Sonia. "Generations of them."

As they approached the next corner the shade of a plumpish woman in regency clothes detached herself from the shadow of a doorway. *"'Ullo moi lover,"* she vibed conspiratorially to Moon. *"Woi don't ee ditch that skinny doxie and 'ook up wi' me? She don't look too 'ealthy if'n ee asks me, know what Oi means?"* Eyeing up the inspector, she winked suggestively. *"Oi can take on ee and yer 'andsome friend 'ere together fer a special rate."*

Whatley betrayed his own latent psychic talents by jumping like a startled rabbit when her ghostly elbow dug him in the ribs. "What the fuck was that?" he exclaimed.

"Just an over familiar ghostly whore," replied Sonia, emphasising the last word acidly. "Who'll piss off if she knows what's good for her." Sonia had gone into full glower and Moon was worried that she might cause serious bodily harm to their potential witness.

"Calm down, love, she's just a working girl trying to ply her trade," he cautioned.

"Damn right," said the ghost bitterly, placing her fists on her ample hips. *"An' trade's bin awful slow of late wi' all these 'ere pesky newcomers takin' ower me patch an' wearin' next t' nothin'. Oi tells 'em t' sling their 'ooks but they just ignores me. An' all me pertential clients ignores me too! Oi mean wot is a girl t' do. Am Oi losin' me looks do yer think?"*

She burst into tears and rested her head on Sonia's shoulder. Sonia gave Moon a look of sheer panic. "I thought she didn't like me," she mouth in surprise. Moon shrugged, looking helpless, gesturing that he had no more experiences than Sonia in comforting distraught, eighteenth century prostitutes. Small blue sparks illuminated the night as she summoned her ghost sense and patted the sobbing spirit on the back. "It's okay, love. I'm sure business will pick up soon," she lied consolingly, while signalling to Moon with her eyes that she needed some help on how to proceed. The prostitutes standing under the nearby street lights on either side of the road watched the apparent pantomime with puzzled interest. Street theatre didn't usually come this far out from the city centre.

"What's your name?" Moon asked the ghost, touching her gently on the arm.

"Rosie," she vibed tearfully. *"Rosie 'Ardy."*

Moon paused, trying to think what to say next. "We're sorry to hear of your troubles but we're trying to help some girls who've gone missing around here. I don't know if you've seen anything over the last few weeks: girls being taken away somewhere, possibly after a struggle?"

Rosie composed herself, wiping her nose on the back of her hand. *"Well, Oi've seed a lot o' bad things 'appenin' roun' 'ere over the years but just recently Oi've thought there moight be a gang o' whoite slavers in town. Weird lookin' coves in dark robes; one o' 'em 'ud be dressed pretty normal like an' e'd go up t' one o' the girls on the street an she'd follow 'im t' some out o' the way spot then 'is mates wud 'ave at 'er an' bundle 'er off into the shadows."*

Moon explained this to Inspector Whatley, who asked, "How often has she seen this happen?"

"Is yer friend deaf?" asked Rosie when Moon turned back to her.

"You could say," replied Moon. He tried to remember what passed for a police force in Rosie's day. "He works for the parish constable sometimes."

Rosie looked Whatley up and down. *"Poor sod. Looks well enough on it, though."*

Moon stifled a laugh. "What did she say?" asked Whatley, looking a little defensive.

Moon grinned. "I just told her you were her era's equivalent of a policeman," he explained in Whatley's ear. "They weren't too highly thought of in those days."

"Well, some things never change, do they?" replied Whatley. "Any chance of an answer to my question?"

"Rosie, how many times have you seen these men in robes?" asked Sonia, who still had her hand around the ghost girl's shoulders.

"Oh, 'bout five or six toimes by moi reckonin'," replied Rosie. *"Oi was curious what they were up to, you know; with business so slack loike. Ye gets bored and wants to know what's goin' on. Hid mesel' well though, there's a lot o' 'arm can come to a girl wot's not careful."*

Poor Rosie, I don't think you were careful enough, thought Moon sadly, examining a fine red line that ran across the pale skin of Rosie's throat; *once, at least, and that's enough...* Aloud, he said, "Where did they take the girls, any idea?"

"Somewhere down road towards the city," vibed Rosie. *"Oi doesn't feel loike goin' down there often no more fer some reasun."*

Probably the limit of your haunting, thought Moon. "Was there anything you remember about the men, apart from the robes that is?"

"Well, the one who din't wear no robe were a skinny cove. Looked t' be in 'is late twennies, pale skin, pale 'air an' 'orrid pale blue eyes, wot you cud see o' 'em behoind those roun' steel-rimmed spec'acles. Oi've ne'er seen 'im up 'ere 'ceptin those few toimes 'ee were 'ere doin' mischief. Oh, an' all o' 'em wore one o' these odd pen'ants; shaped loike a figure eight on 'is soide, wi' a starin' eye in each o' the loops, almost like one o' they 'domino' masks as the nobs wear when they goes to their balls." Rosie paused in thought. *"No, that's all Oi c'n tell 'ee."*

"Thanks, Rosie," said Sonia. "I wish there was something we could give you in return."

"There might be," said Moon, and then whispered conspiratorially in Sonia's ear.

"Do you think so?" asked Sonia.

"Yes," replied Moon, moving round to the other side of Rosie and placing a hand on her arm. "Hold tight, Rosie, this might tingle a bit..."

"Ooh!" exclaimed Rosie in surprise as Moon and Sonia both channelled a tiny bit of their life energy into her. *"Tha's **noice**! Wot is it?"*

"Just a bit of a boost," replied Moon with a wink. "We thought you needed one."

"Well, thank ye both, Oi feels wunnerful." Rosie beamed. She looked up the street. *"An' 'ere comes some likely lookin' gents t' top off the evenin'!"*

Moon and Sonia backed away as three ghosts dressed in roundhead uniforms weaved drunkenly down the road. *"'Ello, foine Sirs, d'ye fancy spennin' a bit o' time wi' Rosie?"* cried Rose, sidling in between the two more sober looking soldiers. *"Well of course yer do! C'mon me 'andsomes, there's a nice big feather bed an' sum good ol' cider back at Rosie's place if'n ye've still got sum silver on 'ee?"* The most drunk of the three companions lifted up a heavy purse and jingled it. *"'Nuff said, let's be off,"* replied Rosie enthusiastically. *"Oi'm feelin' full o' energy t'night, boys, so ye're in fer a treat!"* At which Rosie led her new companions away through a nearby wall.

Sonia regarded Moon with a look of astonishment. "...How?" she managed to utter finally.

"I've no idea," replied Moon shaking his head. "Perhaps she really has got a ghostly feather bed hidden away somewhere in the spiritual dimensions. It's probably best not to dwell on it."

"But I thought that they couldn't communicate with ghosts from different eras."

"From what I've seen some can and some can't; it depends on how fixed they are in the time when they died. Who knows, perhaps our little 'gift' helped Rosie to see out of the box. Anyway, it looks like she's a bit happier than she's been for a while, poor girl."

"What just happened?" asked Whatley, sounding bemused and a little annoyed. Moon and Sonia explained as best they could, giving the inspector the abridged version of Rosie's description of the abductors at the same time. "Oh? It's a good thing she's a ghost then or I'd probably have been expected to arrest her."

"Yes, well prostitution was a little more respectable back in the seventeen hundreds," replied Moon.

"Doesn't sound good though, nutters in robes abducting young women off the streets after dark," observed the inspector. "I wonder where they're taking them."

"Wherever it is, Inspector, I'm afraid that it's unlikely the victims are still alive," replied Sonia sadly.

"What makes you so sure?"

"Because I'd lay odds that Rurik, that's the name of our Ghost Eater by the way, is behind this and we think he's using the energy released when his victims die as a source of power."

Whatley froze in mid-step. "What makes you think that?"

"Jerry and I have learned a lot about how ghosts interact with life energy recently, Art. The living work on a higher level of spiritual energy than ghosts do so it seems obvious that all that energy is released in one go when someone dies…"

"So if Rurik's there when someone dies he can absorb all that power at once," explained Moon.

"Yes," added Sonia. "That's why he sent all those people on killing sprees, so he could feed off the results, but now he doesn't need to waste energy running around trying to be there when a victim dies because he has others to bring them to him."

"Oh, God!" Whatley's eyes widened as the implication hit him. "He's started a cult…"

Moon nodded. "Probably with himself in the role of God. It makes perfect sense, and it's very similar to what Uri said he did in Russia. His followers will be his eyes, ears and hands, bringing him victims and keeping a watch for potential enemies or allies. That's what he meant when he said he had chosen Bristol to start from. I doubt if he's intending to leave it at that, though; he may well have plans to take over the whole country."

"But I can't fight this," muttered the inspector despairingly. "You can't arrest a ghost!"

"No," replied Moon. "I'm afraid that's going to have to be our side of the job. But what you can do is track down this cult. They are killing people after all and they're human, so you *can* arrest them…"

"Right," the policeman nodded in agreement. "I'll see if I can get an ID on this 'skinny cove' of Rosie's. Although I'm not clear how I'm going to pin anything on him with an eyewitness who's been dead nearly three centuries. And you and your colleagues will have to sort out the other side of the problem." He pulled a reluctant face. "I can't help feeling you're getting by far the worst part of the deal. If there's anything that I can do to help please let me know."

"Well, there are humans involved now," observed Moon, "so we may well need you to call in the cavalry when we finally do track down Rurik."

Sonia hugged Whatley's arm. "Don't feel too bad about it, Art," she said. "If Rurik manages to get dug in here everybody'll be in trouble. We're just looking out for ourselves, really."

Whatley smiled. "Thanks."

They walked down the road as far as the railway bridge but the ghosts they encountered were either too caught up in their own past lives or too suspicious to be of any help. Whatley tried asking the living prostitutes they encountered and they had a little more luck there. One girl, so young that Moon felt tears welling up behind his eyes as they spoke to her, had seen some men wearing what appeared to be black robes heading up the side road towards the station. "But that's crazy," commented Moon. "They couldn't be taking their victims onto the train, could they?"

"There's no passenger service that late," replied Whatley. "Maybe they have a hideaway somewhere near here, possibly off the railway track. I'll get some uniforms onto it when I get back to the station. Now, I think that's all we're going to find out this evening, don't you boys and girls? Do you fancy a lift home?"

"Inspector, you couldn't get me away from this rotten place fast enough!" Sonia sighed. "We've touched too many broken lives for one evening."

"Ditto," agreed Moon.

"Gets depressing, doesn't it," said the inspector gloomily. "But you get used to it."

"I hope I never have to." Sonia looked entreatingly at Moon. "No more tours of the red light district, eh love."

"Not if I can help it."

Chapter 21

It was still over an hour before closing time so Moon and Sonia asked Inspector Whatley to drive them to the *Hangman's Rest* instead of going straight home. On the way Moon phoned Uri and the girls to see if they could meet up to discuss their night's findings. Uri's cell phone was turned off but Karen Maddocks, who answered the phone at the house, said they had already gone out for the evening. She wasn't sure where they had gone but it was probably the pub. "Trust Uri," Moon grumbled to Sonia. "First real lead we've had for months and he's incommunicado."

As Whatley dropped them off he said, "You two take care now. I may not be able to help much on the supernatural side of things but I don't want you taking unnecessary risks."

"If we can't deal with this I think you'll have a lot more than our safety to worry about," replied Moon grimly.

As they entered the pub Sonia asked Moon, "Jerry, do you think it could really go that far? Could we even be killed?"

Moon looked at her gravely. "Yes, I do. Face it, we could both have died a few weeks ago over in Leigh Woods and I've understood that this could be a deadly business ever since I was nearly swallowed whole by that *thing* in St Andrew's Cemetery. The trouble is I don't think there's any way for me not to be involved. I'm the only man with the tools for the job... plus Bristol's supernatural equivalent of the Mafia has promised to come gunning for me if I don't do it. No one's expecting you to risk your life though. You could pull out and take a back seat any time if you feel it's getting too much." He gently touched her cheek. "But if I do pursue my 'gifts' like you've been encouraging me to do I doubt this is the last time it'll get dangerous; so you may want to pull out on me as well..."

"Not on your Nelly!" said Sonia, reaching up and kissing him. "I just wanted to know how high the stakes were. You're not getting rid of me that easily, Jerry Moon," she shrugged.

"Anyway, it sounds like life is going be pretty fucking awful if Rurik wins so, if you're going to put him back in the ground for good, you'll need all the help you can get."

Moon grinned. "I guess so. But I'm glad you've decided to stick with me and not just because I think we work well as a team. Just in case I haven't said it recently, I love you, Sonia…"

"Hey, Moon! Stop snogging by the door and buy a drink!" yelled Kate from behind the bar. "You're putting the other customers off their beer *and* blocking the entryway so get your arse in here before I have to ban you both for being a fire hazard." Moon shrugged and he and Sonia walked up to the bar to a chorus of cat calls.

They found Uri sitting in a corner in hot conversation with some people that Moon vaguely knew as members of the Goth music scene, but Charli and Roanne were nowhere in sight. Moon recognised Stroggy, the lead singer from *Stoker's Kiss*, who had invited him to the gig where he had met Sonia. Avril's boyfriend Roger was also there along with Yvonne, the female singer from *Unquiet Grave*, and a tall, platinum-haired, skeletal Goth who Sonia, with mild awe in her voice, whispered was Jareth, the keyboard player for *Phantail*.

"Do you mind if we join you?" asked Moon, trying to indicated to Uri with his eyes that they had something important to tell him.

"Yes, actually," replied Jareth dismissively. "Piss off!"

Moon felt himself bristle with indignation. "Now, there's no call for…"

"Jareth!" admonished Uri. "Please, there is no need for rudeness. These are friends of mine."

"Sorry," mumbled the cadaverous musician, taking a sip from his drink. Moon recognised it as an *Ayesha's blush*, a cocktail heavy on strawberry and blackcurrant syrup, backed up with a liberal dose of vodka. It tasted disgusting but looked like blood, which was why a lot of the more poserish Goths drank it.

Uri turned to Moon. "My friend, we have some important band business to deal with. It should only take half an hour or so, can it wait?"

"Half an hour? Yes," Moon nodded. "But it is important. You know? To do with your old associate Rurik."

Uri's eyes widened. "Ah, well, I'll try to complete my business with these gentlemen as soon as possible." He turned back to the table. "Forgive me, guys, I'd like to wind this up quickly. Moon here has brought me news of a potential album deal that *Blood Velvet* has been negotiating for some time. Do you mind if we set aside the pleasantries and just get on with it." There was a variety of nods and general assents from the others. Uri turned back to Moon. "Very well, if you and Sonia could go and find yourselves somewhere to sit I'll be with you as soon as possible."

"It's like he's holding court," commented Moon as they headed for an empty table.

"He's very well respected in the Goth music scene," replied Sonia, "but I think he puts on the act a bit just to impress them."

"Or maybe that's just the way the men in charge acted in his day. He grew up in a time of serfs and overlords remember."

"And that really bugs you, doesn't it?" Sonia smiled knowingly. "You're a true egalitarian, aren't you, Jerry?"

"I suppose so," Moon shrugged. "I just don't believe in undeserved privilege. Or even worse privilege that's been taken by force and maintained with brutality and subjugation, which is what they had in the Middle Ages. Regardless of all the airs and graces they attached to it, when you cut to the quick the so called nobility was nothing more than a bunch of highly successful thugs."

"So, do you think Uri's a *thug* then?"

"No, but I'm sure Rurik is. Uri just grew up in a privileged class of the same society and retains a few mannerisms which hark back to those times, while Rurik is your full blown, 'might is right' warlord and probably the worst of a very bad lot."

Sonia laughed. "That's what I like about you, Jerry; you have a really clear sense of what's right and wrong. Most of us just muddle along doing the best we can but you really think this stuff through, don't you?"

"Well, I like to know all the background information before I decide where I stand on something, if that's what you mean…"

"Yeah, that's it. But when you do decide something's right you really go for it. That's probably why the 'Powers That Be' decided to give you your Gift; they knew that you have the crusader mentality required to follow things through."

"'Crusader mentality', is it?" Moon grinned ruefully. Then he shook his head. "I'm not too keen on the old 'Powers That Be' idea either. It suggests that the universe is far more precisely organised than I'd give it credit for. Anyway, what's a cynical young thing like you doing hooked up with an old 'crusader', eh? Aren't you afraid I'll lock you up in a chastity belt?"

"Oh, I know a good locksmith," smirked Sonia. "Anyway, maybe I've a touch of the crusader myself. You never know."

"What is all this about crusaders?" asked Uri, who had concluded his other business. "Dreadful people! They plundered the entire Middle East for glory and gold. I never met one that I liked; even the ones I fed from gave me terrible indigestion. Too much spicy food in their diet, don't you know."

"Oh, we were just discussing our mutual penchant for unpopular causes," replied Moon. "Speaking of which, we have a possible lead on Rurik."

Moon and Sonia described their trip to Stapleton Road and their suspicions that Rurik was gathering a cult of followers around him. "Building himself a cult, eh? That would be very much Rurik's style; why waste your time hunting for victims when you can subjugate someone into bringing them to you? But no suggestion of where he might be hiding?"

"One of the witnesses said she thought she'd seen some men in dark clothing hurrying towards the railway station late one night but whether they have a hideaway somewhere near to the railway line or they had a vehicle hidden away up there we don't know," said Moon.

Uri sighed and said, "I suppose the next thing we need to do is search the area around the station for clues to where they're hidden."

"But Inspector Whatley's got the police doing that," Sonia pointed out. "Surely we'd just be going over the same ground."

"With all due respect to the forensic capabilities of the police force," Uri smiled wolfishly, "they do not have access to the range of senses that a vampire commands, or you and Moon for that matter. We need to check the area for Rurik's supernatural presence and Moon can ask questions of any ghosts we might encounter."

"Does that mean we have to go there again tonight?" asked Moon despairingly, taking a deep sip from his pint of Ostrich.

"Yes, I'm afraid so" replied Uri. "We need to strike while the iron's hot. Rurik may not fear the police but his ghouls will so they may decide to move their hideout when they realise the police are onto them. Drink up, you two, and I'll give you a lift."

"I'm not keen on flying, Uri, and I doubt you could carry both of us by yourself. Where are Charli and Roanne anyway?"

"Oh, they're out clubbing. We usually go together but I had that piece of business to handle. But... we won't be flying, come outside and see."

Moon and Sonia finished their drinks and followed the vampire, who was grinning like a schoolboy. He led them to a space in the parking lot hidden from the surrounding street lights by the shadow of an outbuilding. Moon gave a low whistle. "That's just beautiful, Uri."

"Isn't she?" said Uri proudly, beaming all over his face. "She's a custom job; a Harley Evo chopped chassis combined with a VW Beetle at the rear, with a rear mounted V-Twin engine. She was just delivered this Wednesday. There's a guy up in Cheshire who builds custom trikes like this for a living, so we sent him the specs a few months ago and here she is!" Uri caressed the chrome handlebars with a pale, long-fingered hand.

Sonia ran her eyes over the silver-chrome fixtures: the filigree tooling on the ends of the tailpipes; the dark scarlet leather upholstery on the seats; the batwing motifs on the bodywork; the fringed black leatherette fold-back canopy, and the fanged, screaming, chrome skull which held the headlight in its jaws. "Suits you," she said dryly, barely holding back a giggle. Internet fangs were one thing but you could take Goth kitsch too far.

Uri climbed into the saddle, managing to look extremely cool despite the gothic overkill. "Indeed it does," he said, undisturbed by Sonia's sarcasm.

"You look like the cover-boy from a *Meatloaf* album," commented Moon, less amused than Sonia by Uri's choice of transport. This was quite a *beast*!

"Well, let's be off," said Uri, donning a mat black helmet with silver bat wings airbrushed onto its sides and a pair of reflective sunglasses.

Moon climbed in the back and noted with approval the rear seat belts and the sturdiness of the roll-over bar, which looked very secure despite of the chrome gargoyle which perched in the centre with its wings spread down either side. "Buckle in," he advised Sonia, doing so himself.

The ride through the inner city back to Stapleton Road was far from exciting, as Uri probably didn't take them above forty all the way, but it was a very smooth ride with the V-twin purring away behind them like some huge contented predator. Within ten minutes they had pulled off up the side road to the railway station. "Aren't you worried about leaving her out here?" asked Moon as he and Sonia clambered out of the twin bucket seats at the back of the trike. "It's not a very safe area."

Uri smiled knowingly, passing his hand over the top of the vehicle, and Moon noticed a faint blue glow, which spread out to surround it like a pulsing mist, and shivered as an inexplicable chill ran through his bones. "One of the advantages of being a vampire," explained Uri, "is that we can create an aura of fear around an object. Most people will not be able to look at it now for more than half a minute or so without feeling compelled to run away in terror. If anyone was to try to sit on the trike or drive it away they would be driven temporarily insane with fear."

Sonia averted her eyes from the trike, grimacing as an involuntary shudder wracked her body. "I don't doubt it," she squeaked almost hysterically. "Can we move away from it? Like *now*!"

The skull-shaped headlight seemed to be leering hungrily at Moon. "Yes please," he replied thickly through a suddenly dry mouth. Uri laughed at their discomfort as they made their way quickly up to the station. "You really do enjoy some of this 'undead fiend' stuff, don't you?" commented Moon, annoyed by his friend's amusement.

"Oh, yes, but only in small doses and I can give it up any time I like," replied Uri. Moon wasn't sure if he was joking.

The station was deserted, the last train, the ten thirty-eight to the central station at Temple Meads, having passed through about ten minutes before. It had that eerie, empty feel that unstaffed stations have at night, so it felt haunted even though Moon knew for certain that it wasn't. "Look at this mural!" cried Sonia in delight, pointing to the platform wall where the famous Victorian cricketer W.G. Grace demonstrated his technique to three modern day local children. Along the wall were a number of other figures representing the history of the area, from a sepia-toned Victorian lady in a poke bonnet to a family of Afro-Caribbean immigrants in of the nineteen-fifties.

"Haven't you seen it before?" Moon pointed at the picture of Grace wearing a bowler hat and suit instead of his more famous cricket whites. "He used to be the local doctor in this area when he wasn't playing cricket. See, there's his Gladstone bag on the floor next to his feet."

"That's a hell of a beard for a doctor," replied Sonia. "Did you know him then?"

Moon suddenly realised that Sonia had no idea who W.G. Grace was. "No, he lived in the Victorian era. He was probably the most famous cricketer of his time; W.G. Grace, haven't you heard of him?"

"Oh, was W.G. Grace a cricketer? I thought he was a Victorian prime minister or something."

Moon chuckled. "I guess you do learn some things from the boys' comics that girls never find out."

"Yeah, 'cos we've too much sense to be interested in them," replied Sonia with a mock sneer. "Who wants to learn stuff about boring old cricket anyway?"

"Better than all that fluffy stuff about make-up and boy bands, nyeh!" replied Moon loudly, getting into character.

"Er, forgive me for breaking up this wonderful show of immaturity," admonished Uri. "But we are looking for dangerous people in the dark so perhaps it would be better if we did not draw attention to ourselves."

"Oh, okay," replied Sonia, lapsing into seriousness.

"Yeah, sorry, Uri," added Moon, looking sheepish in the dim glow of the station lighting. "You getting anything?"

"Not here," answered Uri, sniffing the air. "Too many people have been here over the last few hours. Plus a couple had sex in the shelter before the last train arrived. All those pheromones really screw up my sense of smell. How about you?"

"Zilch, I'm afraid. The station's not even haunted, which is unusual for such a public place; there's normally at least one marooned spirit hanging around where lots of people congregate regularly."

"Well, I suppose we ought to look further along the track," replied Uri. "You take one way and I'll take the other. And watch out for trains, there's still freight traffic at this time of night."

They headed off in different directions along the line, Uri going northwest towards the coast while Moon and Sonia made their way south-eastwards towards Temple Meads Station and South Bristol. They walked for about fifteen minutes, having to leap from the track at one point to avoid a passing freight train but saw no sign of anywhere that might be a suitable hideaway for Rurik's cult. They encountered one spirit: the ghost of a railway worker who had died in an accident while checking the tracks in the nineteen-thirties, but he had seen no people in robes, despite having walked up and down the track between Stapleton Road and Temple Meads every night since the September of 1932. At that point they gave up and returned to the station, where they waited another ten minutes until Uri alighted beside them, having flown back down the line. "Find anything?" asked Moon. "We drew a blank."

"Possibly," replied Uri. "I scouted the track for about two miles in that direction then flew along the rest of it up to the entry to the tunnel under the Downs. There's a point just before the next set of lights where at least five people congregated recently and there's still a lingering scent of fear. I'm wondering if they got onto a train there instead of at the station, which means that their lair could be anywhere along this line."

"But Inspector Whatley said the victims went missing after the last train had gone…" A slow wave of comprehension spread over Moon's face.

"Yes, of course, the freight service," said Sonia, catching on.

"If they had an accomplice on the train they could put their victim on board here and get off anywhere between here and the coast," observed Uri. "That's a lot of train line."

"Ten to fifteen miles' worth, I reckon," agreed Moon. "And Rurik's hideout could be anywhere along that stretch. Or a few miles either side; there's nothing to say they didn't have transport at the other end."

"Perhaps Inspector Whatley will come up with something," suggested Sonia. "I mean, if they've got accomplices on a freight service it's probably going to be the same train every time, isn't it?"

"Of course! You're right, I'll phone Whatley in the morning and ask him to look into the freight train times and see if his team can come up with a match."

"Then I think we can say our work here is done for the night," said Uri with a lopsided grin. "Shall we see what my new baby can do?"

Uri took them home via the scenic route, taking in a stretch of the M32. At one point he had the trike roaring along at over ninety miles per hour and Moon speculated sourly that he and Sonia would be picking dead bugs out of their hair for most of the next month.

Chapter 22

It was just after eleven the next morning when Moon woke up to the mouth-watering aroma of cooking bacon. Sonia, who was more of a morning person than Moon, was already out of bed but understood by now that Moon needed to lie in on his 'turn-around' day for nights. He threw on his jeans and a T-shirt and, after a quick detour to the bathroom, stumbled downstairs in pursuit of Sonia's cooking. She was standing in the kitchen watching the grill and listening to Radio One. "Hello," she said. "I thought the smell of breakfast might get you downstairs." She added the rashers from under the grill to those on a plate she took from the oven and placed them in the middle of the kitchen table alongside a loaf of bread, a bottle of ketchup, a rack of toast and a bowl of heated up tinned tomatoes. "Help yourself," she said, indicating a place at the table. "Tea's in the pot."

"Thanks," said Moon. He poured himself a cup of tea in Sonia's dragon-claw mug, which had become his favourite, then started to build himself a bacon 'buttie'. "Is Avril around?"

"Yeah, she should be down in a minute. Why?"

"It just occurred to me while I was waking up that dark grey and purple robes might look black under those yellow street lamps at night."

Sonia paused with a dish of fried mushrooms in her hand. "Oh, you mean those idiots who pissed Avril off yesterday evening?"

"Yeah," replied Moon, taking a bite from his sandwich. "It would be a bit of a coincidence for two new cults to appear in Bristol at the same time, wouldn't it? This 'Returned Master' character that Avril described... don't you think that might possibly be Rurik?"

"Now you come to mention it. From what Avril told me this morning, what her culties were preaching sounded very like what you told me that nutter who attacked you a few weeks ago was ranting about."

"Really?" Moon put down his sandwich and regarded her curiously. "Did Avril give you any details?"

"Yeah, they told her that their 'Returned Master' is the one true god but a jealous splinter group among his servants stole the source of his power aeons ago, which is why the world is as fucked up as it is. Now, with the help of his worshippers, he has returned and, once he has gathered enough followers, he will overthrow the false gods and their followers, including everyone who doesn't worship him of course, and return to his rightful place as ruler of the universe. It goes without saying that the faithful will have all the choice jobs in his new administration."

"I think we've got a match there!" concluded Moon excitedly.

"A match for what?" asked Avril.

"Oh, those weirdos who bothered you at the bus stop yesterday," said Sonia quickly. "We think we may have met some of them last night."

"Yeah," confirmed Moon. "Avril were they each wearing some kind of pendant?"

Avril helped herself to some bacon and tomatoes. "Come to think of it they were. It looked like a mask, you know the sort cartoon burglars wear, with little red eyes."

Moon shot a significant glance at Sonia. "That sounds like them."

"Look," said Avril irritably. "I know you guys have some great secret that you're always whispering about when you think no one else can hear you. I know Uri and his weird women are involved somehow and I *think* that you probably helped the police catch the guy who murdered Dominic and the others. I'd also give ten to one that you're up to something like that now, so do me a favour and don't try to pull the wool over my eyes."

"Sorry, Avril." Sonia circumnavigated the table and put her arms round her friend's shoulders. "It's just that we know you're not too keen on anything supernatural and what we're doing is pretty much as supernatural as you can get."

They could see that Avril was lost in internal conflict for a moment, then she sighed, "Yeah, well, I know I'm the first to leap in and pooh-pooh any talk of that sort of thing but I suppose it's time to confess the truth. It's mainly because it just gives me the screaming willies, if you have to know. When I was little there was this invisible *thing* that used to bang up and down the landing at night in the old house we lived in. I used to feel it watching me from the top of the stairs when I was on my own. It scared me witless. The day we left there was the happiest day of my life. When I told my mum she insisted that it was all nonsense, which was the perfect get out for me. You know 'things can't hurt you if you don't believe in them'."

"But you do believe, don't you?" asked Moon. So there was more to Avril's dislike of the supernatural than she had led them to believe.

"Yeah, well I suppose I don't have any choice really, do I? What, with Mulder and Scully sharing the room next door." She gave a begrudging smile. "I mean, either you two are totally loony, or from what I can gather there's some heavy shit going on."

"How about a megalomaniac ghost who's trying to take over the world, is that heavy enough for you?" asked Sonia.

"No way!" exclaimed Avril. "I thought it was just another murder investigation. You can't be serious?"

"As far as we can tell, that's what's going on," replied Moon. "Of course that could all be horse feathers and Sonia and I might simply be certifiably insane. You'll have to judge that for yourself."

"Don't tempt me. Anyway, what do the 'Disciples of the Returned Master' have to do with all this? From my brief encounter with them they were a bit weird but seemed harmless enough in an evangelical kind of way."

"We think they've abducted several young women, who they've probably sacrificed to their new 'god'," Sonia answered bluntly.

"No!" cried Avril, a look of horror spreading over her face. "So, if I'd have been stupid enough to go with them, they might have done that to me?"

"I hadn't thought of that," said Moon with alarm. "They may not just be abducting prostitutes. They could vet their new recruits and any that wouldn't be missed could end up as a snack for Rurik. I'd better try to contact Inspector Whatley as soon as possible. The police should be able to find the address of the cult's base. Can I use your land-line?"

"Sure, help yourself," replied Sonia, with her arm still around Avril's shaking shoulders. The poor girl was finding it hard to adjust to the possibility that she might have had a narrow brush with death.

Moon phoned Whatley on his mobile number and got through almost immediately. "Hi, Inspector, Moon here. We went back to Stapleton Road Station last night with Uri and discovered a few more leads."

"Go ahead, Moon," replied Whatley. "You've caught me 'off duty' but that's only a relative term for a policeman."

Moon explained their suspicions that the abductors might be using one of the freight services to carry them and their victims further up the track. He also mentioned Avril's encounter with the Disciples of the Returned Master and his speculation that they may also be selecting victims from among their converts. "What do you think, Inspector? Any use?" he asked on winding up.

"Hmm, yes," said the inspector. "I'm working this afternoon so I'll phone the station once we've finished speaking and get someone started on looking through the times of the freight services running to the coast. Last night was our first indication that there might be a connection to the railway so all I've managed to do so far is arrange for a handful of uniforms to go over the area around the station and look for clues. I'll also see if we can track down these Disciples of, what's his name?"

"The Returned Master."

"Ah, yes, the Disciples of the Returned Master. We'll ask them if they'll provide us with a list of their members. Perhaps one of them will be our train driver."

"Is that wise?" asked Moon. "Surely it'll tip them off that we're onto them."

"Possibly, yes. But the trouble with dealing with a religious organisation is that we have to treat them as if they're legitimate until proven otherwise. However, we only need to tell them that we suspect one of their members could provide us with information concerning a crime, so they don't have to know it's in connection with the abductions. It's very unlikely that many of their number except for a core cabal are aware of the shadier side of the organisation, which means that, unless we are unlucky enough to end up contacting a member of that core group first off, they may unwittingly provide us with what we need."

"You're a devious man, Art Whatley," Moon laughed.

"I'm a police detective, Moon. It's in my job description."

An old friend of Sonia's from Reading was visiting family in Bristol so they had arranged to meet up for an afternoon of shopping and seeing the sights. This meant that Moon had the rest of the day to himself, so he decided that now was a good time to head back to his flat and do some work on his current article. His walk home took him up the steep hill of Clifton Vale and Goldney Avenue to a complicated junction with Regent Street, Clifton Wood Road, Lower Clifton Hill and Clifton road. A sixth branch of this junction was a wrought iron gateway which led to Birdcage Walk, the pathway that ran through St Andrew's Cemetery. This was the first time he had contemplated walking through the cemetery since his nearly fatal encounter with the Shadow Beast several weeks earlier. The idea was scary even in daylight but, he reasoned with himself, he now had the power and knowledge to combat supernatural beasties on his own so it was time he faced up to his fears.

The tree-covered walkway was pleasantly shady in the July sunlight and the cemetery seemed extremely quiet and peaceful, despite the heavy rush hour traffic streaming along the Queen's Road up ahead. His trepidation diminished as the quietness relaxed him and he decided to stop for a few minutes to soak in some of the place's atmosphere, thinking how ironic it was that somewhere so pleasant in daylight should be so perilous at night. As he gazed over the graves the shadows under one of the yew trees coalesced into a shimmering green figure, which beckoned to him to approach. Curiosity overcoming his wariness, he opened the wrought-iron gate on that side of the path and navigated his way through the gravestones to where it stood. As he approached the hazy form resolved into that of a slender woman, dressed in a dark green gown bearing a raised pattern similar to the herringbone pattern of yew branches; at the gown's bottom hem, which was decorated with a scattering of red buttons the size and shape of yew berries, this pattern faded to the lighter green of younger leaves. Her underskirt, which showed at her forearms and below the hem of her gown, was the reddish-brown of yew bark. The woman's skin was very white with a slight tinge of green, like freshly stripped wood and there were yew leaves and berries strewn through her long auburn hair. This was definitely one of those *Other People*, like the Jenny Greenteeth, but he suspected this one might be slightly more benign in nature.

"Welcome, Jeremy Moon." She indicated a small wrought iron park bench nearby, *"Come, sit in my shade, for we have much of great importance to discuss."*

Moon sat down on the bench and briefly contemplated his old friend the squirrel, who was scampering towards him in hope of a free lunch. "Who are you, Lady?" he asked, gazing up into her fathomless dark green eyes.

"I am Ioho, daughter of the yew, and you," she said with a hint of teasing in her voice. *"You are Jeremy Moon, who walks between the worlds and is our best hope against the Defiler who has come to these lands. None of the Fay Folk, Dark or Light are safe from him; even the Black Terror who haunted this place for centuries was not strong enough to prevail against him. And with each of us he takes he gains in strength."* The squirrel, realising Moon had no food with him, sat on his haunches and scolded Moon loudly before bounding up into the yew tree's branches.

"You mean the Shadow Beast?" asked Moon. "Rurik ate the Shadow Beast? I can't say I'm sad about that," he smiled grimly. "But are you saying even nature spirits like yourself aren't safe from Rurik? How could he have become so powerful?"

"There is a deep thirst in the heart of humanity to conquer and rule over each other and over the earth that bore you. The Great Mother tolerates it because it is important for your development as a species; it is her hope that you will eventually learn to control it before it destroys you because, controlled, such a drive could be of great benefit to yourselves and the

world you live in. Imagine what your race could achieve working hand in hand with the Mother instead of trying to dominate her... But I digress; in Rurik that drive has swollen out of all proportion. It was already very strong in him when he was a man, but the sorcerer who cursed him chose to use his thirst for power against him, unaware of how great that desire truly was. The sorcerer tied Rurik's vampiric nature to that thirst so he would have dominion over his servants..."

"Ah, using what already existed to empower his spell?" Moon nodded his head. "Uri explained that sort of thing to us."

"Exactly," replied Ioho, seeming a little irritated by his interruption. *"Unfortunately, by extending that power of dominion, the curse went further than he intended. It granted Rurik power over the land under his rule and those of our kind who are tied to that land as well. If this city and its environs were to fall under Rurik's domination we Fays would be so warped by his malign presence that we would become terrible and unrecognisable. Unable to serve the Mother, our hearts would be locked in permanent agony, the countryside would be blighted with unnatural growth and disease and no beast, including you humans, would develop naturally for all would bear his heinous mark. We, the Fay, would be twisted so terribly as to be a horror even unto ourselves and a deathly terror to humans. You see, Jeremy Moon, how important it is that you do not fail?"*

"So that's you're angle, is it, Lady Ioho? This isn't so different from the 'sort this out or else' threat your opposite number landed on me. I'm getting tired of hearing this sort of thing. Why should it fall on my shoulders to deal with this mess?" Moon fixed the tree-spirit with a defiant glare.

"Ah, we know you met with a representative of the Dark Ones, and of course all they offered were threats, that is their way." Ioho shook her head, scattering a fine rain of twigs and berries on the ground. *"No, we of the Light wish to offer our help. My brothers and sisters are everywhere, so wherever you finally encounter this abominable violator of the Great Web some of us will be near enough to hear your call and, although we seldom reveal our power, we are very potent. Call on us when you need us and we will be there. But to answer your*

question; it falls upon your shoulders simply because it does, for you are the only one present with the talents required to nip this threat in the bud. You are the one who must decide whether you wish to act or no. But we thought you had already chosen to do so, for your actions suggest you have."

This set Moon aback. Of course he had chosen, hadn't he? So what was the point of moaning about it now? "I suppose I have chosen," he replied. "It's just that all this has come upon me so suddenly I didn't realise I had."

"And you must also realise that you are not alone," continued Ioho with an edge of reproach. *"Your friends and your Lady are also deeply entwined with you in your task. Much of its peril falls also on them."*

Moon pondered this for a moment. "Thank you, Lady," he said eventually. "I suppose I have been a bit selfish. The help you offer will be very welcome. But don't you know that I'll be working with vampires; creatures not that different from the enemy when all's said and done?"

"They bear little resemblance to the rogue known as Rurik." Ioho smiled at the suggestion. *"As vampires they may be beings of the darkness but the darkness exists to balance the light. They are a natural part of the Great Web of Being and work to sustain it as do you and I. Besides, your friends seem to have chosen to serve the Light."*

Moon shrugged. "I guess so. I just thought you might object."

Her laugh was a pleasant rustle of leaves. *"I might object? Oh, how little you know, young one. Who could understand the complex interplay of Dark and Light more than I; whose very flesh though poisonous conceals the power to heal and whose image has long been a symbol of both death and rebirth?"*

Moon looked up into those dark, pine-green eyes. "I'm glad that I amuse you," he said with slight bitterness. "I'm the one who's had to work his way through this blindly, you know. The things that seem to be patently obvious to beings like you don't fall into human heads all that easily!"

"I am sorry, Jeremy Moon. I know that it is hard for you humans to grasp the music of the Web, which plays so loudly for

us. But it is there for those who will listen and it resounds with all the answers you seek."

"Speaking of answers," replied Moon conspiratorially, "is there any chance of you being able to point me to where Rurik's hiding out?"

A frown creased Ioho's beautiful forehead. *"It is hard for us to tell, Jeremy Moon."* She shook her head sadly. *"If this were still countryside I could locate him in an instant but this is a city, where the great Web is violated in many ways; against so much background destruction, it is impossible to isolate the influence of even so monstrous a foe as Rurik. I am sorry."*

For an instant, Moon had a flash of insight into what it was like for these servants of Nature who have to cope with living and working in a city. The constant battle they must be involved in to hold up the banner of Life against the creeping grey terror of urban death. And, as cities go, Bristol was comparatively green so what must it be like for those struggling against the industrialised towns in the North, for instance? "It's okay," he replied, reaching out his hand in consolation.

"Touch me not!" she vibed urgently. *"I am the spirit of the yew and bear the essence of its poison; contact with me would be harmful. But thank you for the gesture."* She smiled gently, *"If you would find Rurik, search for a blighted place. He cannot help but reveal his presence by the influence he has upon the surrounding land."*

Moon considered this new suggestion. "Thank you, Ioho. That could be very helpful. And thanks for the offer of help too, we're going to need all the power we can muster to conquer Rurik." He rose from the bench. "I'll drop by next time I'm passing through."

"I'll look forward to it. Take care, Jeremy Moon; we have so few champions left among your race that we can't afford to lose even one."

Me? A champion? thought Moon as he made his way up to the Queen's Road. *And I wonder what Sonia would say to being called my 'Lady'.* He considered this for a second, *but she is though*, he grinned to himself.

Moon spent the rest of the afternoon working on his Blues-Folk article, which was due for submission the next Friday, and by four o'clock it was almost finished, except for the final read through and tweaking that he did before sending it off to the editor. He pushed back his chair and saved the document onto his hard drive, backing it up on a flash memory key just in case. By the time you've unwittingly sacrificed one or two important files to the capricious god of computers you quickly learn to back-up everything, he thought, philosophically. Then he got ready to go out.

He was having tea at Sonia's that evening then they planned to take Sonia's friend, Ellie, for a tour of the bars around the Watershed area. As he left the house his mobile phone played the first few bars of 'Hanging on the Telephone'. Cutting off Debbie Harry in mid sentence, he answered to find a smug sounding Inspector Whatley on the other end. "Hello, Moon. I'm just ringing to let you know that we seem to have a match. There's a freight train that runs a chemical shipment for one of the factories at Avonmouth twice a week, on Tuesdays and Thursdays, which corresponds quite well with our disappearances."

"Great! Any lead on the cult connection?"

"Not yet, the secretary at their headquarters was very helpful and gave us a copy of their membership database but we're still sifting names at the moment."

"Well, it sounds like a good start anyway." Moon was walking along the street towards Redland Road, which led up towards Clifton and his usual route to Sonia's. He felt much happier about going through the cemetery again, now that he knew the Shadow Beast was out of the picture. "Keep me posted as to how things are going and I'll let you know anything new from my end, okay?"

"Okay, Moon, bye for now."

As Moon turned off his phone an urgent voice in his head shouted, *"Watch out behind you! Move!"* He looked back just in time to see a silver Toyota Land Cruiser mount the pavement four metres behind him, moving at speed. Lacking anywhere else to go, he threw himself into the road, nearly losing his left foot to its right rear wheel. "Fuck!" he hissed, breathlessly, struggling to pick himself up from the tarmac. The cruiser screeched to a halt and he expected the driver to climb out and apologise, but instead he heard the clunk of badly handled gears grinding into reverse. Without pausing to think, he flung himself out of its path just as a Mini came round the corner of the previously deserted side street, its brakes screaming as its driver swerved to avoid Moon. The cruiser quickly sped off, now there were witnesses present, and Moon lifted himself, shaken and dirty, to his feet.

"What the hell do you think you were doing? I darned near killed you," the pretty young driver of the Mini, who had stepped out of her car, asked angrily. She was wearing tennis whites, as was her equally young and pretty companion.

"Trying to survive," replied Moon, fighting the anger building up behind his adrenalin rush. "Look, you didn't manage to get that bastard's licence plate number, did you?"

"What bastard?" asked the tennis player, with a perplexed frown.

"That Toyota, he forced me off the pavement then started reversing. I'm pretty sure he was trying to kill me."

"Oh?" replied the girl. "Sorry, no. How about you, Sherry?"

The passenger shook her auburn curls. "No. The driver wasn't much to write home about though. Pale, scrawny, spectacles; looked a bit of a runt."

"Okay," Moon sighed. "Sorry I interrupted your day."

"Are you all right?" asked the driver as she climbed back into the Mini.

"Just a couple of bangs and scrapes, it's nothing permanent."

"Okay," the girl smiled. "Take care and keep an eye out for rogue Toyotas."

"I will," he promised as they drove off waving. "I certainly will." He looked around at the empty gardens and overhanging trees. "It's okay, you can come out now," he said, stirring up his ghost sense.

A tall, slender figure detached itself from the trunk of one of the tall rowans planted at intervals along the roadside and stood half invisible in its dappled shade. "*Hello, Jeremy Moon,*" it vibed, running pale grey, twig-like fingers through its leafy hair and bowing slightly like a tree in the wind. *"I thought you could do with some help."*

"Thank you." Moon regarded the nature spirit with interest. This one seemed to be male, with a young, child-like face despite his height. He wore greenish brown leggings, dark green turn-topped ankle boots and a long waistcoat, bearing an embroidered rowan-leaf and berry pattern, over a loose sleeved green shirt with small clusters of berries embroidered at collar and cuffs. His green-blond hair was crowned with a circlet of berries and his eyes, the most unusual part of him, were the same bright red as those berries. "It seems the Lady Ioho is living up to her promise. What do I call you then?"

"My name is Luis. I am the spirit of the Rowan," he gestured up at the tree above him.

"I'd kind of guessed that," replied Moon, getting back on the pavement and dusting himself off. "I don't suppose *you* managed to get his licence plate number, did you?"

"What is a 'licence plate number'?" asked the tree spirit, frowning perplexedly.

"Oh, don't worry. It's a human thing to do with cars, that's all."

"Oh," replied Luis noncommittally, turning as if to go back into his tree. Then he paused as if he had though of something important. *"You know those things will destroy your people,"* he said, gesturing towards a parked Volkswagen. *"They poison both the air we breathe and the way you live."*

"So some people try to tell us," replied Moon warily. "But most of us aren't listening."

"Ah!" said Luis. *"So it is as they say: 'fall or rise, Humanity must go its own way'."*

"Doesn't that worry you?" asked Moon, slightly piqued.

"Not unduly," the spirit gestured at the sky and the trees. *"Our fate is not tied to yours but to the Earth. If Humanity fails we will be sad but another species will inevitably move in to take your place. Nature is more robust than you might think and Life on Earth has weathered greater storms than your young race can make. If your adolescent folly drags you all into the dark we will but weep a while then pick up our joy and carry on. We have the Great Song to sing and the Great Dance to dance. If*

Humanity is there to join us in the end we will be very glad but – what is it that you humans say?– we are 'not holding our breath'. Farewell, Jeremy Moon, I am glad to have been able to help our champion. And take care, for it seems our enemy intends to slay you before you can find him."

"Yes, it does, doesn't it?" A stab of fear ran through Moon. He looked up searchingly into Luis' strange red eyes and saw the compassion he hoped for. It was diluted, however, by such a lofty ancientness that had seen the human race evolve from its apelike ancestors and the millions of transient lives in between. "You don't really care that much, do you?"

"I care enough," replied Luis, pausing with one hand merged partway into his tree. *"I can only imagine how hard it is to live such a short existence and be forever fearful of its ending. But we won't lose you, Moon, or any of the others. You must understand that your spirits are like salmon, leaping in and out of the stream of this world. In the end you will join us in the Great Song and tread with us the Great Dance, whatever form you may then inhabit."* Luis smiled and the gentle, joyous fire in his eyes flooded into Moon, chasing away his fear. *"Until then, Jeremy Moon,"* he said as he faded back into his tree.

"Until then, Luis." Moon patted the tree trunk. Then he shrugged and resumed his journey.

Chapter 23

The rest of the walk to Sonia's was a nightmare for Moon, who spent most of the journey looking over his shoulder, expecting to see the Toyota Cruiser hurtling after him to finish its job. But the Cruiser failed to materialise and the walk was uneventful except for that first perilous encounter. By ten past six he was letting himself into Sonia's flat with the key she had given him.

He was greeted by the sound of female voices and laughter accompanied by the smell of cooking emanating from the kitchen. Sonia, Avril and Ellie were seated around the kitchen table chatting and as he entered Sonia raised her head and said, "Hi Jerry, this is Ellie, my old friend from school. Ellie, meet the love of my life, Jerry, but he'd prefer it if you'd call him Moon."

"Hi, Moon," said Ellie brightly with what Moon thought might be a slight Scottish accent. She was what Moon tended to think of as a 'fluffy' girl, very blonde with a soft, gentle face and enormous blue eyes, made larger by skilful application of a tasteful amount of eye shadow. The sides of her almost white hair were pulled back and held by a lacy blue ribbon. Her slim, curvaceous torso was wrapped in a soft, powder blue cashmere sweater over a matching cord miniskirt and her long legs shimmered under satiny, pale blue tights. She looked like a fourteen-year-old's wet dream. The only thing that marred all that fluffy blue perfection was an oversized pair of slippers in the shape of stuffed pandas. How on earth had Sonia and this fluff-pot become friends?

"Hi, Ellie," he replied with a smile and a nod. "Did you guys have a good afternoon?"

"Oh, yes indeed. I don't get to Bristol often enough for my liking, the centre's great for shopping."

"We did a lot of the craft stalls in the market then took a bus up Gloucester road to have a look in the speciality craft shops up there," explained Sonia. "Ellie's a real crafty type."

"Yes, I do a lot of beadwork and I've got a thing for dolls' houses. See what I found." She pulled a tiny pot-bellied stove out of one of at least fifteen small, pink and white striped paper bags on the table. "Isn't it lovely? I normally get this sort of stuff off the Internet but this was a bargain." She indicated the small packages. "They had a sale on and I got a bit carried away."

"You should see what she does with them, Jerry," said Sonia enthusiastically. "It's not just your boring old Victorian town house stuff; she does fantasy scenes as well. She made this wonderful fairytale castle a few years ago with owls in a ruined turret and unicorns in the garden. She's got a real talent."

Ah, thought Moon, *now I see why they're friends.* Ellie obviously shared Sonia's love for fantasy, although he suspected Ellie's tastes didn't run quite as dark as Sonia's did.

"Tea's in the oven. It'll be another twenty minutes, sorry. Ellie and I were a bit late home," said Sonia, pointing to the ancient gas cooker, which had several pans balanced over its none-too-even rings with their contents bubbling merrily. Then she caught his eye and gave him a sharp, questioning look. "Is something wrong?"

Moon thought he had managed to recover from his earlier brush with death but Sonia knew him well enough now to recognise the tell-tale signs of stress. "Oh, it's nothing, I'll tell you about it later," he muttered, gesturing towards Ellie with his eyes.

Sonia raised an eyebrow. "Oh? Okay."

The meal was Avril's steak and kidney pudding, which tasted alright, but always left Moon feeling like he had eaten a mattress in gravy. Afterwards he volunteered to do the washing up while the girls retired to the sitting room with tea or coffee to watch 'Ballroom Fever'. The show paired up celebrities with members of the public and put them through intensive dance training with weekly competitions to stay in the running for a large cash prize; it really wasn't his sort of thing. "I'll dry," said Sonia as Ellie and Avril left the room.

"Are you sure?" asked Avril. "It's the semi-finals."

"Yeah, I need to talk to Jerry," she replied, rolling her eyes as if to imply boyfriend problems.

"Oh, okay, we'll let you know who wins."

"Now," Sonia rounded on Moon once the others were safely out of earshot. "What's happened? You looked well stressed out earlier."

Moon sighed and gave Sonia a worried look. "I was nearly run down in the street on the way over here, and the driver of the car matched the description that Rosie the prostitute gave us for the ring leader of the bad guys she saw."

"God, Jerry!" gasped Sonia, looking stricken. "We need to put an end to this thing before one of us gets killed. I don't want to lose you, having only just found you."

"The feeling's mutual," he assured her. "Look, I'll contact the Inspector as soon as possible but I doubt he can do much about it without witnesses. We need to be really careful tonight though. If Rurik's guys are likely to be out trying to kill us, we ought to make sure we don't get separated and only go to places where there are plenty of potential witnesses if they try anything. Where were you planning to go?"

"Well, there's that new cocktail place down by the docks and then I thought we'd move on to one of the clubs along by the Watershed."

"Okay. Do you mind if we pop over to the *Rest* for an hour or so first? I'll give Uri a buzz and see if he can organise some back-up."

Sonia didn't look very happy. "Okay but…"

"But what?" asked Moon, surprised by her hesitancy.

"Well, Uri and the girls *are* very Goth," she sighed.

"Yeah, they're vampires; you don't get much more Goth than that."

"Look, Jerry. Ellie and I go way back but she doesn't know I'm into this scene at all and I'm not sure how she'll take it."

Moon suddenly realised why he had been feeling something was out of place since he had arrived. Sonia wasn't wearing her usual Goth make-up, just normal foundation with light eye shadow and medium pink lipstick, so she looked much less anaemic than she usually did. Her clothes were different too; she wore a pastel purple halter-neck with white flowers around the top and a dark purple miniskirt with white lace around the bottom. "Oh, I *see*," he said. "Look, if Ellie's as good a friend as you think she is then she won't mind you being a Goth and I'd much sooner have Uri around if things are going to get rough. If you don't want to, though, I'll go with your decision but I don't think it's wise."

Sonia bit her lip then looked at Moon with resignation. "I guess you're right. You phone Uri and I'll tell the others about the change of plan."

Moon found Uri's home number on his mobile and dialled it, hoping that one of the vampires would pick up. He still found their cosy home arrangement oddly disturbing, as he felt instinctively that they should live in a remote castle or half-ruined abbey, not in a pleasant suburban house with a normal middle class family. Roanne answered, her soft Welsh accent sounding even more musical over the phone. "Hello, Moon, what can I do for you?"

"Hi, Roanne, isn't it?" Moon paused. "How did you know it was me?"

"Supernatural vampiric powers," replied Roanne, a little overdramatically Moon thought. "I sensed your aura when I heard the phone ring."

"Oh? Okay..." replied Moon and was greeted by a peal of giggles on the other end of phone.

"God, you humans are so gullible sometimes!" laughed Roanne; "We've got caller display, that's all. There are some things even vampires can't do."

"I'm glad to hear that," replied Moon, smarting slightly at being caught out. "Anyway, I'm phoning to ask you and the others for a bit of a favour. This Rurik business is starting to come to a head and I need some back-up for tonight."

"What? Have you found out where he's hiding?"

"No, but one of his happy little elves tried to kill me with a four-by-four this afternoon and I'm worried that they'll try again when we're out this evening. Sonia's got a friend visiting so we have to play 'business as usual' and we'd really welcome some supernatural muscle to cover our backs."

"Oh, I see..." Moon could hear Roanne sucking her teeth on the other end of the phone then she gave a small intake of breath. "Look, it's not such a good night for us. *Blood Velvet* are playing a small set at the start of the 'Necrofest' at the *Rest* this evening. Just four or five songs but we've got to be there. Charli and Uri are there already setting up and I was just on my way over there for the rehearsal when you called."

"Bugger!" swore Moon. "Is there nothing we can do? I wouldn't have phoned if I didn't think we really need some help tonight."

Roanne paused then came to a decision. "I know; why don't you guys come over for our set? I'll have some complimentary tickets left for you at the desk. How many of you are there?"

"Five, I think, if Roger's coming."

"Okay. I'll get five tickets set aside for you at the admission desk. Will you be okay getting there?"

"Yeah, we'll phone for a taxi. I really appreciate this, Roanne, I owe you one."

"I'll expect payment in blood," she replied, jokingly. "Bye, Moon, I'll see you at the Rest."

Moon laughed. "See you, Roanne, and thanks again."

As he turned off his phone he became aware of raised voices in the living room. "Goth! Sonia, you're a bloody Goth? No way!"

Moon walked through the short hallway to the lounge, hoping that Ellie was going to be less difficult to convince than it seemed. When he entered the room Sonia and Ellie were seated next to each other on the ageing sofa and Avril was in the more comfortable of the two mismatched armchairs. None of them looked too pleased. "Is this your influence, 'Moon', getting her mixed up with a bunch of weirdos?" asked Ellie, her blue eyes radiating an arctic chill.

"No, actually," replied Moon. "It was the other way round. Sonia introduced me to the Goth scene, she'd been involved for some time before I came along."

"Yes, and some of those weirdos you're dissing are the best friends I've ever had," broke in Sonia. "I came here needing some way I could fit in and this was it. They accepted me willingly, despite the issues I had getting over Craig, and they're really non-judgemental and very protective of their own."

"Oh well, I guess I can just treat tonight as a field trip to Weirdville," Ellie grimaced. "I'd ask to borrow some black widow's-weaves if you had anything that'd fit me."

"They wouldn't suit you," replied Sonia with a small grin. Inaccurately, Moon thought, considering Ellie would look gorgeous wearing a potato sack. "But that reminds me, I need to change if we're going to go to the *Rest*."

Moon remembered his news. "Before you go, Roanne's wangled us some complimentary tickets for the 'Necrofest'. They're playing the first set so they won't be free until about nine; just in case you want to wear something a little more striking for the gig."

"Great!" replied Sonia, "I forgot 'Necrofest' was on because Ellie was visiting. C'mon, Ellie, we can't have you going to your first Goth band fest dressed all blue and fluffy. I'm sure we can fix you up with something suitably 'weird'."

Moon sat in the living room vaguely flicking through the TV channels as he waited for the girls to come back downstairs. Judging by the shrieks and giggles coming from Sonia's room they were going to be a while. Saturday evening TV hadn't improved, despite the addition of scores of cable channels. He reflected as he watched a parade of infomercials and soaps flashing on and off. Then something caught his eye. "That was the Bristol Downs, wasn't it?" Flicking back from the re-run of 'Dad's Army' that his channel surfing had stopped on, he caught the end of a news item on a local community channel. "...nd the City Council have no explanation for this unidentified blight, which has devastated the grass and other vegetation on this small area of the Downs, between Ladies Mile and the Circular Road. There is strong government denial in response to rumours that this results from leakage from toxic gas containers stored here during World War Two..." Moon, turned down the volume and watched the next few seconds of footage carefully, trying to fix the location in his head. Ioho's musical voice was ringing again through his mind. *"If you would find Rurik, look for a blighted place..."*

"A blighted place?" he whispered to himself. "I wonder what's under there."

Fifteen minutes later Sonia and Avril came downstairs and stood on either side of the doorway, presenting Ellie in her new role of Goth chick. Moon had to admit that it suited her well. Her long blonde hair was held back with a fluffy black elastic tie, emphasising the heart shape of her face, which was covered in white base on which someone, Moon guessed Avril, who was good at such things, had painted a delicate spider web coming up around her right eye to her scalp, the spider itself dangling from beneath her lower lid like a black teardrop with a small red, adhesive gem for the body. The rest of her eye make-up was a cunning combination of purples and pinks, complemented by the dark, sparkly purple of her lip gloss. The spider theme continued to her ears, from which dangled tiny silver spiders and the top of her dress, which Moon recognised as one of Avril's, who was more Ellie's size, had a frill of black spider-web lace around the neck-line. The dress was corseted, with black silk ribs outlining dark purple taffeta panels, and it flounced out around the hips like a French maid's outfit, showing more spider web ruffles and a hint of frilly black panties. Neither Avril nor Sonia wore Ellie's size in tights so Sonia had lent her a pair of spider-web stockings, which left a larger than normal gap at the top of her long legs that Moon couldn't help noticing. The stiletto-heeled ankle boots with silver tips were Sonia's as well. "You look... great!" said Moon, trying to walk the narrow tightrope between complimenting the girls on their efforts and upsetting Sonia by over-enthusing about how gorgeous her friend looked. "And you both look stunning as well," he said to Avril and Sonia, who were also decked out in Gothic finery.

"Charmer," replied Sonia, flashing her Internet fangs. "But now you're too dowdy to go with us now. Grab him, girls!"

Their taxi arrived ten minutes later and the driver gave Moon a quizzical look as he climbed into the front seat. "Halloween come early has it?" he asked dryly after they had told him their destination.

"Something like that," replied Moon, from behind a mask of Goth make-up. He gestured with his eyebrows towards the girls in the back seat. "It wasn't my idea," he whispered.

"Oh?" replied the cabby, nodding to confirm his membership of the brotherhood of long-suffering males. "The things we do for love, eh?"

Chapter 24

They arrived at the *Hangman's Rest* just after quarter to nine. Moon paid the taxi driver, who gave Ellie's legs one final long appreciative look before driving off towards the city centre. "Are you sure I shouldn't have worn a longer dress?" she commented, hitching down her taffeta frills and trying to pull her stockings up further.

"No, you look fantastic," replied Avril, shaking her head enviously. "I just wish I had your problems."

"Foin lookin' doxy you 'as there, mate," whispered a villainous-looking spirit, who Moon knew often haunted the entrance of the car park. He leered suggestively at Ellie. *"'Ow much?"* he asked Moon, winking lewdly at the girls.

"Not for sale, George," Moon vibed back.

"Buggery!" swore the ghost. *"An' Oi does loike moy doxies. Are 'ee sure, Moon?"*

"Of course he's sure," replied Sonia, who was listening in on the conversation. *"Now, sod off!"*

"She'm got a mouth on 'er fer a sickly lookin', toiny titted 'ore, that one," said George, frowning at Sonia.

"You're no oil painting yourself, Puss-face!" retorted Sonia, shooting a dagger-filled glare at the lusty spook.

"Darling, we're not alone," interjected Moon, nodding at their companions and taking Sonia by the arm. *"See you later, George."*

"Hey! *I can hear you,"* vibed Sonia in surprise.

"Yes, it has possibilities, doesn't it?" observed Moon. This was the first time he had used silent ghost speak around Sonia since she had begun to develop her own psychic gifts and it hadn't occurred to him that they might be able to communicate that way.

"Is something wrong?" asked Ellie. "Sonia, are you sick."

"No, just felt a bit nauseous there for a second. I'm fine now."

"Are you sure you don't want to go into the main bar and sit down? We could get you a glass of water."

"No, I'm alright; let's just get into the gig. Okay?" Sonia looked up at Moon. *"Who was that little maggot?"* she asked in ghost-speak as they headed towards the sound of *Blood Velvet's* opening number. *"One of those bits of gallows' bait you said haunt this place?"*

"Actually, Gallows George was the local hangman a few hundred years ago. He stays around because he misses the old days." Moon grinned. *"These days he has several fast friends among the people he executed. Funny old world, isn't it?"*

"I guess so."

They were joined by Roger, who was waiting for them outside the function room door, then they stopped at the ticket desk, which was the same beer-stained bar table at which Moon had first met Sonia and Avril several months earlier. This time it was being manned by the diminutive Ragger and his girlfriend Suzy, an attractive white-blonde punk-goth. The sides and back of her hair were shaven in a kind of shaggy Mohawk, which showed off a coiled dragon tattoo that ran around the back of her head from left to right. Suzy was over six foot tall and had piercings in just about any place you could conceivably have one. When Ragger had first introduced Moon to Suzy he had thought the two of them were an odd couple, but he had come to know Ragger on a more friendly basis over the time he had been visiting the *Rest* and had grown to recognise the strength and love in their relationship. Suzy was rather shy, despite her size and taste in metal-wear, and Moon suspected they had both been victimised at school because of their unusual heights, which might explain the powerful bond that had grown between them now.

"Hi, Moon, how goes it?" asked Ragger, treating their company to a cheeky grin. He noticed Ellie. "Hey! A new face, aren't you going to introduce us?"

"Hi Ragger, this is Ellie, she's a friend of Sonia's; Ellie, meet Suzy and Ragger, two stalwarts of the *Hangman's Rest*."

"Oh, I'm a bit too short to be a stalwart," said Ragger, self-effacingly. "Although some people might agree to the 'wart' part." He grinned again and stuck out his hand. "Nice to meet you, Ellie, and welcome to the *Rest*."

"Pleased to meet you," replied Ellie, shaking his hand with obvious amusement. "And you too, Suzy," she smiled up nervously at the tattooed and pierced Amazon who towered over her.

Suzy smiled shyly and muttered a muted, "Nice to meet you."

"The great buff and beautiful one told me to put aside some tickets for you," said Ragger, whose impression of Uri hadn't improved over the last few months. Grabbing a rubber stamp from the table, he pressed it onto the back of Moon's hand, leaving the black outline of a grinning skull with a rose in its teeth imprinted on his skin. As he did this Ragger caught Moon's eye, looked over at Ellie and whispered conspiratorially, "Wow! Legs!" then rolled his eyes and whistled softly.

"Yeah," Moon whispered and nodded. "Quite phenomenal, aren't they?"

"Are you two through ogling my friend?" vibed Sonia testily. *"Or do you want me to ask her to let you have a closer look? If she can avoid treading on your tongues, that is."*

Moon was beginning to wonder if being able to communicate with Sonia by vibing was a good thing. *"Sorry, love, but you have to admit they are very nice legs, and you and Avril have displayed them to wonderful effect. Blokes just can't help being appreciative of that sort of thing."*

"Okay, but just remember that I'm wearing a miniskirt too. A few more appreciative glances in my direction wouldn't go amiss!"

Moon checked out Sonia's short but shapely legs, looking very nice under a pair of fine, slightly sparkly, black tights with a border of stylised batwings running down the outside of each. *"Your legs are lovely,"* he replied truthfully. *"It's just, well, stockings... You know, that little gap at the top does strange things to the male libido."*

"You never told me that you had a lingerie fetish." They entered the function room and were greeted by a wall of sound and heaving bodies.

"I don't," replied Moon petulantly. *"No more than any other guy, anyway. I think it's just plumbed into our genes; you know, like poor personal hygiene and an aversion to weepy movies."*

"What does everyone want, it's my shout?" he said as loud as he could over the sound of the band. *Blood Velvet* were playing one of their livelier numbers. It was called 'Violet Moonshine', and it combined a traditional gypsy violin dance with Roanne's heavy bass guitar and ethereal vocals, supported by a strong, pulsing rhythm from Charli on drums. Uri leapt around the small stage like an electrified demon, sawing at his violin with his bow, so passionately that Moon would not have been surprised to see smoke rising from it. Down at the front several Uri look-alikes of assorted shapes and sizes attempted poor impersonations of his style. "God! He's got a fan-club," Moon muttered under his breath.

"Sad, isn't it?" yelled Avril, nodding at a rather overweight Uri clone. "They don't seem to be able to understand that they look utterly absurd!"

Moon glanced at Avril's generous figure, trussed up in an artful combination of black lace, purple velvet and corsetry, combined with well applied make-up to give her the required blood-starved undead look, and thoughts of pots and kettles filled his head. "Aw, give them a break," he yelled. "They're enjoying themselves. Where's the harm in it?"

Despite the crowd at the bar, it didn't take long for Moon to get attention because Kate was serving and she was still pleased with the free publicity his article had given the *Hangman's Rest*. Leaving the bar with their drinks on a tray, Moon found his way blocked by a mass of gyrating bodies. *"Where are you?"* he vibed at the top of his ghost-voice. *"Over here!"* came replies from several different directions, but Moon recognised Sonia's vibe and, studiously ignoring the beckoning arms of an assortment of spirits situated around the room, he made his way carefully to a small table in an alcove, where the girls had established themselves out of the main blare of the music.

"They're really good!" Ellie shrieked over the music, nodding towards the band.

Moon nodded his head vigorously then paused in mid-nod as he glanced towards the stage. Wispy blue tendrils of spirit energy drifted towards the band, where they coalesced into three distinct streams and seemed to earth themselves in the foreheads of each of the vampires. He vibed Sonia and nodded at the stage, *"Do you see?"*

Sonia gazed at the band. *"Yeah, I think I do. Are they somehow feeding off the audience?"*

"Uri told me about this, they feed off the energy and belief generated by their fans. He reckons it's totally benign but it's still weird to watch it happen."

"It's actually quite beautiful," replied Sonia. *"A true symbiosis, they give the audience music and a really great time and we give them power."*

"Plus plenny to spare." It was one of the ghosts who had answered Moon's hail earlier on. Up close Moon recognised him as Dick, the card-sharp, who haunted the window corner in the main bar and, to Moon's surprise, he was glowing with bright blue energy.

Moon watched tiny sparks of lightning flickering at the edges of the ghost's translucent frame. *"So that's caused by the energy build up in here?"*

"Aye, an' it's wunnerful. All this life energy fillin' the place gives a body a real boost."

"Who's your friend?" asked Sonia.

"Sonia, this is Dick. I don't really know much about him except that he haunts the barroom."

Dick doffed his floppy hat, revealing the thin bald dome of his skull, and said, *"Richard Reese M'dear, gen'lman gambler an' frien' t' the ladies."*

"And that's a line I bet you've used a million times," replied Sonia.

"Hey everybody!" squealed Ellie excitedly, pointing in the general direction of Dick. "Do you see a kind of glow in the air over there?"

"Best scarper," vibed Dick and blinked out, appearing elsewhere in the crowd.

"Oh, it's gone," said Ellie disappointedly.

"I suppose it was a trick of the light, love," replied Sonia. *"Might have guessed she'd be a borderline psychic, the number of late-night discussions we've had on the subject,"* she vibed to Moon.

"Yeah," said Moon. "There's a lot of smoke in the air in here, I guess a stray wisp got caught in one of the stage lights."

"You must be right," Ellie agreed reluctantly. "But just for an instant there it looked like a face. Old places like this, you know, they soak up a lot of psychic energy." Moon nodded in mild agreement, as if it were something to which he hadn't given much thought.

Avril looked sharply at Moon and Sonia. "It's okay," Sonia mouthed while Ellie's head was turned towards the stage.

They stopped trying to communicate over the music and sat back to enjoy the show. When Uri announced their next number, 'Lilies and Lace', Sonia dragged Moon to his feet announcing, "We're going to *dance* to this one, see you later guys."

The song was a slow, romantic number with a waltz-like beat. Uri's violin added a clear and soulful counterpoint to the combination of Roanne's soprano and Charli's keyboard accompanied mezzo-soprano. "This is beautiful," commented Moon, as he and Sonia held each other tightly on the dance floor.

"Yes, I've been wanting to dance to this one with you ever since we first met," she replied, reaching up with her mouth and kissing him.

"Mmm!" he replied, returning the kiss and holding her closer, as the wistful melody seemed to become part of their souls and made them feel like they never dared part again. Then, after what seemed like an eternity frozen in crystal, the number finally drew to a close. "Wow!" said Moon, wondering what they had just shared. "Was that magic?"

"Perhaps it was just our magic for each other," replied Sonia. "Don't try to analyse it, you'll ruin it."

"I suppose so," replied Moon reluctantly. He hated things he couldn't explain. "Looks like Ellie's enjoying herself anyway," he commented, nodding over to their table where Avril and Ellie sat chatting with Roger and a tall, rangy Goth with what looked like natural dark hair, as opposed to the dye-jobs a lot of Goths affected.

"I should say so, that's Rufus, the guitarist from *Unquiet Grave*, and he looks pretty smitten."

They returned to their table, where Moon and Sonia had to share a chair to make room for the newcomer. "Rufus, this is Moon," said Avril. "And, of course, you know Sonia."

Rufus nodded. "Hi Moon, I read your article in *Venue*; good stuff."

"Glad you liked it," replied Moon. "They've given me a regular slot for music related items now. My next one's due in next month's issue. It's about the local blues guitar scene."

"No, really? I'll have to keep an eye out for that one." The enthusiasm of Rufus' reply surprised Moon as the *Grave*'s music was at the heavier end of the Goth scene. "My dad plays blues guitar around the local circuit. Donny MacRoss, perhaps you've heard of him?"

"Yes, I had a short interview with him a couple of weeks ago. I like his stuff."

"Dad taught me all I know about guitar," yelled Rufus over the start of the next number. "I still try to find time to go to his gigs when I can." Rufus tried to continue but his voice was overwhelmed by a screaming guitar chord. Uri had hung up his violin and picked up what looked like a genuine vintage Strat, his long fingers dancing over the strings as the band played the intro to a song that Roanne announced was called 'Baroquetta'. The starting riff sounded like a Bach fugue as Uri's fingers traced an almost mathematical progression up his guitar's neck, mirrored exactly by Roanne's long but dainty digits walking up the strings of her bass. Charli played counterpoint on her keyboards, her long, blue-black hair flicking wildly as she poured her energy into the music. Suddenly, she executed a wild turn, dragged her drumsticks from a quiver on her hip with a flourish, and attacked her electronic drum-pad with equal fervour as the song went into the first verse. Uri and Roanne started singing a West Coast Rock style duet:

"Your face is an echo from long ago,

Your beauty is young but you seem so old,"

Uri sang in his rich, chocolaty baritone, his dancing fingers switching to chord shapes as he concentrated on the words.

"And now I'm here to steal your soul...
Sad Baroquetta!"

Roanne's soprano took on an eerie edge as she played the part of a tragic ghost who stalked the centuries, desperate for love but cursed with a terrible hunger, that drove her to consume the soul of every man who tried to love her. Moon wondered which of the trio had written the song and if it was possibly autobiographical. The song concluded when Baroquetta finally found a lover so passionate that, instead of her curse consuming him, their love consumed them both, transforming them into a single eternal flame. Moon was puzzled slightly by this but thought that songs didn't necessarily have to make sense, did they?

This was officially the final song of the set but at the demand of the audience *Blood Velvet* played another adapted gipsy violin piece for an encore then wound up, despite further demands from the audience, to make way for the main bands of the evening. Their set over, the band helped the roadies stash away their instruments then walked out into the audience, stopping to acknowledge greetings and congratulations as they made their way to Moon and the girls' table.

"Well, Moon," said Uri. "Roanne tells me you've been having some problems."

"Yes," replied Moon. "But I'd rather not talk about them here," he nodded almost imperceptibly towards Ellie. "Uri, I'd like you to meet Ellie, she's an old friend of Sonia's."

Uri bowed and kissed Ellie's hand. Somehow, with Uri dressed in his stage gear of black satin and white lace, this didn't seem at all out of place. "*Ya ochen ocharovan,*" he said as he placed a kiss in the palm of her hand. "*Vui, ochen krasaveetza* - You are very beautiful."

Moon could see the blush riding up Ellie's neck, even through her pale make-up, as she looked up, tongue-tied, at the blond giant. "Oh don't pay him any notice, love" said Roanne irritably. "He'd like to think that he could charm the birds out of the trees if we'd let him."

"I think he probably could," replied Ellie, raising her hand to her neckline. "Somehow, 'Hi, Uri,' doesn't seem to cut the mustard after that introduction."

"When it comes from one as charming as you it is eloquence itself," replied Uri. "Hi, Ellie."

"Oh, leave it off!" complained Roanne. "Honestly, he's always like this after a gig. Too much adoration, it makes him think he's the bee's knees! Isn't that right, Charli?"

"Indeed," answered the quietest member of the trio. "He can be quite exasperating."

"*Boszhe moi*!" Uri caressed his forehead in mock despair and fixed Moon with a twinkling eye. "Celtic women! Have nothing to do with them, my friend. Once you let them into your life you get no respect; no respect at all!"

Uri seemed more Russian than usual and Moon wondered if all the energy he had absorbed during the performance had left him a little drunk. In fact all three vampires seemed to be very exuberant, even Charli who was now chatting away with Roanne and the girls. "I'm sure there are compensations, Uri," he replied, glancing at Roanne's near perfect bottom.

Uri smiled mysteriously. "Oh, yes, there are." He checked that the others were deep in conversation then asked, "What's this about one of Rurik's followers trying to kill you?"

"The ring leader of the bunch behind the abductions tried to run me down in his four-by-four this afternoon. I guess Rurik must know we're onto them. We wouldn't have come out but Sonia and Ellie had made previous plans and we thought we'd better make it look like 'business as usual'."

Uri shook his head. "Oh, Moon! I hadn't expected things to escalate this far or I wouldn't have insisted that you get involved."

"It's not your fault, Uri; there are a number of other supernatural parties who are just as insistent, if not more so. I suppose it's just a job I was meant to do." He grimaced. "Anyway, we finally have a clue to where Rurik's hiding out."

"We have?"

"Yes, one of those 'other parties' I mentioned told me that If I wanted to find Rurik I should look for a 'blighted place'. Oddly enough, there was an item on the local news tonight about a strange disease that's affecting the vegetation on a section of the Downs up between *Ladies Mile* and the *Circular Road*. Have you any idea what's up there?"

"Of course I do! The Severn Beach Line of the Severn Valley Railway runs right under that area. I remember them digging the tunnel for it in the eighteen eighties." The vampire stroked his chin. "What else is under there, I wonder? Because of this city's smuggling connections, there are many secret, hidden away places in Bristol. The Ministry of Defence moved into several of those during the Second World War, no doubt making their own modifications and extensions. There could be a substantial complex down there for all we know."

"Yes, well I think that's worth investigating." Moon looked over at the girls. "But not tonight. Tonight we want to show Ellie a good time. Have you any suggestions?"

Uri nodded enthusiastically. "I know just the place."

Chapter 25

The night seemed strangely quiet after the noise of the band when they left the smoky humidity of the pub for the slightly cooler environment of a mid-June evening. Roger and Rufus were playing later in the evening so they couldn't come along with the rest of them. Rufus had virtually begged Ellie to stay and hear their set but this had only succeeded in making Ellie think he was too keen on her. The streets were virtually unpopulated, because most of those out for their Saturday night fun were already in the bar or club of their choice, although their small party of Goths did receive a few cat calls from a group of ageing skateboard punks, who were practising their manoeuvres on the footpaths crossing College Green. It was a fifteen minute walk from the *Rest* to the bottom of Park Street, where Uri led them down a side alley to an arched doorway with a small neon sign over it, which read: 'Encrypted'. "This is the place," he said," opening the door, "We won't have any trouble getting in here dressed in Goth gear; the manager's a Goth himself."

They walked into a small entrance hall that looked like the chapel of an old-fashioned funeral parlour mated with a 1930's theatre foyer. It was all purple plush velvet and silver cherubs. On closer examination, Moon realised that the latter had bats' wings and tiny fangs protruding from under their chubby baby lips. The girl in the ticket booth, who was dressed like a Hammer Horror version of Alice in Wonderland, broke into a wide grin when she saw Uri. "Hello my luvver!" she cried in what Moon hoped was an exaggerated Bristol accent. "How's my favourite vamp then?"

"All ze better for zeeink you, my tasty leettle morsel," replied Uri, producing a very bad Bela Lugosi impersonation from behind his raised arm. The pair leant over the desk and kissed passionately.

Sonia nudged Roanne between the ribs, eliciting a surprised flash of fangs. "I guess they know each other then?"

Roanne gave the ticket girl an icy look. "Oh yes, they know each other. Lizzie's one of Uri's 'blood donors'. He's even suggested we invite her into the 'family'. He says he enjoys her vitality but she's had a double veto from Charli and me. Both of us find her extremely tiresome, to put it politely. The prospect of spending eternity with all that fucking chirpiness is, quite frankly, our idea of Hell."

Not for the first time, Moon found himself wondering about the nature of the relationship between his three vampire friends. "I know what you're thinking, Moon," said Charli, who was suddenly standing very close to him. "Yes, we are lovers, all three of us." She caressed Roanne with a long, sultry glance which could have set the air on fire. "But we aren't selfish, you know, in five hundred years you learn to share. You and Sonia might want to consider that some day."

Moon cleared his throat, which had suddenly become very dry. "Yes, we'll think about it," he managed squeakily.

"Not this side of hell we won't!" vibed Sonia emphatically. *"They may be the good guys but they're still bloody predators one way or another."*

"I was just being polite," Moon vibed back.

"Oh yeah? Then why have you gone three shades pinker? I know you men..."

"Forgive me for butting in on this charming little lovers' tête-à-tête." Charli's voice rang clearly in their heads. *"But we vampires also know the language of ghosts, as do many other 'predators' that might not be so friendly. It is not a closed channel, so to speak."* Both female vampires were regarding them with arched eyebrows.

Now was Sonia's turn to blush. *"I'm sorry, I didn't know you could hear us."*

"Nonsense," replied Roanne, her hidden laughter tinkling through their spirits like breaking icicles. *"It's good that you're wary of us. We really **are** predators, no matter how hard we fight to retain our humanity. That kind of wariness could save your lives. It's a good instinct."* Roanne gave Sonia a teasing look. *"The offer still stands though."*

Sonia's blush darkened from pink to red. *"Erm... We'll let you know."*

"Are you okay, Sonia? You look a bit flushed." Ellie's face was a picture of puzzlement as she looked from her friend to the two female vampires and back again; she must have sensed their unspoken exchange but was uncertain what she had experienced. Moon was surprised that the couple who had just entered behind them couldn't feel the sexual tension being generated by Charli and Roanne. It was almost tangible.

"Yeah, fine," replied Sonia with a wary glance at Roanne, "it's just a bit warm in here, that's all."

"Children! Play nicely!" Uri's warning vibe was a thunder of authority. *"I apologise, Moon... Sonia, it's the rush after the concert. It makes us a little giddy so our vampire natures are harder to control."*

"I'll make a note of that for the future," Moon replied dryly.

Ellie, who had missed all this, was still fussing over her friend. "Are you sure you're okay? You weren't too well earlier, were you? We can go home if you want, I don't mind."

"I'm all right!" said Sonia emphatically. Then she whispered, "It's just the time of the month that's all. I always get a bit flaky around the start, remember?"

"Oh? Yes, I remember," Ellie nodded. "Well, let me know if it gets too bad and we can go if you want to." Sonia had obviously referred to an old problem that Moon was finding himself having to adjust to. Sonia's anaemic look sometimes wasn't just make-up.

They entered the main part of the club via a small bar and picked up some drinks on the way. The place was hot and smelt of perspiration, stale alcohol and mildew. It was impossible to have a cellar this close to the river without some damp breaking through. The dance floor was packed with couples, mostly Goths, but quite a few were more conventionally dressed and Moon was surprised to see that one or two others wore fetish gear. "There is a private section for those who want to play adult games," Uri spoke softly in his ear. "You would be surprised to know how popular it is."

"Really?" replied Moon, jumping at the potential subject for a new article. "Do you know anyone who might agree to an interview?"

"Oh, I think that might not be hard to arrange," replied Uri with a twinkle in his eyes.

Roanne gave a snort. "He's pulling your leg, Moon. We own the place."

"You do?" asked Sonia. The vampires seemed very talkative tonight. Moon thought it was probably another side effect of their overdose of life-force.

"Oh yes." Roanne shot a surreptitious glance at Avril and Ellie. "It's been in the 'family' for years. It started life as a coffee house in the seventeenth century."

"So your 'family' has always tiptoed on the edge of propriety then?" observed Moon with a slight smirk.

"We've never seen the point of *stupid* rules," explained Uri. "But we've always tried to stay on the right side of the law."

Uri bought the first round of drinks and they found a table on a raised wooden dais set back from the dance floor. "Do you own any other businesses in the city?" Moon asked Uri covertly, hoping to gain further insight into his friend's lifestyle while he was in a candid mood.

Uri lowered his voice. "A few, yes. The girls and I have been living in Bristol for centuries; it's amazing how you collect things if you hang around long enough."

"Like property?" asked Moon ingenuously.

Uri laughed. "Yes, like property."

Moon privately revised his estimate of the vampires' material wealth. He had assumed they were merely well off but he was beginning to suspect they were multi-millionaires.

A tall, handsome, dark-haired thirty-something man, wearing a slightly outdated dark blue business suit over an open collared white shirt, walked with self-assurance up to their table. In the part yell, part pantomime language of an experienced night-clubber, he asked Ellie if she wanted to dance. Moon saw the flash of 'chemistry' between them as she nodded her enthusiastic reply. *Looks like someone's in for a lucky night,*

Moon commented to himself, as those long legs went past his face.

Sonia nudged him. "Fancy a dance yourself, you old letch?"

"Less of the old!" he grumbled as she dragged him out onto the dance floor. Uri took their lead, gliding gracefully onto the floor with Roanne and Charli on either side of him. They flowed into a sinuous dance that was, inexplicably, powerfully erotic, even though it contained nothing which could be identified as overtly sexual. "I'm down here!" yelled Sonia irritably, dragging his attention away from the gyrating vampires.

"Sorry," replied Moon. "I was just wondering how they do *that*."

Sonia glanced over to where a growing space was forming around their friends as other dancers stopped to watch in appreciation. "Oh, just more vampire crap," she commented sarcastically, "if we ignore them they might stop."

"They don't seem too bothered whether people are watching or not."

"Don't you believe it! They're as drunk as skunks on the energy they sucked up earlier and they're going for dessert. Only, I guess it's sexual energy they're lapping up this time."

Moon concentrated and found he could just make out pale violet wisps of energy floating towards the vampires. "You're right, I can see it. I wonder if that's one of the reasons they run this place the way they do…"

"Yes, and just guess what Charli and Roanne would be up to if we took them up on their, oh so tempting, offer. They don't do anything that's not to their advantage."

Moon considered this for an instant. Charli and Roanne's earlier antics must have touched a raw nerve for Sonia to be quite so scathing about their friends. "So? That just proves that they're more human than we'd like to think they are." He turned from half watching the vampires to gaze into her dark, cinnamon-brown eyes. "They've done their best to achieve a lifestyle that avoids the destructive drives in their nature. I don't think it's fair to judge them on how they…"

Moon's voice dwindled as he saw Ellie stepping off the dance floor with her handsome stranger, bag in hand as if she intended to leave. "Looks like Ellie's not coming home tonight," he commented, nodding in their direction.

As Sonia turned to look, they both caught the crimson flash of twin rubies through the open neck of Ellie's companion's shirt. "Jerry!" cried Sonia in alarm.

"He's one of them."

Sonia's face was a mask of shock as Moon turned to her. "We have to stop them," he shouted against the backbeat of the heavy trance number that the DJ had just chosen. "You go and get the guys and I'll do my best to catch them before they leave."

Moon rushed through the entrance doors just in time to see Ellie and her abductor's taxi pull away from the kerb. He yelled and ran a short way up the hill after them but there was nothing he could do.

Sonia, Avril and the vampires appeared at the club entrance. Uri and the girls had the strange, pumped up, feral look that he had learnt meant they were gearing up for a fight. Their long hair whipped around their faces as if they stood on a stormy hill top and the psychic energy pouring from them hit him solidly, like a storm-force blast. "They've taken a taxi!" Moon yelled. "But I think I know where they're headed!"

A brief explanation followed then they all slipped into the nearest deserted side street. "You don't have to do this." Sonia looked anxiously at Avril. "Jerry and I know what to expect and we've got a few tricks up our sleeves if we're attacked. You don't have any."

"Sonia, I've been doing kick boxing for ten years and made the regional finals three years running," said Avril sarcastically. "You're going up against humans as well as the ghoulies and ghosties tonight so you might need a bit of extra muscle. Anyway, I wouldn't miss this for the world, so you'd better not try to stop me."

While this exchange was taking place Moon was on the phone to the police. He tried the emergency line first but was told nothing could be done on the vague suspicion that someone of adult age might be in danger from their evening pick-up. In desperation he dialled Whatley's mobile number. The inspector answered groggily just before Moon expected to be diverted to voicemail. "Moon, do you know what time it is? This had better be important!" Moon could hear Mrs Whatley snoring robustly in the background. At least he *hoped* it was Mrs Whatley, for all he knew the inspector could be having an affair with a sumo wrestler – it would account for the frightening volume of the staccato rumble issuing from the handset.

"Inspector, one of Sonia's friends has been kidnapped by the cultists and I think I know where they've taken her."

Whatley woke up very quickly. "You're certain of this?"

"As certain as we can be. Ellie was picked up by a man wearing one of those cult pendants and they took a taxi towards the Downs, which is where I think Rurik is hiding. There's a blight affecting the grass and foliage on the part of the Downs that lies over the Severn Beach line tunnel, which my 'contacts' have told me is a probable sign of his presence. I think he must have found some kind of hidden installation or cave system under there."

"I'll check that out," replied Whatley. "I don't suppose there's any chance of me convincing you to wait until my men arrive?"

Moon shook his head. "Sorry, Art. These guys are killers; we can't afford to leave Ellie with them any longer than we have to. Relax, we're well prepared and probably better equipped than your constables are to face what's under there when all's said and done."

"Okay, Moon, but take care, okay?" Whatley's concern seemed to radiate through the phone.

"Of course I will, I'm not planning to become ghost fodder any time soon. See you up there." He disconnected after Whatley's goodbye and turned to the others. "Right, we've got police back-up on its way, so let's get going and rescue Ellie."

Chapter 26

Trembling in Uri's steely embrace, Moon clenched his eyes tightly shut to block out the cityscape rushing by beneath them. "Not much further, my friend," Uri shouted consolingly into the wind. "I can see the ventilation shaft now. I'm just going to drop straight into it so don't be surprised if it's dark when we land."

Moon felt the change in the air as they entered the concrete shaft and heard the snap and scream of tortured metal as Uri brushed through the vent's rusting protective grill as if it were as insubstantial as a spider-web. Then they were mercifully back on solid ground. Moon opened his eyes and could just vaguely see the horizontal portion of the shaft running off into the darkness to his right. Dead trailers of bramble and old man's beard tangled down chaotically from the upper shaft and he had to brush his hand across his face to ward off the ghostly caress of cobwebs. "How the hell are we going to see where we're going?" he whispered breathlessly. "We'll break our necks!"

"The girls and I have excellent night vision," replied Uri, his retinas flashing blue in the dark as they caught the meagre light from the mouth of the vent. "You'll be safe if you let us guide you."

"I guess that's how it'll have to be…"

Moon was interrupted by a joyous whoop from above. "Whoo! That was some trip," Avril gasped excitedly as Charli deposited her beside Moon. "We must do that again sometime."

"Shush!" hissed Sonia, who had landed a second later with Roanne. "We're trying to sneak quietly into a stronghold of evil and you insist on yelling your head off. I knew it was a mistake to let you come along."

"Don't be such a killjoy, Sonia." Avril was uncowed by her friend's sternness. "They won't hear us from here."

"I just hope they haven't posted lookouts, that's all," commented Moon. "If they have that's our element of surprise gone straight away."

"Don't worry, my friend." Uri shook back his white-blond mane and sniffed the air. "If there were other humans within earshot I would smell them. Here, I only smell rats. Shall we be off?"

They crouched down and made their way along the ventilation pipe, which was about four feet high, until Uri, who was leading the way because of his superior night vision and strength, stopped sharply. "Another set of bars," he whispered. He sniffed the air. "And something else…"

"What is it?" asked Moon, peering around Uri's broad shoulders to where a dim light shone through the grille.

"If I didn't know it was impossible I'd swear it was another vampire." He ripped the grille from its fixtures. "We'll soon find out."

There was a shuffling noise and an unkempt figure with wild hair and a straggly beard appeared through the opening. Moon thought it might be a tramp who had sought shelter in the tunnel beyond but then it snarled like an angry puma and leapt on Uri, its clawed hands seeking his throat. Without effort, Uri punched straight through its chest with one hand, taking out its heart. The unfamiliar vampire had time to look stupidly at the gaping hole in his chest before he burst into flames and was quickly reduced to a pile of ash. "Thank the Gods for *Buffy* and *Blade*," said Uri. "If their storylines didn't make vampires die so neatly in the modern imagination this would be very hard to explain to the police."

"It *was* a vampire?" asked Moon.

"Yes, it was," Uri replied wearily. "It seems Rurik has regained his power to infect others. This is bad news for us, my friend. We don't know how many more of his people Rurik has turned."

They slipped one by one past the broken grille into the tunnel beyond. A gas-powered camping lantern hung from one wall, dimly illuminating the track for a few paces on either side but no more of Rurik's minions waited for them. It would seem the master vampire and his cult weren't expecting trouble.

"Shouldn't we take this with us?" whispered Avril, reaching to take the lamp from its hook.

"No, leave it." Uri shook his head, his pupils huge and owl-like from their trip through the darkness. "It would only give us away and the three of us can see well enough in the dark to prevent you humans from injuring yourselves. We're also powerful enough to deal with most of the opposition should they attack us in the dark... Moon, what are your small friends doing?"

Moon jumped a little at Uri's abrupt question and looked around. The little ghost balls, which he had grown to ignore as he had become familiar with their presence, had ceased their constant exploration of their surroundings and were hovering very still around his head, leaving only the front free so he could see and speak. "I don't know." He regarded his ghostly halo with puzzlement. "Perhaps they sense Rurik nearby and they're afraid."

"They don't look afraid to me," observed Roanne. "They look like they're spoiling for a fight."

"What're they talking about?" Avril asked Sonia, trying to see what the others were looking at.

"At first Rurik's power came from sucking the life out of ghosts," Sonia explained. "Jerry told me that there's a kind of left over essence, a tiny blue glowing ball of life force. For some reason they latch on to him when they find him and now it seems they're acting oddly."

"Oh, right..."said Avril with a puzzled look. "This sort of thing happens to him a lot, does it?"

"From what he's told me this is a bit weirder than usual but not much!"

"Well, I'm glad you've got him, not me. Give me Roger any time – there's nothing more dependable than a bass player."

"Oh, being with Jerry has its compensations." Sonia looked over at Moon fondly.

"Yes, I've heard," replied Avril archly. "I'm surprised there haven't been complaints from halfway down the street."

Sonia hit her friend on the shoulder. "You're not supposed to mention that sort of thing."

"If the ladies have finished gossiping, we need to go this way," said Uri quietly. "Please refrain from talking and if we must speak we should keep our voices as low as possible. Sound travels far in tunnels and if there are more vampires they will hear the slightest whisper."

They set off with Uri and Charli at the front and Roanne protecting their rear, hugging close to the tunnel wall in case one of the overnight freight trains came through.

There was a glimmer of light ahead and Uri suddenly hugged closer to the wall waving his arm against the grey glow indicating for the others to do the same. "What is it?" Moon whispered, urgently.

"A doorway in the wall with two guards."

"Are they...?" A snarl, from above Moon's head, answered his question for him. They were vampires, nothing human could scurry up a wall like that.

Charli reached up calmly from the other side of Moon and ripped the woman's head off, leaving Moon brushing ash and embers out of his hair. "They're only fledglings," she hissed through her fangs. "Cocky and inexperienced; no great threat unless they catch you by surprise."

"Allow me," said Avril enthusiastically, stepping away from the wall and, running up to the other vampire, who was approaching more cautiously, she performed a perfect side kick through its chest, jumping back to shake off the embers. "Whoa! That was hot!"

"Yes, and that was very stupid," said Uri coldly. "You're lucky you caught him by surprise. Please, Miss Avril, don't tackle the monsters on your own. You don't know what you're up against. At best you'll end up dead but, more likely, you'll end up one of them."

"I guess being a vampire would be pretty cool," replied Avril, her eyes still bright with adrenalin.

"Don't devalue your humanity so," counselled Charli. "You would lose the comfort of family, normal human relationships, children and all your life you would have to fight to suppress the instincts of the killer beast raging within you. We may joke about bringing others over but the truth is that we have not done so in the five centuries since we chose to resist our inner evil. We would not wish this travail on anyone else."

"This must be our way in," whispered Moon from beside the reinforced steel door. "Uri, do you sense anyone else nearby?"

Uri stilled and cocked his head from side to side. After several seconds he replied, "Not nearby, no. But Rurik is definitely in there, I can feel his stinking presence almost as strongly as I did when he was my master all those centuries ago."

"Can you get through that?" Moon nodded at the door.

"Not on my own but there are three of us. My ladies, your strength is needed here!" The three vampires braced themselves against the heavy metal door and pushed hard with their shoulders. The steel held for a second then burst inwards with a mighty crack and the screeching of twisted metal against the tunnel walls.

"I guess our presence here's no longer much of a secret," commented Avril into the following silence.

Like a bull in a china shop, thought Moon to himself. "Avril's right, we need to be twice as careful from now on. What do you think, Uri, a triangular formation with you and the girls at the points?"

Uri thought for a moment. "Yes, that should work. I'll take the point and Charli and Roanne the two rear apexes. Good thinking, Moon, we'll make a tactician of you yet."

They got into formation with Moon behind Uri and Sonia side to side with Avril in the middle. The concrete-lined corridor was just wide enough to let them pass. "This looks like it must be Ministry of Defence," whispered Sonia, peering into an open doorway through which rusted army bunks could be seen in disarray, dimly illuminated by the sparse light of widely placed electric ceiling lamps. "World War II, do you think?"

"Cold war more likely," replied Moon, kicking aside a yellowed page of newspaper. The date was almost unintelligible but he could vaguely make out: "'…th Mar.h .962'. Nineteen sixty-two – Cuban Missile Crisis – that would be about right. I wonder what they used it for."

"Probably a command bunker." Uri pointed out what looked like a control room with a fading world map on the wall and ranks of radio consoles along both sides of a central aisle.

"Would make a good news story." Moon poked his head into the room and gazed around with interest.

"Yeah, and it would probably get you locked up," observed Sonia. "This is government secrets type stuff... makes me feel like I'm committing treason just being down here."

"We have worse things to worry about than the government," said Roanne. "I think we're getting close." She nodded at a set of double doors standing slightly ajar in front of them. "I can definitely feel something big and nasty through there."

They approached the doorway with caution. "Why's there no guard?" Avril whispered, glancing around uneasily.

"Perhaps Rurik doesn't think we're much of a threat," replied Uri.

"Well, let's show him different then!" snarled Avril.

They burst through the double doors into what must have originally been the installation's canteen. Chairs and tables had been stacked on either side to clear a large area of tiled flooring around which stood roughly thirty people dressed in normal street clothes. This somehow insulted Moon's sense of propriety; if you were going to be part of a sinister cult you should at least have the common decency to wear a cowled black robe.

In the centre of the floor, spread-eagled naked on what looked like a stainless steel serving counter, Ellie lay struggling. Her hands and feet were secured at the corners with rope and she looked tiny and vulnerable before the monster which stood at her feet.

"Ah, Uri." Rurik's voice was a low, gut clenching growl. "I am so glad that you made it in time to see this. This is the first true meal I have taken since the one you robbed me of so long ago." Rurik was also naked. He towered over his cronies by more than half the height of a tall man. A shaggy black mane of hair covered his head, neck and most of his torso. Over the rest of his hugely muscled body and the great, bat-like wings that spread out at each side, the skin was mottled purple and red. His face was like the mutant offspring of a man and a bat, with giant shell-like ears and a dripping, wrinkled, pushed back nose, twitching over a slavering fang-filled mouth. From between his legs, throbbing and erect, thrust an equally ugly penis. "First, I will have her and then I will feed off her and you can do nothing this time to prevent it, you tender hearted weakling!"

Chapter 27

Rurik's lurid words spurred Ellie to struggle more ferociously against her bonds. She screamed furiously against the gag in her mouth, the sound she made becoming something close to an angry roar as she fought to break free. Moon realised with a kind of pride that she was more furious than afraid.

"You don't expect me to stand by and let you destroy someone in my care, do you, you arsehole?" shouted Uri as the vampiric power expanded into him from wherever it normally lay hidden. As it unfolded through him he appeared to grow in size and his face contorted into a snarling mask. The girls moved in on either side of him so they could present a combined front to the ancient vampire lord, their own sleek bodies rippling with barely contained power.

"Shit!" commented Avril, her face a picture of unveiled astonishment. "Is *that* what they really are?"

"No," Rurik replied to Uri's rhetorical question, a sly smile passing over his face. "I expect you to help me!" Then his massive brows knitted together in concentration as he summoned up the full force of his evil will.

Uri groaned and half turned towards Moon, hands grasping the air as he fought to restrain himself. "Sorry, my friend," he gasped through gritted teeth. "I should not have come here. I forgot…"

"Yes!" laughed Rurik. "You forgot that you belong to me body and soul. Forgot the liege-hold I had over you even before we became what we are now. You have grown stronger since we parted, Uri, I'll give you that. The old Uri could never have dreamed to resist me as you do now, but you'll never break the hold I have over you and your bloodkin."

Moon risked a quick look around; Charlie and Roanne were also struggling to prevent themselves from attacking their friends.

"Seize them, my people!" Rurik roared to his cult, "their blood and bodies will be yours tonight, I promise you. Fear not the vampires, they are entangled in my will like flies caught in a web."

There was a moment's hesitation then the cultists swarmed around them, ignoring the vampires and grabbed for the humans. There was an agonised groan from Moon's right and a short, flabby man crumpled to the ground clutching his knee. The foreleg beneath twisted at an unnatural angle, causing Moon to wince involuntarily. That *had* to hurt! "Yes, and there's more of the same for any of you bastards that try to come near me!" yelled Avril menacingly.

In the short pause that followed Moon looked regretfully at Sonia, who shrugged. "I think we're fucked," she said, her eyes searching desperately for a way of escape. She kissed him hard on the lips. "It was nice knowing you, Jerry Moon!" Then the enemy rushed them again and they were fighting for their lives. Four men surrounded Avril and managed to wrestle her to the floor, although one was unconscious and another was missing an ear by the time they had her pinned.

Moon knocked one assailant aside with a roundhouse punch to the jaw and found himself face to face with the loony evangelist from Gloucester Road. She still looked crazy but now she had fangs. The surprise of seeing her free of custody must have registered on Moon's face. "We has very good lawyers," she explained with a mocking grim. "Now the Master say I can 'ave you body an' blood," she hissed. "I not sure which I wants first!" she laughed and slashed at him with her knife. "Blood, I guess."

"Sorry, bitch, all mine!" shouted Sonia as she lunged past Moon and pierced the other woman's chest with the sharp point of a broken chair leg. Their assailant screamed furiously as she burst into flames. In a last act of madness, her knife snaked forward out of the engulfing flames and raked down Sonia's right arm, leaving a long dark gash from wrist to elbow. "Shit!" yelled Sonia, trying to stem the flow of blood with her hand.

Within moments it was all over, Moon and Sonia were held firmly by beefy disciples and Rurik stood smugly before them again. "Well, Seer, your ragamuffin army seems to have failed you. So sad!" He forced his twisted lips into a mocking moue. "All that remains now is for you to die. But you have brought two most tasty morsels for tonight's repast. He gestured at Sonia and Avril. "So I think I will deal with them first." He gestured lewdly at his freshly aroused penis and Moon felt hatred rise in him like a cold tide. The intensity of the emotion astonished him, bringing with it the stark realisation of how much he loved Sonia. "...After I've finished with Gregory's gift of course," Rurik rasped hungrily as he turned back to where Ellie struggled on the makeshift altar. "Hold her," he ordered Charli and Roanne and, although tears of anger and desperation fell from their eyes, they were powerless to disobey.

Ellie was far from content to play the placid victim, however, and as the vampire moved to position himself between her legs, her struggles freed her left ankle, allowing her to draw her leg back as far as it would go and drive her heel hard into Rurik's groin with a force that made Moon gasp. The monster howled and doubled over clutching his bruised balls. The pain provided sufficient distraction to break Rurik's concentration and free Uri and the girls from his control. Snarling like enraged tigers, they turned on the surrounding cultists with angry vigour. Uri swooped down on Rurik before he had a chance to regain his composure and began kicking his former master repeatedly in the nuts. "That's the problem with returning to the flesh isn't it, Rurik? It hurts!"

"It only adds greater pleasure to what I intend to do to you," hissed Rurik painfully, raising himself from the ground with the tips of his huge wings. "A vampire can be tortured for a long, long time and never die." His mouth split into a jagged, fang-filled grin as he reasserted his will on the vampires, despite the obvious pain caused by Uri's efforts to keep him distracted. "I will hear you beg me for death ten thousand times before I tire of it."

Moon saw Uri and his ladies stiffen as Rurik's dominance robbed them of any hope they might have had for victory. *"If you intend to call for aid, now would be a good time,"* a dark, earthy voice rumbled through Moon's mind.

"Yes, of course I need help!" Moon vibed impatiently. *"Isn't it obvious?"*

"Nevertheless, you must still ask," replied the voice. *"It is the rules."*

Moon realised that, whoever this potential saviour was, he wasn't very bright. *"Alright,"* he replied, ducking a cultist's hurtling fist. *"Help... Please!"*

At Moon's silent bidding dark, blocky figures flowed lava-like out of the concrete floor. The ancient lino floor tiles cracked and burst aside as they rose like living statues into the flickering light of the candles and launched themselves violently at the cultists. "What the hell are those?" Sonia's eyes were wild with anticipation of more trouble.

"Gnomes, I guess," replied Moon, realizing Sonia hadn't heard his silent conversation. "I think they're the cavalry..."

"Bit on the large side for gnomes, aren't they? And where're their pointy red hats?" asked Avril, who had broken free of her captors, leaving another one unconscious and the other wishing he was. *She has some issues to work out, that girl*, thought Moon, shaking his head.

"Racial stereotypin'!" rumbled a nearby gnome, bashing two cultists' heads together. "'Gnomes', as in 'spirits of Earth', yes? 'Sides we only wears the red hats fer weddin's an' foonerals. 'S a sign o' respec', see?"

"Okay," Avril nodded incredulously.

It was hard to tell how many gnomes were in the room because they seemed to blend in and out of each other as they passed, like soft clay, but Moon estimated about ten. They made quick work of Rurik's troops and two of them had taken on the vampire prince himself, wrapping themselves around him like a cage of living rock. As their enemies were subdued more of them left the fray to help contain Rurik, who was putting up a strong fight, snapping limbs off his captors and casting them away to prevent them from reforming. The gnomes were quickly running out of substance as they manifested new arms and legs. It wouldn't be long before they satisfied Avril's earlier expectations of size. "Hurry, seer," cried one, whose granite skin was shot through with veins of silvery metal. "We cannot hold him long!"

Moon looked at Uri. "If only we had the sword you used last time…"

"It would not work, my friend." Uri shook his head. "It would only kill the body he possesses. His foul spirit would live on as powerful as ever."

"Why don't you try ghost zapping him?" suggested Sonia, her eyes bright with desperate hope.

"Zap something as powerful as that monster?" asked Moon incredulously. He shrugged, "Well, I suppose can give it a try."

"Perhaps we all should," suggested Uri, a blue flame of ghost light snapping out from his forehead and piercing Rurik's chest.

Rurik laughed. "You will have to do better than that, you weakling!" he roared, snapping off random bits of gnome as he fought hard against his captors.

"Now! All at once!" shouted Moon, concentrating and sending a tendril of ghost energy lashing out against Rurik. Sonia, Uri and the girls followed in suit. Rurik growled in agony but he still wore the same triumphant grin.

"It's no use," yelled Charli in frustration. "There's too much of him!"

Roanne nodded in agreement, turning wearily to look to Moon for any other suggestions. Then her eyes widened with amazement. "What's happening with *those*?" she asked, indicating the ghost globes, which were whirling and closing around Moon's body. The vampire gasped as a pale nimbus grew between the tiny lights and Moon. "They're doing something to his aura!"

Rurik's laughter tailed off as he regarded Moon incredulously. "What kind of trick is this, Seer? Do you try to scare me with these tiny ghosts?" he laughed. "But… I *eat* ghosts!"

Moon could feel the individual energies of his small companions entwining with his spirit. He sensed their cold anger and determination engulfing him and stifling the wave of panic that welled up from inside. A feeling of clarity overwhelmed him, bringing with it a sudden realisation… "You know what,

Rurik?" he smiled sardonically. "I think they're about to return the favour!"

Moon lashed out once more, a filament of pure, white flame extending from his body towards the vampire lord, who countered instinctively with his own red fire. The two threads of energy collided and entangled. Then, to Rurik's horror and astonishment, Moon's thread began to pull back, drawing pulsing red streamers of the vampire lord's stolen power along with it. Around Moon ghostly forms began to take shape: Connor O'Flynn, the navvy; Gordy, the hospital spook; Dominic and several others whom Moon did not recognise. Then Rurik roared in pain as other tiny pinpoints of light began to flow out of his body towards Moon, punching glowing scarlet holes in the vampire's distorted flesh. "You cannot do this! It is impossible!" he cried, trying to pull the little balls of energy back into himself with his massive claws.

"Well, I guess I can," replied Moon. "With a little help from my friends, that is. That's the trouble with being a bully, Rurik. It only works while your victims are afraid of you. Once you've hurt enough people badly enough they get together and fight back." The new ghost balls took their places beside Moon and began to return to human shape. He realized that these must be the victims of Rurik's cult, who had been taken before they could pass over. Their sheer numbers amazed him; there must be at least forty people here whose lives had been sacrificed to this false 'god'.

Rurik's victims began to take on more solid forms as Moon channelled their stolen energy back into them. At his left Sonia released an astonished gasp. "I see them!" she whispered with startled awe.

Moon wished he could explain what was happening but could not let his concentration falter. Even this slight distraction loosened his hold on Rurik and he felt the flow of energy reverse for an instant. *"Not on your life, you bastard!"* the silent yell of an unknown spirit reverberated through Moon and the joint fury of his invisible allies fed him with white hot power. With the slightest hint of extra concentration he regained control of the flow and Rurik howled with frustration. If what now stood pinned between the unyielding gnomes could still be called

Rurik. Its form had diminished to mere human proportions, the great wings had almost dissolved into the, now pasty, flesh and that terrible face was fast losing its demonic aspect. Moon was beginning to recognize those features from somewhere.

A sudden rush of elation, mixed with a touch of deepest gratitude, flowed through him accompanied by a wonder-filled cry of recognition: *"Mary! My Love!"* as Connor O'Flynn finally passed happily into the Light, leaving an echo of peace behind him.

One by one, others began to pass over. The psychic backwash of their passing was intoxicating and almost too euphoric to bear. Sonia and Avril were embracing each other and weeping freely. Uri had gathered his ladies to him in a sort of shell-shocked huddle and Moon realised that his own face was drenched with tears. "Ha!" Rurik's laugh was a bark of abhorrence, cutting across the epiphanous atmosphere like a jagged knife. "Weaklings! Look at you, so clogged with sentiment! You disgust me!"

"No, not weakness," said Uri quietly, raising his head to regard his enemy with pity. "This is what you and those like you cannot understand." He raised a hand, to indicate his companions and the remaining ghosts. "This..." he choked slightly on his emotion, a crimson stained tear running down his cheek. "This is what makes us human. When we stand together against evil, this is our greatest strength. And it will be your downfall."

"Yes!" agreed Moon gently, and the remaining spirits' voices took it and transformed his affirmation into a word of power, ripping the remaining energy out of Rurik.

"No!" The word echoed out of the vampire lord's mouth, a final wailing denial of his defeat, until his body dwindled further and all that was left was unmistakably the pale-faced ringleader, who had tried to run Moon down with his Toyota. He was also unmistakably very, very dead. Moon considered attempting CPR. Did his nurse's duty of care extend to murderous arseholes? "Oh bugger!" he whispered under his breath, it probably did.

"Many come," vibed the leader of the gnomes. *"We must leave."*

"Thank you for your help," replied Moon with a grateful nod.

"Farewell," replied the gnomes, gathering up their broken limbs before they merged back into the bedrock.

"Goodbye," said Moon and the others who had heard their words. He turned to Uri. "That'll be Inspector Whatley and his men on their way. I think you'd better make yourselves scarce."

Inspector Whatley arrived in the underground complex with his squad of police officers to find Moon, Sonia, Avril and Ellie surrounded by the dazed and bemused remnants of Rurik's cult. Several of the cultists were lying wounded or unconscious on the shattered linoleum. However, the last remaining progeny of Rurik's fresh brood of vampires were showing signs of rapid recovery. Moon was performing CPR on the cult leader, which confused several of the officers so much that they dragged Moon away from the body and had him in handcuffs before the girls had a chance to argue his innocence. It was Whatley's timely entrance through the, now shattered, doors of the old canteen that saved Moon from further rough treatment. "Ease off, lads! I know he looks like trouble but you can't arrest anybody for doing a bad Alice Cooper impersonation, he's still on our side."

Moon raised his fingers to his face and they came away black at the tips. The tears that had recently coursed down his cheeks had obviously spelt ruination for the girls' make-up job. The gods alone knew what he must look like. A quick glance at Sonia's mascara-stained features confirmed that 'Alice Cooper' was probably quite accurate. "Hello, Inspector, what kept you?"

"Now, Moon, we came as quickly as we could. Any chance of explaining what's been happening?" He glanced around at the wrecked floor and the groaning bodies of Rurik's supporters. "Did you do all this? You and these three little girls?"

"It's amazing what strength you can muster when your life's in danger, Inspector," quipped Sonia.

Whatley turned towards her and used the movement to mask a surreptitious wink in Moon's direction. "I suppose so, Miss Crest, but I'll need a fuller explanation than that, so I think we'd better all adjourn to the station so we can take your statements." He waved to a woman police constable and pointed to Ellie, who had wrapped herself in a mouldering tablecloth, which barely hid her nakedness. "Constable Ingles, could you find this young lady something to wear, please."

Moon handed Constable Ingles his jacket. "Here this might help."

There was a sudden strangled scream from the back of the room. A policeman was struggling in the grasp of one of Rurik's vampiric offspring. The wretched creature had probably once been a clerical worker, judging by his grubby, ill-fitting two piece suit and burgeoning paunch, but his eyes were now slits of glittering red as he looked up from his victim's throat, a river of crimson coursing down his chin.

"Help him, lads!" yelled Whatley angrily as several uniformed figures converged on the vampire and his victim. "Round up the rest and don't be too dainty with your truncheons." He shook his head. "This is a rum bunch and no mistake. God alone knows what they're cranked up on!"

The remaining vampires gave the police a bit of a run for their money but greater numbers and expert use of truncheons shortly had them cuffed, subdued and dragged off to a riot van waiting by a long concealed entrance near the Downs' water tower.

"I'll take these people to the station in my car," Whatley told his remaining officers. "Mr Moon is the consultant who helped us with the 'vampire killer' case. He was the one who alerted me to this business and we have a few things to discuss – *like how we're going to explain all this away without mentioning ghosts and vampires!*" he added under his breath as the officers left the canteen. "You've handed me a tough one, Moon."

"I know," replied Moon as they made their way back to the surface. "There's no way we're going to be able to tell the truth about all this." He looked grimly back down the tunnel. "I'll tell you one thing though, you ought to get a squad to search this place thoroughly right away. If I'm right the body count for this one's going to be huge."

Whatley's gaze followed Moon's to where the police torches reflected off the mouldering government issue paint work. "Oh shit! I hope not. It took me an age to get anyone in the MOD to admit that this place even exists. It's still classified 'Top Secret'."

"Well, I don't think it will be much longer…"

Moon's comment was cut off by a cry of "Sir! Over here… Oh, God!" and the sound of someone being noisily sick on concrete. A faint whiff of corruption mixed with vomit wafted up from below.

"It looks like you're right, Moon." Whatley's face was pale in the torchlight. "I think I'll let my sergeant and the Scene of Crime boys handle the rest of this. Let's get back to the station."

Moon thought their trip to the police station must have been one of the oddest on record, with a senior police officer and four witnesses using the time available to fabricate a tale believable enough to fool the criminal justice system. By the time they got there Moon and the three girls were word perfect in every detail.

Chapter 28

Moon woke to the sound of a fist pounding on Sonia's bedroom door. The flashing display on her digital alarm clock read 1:32pm. Sonia groaned and spun irritably on the other side of the bed. "What the fuck do you want?" she yelled, poking her face bleary-eyed from under the duvet. They had arrived home around five in the morning once all their statements had been given and they had all been checked over by the medics and pronounced fit to leave.

"Sonia, it's me, Ellie. My train goes at two-thirty and I thought you'd at least want to say goodbye after nearly getting me raped and eaten by vampires!"

"Oh, hang on!" Sonia wrapped herself in the duvet and stumbled over to the door, leaving Moon suddenly naked on the bed. He swiftly grabbed Sonia's teddy bear, which was bright red with devil's horns and a cape, and managed to cover the worst of his nakedness before Sonia opened the door. "God, Ellie, I'm sorry," Sonia apologised through a tangled veil of bed hair. "You know, this hasn't been a typical Bristol weekend." She paused, obviously realising how absurd this statement was. "Are you okay?"

"I'll survive and it'll be something to tell the grandchildren. What interesting lives you live over here. I'd be tempted to move here if I thought I could survive the excitement! That guy Rufus is really cute." She and Sonia grimaced simultaneously and nodded, "Intense, yeah? But cute. That's the reason I ended up going off with that other bloke, you know, Rufus came on to me so strong in the pub it left me desperate for something quick and uncomplicated. I'd love the chance to experiment with the Goth scene a bit too. It seems to be a lot cooler than I thought it was." She looked over Sonia's shoulder. "Oh, hi Moon, nice... teddy!" Moon smiled resignedly and waved.

"We don't normally have to fight off plagues of vampires," said Sonia reassuringly. "Why don't you pop up here for a few weekends and see if Rufus is worth the effort. That way you can play at being a weekend Goth at the same time."

"I might just try that. I'll see you downstairs. I'd keep the bear Moon, it suits you." The offending toy thumped off the back of the door as Sonia closed it.

"Hey! Be careful with that, they don't make them any more."

Moon and Sonia managed to get up and ready in time to join Ellie, who was now back to wearing an outfit in her signature powder blue, for the two bus journey to the station. Moon often wondered why Bristol's Temple Meads Station was so far from the city centre. He supposed that it was probably because the city of Bristol was so well established by the coming of the railways that there was no room for it any further in. They said goodbye to Ellie at the barriers with the usual promises to keep in touch. Ellie surprised Moon by hugging him hard and saying shyly, "Thanks for coming to get me. Sonia told me it was you who worked out where to find me."

"Just doing my job," Moon shrugged. "If the local 'Fairy Mafia' are right about me, that is."

"I think they are," Ellie laughed. "There's a real sense of destiny about you, you know."

"Oh, God, I hope that doesn't mean there's going to be more of this crap!" moaned Sonia. "One big bad nasty trying to take over the world is enough for one lifetime."

"We can but hope," observed Moon absent-mindedly as he watched a Victorian couple wander nonchalantly through one of the walls of the W H Smith kiosk, followed by a red-faced porter pushing a loaded trolley. He wondered briefly if they were left over victims from a nineteenth century rail tragedy or were just frequent travellers having fun reliving a past trip. "But I don't think the Spirit World's done with me yet."

"Well, let me know what happens," cried Ellie as she passed through the ticket barrier. "And if you ever need any help…"

"We know…" joked Sonia.

"Call someone else!" they chorused.

"Do you think we'll have any trouble from the Law about all this?" asked Sonia on the bus home. The subject had clearly been bothering her.

"Well, we came up with the most plausible story we could, given the circumstances."

"Yeah, but it's a bit 'News of the World', isn't it? 'Crazed Drug Cult in Satanic Sacrifice Shocker!' sort of thing. Doesn't sound real to me somehow." Sonia shrugged noncommittally.

"No, not if you put it that way. But the evidence is all there. Nearly forty people dead in suspicious circumstances demands an explanation. I think the public will probably swallow anything they're told as long as they're sure those responsible are out of circulation. I guess we'll be seeing the first headlines in a couple of days. I just hope the press don't connect us with it. The last thing we want is reporters invading our lives."

"Oh, God, no! And what about poor Ellie, if they find out she was nearly their final vict…"

Debbie Harry's voice burst into song from Moon's mobile phone and he stopped her in mid 'hang…' by pressing the receive button. "Hi, Moon? I hope this isn't an inconvenient moment but I just had to tell someone about this before they start tapping my phone." Inspector Whatley sounded sickened and a little frightened.

"What's wrong, Art? You sound terrible?" Moon raised his eyebrows at Sonia, who mouthed a silent question.

"I was called in early for the night shift because three of our suspects mysteriously dropped 'dead' at sunrise."

"Oh, I see…" said Moon. They should have expected this but Moon and Sonia's only previous experience of vampires had been Uri and the girls, who were old enough and powerful enough to resist daylight. It seemed that fledgling vamp underlings were not so resourceful.

"That's not the half of it. When we started shipping them out to the morgue one of them got partially exposed to direct sunlight. Talk about instant revival, she was up off her trolley and laying into our guys like a wildcat trying to get back into the shade. Then she spontaneously combusted. Poor old 'Hammer' Harris and Jimmy Pearce have both got second degree burns and Sally Handley had both cheeks gashed by that thing's claws."

"Poor girl," said Moon, remembering a pretty young woman police constable.

"Yeah, she won't be able to sit down for weeks!"

Whatley's voice was shaking with emotion and concern for his comrades but Moon could detect something else. "What's all this about someone tapping your phone?" Sonia's eyes widened with surprise.

"Yeah, I was just getting to that. When they called me in I was thinking: 'Well there goes our cover-up,' but by the time I was behind my desk this ministry type in a pin-stripe suit was ushered into my office. *Very* expensive pin-stripe suit, you understand?"

"Someone high up?"

"Stratospheric, I reckon. The report of the incident had gone up the line like a bloody rocket and this guy was the result. I guess the Secret Service connection with those tunnels might have drawn things to their attention but they were still far too quick to pick this up. They must have a system in place to identify this kind of thing and feed it in their direction."

"So he was Secret Service?" Moon was whispering now and checked their fellow passengers to make sure no-one was listening too closely, but they all seemed preoccupied with their own concerns.

"I don't know. He said he was with S Branch, but what they're a branch of he didn't say. I asked if he was sure that was just one 'S' but he didn't seem to get the joke. All I know is that they took custody of the remaining suspects, the 'corpses', all the evidence and paperwork and bundled everything into a grey, unmarked truck. They downloaded everything off the system as well, then made us wipe all we had relating to the case off our hard drives. All 'in the interests of national security'. Made us sign extended versions of the Official Secrets Act as well, which is why I'm hoping this gets through their net before they can catch it. They'll probably be visiting you next anyway. I guess it depends on how well your statements stand up to scrutiny, eh?"

"Thanks for the warning, Art. I'll find some way to let you know if you're right."

Moon made Sonia wait until they got home before telling her the whole of Whatley's story. "Looks like a good thing Uri, Roanne and Charli split when they did," observed Sonia. "If these S Branch types are interested in collecting vampires I think we ought to warn them, don't you."

"Yes, I do. And if they do turn up on our doorstep we need to stick entirely to our original story. It might not just be vampires they're interested in. I'm not keen to end my days in a hidden government bunker having my brain dissected to see how I talk to the dead."

"We need to warn Ellie somehow too. Perhaps we could risk a phone call before they get onto us."

So Moon phoned Uri's home and left a message that they needed to meet as soon as possible to discuss 'some important developments from last night', and Sonia called Ellie's mobile and explained as obliquely as she could that she may have some unexpected visitors asking about her ordeal and emphasising the need to 'get the facts right'. "I think she understood," said Sonia with a sigh. "I arranged to go up and visit her tomorrow. She was a bit taken aback but I'll explain everything when I get there." She looked up at Moon. "I'll be throwing a sickie so you'll have to cover for me if the boss calls."

"Okay, we need to pop round to Uri's this evening and clue them in."

"God, this suddenly seems so cloak-and-dagger! I hope it turns out that we're worrying about nothing."

"So, you think this S Branch could be a branch of the Secret Service with a heavy interest in the supernatural?" asked Uri. "That may be. I have suspected for some time that there must be something like this in operation. The Church certainly used to have something of the sort and one would expect, in such increasingly secular times, that the Government would inherit the function."

"But what's the point of keeping such things secret?" asked Sonia. The five of them were sitting in the comfortably messy lounge of the vampires' private apartments in the Maddocks' house. The piles of magazines and books and the pile of DVDs by the TV hinted at something with which Moon was all too familiar: the long hard struggle to avoid the boredom you can experience when your lifestyle is several hours out of step with other people's.

"This is the age of reason, sweetheart," explained Roanne, running a long finger down the back of Sonia's hand. She seemed to be amusing herself by coming on to Sonia, having seen how freaked she had been when she and Charli had propositioned them in the club the night before. "You can't build a civilization on science and rational thought when people are still scared about the monster under the bed. So I guess they feel it's worth expending the effort to sweep inconvenient evidence under the carpet to maintain the status quo."

"Don't tease Sonia, darling," reprimanded Uri. "If she doesn't want to play it's impolite to labour the point." Roanne wrinkled her nose and rolled her eyes whilst removing her hand.

"Anyway," said Moon quickly. "Roanne may be right but I was thinking they might have more interest along the lines of possible military and espionage applications. Ghost-speak would be a really useful talent for a spy, for instance, or what about using ghosts for surveillance."

"Whatever they're interested in, we don't want them focusing that interest on us, thank you very much!" said Charli, shaking her head. "Is there anything we can do to keep them off track?"

"Some of our family members have pretty high up positions in the government. Perhaps they could throw a few spanners in the works," suggested Uri. "If we alert them to the possibility they could keep an eye open for anything pointing suspicion towards us. One or two of them might even be able to get transferred into the S Branch itself."

"You're beginning to sound like the fucking Mafia," complained Sonia.

Uri paused with his coffee cup near his lips. "My dear, this is so important to us. We live in relative comfort, hiding in plain sight. It is a long time since we've been forced underground, which is much less pleasant, you know. We want to do what we can to prevent it becoming a necessity."

"I suppose so. I'd just be happier if you didn't have this sort of secret society that you've wrapped around yourselves. It makes it hard to trust your motives."

"Ah!" replied Uri, a dark hint of laughter in his eyes. "You think it makes us seem mysterious and sinister?"

"Well, not so much you, now I know you, but the idea of such a closely knit family in this day and age, which has members in high places all working to keep something secret. You know…"

"There are other families out there which are just as secretive and nepotistic, and who are working towards much worse ulterior motives, believe me!" said Roanne earnestly. "Most of the upper echelons of society for a start. At least the Maddocks and the Llewellyns have fairly altruistic goals."

"I suppose so."

"So we're agreed that we'll do what we can to avoid drawing attention from this bunch?" Moon attempted to sum up their discussion. "Sonia and I will do our best to throw them off the scent if they approach us for information and you'll do what you can to get information on them and their goals via your 'family' connections."

"That is the general idea," agreed Uri. "Can Ellie be trusted not to betray us, knowingly or unknowingly?"

"She's a smart girl," replied Sonia reassuringly. "And I'm taking the first train out tomorrow to visit her and bring her up to score."

"Well, that seems to be the best we can do about this problem. You must let us pay for your ticket, Sonia. Rail prices aren't cheap these days."

Confident that they had done all they could to handle this potential threat, they settled down to a relaxed evening of drinks and movies.

Chapter 29

The weeks passed quickly and soon it was mid August. Moon had virtually abandoned his flat to move in with Sonia to get away from the oppressive heat that accumulated in his south-facing bed-sit. Sonia and Avril's place was more protected from the heat by the steep slopes where the Avon Gorge began to level off in the direction of Bristol Centre. There had been no further sightings of the mysterious S Branch and it was beginning to look like they had been dismissed as innocent victims of the vampire cult. Which he was sure was all for the best.

Uri's sources had been able to glean a small amount of information, none of which painted a pretty picture of the S Branch, which had originally grown from a small research unit established during the Second World War to investigate the military potential of ESP. These days their work was based in at least twenty research facilities situated at isolated sites scattered around mainland Britain. The nearest of these was in South Wales, and it was there that the remnants of Rurik's cult had been taken, without trial, for reasons known only to the leadership of S Branch itself. Knowing this, Moon shared Uri's concern and was glad that the vampires' family connections provided them with a way to keep an eye on the activities of the Branch. The hoped they would be forewarned if the men in pinstripes decided that they *were* worthy of additional attention but with luck that would never happen. For now, however, they would try to live their lives as normally as possible.

At eight thirty-three pm on Friday twentieth of August Moon walked into the courtyard of the *Hangman's Rest*. He was wearing a long black satin frock coat, which had been made for him by one of Sonia's friends who supplemented her online copywriting and proofreading business by tailoring period and fantasy clothing for the Goths, re-enactors and role-players in the Bristol area. Beneath this he wore a red silk shirt with frills spilling out at the collar and cuffs and black jeans tucked into cuff-topped knee high boots. His hair was bleached blond and styled in a Manga-like shag cut and a small black dragon holding a red teardrop shaped gem dangled from his left ear. His white face reflected the yellow of the sodium streetlights, a black crack painted artistically down one cheek, making it look like a cracked porcelain mask. In short, Moon was really 'Gothed-up'. He saluted George the hangman, who was standing near the gates leering at any young women who passed by, and headed for the queue to the function room. There was something a bit odd about the clothing of the people in the queue ahead of him, odder than the normal Goth oddness, that was, but he couldn't quite put his finger on it.

Avril was manning the ticket desk with Sonia keeping her company. They were both in extreme Goth mode. Avril wore a corseted gown of black taffeta, which was cut low enough to show a dark hint of areola and give her spider tattoo a bit of an outing. Her hair was piled up on top and bulked out with extensions so a riot of nylon ringlets tumbled out from under what, despite any reasonable expectation, seemed to be a miniature black cow-girl's hat with a dark red ribbon tied round it. She also wore cuffed gloves with silver pentacles at the wrists and Moon noticed as she moved that her black velvet sleeves had long fringes dangling from them. As Sonia stood to greet him he realised that she was wearing a black and red satin corset and very little else. A wide crushed satin sash hung round her hips and was tied with a large, bustle-like bow at the back, which alternately hid and revealed the fact that she was wearing a tiny thong over her dark red spider-web tights. Her long black hair was piled up and ringletted like a Victorian showgirl's and two long black ostrich feathers rose from the back of her elaborate silver headdress. The stiletto heels on her short, black, button-sided boots were long enough to almost bring their eyes level. As they kissed he felt something heavy bump against his left thigh. "What's that?" he asked, looking down with surprise.

When Sonia stepped back Moon saw she was wearing a red and black garter around her right thigh with a tiny silver derringer tucked into it. "It's okay, it's not real," she said, pulling the dinky gun out and firing it at him with a loud crack.

The sharp, sulphuric smell of percussion caps filled the air. "What's going on?" asked Moon. "Am I mistaken or is there a distinctly Western theme to tonight's proceedings?"

"Oh, wait and see!" said Avril excitedly. "We've got something special planned. It should be hilarious."

Moon looked quizzically at Sonia. "My lips are sealed," she said. "I would have told you but you were working and I don't want it getting to the wrong ears now."

"I'm intrigued. But I guess I'll have to wait until whatever it is happens." He held his hand out to Sonia. "Are you coming in?" Sonia glanced enquiringly at Avril.

"Go on," Avril waved them away. "Moz will be taking over from me soon and I can fend for myself 'til then."

Entering the function room was like walking into an old-fashioned London smog. "I think Bazzer's been overdoing it with the dry ice," explained Sonia, wafting her hand in front of her to clear the air slightly. Bazzer was another part-time barman at the *Rest*, who also doubled up as roadie-cum-soundman when they had a band night. Moon could vaguely see his bearded and pony-tailed silhouette on the stage knocking several different kinds of hell out of the dry ice machine with a spanner. The early crowd and the band were egging him on with helpful comments like "Fire!" and "I don't think it's dead yet, Bazzer!"

With a snort of disgust Bazzer finally disconnected the ageing machine, stood up and aimed a well placed kick at its side. "I reckon that's buggered. If any of the bands on later want atmosphere they'll just have to make it 'emselves."

The first band on was a new group called *The Hangmen*, which included several of the *Rest's* own staff. The lead singer was Suzy, Moz's girlfriend who was looming out of the fake fog like a modern day Valkyrie. Kate played a mean lead guitar alongside her and with two of the bar staff that Moon didn't know too well ('Bat' and 'Cider' were the two names that came to mind) playing bass and drums respectively, they made quite a respectable rock foursome. Suzy's firm contralto had a peculiar, raw edge that Moon thought was perfect for the Led Zeppelin style music they played. Most of the songs were originals and he recognised Kate's acerbic wit in many of the lyrics. "They're *good*!" Moon yelled over the mournful song of Kate's guitar. "Is this what you were waiting for?"

"No, that's later on," replied Sonia. "Just enjoy the show for the moment."

Stoker's Kiss, who were topping the bill that evening, came on at ten-fifteen after a short bar break. "Now, wait for my lead and do what I do," said Sonia.

Moon gave a puzzled nod, "Okay, whatever..."

The band was as good as he remembered from the few times he had heard them play and he and Sonia were soon dancing happily along with the rest of the audience. Then Stroggy lifted the mike to his mouth and announced, "The next number is called *Carpe Jugulum* in tribute to Terry Pratchett's book of the same name. It's a lively one so join in and dance along!"

Over the appreciative response of the audience, Sonia yelled, "Now!" as she dragged him into line with Avril and Roger, who were already linked up with several others.

Moon vaguely noticed Kate and Mozz organising another line behind them but he only had time to ask, "What the...?" before about ninety percent of the audience was performing a Country and Western style line dance to the song, dragging him along with them.

The band managed a few more bars but the music became more and more disjointed as the musicians broke down into fits of laughter. Eventually, Stroggy stopped singing and gasped over the mike, tears steaming down his face, "You bastards! Okay, we give in, this *is* a C&W number! Now can we get on with the gig?"

The audience stopped dancing and collapsed with laughter. "Well don, Stroggy, we thought you'd never admit it!" yelled Kate, twirling a silver six shooter.

"It was worth it just to see you lot strutting your stuff!" replied Stroggy. "Now, guys, reprise in a one-two-three-four!" And, as the band restarted the number, the whole of the *Rest*, including one or two of its more insubstantial regulars Moon noticed, linked arms and performed a near perfect line dance with the occasional fake firearm being discharged at the old oak ceiling. This was likely to become a regular highlight when the *Kiss* played, Moon realised, as he bent to kiss Sonia and pinched her playfully through her spider-web tights.

Later, when the gig was over and Moon and Sonia were outside, he held her against him as they waited for a taxi. "Tell me there'll be lots more nights like tonight," he said, nuzzling her hair.

"As many as we can make, Jerry," she replied, turning to kiss him. "Does this mean we're serious?" she asked, and he could feel the slight edge of trepidation in her voice.

"As serious as you want us to be," he replied. "You know I won't push you."

"Well, I guess that means serious," she shrugged. "I love you, Jerry Moon."

"I love you too. So what's next?"

"We could get a place together." She smiled.

"I guess so." He looked thoughtful for a second. "There's only one problem…"

"What's that?" she looked up sharply, searching his face for lack of commitment.

"Anna, who's going to look after Anna?"

"Oh God, Moon! I'm sure we can sort something out. Some people have trouble with in-laws but me? I have to share my boyfriend with a centenarian four-year-old!" She laughed. "But I wouldn't have it any other way!"

As they got into the cab that drew up next to the pub's gateway, Moon caught a vague glimpse of the moustached face of a man sitting in a black Mercedes parked across and slightly up the road. For some reason this dark-haired stranger with a slight military air about him seemed oddly familiar. He shrugged and filed the thought away for future contemplation.

Major James Hamilton released a sigh of relief as his two subjects rode away in their cab. He thought he had been rumbled there for a moment, but it looked like the male subject hadn't noticed that he had been keeping them under surveillance for several weeks. As he drew away from the kerb to follow at a discreet distance he reached over and blanked the screen of the car's built in computer. On its surface could briefly be seen the Ministry of Defence logo, heading a standard report screen on which was displayed a photograph of Moon and the words:

Subject:	**Jeremy Angus Moon**
Age:	**28 years**
Occupation:	**Nurse, Bristol Royal Infirmary, Surgical Directorate**
Recruitment potential:	**Ethically incompatible**
Status:	**Involved in Bristol Downs' Bunker incident Potential threat to security or valuable anomaly**
Abilities:	**Unknown – possible high level psychic/ psychokinetic**
Plan:	**Investigate extent of threat and consider options of incarceration, experimentation or termination.**

Hamilton shrugged, so far the subject had exhibited little potential threat except to the realms of good taste. However, he glanced fondly down at the standard issue automatic that always rode in his shoulder holster. Give him time to build a case then he would enjoy either capturing the little freak or putting him in the ground.